Commonguy.com

A novel by

Don Miller

Also by Don Miller

INVITATION

Published by Don Miller

ISBN # 978-0-9839612-1-5

Cover design by Leah Henderson

ACKNOWLEDGEMENTS

My special thanks to:

Dr. Dennis Hensley for his exceptional editing services and his advocacy of perseverance.

Leah Henderson for the terrific cover.

My wife Nancy for being her.

Commonguy.com

Prologue

Saturday, October 1, Stanford University, California, 11:58 a.m.

While the assassin stood two feet back from the attic window of the Stanford Memorial Auditorium and scrutinized his target area, Secret Service Agent Anita Vandy, stationed in a third story roof tower two blocks away and across the street, scrutinized hers. She could barely see the stage of the Frost Amphitheater through the trees, but had a clear view of everything surrounding it to the west and south. She had a direct line of sight to the window high up in the Auditorium. She held her long-range weapon in ready position, safety off.

The visiting entourage stood at the front of the stage, waving to the cheering crowd. The assassin's prey stood with his left hand resting on the shoulder of the young boy at his side. The signal man looked back over his shoulder, directly at the Auditorium attic window. The assassin centered his target's temple in the crosshairs of the CheyTac Intervention M200 sniper rifle as the man's head turned strangely toward him.

A fraction of a second before the assassin's brain sent the signal to his trigger finger, the target ducked. Automatically adjusting for the movement as he squeezed the trigger, the killer saw the man bend down behind the boy, saw the boy jerk from the impact of the bullet, and instantly re-aimed for a second shot. He had no chance of getting it off.

Agent Vandy's scope was fixed on the open window in the Auditorium. Something moved. She saw the sniper, took aim, saw his rifle spit fire, and squeezed the trigger of hers. Through her scope, she saw the left side of his face, the scarred side, explode.

All was chaos at the amphitheater. Daryl had seen Littleton look up, turning his head back and to his left. Even with dark glasses hiding his eyes, Littleton's move, its duration and intensity, struck Daryl as out of place. He had started to glance back to follow Littleton's fix when he felt Rory begin to quiver and sink. Rory was swooning, collapsing from the onset of another seizure. Daryl instinctively lurched down to catch him and heard a crack. Then Rory jerked toward him, pitching into his arms. In the next instant, he heard a second crack, and, horrified, realized his son's upper left thigh was a mix of shredded pants and flesh and spurting blood.

Racine, standing to her husband's right, saw the red flow gushing from her son and fell to her knees. Rory was fully engaged in the seizure, bleeding profusely and convulsing on the stage – a sanity-shattering nightmare for his parents. Racine ripped off her jacket, and wrapped it around the lurching wound, trying to slow the flow of blood. Her screams eclipsed the din emanating from the crowd. "Get a doctor! Get a doctor!"

Chapter 1

Fourteen weeks earlier, Saturday, June 18, New York City, 11:07 p.m.

"It's been a helluva day for you, Rand," Senator Dresser congratulated Pritchard, dropping all pretense of formality. "I'll bet you brought in every bit of twenty million, what with brunch, the town hall meeting this afternoon, and this shindig tonight."

"Yeah, Gordy," the President replied, "today's one for the record books. When things are going great it's easy. Everybody wants to hobnob with the Pres. Even Jorgensen was all rowdy and festive tonight."

"The big guy was havin' a blast!" Dresser laughed, picturing the six-foot-six, white-haired giant, his big Texas cowboy hat making him look even bigger. "You *know* he wishes he could switch sides. Being a Democratic governor in Texas when Republicans are soaking in popularity has to be a bad dream for him. If his family ties to the Dems hadn't been so strong, he'd have switched sides back when we were all freshman senators having the times of our lives. He'd love to be on our train now."

The tux and tails dinner party had officially ended at 10:00. Those remaining in the room consisted of the presidential party, close friends and – the largest group – the Secret Service protection staff. Tennessee Senator Gordon Dresser, sixty-four years old, balding, and stout, was President Randall Pritchard's most trusted personal friend. Their lives had intersected twenty-eight years ago when they were both first-term senators, Dresser from Tennessee and Pritchard from Kentucky.

That was when their careers had sky-rocketed, along with Troy Jorgensen's. The three newcomers, two Republicans and the Democrat from Texas, had refused to waste time deferring to their more experienced colleagues. They had teamed up, cosponsoring twice as many bills as any first-term senators in history. All of the bills they had introduced had been calculated to gain them popular support: jobs bills, tax reductions, budget-balancing, veteran recognition and compensation, fraud/waste/abuse crackdown, upgrading educational standards, health care reform. The trio had always presented a united and conspicuous bipartisan front.

The media had insisted on spotlighting them, and the public had loved them. Their bills were voted down more often than adopted, but they'd been popular bills, and the opposition invariably suffered public disfavor. The three had developed golden reputations, while living in the fast lane. They'd gone on fact-finding trips together, partied behind the scenes together, and even taken a few vacations together. At the end of their first terms, their fellow senators had been disenchanted with them, but after each was reelected by a landslide, support, however begrudging, could no longer be withheld.

They were men on the rise, thriving, invincible. And they were womanizers. By the midpoint of their second terms, Dresser's and Jorgensen's wives had both surpassed their tolerance limits and sued for divorces. By the end of the terms, Dresser was single and vowed to remain that way, and Jorgensen was remarried and no longer promiscuous. Pritchard's wife, Justine, was the only one of the three unfazed by her husband's infidelity. She was committed to the long haul, counting her place in the Washington social scene to be of greater value than a faithful husband.

After their second terms, Jorgensen had returned to Texas state politics and worked his way up to governor. Pritchard and Dresser had developed into an increasingly formidable team. Pritchard came to be seen as the leader. His stature rose, and as time passed his name began to be mentioned in Party conversations about future presidential candidates. He looked the part: tall, fit, attractive, and distinguished. His resume of authored bills and senatorial clout were impressive.

His most exceptional trait, his charisma, got honed and polished to perfection.

The most career-threatening predicament Pritchard and Dresser had gotten themselves into had occurred twenty-three years ago in Nashville. They had been invited by Kris Jansen, one of Nashville's wealthiest recording magnates, to a bash at his secluded mansion for a night of no-holds-barred revelry. Anything suiting widely varying tastes turned out to be free for the taking. Pritchard and Dresser avoided the drugs and the underage teasers, but availed themselves liberally of the booze and full-fledged women.

After three hours at the mansion, at most inopportune timing, sirens had blared up the winding, tree-lined drive. Pritchard and Dresser had been in adjacent first-floor suites in the north wing of the mansion, each with two voluptuous companions, when fire had erupted on the second floor of the south wing. That fateful event had spawned a life-altering relationship between Randall Pritchard and his now Chief of Staff, Gaylord Scapeli.

Scapeli had been in charge of security at the mansion. He was responsible for knowing who was in the building and protecting them. That night, the two senators were the highest-profile occupants. Before the fire trucks had screeched to a halt at the south end, Scapeli had personally escorted both men out the north wing rear door and into his waiting sedan. He had ushered Pritchard into the front passenger seat and Dresser into the back. Scapeli had driven out the rear access drive and to the back VIP entrance of the senators' downtown hotel. The fire had been big news the next day. The activity ongoing at the mansion had been described as unseemly and immoral. The media had made no mention of the presence of either Dresser or Pritchard. No public insinuation was ever made.

During the ride into Nashville, Scapeli had talked of his investigative and protective services company, Davidson County Safety Services, directing his conversation to his front seat passenger. Scapeli had teased Pritchard with some juice on Lee James, the likely Democratic opponent he would face in the next senatorial election. Scapeli claimed he had proof James had taken bribes as a Kentucky state representative and that James, father of four daughters, ages eight to seventeen, had kept a barely-of-age black mistress for three years until his wife found out a year ago. As the two senators had exited the sedan Scapeli had handed Pritchard a business card and told him he always maintained availability for new quality clientele.

Pritchard had called him to request a meeting two days later. Scapeli had impressed Pritchard with his political savvy, his possession of useful, damaging information, and his suggestions of various means of securing funds to pay for his services from sources other than Pritchard's pockets. The two men had then struck their first agreement with a handshake. Scapeli had guaranteed Pritchard a one-sided victory in the upcoming senatorial election. That had been only mildly impressive, considering the heavily Republican voter bias. What had turned out to be impressive was Scapeli's systematic destruction of James.

Scapeli had uncovered every speck of dirt that existed on James, and had made sure all of it found voice in the press. After James's credibility had been reduced to nothing, Scapeli had implanted shreds of fabricated accusations into the media network. The result had been more than the promised landslide victory at no cost to Pritchard. James's political career lay in total ruin. He would never again be a factor on the political scene. An unstructured marriage had been born between Pritchard and Scapeli, consecrated by their first collaborative screwing of an adversary. This marriage had no proviso for divorce.

*   *   *

"Your intro was fantastic, Gordy," Pritchard said. "It's always great when you're at these fundraisers."

"Anything I can do for the cause." Dresser smiled. "It's been a *long* time since an incumbent was as popular as you."

"It *is* fun. Back when we were first running for senate, who'd have ever thought we'd be sitting here talking about how easy it is to raise twenty million for a presidential campaign? What a ride we've had. I'd love to sit and reminisce, Gordy, but I have other things to do yet tonight. I've gotta head up to my suite. Thanks again for the introduction, though. You always give fantastic speeches."

The two men stood, Pritchard looking thoroughly presidential, the tuxedo enhancing his six-foot-two inch debonair frame. He exuded confidence and experience with his penetrating brown eyes, thick dark hair grayed at the temples, erect stance, and long stride.

"You're welcome, Rand. Now, you go take care of the rest of that business waiting in your suite." Dresser winked at him. "Have a grand night."

Pritchard was accompanied to the secured floor of the hotel by his Secret Service team. When they exited the elevator, Pritchard nodded toward the agent in charge and said, "You know the drill, Lawrence. Call me if Canada drops a bomb on DC. Otherwise, my day's over. No one knocks on the door, and my phone doesn't ring before six."

When he entered the luxury suite, the lights were dimmed and news was on the TV. He removed his tie, cummerbund, and shoes. Brandy was on the counter awaiting him, already poured. He picked up the glass and sprawled on the recliner across the room from the TV. The news segment was about the political woes of the two Democratic front-runners, Garner Wheeler and Richard Herrington. The two men were mucked in the process of destroying each other.

In the past week, Wheeler had exposed Herrington's heroic Vietnam War record as a far cry from what had been touted. Three soldiers under his command and four surviving Vietnamese victims of his reckless cruelty had come forward with vivid accounts of their experiences. All seven professed receiving thrashings at his hands while they were defenseless. The soldiers had each been hospitalized afterward. The Vietnamese, young women and children at the time, had been left to die. However, they had survived while others in similar circumstances had not.

Herrington's military units had been successful in battle, but all three soldiers claimed Herrington himself had never led or been anywhere near battle unless it was against unarmed civilians, in which case he had been ferocious. Two of the soldiers had produced photographs of young Herrington in action, physically pulverizing defenseless women and children. Herrington's run for the presidency was over.

Vengeful as ever, Herrington and his camp had thrown dung back at Wheeler yesterday. Herrington had been claiming for the past month that Wheeler had siphoned millions from the Illinois state coffers during his eight years as governor. Until yesterday, all Herrington had produced in the way of evidence was a few low-tier bureaucrats claiming that hundreds of thousands of dollars had disappeared from their departments' accounts. Yesterday, however, Herrington had published a complete accounting of exactly how much had been pilfered from each department, along with a detailed record of the money trail, naming the specific banks in Switzerland where it was now parked, all in accounts controlled by Wheeler.

The media scoop today was that Herrington's accounting was standing up to scrutiny. The position of the Wheeler staff was denial and a contention of sour grapes. However, they had not attempted to explain what might have happened to the alleged missing funds. The consensus of independent analysts was that it was unlikely Wheeler could come up with any explanation that would withstand investigation. If he couldn't, his run for the presidency would also soon be over.

Pritchard could hardly contain himself. Everything was unfolding exactly as Scapeli had predicted. It was as if Scapeli had set the whole scenario in motion before either candidate had even announced any intent to run. *Who knows, maybe he had. If anyone alive could pull off something like that, it was Scapeli.* He was fortunate to have Scapeli on his side … or at least, not opposing him.

The report of the demise of the Democrats transitioned to a scene of a political rally in front of the State Capital Building in Des Moines, Iowa. Speaking from the top of the steps was Marten, the irritating Independent who had appeared from nowhere. Pritchard's expression turned into an involuntary snarl. The occasion for the speech was Marten's filing for presidential ballot access in Iowa, bringing to forty-three the number of states in which his name would appear on the ballot. How was this nobody, with his simplistic, unrealistic ideas on how to run the most complex government in the world, getting this much attention? *How did this moron get his name on forty-three state ballots?* It now looked as though there was a chance he could be on the ballot in all fifty states. That was unheard of.

No Independent had ever accomplished that. And this guy had nothing. *Not a damn thing. Not even a brain.*

Regardless, Marten's name would be on the ballot; Marten, along with his Republican traitor Vice Presidential sidekick, DeCamp. DeCamp was a small-time state representative in Ohio, an unknown. One thing was for sure about him, though. *That son of a bitch will be castigated from the Republican Party forevermore.* Pritchard hadn't yet talked to Scapeli about this Independent ticket. Even though the novices didn't stand a chance and were no threat, Scapeli would certainly have been tracking their every move. It was time to deal with them. *Time to end them.*

"Hey, Rand," called an inviting, sexy voice from behind the door to the bath, "are you coming in? The water's perfect."

He'd been so absorbed in the plight of his opponents that he'd forgotten all about Lynn. *Boy, I must be slipping. Shake it off. Today's been fabulous. The election's in the bag. Marten is not a problem.* "I'm comin' in."

He swung open the door to the huge, luxurious bath. The whirlpool in the mirrored corner of the room was big enough for a cheerleading squad and there was Lynn, lounging naked in the middle of it, waiting for him. He loved it when she was assigned to his travel security detail. *How can a woman as enticing as that be the best sharpshooter in the Secret Service?* This would be the perfect end to a perfect day.

*   *   *

Forty-eight hours later, Gayle Scapeli stepped off the elevator into the Center Hall of the residence floor of the White House. Glancing left as he crossed the Hall, he saw First Lady Justine Pritchard, tall, sleek, and elegant, even at 11:00 at night, entering the Hall from the Queen's Bedroom suite, her quarters. "Good evening, Justine."

She nodded coolly, said nothing, and turned to descend the staircase.

The door to the living room suite converted to night-office-suite across the Hall was open, and Scapeli walked in. The President, still dressed formally minus the jacket, stood tall, gazing out the window, brandy in hand.

It had been a long day, but a good one. In the morning, sandwiched among a dozen photo ops with the likes of the CEO of a major television network, the president of the Autoworkers Union, and the Prime Minister of Great Britain, he had publicly signed a major trade agreement with the President of China. Television cameras had also been present in the afternoon when he had signed the tax reduction bill his Administration had submitted to Congress after budget projections were issued predicting a surplus next year. He had dined and spent the evening with the majority and minority leaders of the Senate and House and laid out his strategy for a bipartisan initiative to construct a high-speed rail system to connect New York and Los Angeles.

"Good evening, Mr. President," Scapeli greeted.

Pritchard turned toward him. "Hello, Gayle. Thanks for coming. These meetings seem to get later and later." There was no need to offer Scapeli a drink. He never touched the stuff. "Have a seat." Pritchard motioned to the sofa.

His relationship with Gaylord Scapeli was bizarre for a President and his Chief of Staff. They were not friends, although their association went back twenty-three years to that debacle at the Jansen manor in Nashville. Their dependence on one another had intertwined ever more intricately over time. Pritchard knew their continuing alliance existed solely because they both understood exactly what each could do for – or to – the other. Neither could afford to alienate the other.

Scapeli's Italian bloodline emanated through his dark, angular features.   At five-foot-ten, one-hundred-eighty-five pounds, he was sinuous. He worked out hard every morning before 6:00. An expert in martial arts, Scapeli would be the wrong fifty-eight-year old man for a street thief to target in a back alley. He had served in the Army for fifteen years, the first three as a Ranger, the next four in college mastering foreign languages, and the last eight in some kind of espionage role that Pritchard had been unable to probe, though he had tried. Scapeli's skills in observation surpassed those of anyone Pritchard had ever met, including everyone on his Secret Service protection detail. Scapeli's phenomenal ability to set up future events to turn out in accordance with a planned outcome had been demonstrated on multiple occasions. Gaylord Scapeli was not a man to cross.

"You want to talk about Marten and DeCamp?" Scapeli asked, still standing. Then he added, nodding toward the closed bedroom door, "Who's in there?"

Pritchard marveled at the man. The door was closed and the bedroom light was off. The walls were sound-resistant and she had not made a peep. Scapeli was aware the First Lady was just down the hall, and yet he instinctively knew the adjacent bedroom was not empty. *Well, maybe it isn't all instinct. He knows me well.*

"Janice? Don't worry about her. The walls are soundproof. Even if she could hear us, who's she gonna tell? She's painfully aware Justine will instill a death wish in her if her presence here ever becomes news."

"Turn up the TV." Scapeli motioned to the table as far from the bedroom as they could get. "Let's talk there."

Pritchard carried his drink to the table and sat. Scapeli walked to both doors connecting the suite to the corridors, quietly closed them, and sat next to the President.

"Marten isn't anywhere near left field," Pritchard began, agitated. "Hell, he isn't in the ballpark. Not even in the parking lot. Nobody's gonna vote for a President who's never held public office. His crazy-ass ideas couldn't *possibly* be implemented. *Anybody* can see that."

Scapeli's reproachful look transmitted a familiar message to Pritchard: admonishment for carelessness in conversation. He spoke quietly, forcing Pritchard to lean in to hear, shifting the tone of the meeting to guarded.

"I started watching Marten when they announced they'd seek ballot access in Arkansas last October. After they did that and then did it again in Nebraska and Nevada, I watched closer. Getting ballot access in those three states isn't hard. But, some of the other states they've pulled off are, especially North Carolina and Texas. Without any political organization, I didn't think they'd get near enough signatures in either state. But they did."

"How'd they do it?" Pritchard asked, now speaking as softly as Scapeli. "A billionaire backer?"

"No. They're just using the Internet and volunteers. They haven't done any advertising and claim they won't. Unfortunately, they've got the media's attention. People are buying into propositions they're preaching on the Web.

"Marten and DeCamp," Scapeli continued, "took sabbaticals in April, and Marten's taking the rest of the summer. He worked their campaign full-time in May, which got them on the Texas, North Carolina, and Massachusetts ballots. DeCamp'll join in after the Ohio legislature adjourns in July. Their wives are organizing their volunteers. They haven't employed anybody and haven't asked for contributions, at least not publicly. It's intriguing."

"*Asinine* is the word I'd use," Pritchard replied, getting more worked up. "And if that turncoat, DeCamp, took leave from his Ohio Rep seat, I'll see to it that it's permanent. What's Marten, an architect, right? What could he possibly know about running this country? Every one of his hair-brained ideas would *bury* any President stupid enough to push them."

"Calm down, Rand," Scapeli hissed insistently. "Marten and DeCamp are not going to threaten your reelection. Herrington and Wheeler destroyed each other exactly the way it was planned from the beginning. The Democratic ticket is going to be Catcher/Bartolo, like I told you it would be. And that ticket has no chance of posing any threat. What they *will* do is attack Marten and end his bid. Catcher and some special interest groups are going to rip Marten and DeCamp to shreds. Their ads are already making Marten look like a fool."

"We ... I ... should take the lead in exposing how disastrous Marten's plans would be."

"No," Scapeli retorted. "Officially, this Administration won't acknowledge that a Marten/DeCamp ticket exists. If we notice they're running, we add an ounce of legitimacy to their bid. We won't do that. Catcher will front the attack. If there's backlash, and there will be, he gets it, not us."

"How you gonna control what Catcher does? Which special interest groups? What'll you do if Marten survives it?"

Scapeli looked exasperated. "How many years have I been doing this crap for you? Have I ever failed? Are Herrington and Wheeler out of the picture? You don't need or want to know the details, but believe me, Marten will get annihilated. Catcher will lead the assault, and that'll make him even weaker. Don't worry about how, Rand."

"All right, Gayle. I'll leave it to you. But I want Marten, and especially DeCamp, gone before the convention." He downed the last drops of brandy, glancing at the half-empty bottle on the counter.

"You'll like the way it works out. Concentrate on your end. Keep politicking. The economy is going great. International support is strong. You're more popular than any incumbent ever. For the next four months, steer this machine where it needs to go. Win it bigger than ever. Start your second term riding the biggest victory margin the United States has ever seen. You go into your second term like that, and you'll be set to establish your legacy as one of the greatest presidents in this country's history. I'll sweep the dirt away. You drive the legacy."

"What about Borster? Have you planned anything for him yet?" Pritchard changed the subject. "He pisses me off more every day."

"By the middle of August, the Vice President is going to decimate his own reputation. The Party and the public will demand that you kick him off the ticket."

"How ..."

Scapeli held up his hand, cutting Pritchard off. His signal was perfectly clear: *You don't want to know.*

For the first time since Scapeli walked into the room, Pritchard smiled. "Gayle, I'm glad we're on the same side. We're different, but we make a formidable team."

Scapeli rose to leave and now spoke loudly. "Good night, Rand. By the way, before the night is over, make damn sure Janice understands exactly the hell she'll face if she ever lets it slip that she was here tonight."

"Don't worry, Gayle, she already knows. If anyone ever accuses her of knowing me personally, she would lie about it to a judge sentencing her to hang for perjury."

Scapeli turned and walked out of the room.

Pritchard poured a refill.

Janice, lying naked in bed, waiting for Pritchard to return, slipped the miniature receiver/recorder out of her ear and into the inside zip compartment of her small purse lying on the nightstand. *I'll wear him out and get that sensitive little microphone from under the table after he's snoring.*

Chapter 2

Eighteen months earlier, Sunday, December 14, Carthage, Ohio, 2:10 p.m.

Rarely did a month pass without the two families spending at least one Sunday afternoon together. Daryl Marten and Cleve DeCamp had a friendship with deep roots, dating back to elementary school. Daryl had married Racine Santana twenty years ago, the summer she had graduated from college and he had received his degree in architecture.

Cleve had married Melinda Richards, a hometown girl, that same summer. Cleve was medium height, not fat but showing signs of expanding, dark hair partially covering his receding hairline. Melinda was an inch shorter than him, with shoulder-length, auburn hair and a figure that had been hourglass ten years ago.

After finishing a late lunch, the Daryl and Racine's three sons, Jeremy, Kyle, and Rory, and Cleve and Melinda's two, David and Bobby, descended to the Martens' basement to play ping-pong and watch the annual slugfest between the Cincinnati Bengals and the Cleveland Browns. Racine, Melinda, and their two daughters remained in the dining room, chatting. Daryl and Cleve headed for Daryl's study. When Cleve had called Thursday night, Daryl had sensed something was bothering him.

Daryl and Cleve shared fond memories of collaboration from younger days. In high school they had developed a reputation as a pair of idealists, writing political editorials for the school newspaper. After high school they had roomed together at Ohio State, where Cleve had majored in political science, Daryl in architecture. Both carried minors in American History.

They had been active in the campus Young Republicans, contributing more in writing political articles than in supporting campaign and party activities.

Cleve's family had a long tradition in politics, primarily in Ohio, but also in Ottawa, Canada, where they had a clan of distant cousins. After college, Cleve had taken a position as public liaison on his uncle's staff. His father's brother, Ronnie DeCamp, was a state representative in Columbus at the time. Ronnie was later elected to the Ohio Senate and then to the U. S. House of Representatives. Six years ago, at thirty-eight, while Ronnie was still an Ohio senator, Cleve had been elected to a seat in the Ohio House of Representatives.

As Daryl and Cleve took seats in the study, Daryl tried to create an opening for his friend. "Will the groundwork you laid during your first three terms pay off next year?"

"I doubt it. I'm struggling. I'm tryin' to stay positive, but it gets harder every day. Maybe everybody's been right all along. I'm too much of an idealist. That was always our stock in trade: optimism and idealism. We always thought if we lived ethically and morally and if we preached it and worked hard for it, good things would happen. That's what threw us together from the start. Now, I'm losing my grip on it."

"I hear you talking, Cleve, but I'm not convinced. Morality and ethics are your heart and soul. Mine, too. It can't be beaten out of us. Do unto others as you'd have them do unto you. That's it. We couldn't live any other way. I know there are lots of self-serving people out there driving lots of issues. And I'm sure you have to deal with that way more than I do. But, it doesn't matter. Moral, ethical ways are better. Win or lose, they're better. Period."

"Holding onto that might be easier for you than me," Cleve replied. "When I went into politics, I thought it'd be the other way around. I thought being in the thick of it every day, working in *my* Republican Party, with my hands right in the legislation, I could make decency shine through everything. I just don't feel that way anymore."

"Now, *that* I can believe." Daryl grinned. "By the time we finished college, I'd lost faith that *any* political party would ever do much to promote integrity. You didn't have the luxury of letting doubt seep in. There's too much Party history in your family. And your family *has* always been honorable. Your heritage set you up to work within the system. I can believe you're disillusioned with the system, but not that you've lost your roots."

"Maybe, but it's hard to keep going. In twenty years of working with the Ohio legislature I haven't accomplished much. Nothing, really. I championed the good on my uncle's staff, then as a state rep, but it's never made any difference. Nothing came of any of it. Governmental waste is worse than ever. So is outright abuse of power and finances – fraud. When laws are passed, the final version is *always* driven by self-interest, usually from some coalition, but sometimes from one particular company, or even a single person. It's all about votes and money, mostly money."

"What happened, Cleve? You just got reelected by a solid majority. Your voters believe in you."

"My voters like me and my family. I haven't pushed issues that would hurt them. That's all they see. No one thinks for a second that government could be good. They just don't want it to make things worse. All I have to do to stay popular is not contribute to making the government worse than it already is."

"What happened?"

Cleve hesitated. "Uncle Ronnie's in trouble. I'm positive he was straight when he was in Columbus, but when he campaigned for Congress he used too much of his own money. He recovered by accepting bribes and kickbacks."

Daryl's jaw dropped. "Ronnie? No way."

"Believe it. He told the family last weekend. It'll become public knowledge next week. He's finished. He'll resign his office, and have to face the public. Probably file bankruptcy. And do prison time."

"No! I can't believe it." Daryl shook his head. "What's this do to you?"

"Nothing tangible. I'm positive nothing illegal happened when I was on his staff. Even if it did, I had no knowledge. I'm sure I'll take some pot shots from the Dems, but I don't care. I want out anyway. I'm done with the Party and politics."

There was an awkward silence as the two men looked at each other before Cleve went on. "There's more. Last month, when I went to Washington for the welcome bash for new congressmen, I talked to Vice President Borster. I wasn't sure how that happened at the time, but now I think he sought me out. I think he wanted to blow off steam to somebody he thought had integrity, somebody it might matter to. He landed on me.

"Borster's a decent politician. He's a patriot. He lives and breathes the United States of America. He's dedicated to his constituency and puts their wishes above his. He's proud of his record and his nine years as a Virginia senator, and he desperately wants to serve the country.

"He's got nothing in common with Pritchard. He was only on the ticket because Pritchard needed the votes he would bring. Their views on service to the nation and running the Government couldn't be more opposite. When they took office, Pritchard didn't include Borster in the decision-making circle. When Borster pressed for input and more conservatism, Pritchard made it clear his opinions weren't welcome and ostracized him. Nothing gets assigned him except his duty to preside over the Senate. He's not allowed to make public statements or appearances. He's invisible, and he can't stand it.

"Borster also has a couple of thorny traits. He's unforgiving and can be vindictive. I think he wants some dirt to get out on Pritchard, and he's trying to find avenues for it. I think that's why he sought me out. He thought the dirt would drive me nuts and I'd release caged rumors."

Daryl listened with piqued interest, but didn't respond. He didn't want to push his friend.

"Borster says everything the Administration does is for short-term public perception. The number-one goal is getting Pritchard reelected. The number-two goal is establishing his legacy. Foreign policy is developed with the only consideration being how the country will perceive Pritchard's stance. If projecting an overpowering image would be more popular, but quiet back-door compromise would be better for world relations and stability, the strong-arm course is taken.

"Borster claims the Administration controls the Federal Reserve Board. If a drop in the prime rate by the Federal Reserve would result in short-term financial advantage to investors or home buyers, even though it drives the economy ever closer to meltdown, the rate drops.

"If a particular stock jump on Wall Street would artificially turn the market up, boosting Pritchard's ratings, the perfect investor materializes to inhale the desired stock. Later the investor slowly dumps it in exchange for small pieces of cheap stocks that miraculously skyrocket after the transfer.

"Today, the country looks like it's in fabulous shape. Pritchard's more popular than Bush was after nine-eleven. And, according to Borster and his sour grapes, it's all contrived. He claims the mastermind is Gayle Scapeli. He says Scapeli's an espionage guru and has dirt on everybody. Borster's convinced Scapeli has enough on Pritchard to get him impeached and criminally prosecuted if he chose to use it. That could mean the real head of our government is not the person we elected."

Cleve looked Daryl intently in the eyes, almost pleading. "Daryl, the Vice President is biased, but my gut feel is it's all true. And I *hate* it. This is *my* Republican Party. I've devoted my life to it, served it and promoted it. And it's a sham."

"Maybe Borster twisted it out of proportion. Nothing's perfect, and political parties are about as far from it as it gets. But maybe it's not as bad as he painted."

"You might be right, but, Ronnie's downfall, piled on top of that conversation with Borster, plus the empty basket I have to show for my years in the Ohio House, have blown away my faith in our system and my ability to do anything about it."

Daryl searched for something that might give solace to his friend. "Maybe trying to work through political parties isn't the easiest way to improve the world. Remember what we always had the most fun at? We loved publishing our opinions on how the world should work, from our idealist point of view. Maybe we should try that again. Take advantage of the Internet and just put it out there. The way the world should work, according to Cleve and Daryl."

Cleve laughed. "Now, that *would* be fun. It'd have to be under your name though, as long as I'm still a Rep. The things I'd say would be too radical for my colleagues to bear. You were always the best writer anyway. I'd be your ghost support."

"I think it'd be fun, too." Daryl chuckled. "Crazy, but fun. Two old geezers blasting away on the Internet, trumpeting how the world should work. We could revive some of our old editorials and save the world again. Our kids'd be mortified! Maybe we should do it. We could conscript Jeremy and David's services. Make them set us up a blog or something. That'd be the most fun of all, making our kids help!"

Daryl's suggestion had cracked the tension. They were both laughing heartily when they heard Kyle screaming, charging up the basement stairs, "Dad! Dad! It's Rory! Come fast!

Chapter 3

Two weeks later, Thursday, January 1, Carthage, 3:00 p.m.

The Martens and DeCamps were bringing in the new year together, an annual family tradition. Rory had given them a scare two weeks ago.

At age three, Rory had experienced a series of seizures, sudden loss of consciousness, and convulsions. After weeks of tests the doctors had determined Rory had a benign brain tumor the size of a marble. They told Daryl and Racine operating would be risky, and the right treatment would shrink the tumor, possibly even eliminate it, as Rory grew to adulthood. They tried various drugs and found a combination that controlled the seizures and appeared to shrink the tumor.

Rory, a smaller version of his father, with penetrating blue eyes and dark blond hair, would turn ten in February and still took oral medication, but he hadn't had a seizure since he was five. Rory's malady and treatments had resulted in him being less active than most kids, and, seemingly, more insightful and more sensitive to the feelings of others.

None of that mattered to Daryl on December 14, when he catapulted down the basement stairs to find Jeremy shirtless, cradling Rory's head in his arm, repeating, "You'll be okay, Rory. You'll be okay." Rory was lying on the floor unconscious and shaking. Jeremy's shirt, wrapped under Rory's head, was soaked in blood, growing redder by the second.

The blood was from a gash in Rory's head, cut open when he fell against the corner of a bookcase. Daryl and Racine didn't wait for the rescue squad. They carried their son, unconscious, shaking, and bleeding, to their car and sped to the hospital. Upon arrival at the emergency room they were rushed to a trauma room. Within two minutes of receiving an injection, Rory's shaking stopped.

The DeCamps brought the rest of the children to the hospital and stayed the remainder of the day. Rory woke three hours after being delivered to the hospital, weak and with a stitched and hurting head, but otherwise all right. Daryl and Racine spent the night at the hospital. Jeremy, Kyle, and three-year-old Kelsey stayed at the DeCamps'.

By the New Year's celebration, Rory's stitches had been removed and he was back to normal. The doctors had confirmed the tumor was continuing to shrink. They thought his body had developed some immunity to the medication he was taking. They had tweaked the formula, and there had been no recurrence so far.

Daryl and Cleve had continued to toy with the idea of hurling their opinions onto the web. The more they talked, the more they were enticed. It would be like old times, a renewal. Cleve desperately needed one. Daryl was drawn to the thought of refreshing his own optimistic, idealism. Their wives and kids rolled their eyes at the prospect of the two dads posting offbeat editorials on the web. Regardless. the day after Christmas, Jeremy and David were coerced into creating a web site. Today was launch day.

Jeremy and David were both fifteen and best friends. From the neck down, they could've been twins, their tall skinny teenage builds identical. They were smart kids. Jeremy was particularly responsible and studious, to the point that Daryl wished he could temper him with a bit more of a carefree spirit.

Jeremy and David unveiled the home page, entitled "Common Guy." To the left was a subscript: *Reflections of an eternally optimistic American idealist.* To the right was a picture of a blond haired man skipping a flat rock on a still pond that was surrounded by trees sporting a dense mix of orange, gold, and red leaves. The man wore jeans and a white jacket with dark blue sleeves and crimson block lettering on the back, proclaiming: "BOUND TO THE USA." Under the picture was the name Daryl Marten. The remainder of the page introduced the web site:

I'm Daryl Marten, 43 years old, hopelessly in love with my wife, proud father of four, school board member, and partner of two good men practicing architecture in a southwestern Ohio town of 15,000. I've never shed the idealism or optimism of my youth. I am a patriot, proud and thankful to be an American.

I have come to believe the United States is proceeding down paths that are not in the best interest of the nation. More and more, I am convinced it is crucial for our country to change course, and I find myself no longer able to stand idly by. One man is only one man, but I am compelled to try to contribute to changing the trends I believe are weakening our nation. Can my efforts kindle any change? Maybe; maybe not. Certainly not if I don't try. Should I try? Absolutely!

This web site is my attempt to contribute to strengthening our country. I will post one proposition per month, each urging a particular improvement. I will reach out to people, informing as many as I can that the web site exists and asking everyone to visit. If the site attracts significant readership, then whether or not anything comes of my efforts will depend on whether or not many people agree with me, and whether they agree strongly enough to do anything about it: write to local papers, contact elected officials, insist on being heard.

I am energized and looking forward to posting my first proposition in January.

"You ready to go online, Dad?" Jeremy asked.

"It looks good, boys. Do it."

Jeremy grinned and pressed the enter key. "You're on!"

"Let's toast to commonguy.com!" Cleve offered. Champagne was poured for the adults, sparkling juice for the kids. "To bettering the USA." All glasses raised and clinked.

"To the rebirth of DeCamp/Marten team for optimistic idealism," Daryl added.

"Daddy, if it's a team, why doesn't it have your picture, too?" feisty nine-year-old, carrot-topped Bobby DeCamp, a perpetual action machine, asked.

"Yeah, where's Cleve's picture?" Kelsey echoed.

"Well, Bobby," Cleve said, "you know in your Christmas play how Miss Dean was there to help everyone remember what to say, but the audience could never see or hear her?" Bobby nodded. "Well, this is like that. I'll help Daryl behind the scenes, but nobody will know I'm there."

"You mean when Daryl doesn't know what to say, you'll tell him?"

Everyone laughed.

"That'll be all the time!" thirteen-year-old Kyle let out, ducking a punch from his dad. Kyle, as Hispanic looking as his mother and a head shorter than Jeremy, was a fun-loving prankster. He was athletic and an attention seeker, more apt to create mischief than follow any rules, an opposite personality from his older brother.

Jeremy asked Cleve, "Is it because of being a state representative? Could the stuff on the web site get you in trouble?"

"Let's say, we'll be freer to say exactly what we think if I stay in the background," Cleve answered.

"But you'll be doing a lot of the writing?" David asked. "Could you still get in trouble, even if your name isn't mentioned?"

"Daddy isn't getting in any trouble," twelve-year-old daughter Laura DeCamp blurted. "He's the best rep in the state."

Rory said, "I think Cleve and Dad will write things some people might not want put on the Internet. Some people are making rules that aren't always good, and sometimes they make them for bad reasons. Dad and Cleve will show everybody what's wrong and how things should be."

"Then I think I should write some of the stuff," Kyle said. "There are a lot of rules around here that are wrong, and there are no reasons at all for them. I'm gonna dedicate *my* life to changing those!"

"Can I be on your web, Daddy?" Kelsey asked.

"Huh-uh, sweetie. I'm keeping you all to myself. But you can tell me what you think I should write."

"Okay!" She beamed.

Racine wrapped her arms around Daryl, kissed him, and said, "Looks to me like your site's already a hit."

Melinda leaned on Cleve, their arms crossing each other's backs. "I know Cleve's excited about this," she said. "It's already lifted his spirits."

"Yeah," Cleve said. "Last year was disheartening, especially the last two months. It feels good to be excited about something. I'm looking forward to it."

"It's you and me again," Daryl said. "It feels like old times."

"That's cause you guys are such old-timers," Kyle blurted with a laugh.

*   *   *

Late that night, Melinda lay with her head on Cleve's heaving chest, her left hand toying with his ear. Cleve lay on his back, left arm circled under and around her as he stroked the flesh of her back.

"Okay," she said, exhaling. "We've officially kicked off the new year. Let 'em bring it on."

He pulled her up to him and kissed her softly, long. As she laid her head back on his chest he said, "This year could bring endings and beginnings for us. It could be different than any we've seen before."

"You thinking about Ronnie? How bad do you think that might get?"

"It'll be an issue, but that's not what I was thinking about. I'll survive Ronnie's fallout. The Dems will make a halfhearted jab at me, but they know there's nothing there. I was thinking of the web site. It's going to look a bit radical."

"You think that'll impact you? Isn't that why it's in Daryl's name?"

"Lot's of people know how close we are. It won't be hard to figure out we've done this before. If the site starts to get attention, somebody'll put two and two together. If that happens, I'll get some public questions about it."

"That should be easy, shouldn't it? Daryl will say the whole thing is his. Wouldn't that be the end of it?"

"Yeah, it could shake out that way, but that's not what I'd want. I've *had it* with Party politics. I'd want to scream at the top of my lungs that I'm in it up to my ears, that it's Daryl and me together. I'd hate myself if I denied it."

Melinda rubbed his chest lightly. "I know how hard it's been, honey. I don't know what we'd do if you got out of politics. I don't know how we'd make a living, but it doesn't matter. We'll be all right. It hurts me just as much as you seeing you losing respect for what you do. Wherever we are a year from now, whatever you're doing, I'll be right there with you."

"I love you," he said quietly and kissed her again. They held each other without talking for a few minutes. Then he said, "Our life could change. I don't know how much. I already know what we're going to post. We'll say it better, more pointedly, more believably, than we did in college. Somehow, I feel like the country's ready to hear it ... no, more like *thirsting* for it. And the Internet's a fast, free-wheeling medium we didn't have back then, at least not like it is now. It could generate a firestorm. Deep down, that's what I want. I want the firestorm. I suppose that's from twenty years of trying so hard and accomplishing so little. It would feel so, so good to turn out to be right after all. To show 'em all that good really can win in the end."

"I don't know what all that might mean for us, but I know how much you want it, and I hope it happens. Whatever you need from me, you know you've got it."

"I love you, Mel," he told her again. He felt his gut trembling. He didn't know whether it was from his feelings for his wife, because he was so distressed with his career, or because he wanted that firestorm so badly.

Chapter 4

Fourteen weeks later, Saturday, April 11, Carthage, 4:35 p.m.

Daryl proofread Proposition #4. The routine that had developed was to post entries on the second Saturday of the month. Every Friday evening, the Martens and DeCamps gathered for dinner, after which Daryl and Cleve spent time planning, critiquing, and discussing feedback. The work of drafting propositions and editing drafts was accomplished on weeknights and weekends.

After posting Proposition #1, Daryl had contacted everyone in his address books, telling them of commonguy.com, explaining what it was about, and inviting all to visit it after the second Saturday of each month. To anyone who found the postings worth reading, he asked that they forward the site information to everyone in their address books.

The web site tracked hits but was set up without provision for posting responses or comments. Daryl and Cleve anticipated they wouldn't have time to reply to all comments and they didn't want the site to get bogged down with chat, some of which might be off the wall. However, they did want to gauge reader reaction in addition to counting hits. They kept up on the tone of reader opinion by monitoring Daryl's Facebook wall comments and by reviewing independent web sites commenting on their propositions.

Before posting Proposition #4, Daryl reread the January and February propositions.

Proposition #1: What's Worth Fighting For?

When I strip away the intertwined layers of needs, wants, beliefs, and fears, everything that motivates me, then scrutinize these slivers piece by piece to sort the threads of truth into one precept underlying all the stitching, what is the kernel at the heart? I land on a conviction that the objective worth preserving and protecting above all else is the thriving of human civilization into a boundless future. From that precept, it follows that the first consideration in every political act should be its impact on the future of mankind. Although this is a worldwide proposition, American effort toward it must begin at home and then extend to international advocacy and cooperation.

What components are integral to the pursuit of this goal?

1. Integrity in leadership.
   a. The basis of integrity is the concept that each human life is precious.
   b. No individual, regardless of accident of birth or social stature, has any more or any less value than any other.
   c. All rules must apply fairly to all people, including persons who occupy positions of leadership.
2. Optimization of resource utilization.
   a. Our greatest resources are we, the people, and the products of our efforts.
   b. Utilization of natural resources must be redirected to the use of renewable forms only, stopping the exhausting of Earth's nonrenewable natural resources.
3. Establishing a social and political environment that assures the opportunity for all people to maximize their contributions to society.
   a. The divergent gap in human standards of living across the earth must be closed as expeditiously as possible to put all people in a position to contribute to their potential.

b. Wasted efforts and expenditures caused by bureaucracy and political contrivance must be minimized.

c. Everyone must pull his or her weight. There should be no free rides and there must be controls limiting privilege gained by one or more individuals at the expense of others.

This proposition is for the Government of the United States to commit itself, by Constitutional Amendment, to consider the preservation of human civilization above all else in every action it takes.

All future propositions posted on this web site will derive in some manner from this one.

Proposition #2: How Much Do States Waste?

When our nation was founded, the thirteen states insisted that each retain the authority to determine its own modes of operation and pass its own laws, regardless of what the other twelve might do. Over the ensuing two centuries, due to national expansion and unimaginable advancement in communication and travel, it became necessary for the central government to assume ever-increasing control to regulate intrastate activities and pursue national interests.   Today, the holdover authority retained by the individual states is detrimental to commerce and to the efficient use of tax dollars.

1. What makes it acceptable to drive 80 miles per hour on one side of an artificial, invisible line but not faster than 65 on the other, to teach without a master's degree on one side but not the other, to drink beer at 18 on one side but not the other, to run for President with 1,000 signatures on one side but not less than 74,000 on the other?

2. Why is it necessary for an architect to pay to maintain 50 registrations or for a company to pay for 50 certificates of authorization to do business across the country?

3. How much expense and effort are wasted to maintain 50 licensing bureaus for engineers, lawyers, insurers, drivers, vehicles, nurses, boats, accountants, corporations, teachers, ad nauseum, when one central agency would be more effective and consistent at a fraction of the cost?

4. What is the rationale for continuing all the duplicity, inconvenience, inconsistency, and waste? Only this: that's the way we've always done it.

This proposition is to consolidate duplicated state functions into national functions. Would such a consolidation process be easy? No. Would it be fast? No. Would it be possible? Not unless it's begun. It is time.

*   *   *

The Thursday after posting Proposition #1, Daryl had checked the commonguy.com hit count and found 227. He had received 48 Facebook comments, all having an obligatory aura to them, from friends or associates who would have visited any site Daryl would have asked them to. Most of them briefly praised the writing and the nobility of caring about all people. Daryl and Cleve were disappointed with the feedback. However, when they met on the Friday after Proposition #2 was posted, they were animated.

"Hey, buddy!" Daryl grinned at the door, welcoming the DeCamps. "Have you seen any of the blogs that are posting comments about our propositions?" He knew from Cleve's broad smile that he had.

"I found six sites with dozens of comments. And our hits are going up by the hour," Cleve said, entering behind his family. "I checked the count just before we left, and it was over twenty-seven hundred, most of them in the past five days."

"I just looked, and one of the sites had fifty-three posts about Commonguy," Daryl added.

During dinner, the childlike excitement didn't emanate from the children. The two dads couldn't wait to get to Daryl's study to delve into the Web entries. The wives and kids were amused by their excitement. Within forty minutes of the DeCamps' arrival, Daryl and Cleve were poring through the site that had the most postings, sixty-four now.

Daryl pointed at the screen. "Look at this one. 'Commonguy has hit on gold. Why haven't any of our politicians ever thought of consolidating this myriad of redundant state offices?'"

"And this one," Cleve said. "'I'm contacting my state representatives and senators today to support this idea. We could save millions. I'm going to make sure they know about commonguy.com.'"

Daryl scrolled down through positive post after positive post. When he came across a more cautious one, he stopped. "Here's one with a different tone. 'Commonguy's consolidation ideas might sound good in theory, but think about the number of jobs that would be eliminated. How much individual hardship would this create, and what would it do to the economy? This guy would be wise to think things through or maybe talk to some experts before spouting off his farfetched opinions to the world.'"

Cleve was also skimming past positive posts, looking for volatile ones. "Listen to this one. 'Marten is a damned idiot. Our federal government is the most inept and corrupt bureaucracy imaginable. It's bad enough having all of these departments in our state governments, but if you want to see things get really screwed up, turn it over to our national government. Anyone who thinks that would save us money is crazy. If you want to save money, take the obvious action: close down all the damned state offices and get rid of the ridiculous regulations. That would be way better than ratcheting them all up a notch to the federal government.'"

"That's great!" Daryl said. "If we want Commonguy noticed, we *need* some controversy. We might actually get some attention with this thing. Maybe it really will turn out to make a difference. It's gonna be fun!"

"I feel like a kid," Cleve said. "I'm more excited about this than I was for our high school and college editorials.

Wouldn't it be ironic, after working twenty years in state government, to have more impact by going back to what we loved most before we ever started our careers?"

Before they knew it, four hours had passed. They scurried out of the study and found their wives drowsily watching a movie and the younger children asleep on the floor. After half an hour of socializing by those still awake, mostly talking about Web postings, the DeCamps headed for home.

*   *   *

The following Saturday morning, Daryl had added a section to the commonguy.com site for updates. He posted the first one.

Update, February 21

I am excited about the quantity and quality of postings I've seen on Facebook and Internet sites responding to the two propositions on commonguy.com. As I publish more propositions, I will address some of the responses, suggestions, questions, and opposing viewpoints that I become aware of. I invite everyone to visit commonguy.com and, if you feel the propositions are worthwhile, spread the word.

*   *   *

The feedback on Proposition #3 had been more lukewarm than that generated by Proposition #2. Regardless, the hit count for the site was growing exponentially, having now exceeded 15,000. Before posting Proposition #4, Daryl reread #3.

Proposition #3: The Cost of Incompetence

Property damage, injury, and death often are a result of persons making personal, vocational, business, or professional decisions incompetently. Circumstances run the gamut of imagination. An auto mechanic decides to use a similar part he has on hand rather than ordering the correct part for a brake repair. A vacationer starts a campfire in a dry forest without having adequate provisions for fire control. An engineering intern designs a complex structural building component. A nurse injects medication based on an illegible order instead of calling the doctor. A driver passes without sufficient clear sight distance, on and on.

1. For any activity, training and experience are necessary to make decisions with reasonable assurance that intended results will occur and to understand the potential consequences of unintended results.

2. People must understand there are limits to their training and experience and that ignoring those limits puts others at risk.

    a. When faced with any decision, without having sufficient training, experience, or information to be reasonably sure of the outcome, don't make the decision. Send the issue up to a higher level, request qualified help, or obtain adequate information or training first.

3. Costs and hardship resulting from incompetently made decisions can be minimized by infusing an understanding of the concept of competent decision-making into society.

    a. Teach the concept in a mandatory first-year college course, in a required high school course, in junior high, in elementary school, in the military, in naturalization classes.

    b. Promote it in television ads.

    c. Require employers to send new employees to a one-day competency course, and require the course be taken by anyone opening a business.

This proposition is for the government to declare war on incompetent decision-making by making a commitment to educate. The payoff resulting from widespread understanding of the concept and consequences of incompetent decision-making would be incredible.

"Hey, Dad," Jeremy called out as Daryl finished reading. "Telephone."

Daryl walked to the kitchen and picked up the handset. One of the office CAD technicians had some questions for him. It was after 5:00 Saturday afternoon, and half the office staff was working. Daryl felt a pang of guilt, knowing he should be there, too. He'd spent all day working on Proposition #4 and reading postings on the Web.

After working five years for an architectural firm in Cincinnati, Daryl had joined with two partners, Howard Tennyson, a ten-year veteran at the Cincinnati firm, and John Verkler, a member of Daryl's graduating class, to create the firm of Tennyson, Marten, and Verkler. They had opened an office in historic downtown Carthage. The first two years had been lean, drawing primarily from their individual previous client bases. However, by the end of the third year, they had developed a solid reputation for listening to their clients, providing them what they wanted, and dealing with them candidly and professionally. Their clients liked and trusted them, kept coming back, and recommended them to others.

Tennyson, Marten, and Verkler had never lost a repeat client to another firm and had never been threatened with legal action. Now in its fourteenth year, the firm had four associates and fifteen other employees. Over the years the firm had gained a reputation as historic preservation specialists with a strong bent toward practicality and cost consciousness.

Daryl enjoyed his work and career, but his efforts with Commonguy had rekindled his passion for political philosophy and writing. He had all but forgotten how much he had liked that in high school and college. Now, when his mind was free, it rarely drifted toward his projects at work, instead gravitating toward the next proposition or the feedback on previous ones. He knew his productivity at work was slipping.

Daryl answered the CAD technician's questions, hung up, and returned to his study. He knew Cleve was becoming as absorbed in Commonguy as he was, and it didn't appear likely that this project of theirs would be doing any retreating. He put the finishing touches on Proposition #4 and posted it.

Proposition #4: Stop Making Lawyers Rich

Costs of goods, services, and government in the United States have spiraled out of control, partly because the high litigation awards that have become "business as usual" in our courts system, have made skyrocketing fees and prices inevitable. Attorneys promote their services by basing fees on percentages of awards. They maximize their income by luring cases with potential for preposterous awards. Clients are enticed by the promise of zero legal fees and an opportunity to receive a payoff far in excess of actual costs of damage incurred.

1. This practice can be terminated by making percentage-based fees illegal. Require legal firms to base compensation on either hourly rates or fixed fees.
2. Cases do occur where the nature of the crime and the wealth of the perpetrator combine to demand huge punitive damage penalties.
   a. There are no cases for which the plaintiff deserves to receive any compensation in excess of the cost of his or her loss.
   b. Even more so, there are no cases wherein the plaintiff's attorney deserves to reap any portion of high punitive damage amounts.
3. How should restitution and punitive damages be determined and distributed?
   a. When harm is caused by persons or companies, the causer must pay restitution to the injured party in the amount of the actual or calculable costs incurred, but nothing more.

    b. Both restitution and punitive amounts can be calculated fairly and have extensive rational precedents on record.

    c. Award amount calculations should be standardized, publicized, kept updated, and mandated for universal application in all courts throughout the country.

    d. Juries should never be tasked to determine or confirm restitution or penalty amounts.

    e. Mandate that all punitive damage amounts be applied directly to the national debt, with all disbursements administered by the Treasury Department.

4. If an injured party retains a lawyer, the ramifications of that decision are that party's responsibility. Plaintiffs should not be entitled additional restitution to compensate for legal fees.

    a. Every jurisdiction should have a prosecuting attorney's office staffed to represent plaintiffs who do not wish to retain an independent attorney.

    b. The prosecuting attorney must pursue all cases, including those involving harm done without financial loss. For example, an accident that doesn't injure a pregnant woman but causes the loss of her unborn child might result in little or no financial loss, but the entity whose negligence caused the harm must face prosecution. In some cases, restitution might be minimal, but high punitive damages might be warranted.

These changes to our litigation process would benefit all except those who currently receive undeserved compensation from it. All citizens would win equally. Costs of health care, insurance, legal fees, products and services of all types, and eventually operation of the government would shrink, as would the national debt.

Implementing these changes would require integrity, courage, and veracity from governmental leaders, many of whom stem from the legal community. It won't happen without tremendous public pressure. This proposition is for the citizenry to apply that pressure now, cohesively and deafeningly.

After posting the proposition, Daryl read it again and said aloud, "Brace yourself to be attacked by a swarm of lawyers on this one, Daryl."

Chapter 5

Five weeks later, Sunday, May 17, Washington D.C., 6:30 a.m.

On Sundays Gayle Scapeli worked from his residence on the upper two floors of the six-story building he had purchased near 12th and Massachusetts. His morning workout behind him, showered and dressed for the day, he was engaged with his computer.

It had been three weeks since the Trial Lawyers Lobby had first contacted his staff. A week after that a smattering of congressmen had begun to squeak, followed by a few senators. During the past week, the Secretary of the Treasury had requested White House attention to the matter. Scapeli was not inclined to give legitimacy, time, or energy to flash Internet issues. They were never anything more than overnight sensationalism, disappearing as fast as they had surfaced to incite the pandemonium of the moment.

He was disgusted that an Internet flash had seized the attention of the Trial Lawyers, a handful of legislators, and the Treasury Department. Regardless, it had. Like it or not, he needed to become knowledgeable. He called up the culprit web site, commonguy.com.

*   *   *

Gaylord Scapeli understood the traits that had propelled him to his position of power. He was intelligent, quickly comprehended situations for what they were, and knew intuitively what motivated people. The intelligence was inborn. The ability to decipher circumstances and motives had been seared into him during his brutal childhood. He would never have reached adulthood had he allowed emotions to color his view of the situations in which he had to make survival decisions.

He had grown up in Cabrini Green, the most notorious of the Chicago projects. His sister, Jasmine, six years older and to his knowledge his oldest sibling, had watched over him until she was thirteen, when his mother had sold her to a pimp for drug money. He never saw or heard from Jasmine after that. At seven years old, he began fending for himself, stealing, scavenging, whatever it took to stay alive for one more day.

Gayle had two brothers, both of them older than he and younger than Jasmine. When he was eight, he watched his oldest brother die, shot in the face by the owner of a sleazy grocery store during an attempted robbery. A year later, the younger brother vanished. He had a sister three years younger than he. She was living with their mother when, at fourteen, Gayle walked out the door of their decrepit row house apartment for the last time, having decided street living was preferable to remaining one day more with his drug-addicted whore of a mother. He had no clue who his father was. He assumed his paternal ancestry was Italian, since he looked pronouncedly so and his mulatto mother was only one-quarter Italian. He was sure his siblings all had different fathers, though no father had ever came to visit at the putrid dump they slept in.

After taking to the streets, he had never looked back. He assumed his relatives were all dead by now, but he didn't really know or care. The best thing Jasmine had done for him was enroll him in school. Contrary to any reason or expectation, young Gayle had loved learning. It was easy for him and drew him in. Somehow he had stayed in school and graduated in the top five percent of his class.

School had been the easy part of life. The streets were merciless. Availability of food and shelter was sporadic. Staying alive had required him to recognize threats immediately and react spontaneously. More than once it had come down to "kill or be killed." He had survived. By age sixteen he had become emotionless and cold-blooded, conquering even fear.

During his senior year, Army recruiters had offered him a way out that had focused the future course of his life. The

Army's mental and physical aptitude tests identified him as a prime candidate for the crack Ranger outfit. There he had exhibited extraordinary shrewdness and veracity, which had not gone unnoticed or unexploited. The Army had then put him through college and inserted him into top secret covert operations.

After spending eight years executing orders that would never be disclosed, Scapeli, supremely competent and confident, made a life decision. His training and experience had convinced him he could achieve anything by planning and controlling the development of circumstances and the actions of the people involved. He could do that better than anyone he knew. He could induce and coerce others, without them even suspecting he was manipulating them, to act in accord with his blueprint to create whatever result he wanted. At thirty-three, Gaylord Scapeli left the Army, committing to himself that he would live the rest of his life serving his own interests. He would have power, utilizing others in whatever manner necessary to gain it.

By the time he had entered covert operations, he had overcome all human compulsions that could weaken his will or position. He had never used drugs. He had consumed plenty of alcohol between the ages of twenty and twenty-five, but those days were over. He'd had many women during those years, some willing, some not. That was also over. The need for sex was no different than any other addiction. If one had to have it, one became in some measure a slave to it. He would have no family, other than any unknown offspring he might already have spawned, and they didn't matter.

Scapeli created Davidson County Safety Services to be the venue from which he would work his magic. It had been no accident twenty-two years ago that Randall Pritchard had been present at the orgy at Kris Jansen's mansion in Nashville. The fire at the mansion had been no accident. The conversations between Pritchard and him had been no accident. The fact that Pritchard was President of the United States today was no accident. The fact that the President was not free to disregard any demand of Scapeli's was no accident. Scapeli's current position and power had all been planned, beginning twenty-three years ago.

In some ways, getting Pritchard to the top – getting himself to the top – had proven to be easier than staying there. After becoming Chief of Staff, Scapeli had to keep his machinations at arm's length, not traceable to him. His Ranger protégé and now owner of Davidson County Safety Services, Gerald Baron was his most critical asset, the nerve center of his network. Baron knew everything about each of the myriad of individuals who were fraudulent enough or immoral enough or unlucky enough to be caught in Scapeli's web. He understood exactly how the strings had to be pulled, tweaked, and twisted.

Controlling the professional staff in the White House Office, the President's staff, was easy. They were all competent individuals serving at the pleasure of the President. They would do what they were told or be replaced. With one exception, none of the White House staff was ever involved in or aware of the clandestine dealings undertaken to manipulate the political landscape. The closest clean staff member to the President was Greg Jolsen, Assistant to the President for Communications. He controlled public communications and did an excellent job of keeping Pritchard on a pedestal. Jolsen was also savvy enough to execute, precisely and unquestioningly, any directive from Scapeli.

The clean staff member closest and most valuable to Scapeli was Elaine Kosovich. She was forty-seven and had never been married to anything except her job. She was all business: dedicated, efficient, and capable. Kosovich ran the day-to-day operations of Scapeli's office, allowing him to concentrate on whatever issue might be most important to him on any given day. She never questioned Scapeli's direction, and no one on staff ever questioned hers.

The lone exception to White House staff members being kept uninvolved in Scapeli's behind-the-scenes dealings was Lowell Pullman, the National Security Advisor. He interacted with the Director of the National Security Agency, Dennis McGlothlin. McGlothlin was one of the key appointees requiring Congressional approval who Scapeli had considered critical to be under his influence. Funds funneling into and out of NSA could remain undisclosed for national security reasons. Scapeli's maneuverings required a stockpile of untraceable cash, and NSA had to be the source. It had been essential to place individuals in these two positions who knew that Scapeli could and would destroy their careers and lives, should they misstep.

Scapeli's network was imposing. Hundreds of powerful persons were under his thumb, including a major television network president, eleven U.S Senators, twenty-eight U.S. Representatives, seven governors, the secretaries of Defense and State, one Supreme Court justice, the Chairman of the Federal Reserve Board, a plethora of state senators and representatives around the country, and the President of the United States of America. His control extended over an approximately equal number of Democrats and Republicans.

The unearthing of enough closet skeletons to coerce this pool of individuals to do his bidding had required years of meticulous planning and effort. Most of their secrets were born of sexual escapades or fraudulent financial dealings, although some related to family embarrassments, war atrocities, or criminal activities. Two involved murders. Over a third of these skeletons would never have come into being had he not created them, as was the case for the incident at Jansen's mansion in Nashville that had sealed his control over Pritchard.

His system worked well. When Scapeli needed an action, he instructed Gerald Baron. Baron would select a communicator – he had many sources – to conscript the initiating individual. With no mention of Scapeli's name, the person ultimately required to act would have no doubt regarding either the source of the command or the consequence of failure to deliver. So far, Scapeli's objectives had always been achieved, and his involvement had been untraceable.

Scapeli read Daryl Marten's first four propositions. *Save mankind by getting rid of corruption and waste and by taking from the rich and giving to the poor, consolidate redundant state functions into federal bureaucracies, stop people from being incompetent, and force lawyers to stop getting rich from big trial payoffs.* Scapeli laughed aloud, imagining the chaos that would erupt in the House and Senate if any of these propositions actually wiggled their way onto the legislative agenda. He laughed louder at trial lawyers, legislators, and the Secretary of the Treasury actually being worried about it.

He read the entry, posted a week ago: Proposition #5: Crush Fraud. Crush fraud perpetrated by anyone: politicians, corporate and banking executives, TV evangelists, stock brokers, investment administrators. Send 'em all straight to jail and make 'em pay every cent back. *Right.*

Scapeli thought about what might be happening. The concepts proposed by Daryl Marten, whoever he was, would appeal to the American public, regardless of the impossibility of adoption and implementation. Marten had started posting his simplistic pie in the sky notions four months ago. The only reason any legislators would be concerned, or would have even noticed, would be that either their constituents or their backers, probably the Trial Lawyers Lobby, were pushing them. The Treasury Department would not have paid any more attention to Marten naming them to administer punitive damage proceeds than they did any of the other thousands of Web posts suggesting their action, had it not been for the lawyers being up in arms.

He laughed again. He actually liked the idea of pulling the rug out from under the lawyers. *Scalp the scalpers.* It had no more chance of coming to fruition than any of the other propositions, but it was an entertaining little fantasy. Regardless of the concerns of any lobbyists, legislators, or department heads, Pritchard would not be getting involved in this. *What do they want the President to do, tell the quack to stop posting on the Internet? That isn't going to happen.*

Now that the targets of Marten's barbs were becoming aware, rebuttals would come out of the woodwork. Hundreds would blast forth from authoritative sources, bellowing the absurdity and faulty logic of Marten's propositions. Most of the rebuttals would be nothing more than confusing rhetoric, but it wouldn't matter because they would come from judges, chief executive officers, governors, senators – those perceiving support for Marten's ideas to be a threat to their sacred methods of conducting business as usual.

Scapeli found himself looking forward to watching it all play out. Marten's ideas were apparently acquiring some measure of popularity. But there was no way his targets would allow his propositions to receive any real consideration. If the public got too supportive for comfort, Marten would get bought off and become rich. *If he really does turn out to be an idealist and refuses to sell out, he'll start getting threats. If he remains too stupid or stubborn to quit, he'll be lucky to survive.*

Scapeli closed out of commonguy.com. He had other issues to deal with that did require action. The presidential nominating conventions were little more than a year off. It was time to put the wheels in motion to position the Democratic candidates. Scapeli knew who they were going to be. The contenders just didn't know it yet, at least not for sure. It was time for them to throw their hats in the ring.

They had been chosen for several reasons. Illinois Senator and former governor Garner Wheeler and former Secretary of State and retired Army General Richard Herrington both had strong popular and Party backing. They were both ambitious and had long been considering bids for the presidency. And they both had blockbusters in their past that almost no one knew about. Scapeli knew.

Wheeler and Herrington would battle each other hard for the nomination and excite the nation with their contest. As the convention would draw near, with the two running neck and neck, talk would surface about how strong the ticket would be with both of them on it. But, which would be on top? Their antagonism would intensify. Then, from nowhere, they would each obtain devastating, verifiable details of the other's indiscretions, first Wheeler of Herrington's, and then, after the initial smear, Herrington of Wheeler's. The Democratic Party's bid for the presidency would blow apart into a chaotic mess.

The "also ran" for the Democrats would be young Vermont Senator Bradley Catcher, who would find, on the eve of his withdrawal announcement, that his opposition had suddenly evaporated. By default, he would be the Democratic Party's candidate. *Catcher has no chance against Pritchard. He might not carry a single state.*

It was time to put Baron into action.

Chapter 6

Four weeks later, Sunday, June 14, Cincinnati, 6:53 a.m.

Zachary Forrester, junior news correspondent for Channel 4, wasn't scheduled to work Sunday but sat in his cubicle anyway. He had graduated from college a year ago and landed this job last September. The pay wasn't much, but he was excited about his career, and his face was on camera a lot, reporting from all over Hamilton County. The fresh correspondent's eager, youthful face, slight frame, short-cropped light brown hair, and dancing blue eyes were fast becoming a daily presence in Cincinnati households.

For the past six weeks Zach had been following Web postings by and about Daryl Marten and his commonguy.com web site originating from nearby Carthage. Marten's last two propositions urging restrictions on lawyer compensation and a crackdown on fraud had generated a lot of Internet traffic.

Marten was receiving enthusiastic popular support, and, at the same time, getting ripped to shreds by prominent persons. Naysayers proclaimed how outlandish and impractical his propositions were and how impossible they would be to adopt and implement. Federal judges, Fortune 500 company presidents, congressmen, and even two governors had exploded on Marten. Some of the repudiations elucidated in infinite detail why various propositions would be disastrous. Some revolved around how the United States political system worked; asserting that legislative consensus on such speculative schemes could never be attained.

The rebuffs contained lots of verbiage, but little substance to back up the claims of non-viability. The tactics fell into two categories. Most of them offered drawn-out arguments using a plethora of technical jargon. It took hours to read these and actually understand the terms. Zach had waded through two of them, looking up every unfamiliar word. After spending a day on each, he was convinced both were thoroughly inconsistent. The second category of disavowal spewed out generalities, reaching conclusions that might have been logical had the unstated underlying precepts been defensible assumptions, which they were not. Zach's judgment was that the rebuttals, by and large, were deceptive.

Last Monday he had approached his boss, asking if he could request an interview with Marten. The response had been to wait until the next posting, research it, and then come back to explain how he would approach a meeting. That was why Zach was working on his day off. He anticipated the posting of Marten's sixth proposition and wanted to read and research it before Monday morning.

It was there.

Proposition #6: Cost of the National Debt

The national debt is money the federal government owes to holders of instruments of debt service: treasury bills, notes, and bonds. The government issues them to pay its annual expenditures that exceed receipts. The national debt currently stands at $15 trillion. Some of the debt holders are domestic, but over half are now foreign.

1. The annual federal budget ranges from $3 to $3.5 trillion: 24% for Medicare and Medicaid, 21% for Social Security, 20% for Defense, 10% for interest on the national debt, 10% for other mandated expenditures (food stamps, congressional salaries, etc.), and 15% for other discretionary expenditures (grants, special projects, etc.).

2. Annual tax revenues range from $2.5 to $3 trillion: 45% from personal income taxes, 36% from Social Security and Medicare taxes, 12%

from corporate taxes, and 7% from other sources (excise, estate, and gift taxes, etc.).

3. The Government spends about 20% more per year than it receives. Half of this overspending is interest on the national debt.

4. To avoid placing ever-burgeoning debt on our children and grandchildren, this overspending must stop. The solution requires a combination of reducing expenditures and increasing revenues.

5. It is possible to reduce spending for big-ticket items: Medicare, Social Security, and defense. It is also possible to increase revenues enough to balance the budget and to pay off the national debt without increasing taxes on individuals earning less than $200,000.

6. The national debt will have to be dealt with in some manner at some time, and the longer the action is delayed the more severe it will be.

   a. Covering the current cost of interest on the debt could be dealt with by increasing revenues 10%.

   b. Increasing them an additional 5% would pay off the national debt in less than twenty years, at which time this 15% tax boost could be dropped.

This proposition is for the United States Government to stop overspending its receipts and pay off our national debt.

Who could argue against the government living within its means and paying off the national debt without raising taxes on anyone making less than two hundred grand ... except the people making more? This proposition would expand the list of people Marten would irritate to include high-income earners.

Whether workable or not, Marten's propositions were receiving expanding popular support and booming opposition from a diverse group of powerful individuals. This new proposition would intensify the discord. Daryl Marten seemed hell-bent on becoming a hot potato. *And, by God, I'm going to be the first reporter to jump in this fire.*

*   *   *

Late Monday morning, as Daryl rose from behind his desk to head home for lunch, his intercom buzzed.

"Yeah, Jill."

"Zachary Forrester from Channel 4 is on line two for you. Do you want to take it?"

Daryl's heart leapt. He'd been wondering if a call like this might come, hoping for it. "Yes."

Daryl punched the button and said as calmly as he could, "Daryl Marten."

"Hello, Mr. Marten. This is Zachary Forrester from Channel 4. How are you this morning?"

"Fine, Zachary, what can I do for you?" Something in the reporter's voice, a hint of youthful exuberance, had led Daryl to call him Zachary rather than Mr. Forrester.

"It's just Zach to my friends. I've been following the Web traffic generated by commonguy.com. Are you the Daryl Marten behind all the fuss?"

"That would be me."

"Great! I have to say, I'm impressed by your propositions and all the reaction. I'd like to set up an interview. Would you be interested?"

"Sure." Daryl tried not to sound too enthusiastic but wasn't sure he pulled it off. "When?"

"I'd rather not sit on it. We'd like to run it tonight at six. Could you do it this afternoon?"

Daryl's heart was pounding. "I can make that work. What time?"

"How about two o'clock at the Channel 4 studio?"

"I'll be there. I'll look forward to meeting you, Zach."

"And I'm anxious to meet you. I'm excited about what you're doing."

"Great! I'll see you at two."

Daryl had trouble containing himself at lunch. School was out for the summer, and Racine and the kids were all home. They were jubilant that Dad was going to be on TV. Daryl called Cleve. They agreed to gather at the Martens' at 5:30 and have dinner after the broadcast.

Daryl immediately liked Zach. His enthusiasm was infectious, and he seemed to hold nothing back. What you saw was what you got. He was friendly, and Daryl was struck with the impression of trustworthiness, counterintuitive to his expectations for media personalities. The two chatted for half an hour, getting to know each other and planning the three-minute interview. Zach explained they would probably not run the entire interview, but promised he wouldn't allow editing to portray anything out of context. They were both pleased with the tape. They exchanged cell phone numbers, shook hands, and Daryl left the studio shortly after 3:30. He was too hyped to go back to work and called Jill to tell her he wouldn't be coming in but would be on the Channel 4 evening news. Then he went home to enjoy the afternoon with his family.

At 5:05, Daryl's cell phone rang, displaying a number that seemed familiar but he couldn't place.

"Daryl Marten."

"Hey, Daryl," came the excited voice, "it's Zach! Guess what?"

"What?" Daryl replied apprehensively.

"You're not going to be on the six o'clock news."

"Why? What happened?"

"We, my friend – you and me – are going to be on the six-thirty national news!"

"*What*? How?"

"When our editors think we have something really special, they send it to the network to try to get it on national. Once in a great while, it works. It worked today, buddy! They're going to show the whole interview, the whole three minutes!"

"No way! That's incredible! I don't know what to say."

"Me neither, except watch the news! How 'bout you and I have lunch tomorrow? I'd like to come to Carthage and see your office, and maybe see where you live. If you don't mind. Maybe meet your family. No cameras, just talk."

"That'd be great. Noon, at my office?"

"See you then."

As he hung up, Racine and the kids were all staring at him. Kelsey said, "Are you still gonna be on TV, Daddy?"

"What the heck, Dad?" Jeremy added. "What's up?"

Daryl eyed his family, a huge grin on his face. "I'm not going to be on the Cincinnati news after all." He waited a moment, looking at the bewildered faces, and then added, "I'm going to be on the national news! Wait till Cleve hears this!"

The eleven members of both families distributed themselves around the TV so all had a good view. Ten minutes into the newscast, anchorwoman Regina Wasson introduced the segment.

"Since January, an architect from Carthage, Ohio, has been posting propositions on his web site, commonguy.com. Daryl Marten posts one proposition per month, each suggesting a fundamental change in the way our government conducts business. Marten's site has attracted the attention of the public and a few high-level officials and businessmen across the nation. Some view his propositions as radical, some as oversimplified, some as unworkable. Others see them as a breath of fresh air.

"Regardless of the variety of opinions, Marten has undeniably been noticed by some influential people. Our Cincinnati affiliate interviewed Mr. Marten this afternoon. Here's the interview."

The living room, which had been hushed, exploded as Zachary and Daryl appeared on the screen.

"This is Zachary Forrester, with lifelong Carthage resident Daryl Marten who, in January, launched his web site, commonguy.com. We've been monitoring his postings and reactions to them for several weeks.

"Daryl has advocated allowing legal firms to bill only at hourly rates or fixed fees, making it illegal for them to base fees on a percentage of court awards. The goal would be to eliminate frivolous lawsuits and unreasonably high payoffs to lawyers and plaintiffs. He has also advocated the consolidation of duplicated governmental functions, such as licensing bureaus and highway departments from multiple bureaucracies in each of the fifty states into single departments of the federal government. One of his propositions urges balancing the federal budget and eliminating the national debt without increasing taxes on anyone earning less than two hundred thousand dollars annually.

Another suggests that the government vigorously pursue and prosecute the perpetrators of public and private fraud. Daryl, what prompted you to launch this web site and publish your suggestions for governmental change?"

"First and foremost, I'm in love with the United States of America, and I want to see our nation be the best it can be. Second, and I suppose some might consider this a personality defect, I've never been able to shake either the idealism or the optimism of my youth. I'm still convinced that good things come from being ethical and moral, whether we're talking about a person, a business, or the government. Third, it seems to me that decisions being made by our leaders in government and business have been moving further and further away from being ethical or moral. All of this has nudged me to the point that I'm no longer willing to just stand by and watch. I have hope that my efforts might actually make a difference."

"Have you been surprised by the amount of attention Commonguy has drawn?"

"I'd say encouraged more than surprised. From the beginning, we knew we couldn't have any impact unless a tremendous number of Americans agreed with us strongly enough to voice their opinions."

"Daryl, you said 'we'. Is Commonguy the product of more than just your effort?"

"Yes. I have a collaborator. To date, he's chosen to remain anonymous, and I respect his wishes. While I don't claim to be doing this on my own, my name will be the only one publicly attached to Commonguy until such time as he may decide to make his identity known."

"Is there anything you'd like to say to those who support your propositions?"

"Yes. If you agree strongly with any of the propositions posted on Commonguy, please do two things. First, spread the word. Ask as many people as you can to visit the web site. Second, contact your elected representatives. Make them know how much you support those propositions you agree with. None of these propositions have any chance of being implemented unless the United States citizenry clamors for them."

"And do you have any reply to the rebuttals that have been posted on various Internet sites?"

"Yes. One of the objections has been that the proposed changes are too sweeping for our government to consider, that it would not be possible to get enough agreement within our legislative and executive branches to adopt the changes. To that, I say the decisions about how this country runs are and always will be made by 'we, the people.' Our representatives are elected to carry out our common desires as expressed by the majority of each official's constituents. If enough people demand changes, our lawmakers will ultimately be unable to resist legitimate consideration of them.

"To the claim that the propositions are too simple and could not work in practice, I have several comments. Yes, the propositions as written are simplifications of the concepts. The details of implementation of each proposition would take many people many weeks of effort to prepare, and would be documented in volumes rather than on a single page. However, that doesn't mean that far-reaching changes could not work. I've examined as many of the rebuttals as I could. What I've observed is that the arguments attempt to confuse the issues rather than logically address the process or impact of implementation. They use technical terms many people are not familiar with and, in some cases, have invented words that have no definition at all. Every one of the responses I've examined has failed the tests of consistency and logic. In short, I believe they're mostly smoke and mirrors."

"One final question, Daryl. Do you intend to respond to each of the supporters and challengers who publish their opinions on the web?"

"I'd love to do that, Zach, but it would be impossible. I'm excited and encouraged by the interest in Commonguy. But, there aren't enough hours in a day to reply to all of the responses being posted. It's turning out there isn't even enough time to read them all. I track the Commonguy hit count and try to keep up with the breadth of the feedback and absorb each unique perspective. We'll attempt to respond to as many viewpoints as we can."

"Thank you, Mr. Marten, for taking time to visit with us. Good luck to you and your collaborator, and I'll be keeping my eyes on Commonguy."

The screen changed back to Regina Wasson. "If you'd like to know more, take a look at commonguy.com. I did this afternoon, and I'd say the controversy has only just begun. We'll be right back."

The Marten household erupted.   Cleve exclaimed, "Wow, Daryl, you were fantastic!   In all my years in the legislature, I've never been able to do anything like that."

Racine wrapped her arms around Daryl and kissed him. "You were great, sweetheart."

"Are we famous now?" Kelsey asked as Kyle turned a cartwheel.

As the ruckus subsided, Cleve said, "Things could get a little crazy now. Better brace yourself."

As Daryl grinned at him and started to reply, the phone rang. It never stopped. First it was family and close friends, then acquaintances and business associates. By that time, people around the country had found the telephone number of Daryl Marten in Carthage, Ohio. Most of the calls were from supporters already familiar with commonguy.com. There was a smattering of ominous ones.

"Marten, you're out of your mind. You're making some powerful enemies. If I were you, I'd grow eyes in back of my head."

"Are you an imbecile? What makes you think you can put your retarded ideas on the Internet and accomplish anything other than create a riot?"

And the most disconcerting one, "You're a *dead* man."

Chapter 7

Thursday, July 23, New York City, 6:03 a.m.

Daryl and Racine lay wrapped in each other's arms in a luxurious suite at the Times Square Marriott, courtesy of The Insomniac Show. They had arrived at LaGuardia yesterday afternoon, having left the kids with Grandpa and Grandma. Daryl was to be at the studio at noon to prepare for an appearance on Jeff Kramer's show, to be taped before a live audience at 4:00 and air tonight at 11:30.

"Need your nerves calmed?" Racine smiled.

"I'm fine." Daryl pulled her tight to him. "You already went the extra mile last night, just to get me to sleep."

"My pleasure, baby. Don't worry, you'll do great. You're ready."

"I am glad you're here with me. I couldn't pull it off without you. I love you, you know."

She rolled up on top of him and kissed him. "I love you, too, Daryl Marten."

As he held her, Daryl thought back over the past month. Cleve had been right. *Everything's crazy.* Since the interview with Zach, life had become a cyclone.

*   *   *

The night the interview had aired, he'd finally unplugged the phone so he could go to bed. At 7:00 the following morning, he plugged the phone back in. It rang immediately. The calls were all from supporters. After being on the phone fifteen minutes, he unplugged it again and told Racine, "We'll have to get an unlisted number."

He arrived at the office 8:20 to find Jill on the phone, looking pleadingly at him. John Verkler and Howard Tennyson were leaning on the reception counter, listening to Jill and waiting for him to arrive.

He eyed the trio. "Has she been on the phone since eight?"

"I got here at seven and it was ringing," Howard said. "After five minutes, I thought maybe there was some kind of emergency and answered it. They asked for you. Soon as I hung up it rang again. Different person, same thing. Nonstop."

"I'm really sorry, guys," Daryl said. "This came out of nowhere. It's the same at home. I had to unplug the phone."

"What do you want to do?" John asked.

"Well..." Daryl talked as he thought. "I could ask Racine to come in and take calls on our main line. We'll have to call all our clients and contractors and give them our backdoor number. I can call them all if Jill doesn't have time."

"That's probably the best we can do," Howard said. "We could set Racine up in the small conference room. Are you planning on returning all these calls?"

"There's no way. Racy can talk for me. She knows what I'd say."

"Okay. Sounds like a plan, at least for now," John said. "Really, Daryl, this is amazing. I know it's important to you. We're impressed. We just didn't expect the sudden disruption. It'll probably be great for business in the long run. It's just difficult this morning."

"I know," Daryl replied. "I'm not ready for it either. But I'll do whatever it takes to keep us going here. I know you'll both be patient, and I appreciate that. And I apologize for the madness."

*　　　*　　　*

Racine worked the office phone from 7:30 until 5:00 every day that week, leaving the kids with Grandpa and Grandma. She took all Daryl's calls, including the few that were threatening. For the most part, her responses were simply, "Thank you very much for your support." The threats were distressing. It became impossible to give the agreed-upon reply:

"We're sorry you feel that way, but we believe strongly in this. We're not forcing our opinions on anyone, just promoting thinking in different ways to find the best solutions." The worst tirades, like, "Prepare to meet your maker, bitch," unraveled her, and all she could do was slam the phone down.

Early Saturday morning, the family went to Stone Lick State Park for a day of recovery. While the kids were playing badminton, Daryl and Racine talked. There had been no time for that during the week.

"Honey," Racine asked, "are you sure you want to keep going with this? I know how excited you and Cleve were about it. And it looks like it's working, doing everything you hoped. More. But I sure didn't see *this* coming. None of us did. The threats are *horrible*. They scare me."

"I don't know. You're right, we didn't see it. *Couldn't* have. I mean, we thought it'd either be controversial or a dud. But I didn't expect *this*. It'd be hard to quit, though. To start this, then, when it works better than we ever hoped, just when we really get people's attention, say, 'Wait a minute, this is too tough,' and quit … I don't know. Maybe if we don't drop it, six months from now we'll think going on was the worst mistake we ever made. But I'm not sure I can quit. I *will* talk to Cleve, though, and if he wants to drop it, I'll do it. But I know Cleve, and sticking with it'll probably be more important to him than me."

"I'm just scared. I don't want anything to happen to you. I want us to be safe and happy. I'm trying not to worry, but it's been a *god-awful* week. I wasn't going to mention it, but I've seen two cars creep by our house, gawking. I mean, Monday night was really exciting, but after that it's been terrible." Her voice cracked, and a lone tear trickled down her left cheek.

"I saw a drive-by, too, and didn't want to tell you. I'll talk to Cleve tonight, honey."

"I'm sorry, Daryl. I don't want to make it even harder for you. Whatever you decide, I'll stick by you. You're a good man, and you're my guy. And I'm with you."

*   *   *

Cleve and Melinda had their own heart-to-heart talk Friday night, before the Martens' Stone Lick outing. They had kept in close touch with Daryl and Racine and knew what the week had been like for them. Watching the late-night news over a snack at the kitchenette counter, Cleve brought it up.

"It just isn't right to sit by and watch Daryl struggle with this on his own. I'm as much the cause as he is. Maybe more. I should come clean."

Melinda stared at him with a half surprised, half worried expression. "Tell the world? What would that do to your career?"

"I don't know. After seeing this week, probably wreck it."

"That's huge. Don't be too rash."

"I can't leave Daryl and Racy hang out there by themselves. It wasn't a big deal till now. But we *know* what they've gone through this week. It's eating at me. All our talk of ethics and morals, and me just sitting back, letting them take all the blows? How much more hypocritical could I be?"

"Maybe we should all give it up. Just close down Commonguy." She knew it was a futile suggestion, but made it anyway.

"I'd do that for Daryl and Racy, if that's what they want, but I'm not sure what I'd do then. I'm the reason this whole thing got started ... me feeling like I've wasted my life's work. My career in politics and the Party is over, anyway. I've had it with the way our government works. I mean, the way it *doesn't* work."

"I don't know the answer. I know how into this you and Daryl are. But now that we're seeing it really start to click and what it's doing to their lives? I know it's selfish, but I can't make myself want what they've had this week. I guess that's bad."

"We'll talk to them this weekend. The four of us together should decide whether to keep going or fold."

"All right. And if it turns out we decide to stick with it, I'll be in all the way. If we decide that, once it's done, I won't drag my feet."

"I know, Mel. I've seen you in action. Once a machine's in motion, you're better and stronger than anyone. I'm not worried about you holding back."

*   *   *

Daryl had called Cleve Saturday afternoon from the park and arranged to spend the evening at the DeCamps'. After dinner, they waited for the kids to head for the basement, but that never happened. After half an hour of small talk, Daryl nonchalantly asked them if they were going to go play games.

Jeremy responded, "We know you guys are gonna talk about what to do with Commonguy. We lived through this week, too, and we'll be living through next week with you and Mom, and the weeks after that. We want to hear what's going to happen."

Rory said, "We don't have to talk, Dad. We just want to hear. It's as big to us as it is to you guys."

Kelsey ran to Daryl, arms outstretched. "I want to stay with you, Daddy." He swept her up, and she wrapped her arms around his neck.

Kyle simply said, "I'm not leavin'."

The DeCamp children were less vocal, but just as intent on being present. They had heard some of the phone conversations. They knew the Martens' week had been strained and that Jeremy, Kyle, Rory, and Kelsey had spent their days at their grandparents' house.

"Okay, kids," Daryl said. "You're right. Whatever we decide will impact you as much as us. It's fine with me if you stay."

"I'm stayin' right here," Kyle repeated stubbornly.

Cleve couldn't hold back any longer. "After seeing what this week's been like for you, if we stick with it, there's no way I'm keeping my name out of it."

"You don't have to do that, Cleve," Daryl replied. "The Party would have your head."

"Maybe. But I don't care. You know how this whole thing got started. I'm done with them anyway."

"What would you do? Change careers?" Daryl asked.

"Not right away. My term's just starting. Just because the Party doesn't like me anymore, they can't just kick me out of office. Who knows, I might get more accomplished if I'm *not* a Party member."

"What about your lives?" Daryl prodded. "You saw what happened to us and my business this week. You're a state rep. It'd be worse for you."

"We can handle it if you guys want to stick with it."

"What do you girls think?" Daryl asked. "Cleve and I've been doing all the talking, but it isn't just up to us. You've got just as much say in this as we do."

Racine looked resolute. "I've been thinking since this morning. This has been a terrible week, and I *desperately* don't want my life ... our lives ... to be like this. And I don't want any more threats or the fear that comes with *every one* of those calls. I want us to be safe. I want my *kids* to be safe. But even with all that, I'm not gonna roll over and play dead just because I'm afraid of what some fanatic might do if we take a stand for what we believe's right. I don't want the problems or stress that come with Commonguy, but you don't have to quit because of me."

After an awkward minute, Melinda said, "This isn't what I thought I was going to say. Cleve needs to do this. He needs to shout to the world he's part of it. I want him to feel good about his life. Being a full vocal partner in Commonguy will do that. So, that's what I want. I want to keep going and I want to shout right beside him." She laid her hand on his.

"I know I'm just a kid and I said I'd be quiet and just listen," Rory said, "but you can't quit, Dad. You guys have *great* ideas. That's why so many people like them and just some selfish people who don't want to live by fair rules hate them. Even if they try to make things bad for us, we can take it."

"How could we quit?" Daryl asked quietly, Kelsey still clinging to him.

"I'm not afraid of the jerks! Bring it on!" Kyle yelped.

"I'll pound 'em!" Bobby added.

"We're in," David said. "You can count on us."

"Looks like it's us against the world." Jeremy grinned and clapped an arm around David's shoulders.

*   *   *

Update, Sunday, June 21

Last week began with a tremendous boon: a news interview broadcast nationwide. Following the broadcast, the phones at both my home and office began ringing nonstop. Most of the calls were supportive, but a few were threatening. We were unable to handle all the calls, and our week became stressful.

I mentioned during the interview that I have a collaborator. Being unwilling to allow my family to absorb all the stress, and at hazard to his career, my lifelong friend is making his participation known. He is Cleveland DeCamp, the state representative serving the Carthage area in the Ohio legislature. Although Cleve is a member of the Republican Party, I am not. Commonguy.com is not affiliated with any political party. After last week, I'm convinced it is opposed by both major parties. We believe Cleve will fall into disfavor with the Republicans now that his association with Commonguy is public knowledge.

We don't relish the difficulties our families are likely to encounter in the coming months. We do look forward to publishing more propositions. We seek no income from Commonguy, so we won't hire staff. We won't be able to reply to individual contacts, or to read or listen to every message we receive. We will keep abreast of the tone and general content of all feedback, and will address common themes and questions.

That afternoon, the Marten family convened at Rob and Donna Defoe's home on the outskirts of town. They were less apt to be disturbed at Daryl's brother-in-law and sister's home than the home of his parents, Drake and Julia Marten, since all telephones and residences in Carthage listed under the name of Marten had been subject to unsolicited calls and drive-bys. Daryl had suggested this gathering to prepare everyone for what might happen during the next few months.

Rob was a hearty, booming man, five years older than Donna. He owned a construction company founded by his father. Donna had worked as a secretary at the company after graduating from high school and had fallen for Rob and married him when she was nineteen. They had two daughters, ages 17 and 13. Donna filled her days with community support activities. She'd spent most of her time the past week talking with friends impressed by her brother's newfound fame.

Today the kids didn't hang around for the adults' conversation. The six of them headed for the Defoes' horse barn, their habit on summer visits.

"It'll be fine," Rory assured his mother as he hurried off with the rest of the gang, giving her no opportunity to object.

"I'll ride with Jeremy!" Kelsey squealed, knowing full well that was a condition of her release.

"I'll take care of her, Mom," Jeremy said, picking up his elated little sister.

"Racy," Julia started off, "your husband's always had a stubborn streak, but I think we all, especially my grandchildren, would be better off if you'd convince him to get off his high horse about how this country should run. It's got along fine for two hundred years without his help. It doesn't need Daryl Marten to tell it how to run." They all knew Drake and Julia were proud of their children, especially Daryl, but Julia was obviously serious.

"Sorry, Mom." Racine grinned, "You know I've never been able to control him."

"Actually, that's why I wanted to talk to everybody," Daryl interjected. "I don't want to make a big deal of it, but I do want you all to know what I'm doing. I hope no fallout hits any of you, but I can't promise it won't. You all know Cleve is in this with me. Last night we got together to decide whether to throw in the towel or press on. Mom and Dad, it turns out you guys didn't raise quitters. Neither did Cleve's folks. We're not gonna get bullied out of doing what we believe in. We're sticking with it."

"I was afraid of that," Julia said.

Drake looked his son in the eyes. "I admire tenacity. You know I do. But, are you sure? We know you received death threats last week. You've got a terrific wife and four great kids. You've built your practice into a rewarding business. What's so important about telling everybody how you think the country should run? Is it really worth it?"

"You know better, Dad. You've watched me for forty-four years. It's my idealistic and optimistic nature. *You* put that in me. You *know* I can't say I don't care, that I can't say, 'Whoa, this is getting too tough, I'd better quit.' You know that better than anyone."

Drake sighed. "I have to try, Daryl. I'm not young anymore, and maybe I don't look at things the way I used to. I worry about your safety. Yours and Racy's and my grandkids'. All my kids and grandkids, for that matter. I'm not sure this thing won't put us *all* in danger."

"Aw, take it easy on him, Pops," Rob said. "I've had everybody here up in my plane. Hell, I've let most of you take the controls. This can't be any riskier than that."

Rob's construction company owned a Piper Seneca V. Flying was his favorite hobby and he often took the family members for rides. Defoe had an instrument flight rating but preferred to fly during the day, without flight plans, reserving the freedom to change course and destination on a whim. He networked with other small craft pilots and liked to avoid major airports, utilizing private air strips whenever he could.

"It'll be all right," Donna told Drake and Julia. "You let me marry this guy." She nodded at Rob. "What could be more hazardous than that?"

"If you remember," Julia retorted, grinning, "we *did* warn you, but you were deaf."

"And don't forget," Danielle chimed, "I'm a doctor. Whatever happens, I can probably fix it." Daryl's youngest sister, Danielle, was a pediatrician, divorced and childless, five feet eight, shapely, brunette, and still a head turner at thirty seven.

"We raised a flock of idiots." Julia eyed Drake and shook her head.

"Anyway," Daryl said, "we're moving forward. I'm not sure what will happen. But, if any of you get harassed, I want you to let me know. I've told Sheriff Stone about every threat we received. I want to keep him informed, so tell me if anybody bothers any of you."

"All right," Julia said, "if you're doin' it, you're doin' it. We'll deal with whatever happens whenever it does. I'm done with this conversation. It's a nice day and all my grandkids are playing right out there. Let's play cards or something on the back porch and watch 'em ride."

"Sounds great, Mom," Racy said.

*   *   *

The following week, life's stress eased slightly for the Martens and intensified for the DeCamps. Tennyson, Marten, and Verkler automated their phone lines. Almost all calls on the main line related to Commonguy. After work, Daryl listened to those he had time for, trying to keep up on the general content, but deleted more than half without listening to them at all. Daryl had their home phones disconnected, and they now used only cell phones. Racy stayed with the kids and didn't have to hear the threatening calls.

Cleve was ostracized by the Party, but he didn't care. The DeCamps handled their phones as the Martens had, disconnecting their home phones and automating Cleve's office phones.

Daryl had met Zach for lunch the day after their interview. As they left the restaurant he had invited Zach to dine at home with the family the following Thursday evening. That night, as Zach raised his finger to the doorbell button, the front door jerked open door.

"Hey, everybody," Kyle yelled, "the TV guy's here!" Then Kyle turned and ran to the kitchen. "He's here, he's here!"

As Kyle turned and ran, leaving Zach standing at the open, Kelsey ran around the corner toward him, arms outstretched, saying, "Hi, Zach! My daddy likes you! I'm Kelsey! I'm four-and-a-half!" She jumped, and Zach had to lunge to catch her as she kept talking. "C'mon, let's go see Rory!"

Zach enjoyed his introduction to the Marten family. During dinner, Jeremy grilled him about his career. "What's it like to be on TV? When did you know that's what you wanted to do? What's the most exciting story you ever covered?"

Rory asked about his college studies and his hobbies. Daryl and Racine sat back and smiled, listening to the interaction and trying to keep Kelsey off Zach's lap so he could eat.

When dinner was finished, Kyle asked, "You any good at ping-pong, TV guy? It's set up in the basement."

"You'll *never* beat Jeremy," Kelsey quipped.

"I love ping-pong," Zach replied, winking at Daryl and Racine. "I'll take a crack at Jeremy." He followed the four clamoring youngsters down the steps.

Daryl helped Racine clear the table and they listened to the commotion in the basement. After an hour, Daryl went downstairs to rescue a sweating Zachary. The kids eventually settled down and allowed Zach to visit with Daryl and Racine. They talked of their families, college experiences, and careers.

When they finally noticed the kids were silent, Zach glanced at the clock and exclaimed, "Crap! I missed myself on the eleven o'clock."

They bade each other goodnight, but not before Zach had been invited to and accepted dinner next Thursday night. He'd been there every Thursday night since.

*   *   *

On Saturday, July 10, Daryl posted Proposition #7.

Proposition #7: A Fair and Reasonable Tax System

The tax code is so convoluted and has so many loopholes that it has become unwieldy and unfair. It should be replaced with a straightforward system.

1. No taxes should be required of individuals earning less than a necessary income.
    a. This non-taxable income limit should be the amount required for a family of four to pay reasonable living expenses (rent, two economical vehicle payments, and grocery, utility, and insurance bills).
    b. Today, this limit is approximately $40,000 per wage earner or $80,000 per family.

2. The budget should be set to match the current year's tax proceeds.
   a. Include 5% of the current national debt principal in each year's budget for the next 20 years to eliminate the debt.
3. Currently, about 1% of taxpayers earn more than $500,000 per year, and they pay 40% of the total federal income tax. Approximately 10% earn between $120,000 and $500,000 and pay about 30% of the tax. Almost 40% earn between $70,000 and $120,000 and pay 25% of the tax. About 50% earn less than $70,000 and pay less than 5% of the total tax.
4. Every individual would be taxed on income in excess of the non-taxable limit.
   a. There would be no tax deductions, no tax credits, and no separate provisions for filing jointly, individually, or as head of household, except that a two-wage-earner family could average the total income of the two individuals.
   b. Every perk or item of non-monetary compensation received would be counted as income at fair market value.
   c. Unreported income discovered by audit would be taxed double, and interest would be applied from the date the reporting violation occurred.
5. For companies, a modest non-taxable retained earnings limit, 10% of their previous five-year average annual earnings, would be allowed. All business entities would pay taxes of 50% on all retained earnings in excess of their non-taxable amount.
6. Individual tax rates would be heavily progressive.
   a. If personal income over $500,000 were taxed at 70%, and if earnings less than $40,000 were exempt from income tax,

total annual tax revenues would increase by 1 trillion dollars per year.

b. If income between $100,000 and $500,000 had tax pro-rated from 20% to 70% and if income from $40,000 to $100,000 had tax pro-rated from 0 to 20%, tax revenues would increase by another quarter trillion per year.

c. Approximate individual tax rates would be:

INCOME	TAX	RETAINED
$40,000	$0	$40,000
$100,000	$6,000	$94,000
$300,000	$76,000	$224,000
$500,000	$166,000	$334,000
$1,000,000	$516,000	$484,000

Income over $1,000,000 per year would be taxed at $700,000 per $1,000,000.

This proposition is to restructure our income tax apportionment to pay off the national debt in less than 20 years, eliminate taxes on anyone living near or below the poverty level, and increase the tax burden on those who can contribute more with less personal sacrifice.

*   *   *

The Monday evening after posting Proposition #7, as Daryl skimmed through voicemails before leaving the office, a new type of message grabbed his attention. A publishing house was offering him a book deal. He jotted down the email address and took it home. That night, after the kids were in bed, he and Racy answered it:

Thank you for your book offer, but I don't have time to work on a book. I'm not interested in making Commonguy an income-earning venture.

The next evening another voicemail riveted his attention. He returned that call immediately.

When he got home and strode through the door, grinning, Racine said, "Oh, no, what now?"

"Guess what!"

"What?"

"You'll never guess."

"What already?" she retorted.

"You and I are going on a little trip."

"Where? When?"

"A week from Thursday. To New York City. To be on the Jeff Kramer show!"

"You're kidding. On Insomniac? No way!"

"Way! I've gotta call Cleve."

*   *   *

Daryl and Racy entered the studio at 11:30 and waited. At 12:15 they met Cathy Richards, who explained the routine. At 1:00 Jim Morris would meet with them for an hour to discuss onstage interaction. Between 2:00 and 2:30, they would meet with Jeff Kramer for a few minutes to become acquainted. By 3:00, Daryl would go into makeup. At 3:30, Racine would be escorted to her front-row seat.

Morris told them the conversation would be unscripted. Jeff would keep most of the talk light and relaxed. He would work some questions into the conversation that would allow Daryl to choose what he would like to say about Commonguy. Jim went over a list of questions Jeff might ask Daryl. Morris said Jeff didn't always stick exactly to the list. He never strayed too far from it, but Daryl shouldn't be surprised if a question a little different than those on the list popped up. Daryl would be the second guest of the evening and would be on for at least five minutes and not more than ten.

At 4:30 Daryl stood nervously, stage left, as Jeff Kramer introduced him.

"Our next guest is the man behind the Internet sensation commonguy.com." There was resounding cheering and applause. Daryl waited. "Please, let me finish," he heard Kramer chuckle. "Hold on a minute, and I'll bring him out." The crowd quieted a bit. "Ladies and gentlemen, please welcome Mr. Daryl Marten!"

Daryl walked on briskly, looking straight at Kramer, stretching his hand out. The audience was on its feet applauding, whistling, and cheering. The two men shook hands, and Kramer motioned for Daryl to sit. They sat, but the crowd didn't quiet. Daryl looked at the audience, smiled, and nodded his head in appreciation. Kramer held his hands up to the audience, to no avail.

"Please, folks, please." Jeff laughed. "We only have ten minutes. We can't do anything till you settle down." Finally they began to take their seats. He grinned at Daryl and said, "Your reputation precedes you." The crowd started to stand and cheer again. "Now, quit that!" Kramer faked a stern look at the crowd. "We've got business to tend to.

"Daryl is here tonight with his lovely wife, Racine, sitting right there in the front row." The camera panned to a close-up of Racine, small, Hispanic, and beaming. Her face lit the studio monitors for the audience as well as TV viewers. The cheering started all over again. "Hey!" Kramer yelled. "Stop it! I know she's a beauty, but let's not embarrass her."

Kramer opened the conversation. "Well, Daryl, I think the appropriate way to start this conversation, since the audience obviously likes your wife so much, is to ask how you landed her. How did you two meet?"

That was not remotely like any of the questions on the list. Daryl hesitated then dove in. "Well, it's kind of a difficult story."

"Great! That's our favorite kind," Kramer chimed.

"We were in college. I was a junior and Racine was a freshman. It was springtime and I was out late, after midnight."

"This is going to get good! Were you sober?" Kramer teased.

"Mostly. It really wasn't a good situation. I was walking to my apartment and passed a dark alley and heard a bunch of garbage cans crash over. I figured there were raccoons or dogs rooting through garbage. Then I heard a rustling sound like someone being dragged. Then a smack and a thud, like someone hitting the ground. Then a groan. I couldn't make out much in the dark, but I saw a small form on the ground and a big form standing over it, reaching down. I really couldn't tell what was going on and just reacted. I ran at the big form and yelled.

It jerked toward me, and I hit it in the head as hard as I could. It staggered, turned, and stumbled off. The small form lying on the ground, unconscious, turned out to be Racine. I carried her the two blocks to my apartment, called 911, and rode in the ambulance with her to the hospital. I stayed until she was awake and then visited her a half-dozen times during the three days she was in the hospital. That's how it all started." He smiled at her.

"So, you're her knight in shining armor! You saved her."

"No, that's backward, really. Truth is, I was much luckier than she was. I helped her through some danger one night. She's *made* my entire life. She's my best friend, a perfect mother, and my soul mate. That was a tough night for Racy, but it turned out to be the luckiest night of my life."

The crowd stood again, cheering. "C'mon, Daryl. Did you just make that up? If we'd talked about that story before the show, it would've been the first thing I'd have brought up. But, honest folks ...." He eyed the audience. "I didn't have a clue. I thought I was gonna rattle him a bit by throwing a curve ball. Well, it's a great story." He smiled broadly at Racine. "I'm glad your knight showed up when he did.

"Well," Kramer continued, "let's get started. I was going to show an excerpt from the interview you did with ... what's that news kid's name? Forrester ... but let's just show the whole darned thing. Something tells me everybody here has already seen it, but they'd all love to see it again. Roll it." There were more cheers from the crowd, and even more when the clip concluded.

"So, Daryl, has your life changed any since that interview?"

"You can't imagine. Within five minutes of the broadcast, our phone started ringing and it never stopped. We had to have it taken out. Same thing at work. When I walked in the next morning, our receptionist had the phone welded to her ear. My partners and I had to figure out how to continue to do business."

"Do you get any negative calls, hecklers?"

"Almost all are supportive. A few are not."

"How bad do the bad ones get?"

"Bad."

"Have you been threatened?"

"Yes."

"Your life?"

"Yes."

"That's gotta be disconcerting, especially not being used to anything like that."

"It was at first, but I guess we've learned to deal with it a little better."

"How do you do that?"

"We try to ignore them. I mean, we report them, but they're all anonymous and untraceable. What can we do? We just delete 'em and go on."

"Have you considered calling it quits? Giving up?"

"Sure, but we couldn't bring ourselves to do it. Everyone probably knows by now that I have a partner. We met on the Saturday night after the TV interview, my partner and me, our wives, and our kids. It was an amazing evening, really, the eleven of us around the table deciding whether to stop advocating our convictions because we were being threatened. Not a single one of us wanted to quit."

"Tell us about your partner. He's a politician, right?"

"Yes. Cleve DeCamp is a member of the House of Representatives in Ohio. He's a lifelong Republican and comes from a family tradition of Republican public servants. He's become discouraged with our government's performance. And with the lack of results his years of effort have brought."

"It seems, Daryl, that neither of the political parties, especially the Republicans, are particularly enchanted with your project. Is that making life difficult for Representative DeCamp?"

"Very. But he prefers Party harassment to accomplishing nothing. Here's the thing about Cleve. He knows what needs to be done to make our government better. He's worked all his life within the system, trying to make improvements. He's finally given up on working from inside the system, but he hasn't given up on fixing the problems. We go back to grade school. Outside of my family, Cleve's my closest friend. We understand each other, and, when it comes to making this country better, we see eye to eye."

"You've said making money off Commonguy isn't part of your plan. Have people sent you money, just offering support?"

"People have asked if they can donate to Commonguy, but that isn't possible. Commonguy isn't a legal business entity and has no checkbook. So there's nothing to donate to."

"What about book deals or anything like that? Do you think this Commonguy thing might set you up for life?"

That question wasn't on the list. "Funny you should ask that. The answer is no, I'm not trying to set myself up for a book deal. But, the day before I got the call from your show inviting me here, I received an offer from a publishing house for a book deal."

"What'd you do with that?"

"Turned 'em down. My plate's full and I don't have time to devote to a book."

"What about just giving you money, you know, writing you a personal check? Has anyone done that?"

That question wasn't on the list, either. "Several have tried. We've received some checks in the mail just made out to me, Daryl Marten. We've returned them all. I have no intention of making this a business or hiring a staff. What we're doing is advocating what we believe is a better way. If enough people agree and are loud about it, then our elected officials will eventually be forced to consider some of the more popular measures. If people don't agree or don't care all that much, then maybe we're wrong. Either way, Cleve and I are working to make this nation better in the way we believe we should."

"I find all that rather amazing, Daryl, don't you?"

"Not really. We just couldn't sit by and do nothing any longer."

Kramer chuckled. "Okay, we have just a couple minutes left. Let's talk about your newest proposition. It advocates changing the tax structure, right? Actually, I think it might be pretty hard on me."

"Yes, Proposition Seven would shift significantly more of the tax burden onto those making more than five hundred thousand per year. It hits hardest on those making over a million. But, if you stop and think about it, it's much easier for a person making a million to make another hundred thousand, which would net him thirty thousand, than it is for a guy working his tail off for forty thousand to make another thirty. And if you look at the long-term benefit of balancing the budget and paying off the national debt, it seems like a no-brainer to us."

"Listening to you explain what you advocate and why, it seems to make a lot of sense. I'm impressed. We have time for one more question. Somewhere, back behind all of this effort, are you thinking you might become an independent political candidate, say, for example, running for President?"

That question resembled nothing on the list. Daryl was dumbfounded for a moment. After collecting his thoughts, he spoke: "No. I have no political background and no qualifications. That thought has never crossed my mind. I'm sure I'd get chewed up and spit out if I tried that."

The audience was dead silent. "You're rapidly becoming a very popular personality, Daryl … and in the realm of politics. Are you saying if you found yourself having overwhelming popular support to run for the presidency, you wouldn't consider it?"

"The thought's never entered my mind. I don't have a clue what would be involved in running for President. I don't know how else to answer your question."

"Well, let's do this: let's ask the audience. What do you folks think? Would you vote for this man for President?"

The audience exploded.

Kramer laughed as Daryl sat shell-shocked. "Well, sir, if the election were held here in this room tonight, you would win! Maybe you should give it more thought. I'll tell you what, if you decide to throw your hat in the ring, we'd love to have you come back and make that announcement on our show. Ladies and gentleman," Kramer boomed, "Mr. Daryl Marten! Thank you for being on our show tonight. It's been a pleasure."

The applause was deafening as the network cut to commercial.

Daryl stood unsteadily, surveyed the wildly cheering crowd, and managed a weak smile. Obviously shaken, he looked at Racine.

Kramer thrust out his hand, shook Daryl's vigorously, and leaned over for a private farewell: "I hope I wasn't too hard on you, Daryl."

Daryl shook his head almost unnoticeably, mumbled a quick thank you, turned, and hurried off the stage and back to the dressing room. *Why did he ask that? What'll happen tomorrow? Way, way worse than Zach's interview. And we couldn't handle that!*

Racine burst into the dressing room a minute later to find him sitting on a chair, hyperventilating.

"Daryl, are you okay? Talk to me. Don't faint on me."

Chapter 8

Sunday, August 9, Washington DC, 6:30 a.m.

In one respect Gayle Scapell had become like many
other Americans. The first thing he now did on the second
Sunday of each month was read the new post on
commonguy.com. Marten's postings were like clockwork. He
read Proposition #8: Who Should Pay for the Criminal Justice
System?

Subsidize manufacturers for building facilities connected
to prisons. Force criminals to pay for their upkeep. Reward
positive behavior with the best work assignments. Give
uncooperative or violent inmates the choice of solitary
confinement and reduced rations, or death by lethal injection.
Castrate rapists. Sentence violent murderers and anyone
convicted of criminal behavior for a third time to life with no
parole. Operate the prison system at a profit.

This proposition had a harsher tone than previous ones,
but it contained the same inherent paradox. The majority of the
population would love the concept, yet implementation would be
a practical impossibility. *Hell, I like the idea, myself. How
could anyone argue against criminals supporting themselves?*

Scapeli had watched a recording of Marten on Jeff
Kramer's show. That fool, Kramer, had actually given birth to
the notion of a Marten presidential campaign. Marten's reaction
had been predictable, almost collapsing on stage. *That
stammering film footage will be useful if Marten has second
thoughts about running.* There appeared to be no chance of that,
but a plan would have to be devised, just in case.

At 1:15 that afternoon, Scapeli pulled off the road near a secluded picnic spot in Patapsco Valley State Park and walked the short trail to the table. Gerald Baron had arrived an hour earlier, ensuring this particular spot would be vacant at the appointed time. Baron was a nondescript man, fifty-four years old, five-eleven, one hundred and ninety pounds, with a receding hairline.

Baron had served in the Rangers and had impressed Scapeli with his reliability and boldness. Years later, when Scapeli launched Davidson County Safety Services, he chose Baron to be his right-hand man. When Pritchard began his third senatorial term, Scapeli had become his career manager full-time and bequeathed Davidson County Safety Services to Baron. Along with the gift came a never-ending string of covert commissions, all financed from veiled sources accessible to Scapeli, courtesy of the American taxpayer. The activities resulting from today's discussions would be funded by the NSA slush fund. Gerald Baron had become a wealthy man executing clandestine missions, thanks to his benefactor.

Scapeli scoured the surroundings and spoke quietly. "I've got several things. Let's start with Richard Herrington. His Vietnam record isn't exactly as he's touted it. His troops were successful in battle, but he never led them when that would've put him in personal danger. He abused his soldiers. His treatment of locals was worse. He took whatever he wanted from them, enjoyed beating people. Lots of women and children died. None of it ever went on his record record, but a handful of soldiers and Vietnamese he thrashed are still alive. Find those survivors and document what he did to them. Get names, detailed descriptions, and specific dates. Investigate the details and make sure they can't be disproved. Get some pictures."

"How soon?"

"I won't use it before June, but I want it ready by the end of February. All true and meticulously documented."

"You'll have it."

"Now, Garner Wheeler. When he was Governor of Illinois, he pilfered millions. It went to several Swiss banks. I need a precise accounting. I want to know how much from each department, how he did it, and the dates money transferred out. Identify the banks that received the money, the amount each received, and the dates they received it. Don't concern yourself with what it'll cost to get the information. Just let me know what you need to cover your expenses."

"And leave no clues that anyone is probing?"

"Don't raise a single suspicion."

"Same time frame?"

"Yes."

"Done."

"The next task is easier, but I need it sooner. Have you heard of Daryl Marten and his Commonguy web site?"

"The wannabe philosopher and his Republican sidekick, Decamp? Yeah, I know who they are. I've been wondering when you'd want to talk about them."

"I want the dirt. Every act either of them ever committed that they wouldn't want anyone know. Same for everybody in their families. And I want to know what and who is most important to them."

"No problem. When?"

"Mid-October. I don't know yet what I might need to do about them. Probably nothing. But I want this soon enough to carry out a plan if we have to."

"Okay. That it?"

"No. One more task. I haven't decided yet how I want to deal with it. I want to meet again in a month and get your ideas on scenarios. I'll be thinking, too. Between the two of us, I want to come up with the perfect plan."

"This sounds like the most fun of all, Gayle. What is it?"

"Borster's getting insistent on being a player, and it's not gonna happen. He's got enough trash on Pritchard to force the issue if he decides he doesn't care anymore about the Party team and threatens to go public. And he might just do that if he thinks we're going to drop him from the reelection ticket. He's a loose canon.

"The problem with nailing him," Scapeli continued, "is that he's too clean. I don't have enough on him to keep him in line. I didn't want him on the ticket last time. We only carried him because nobody else could pick up enough votes to guarantee the White House. I'm not bringing him along this time."

"I work miracles, Gayle, but the death of a Vice President, if that's what you've got in mind, would be scrutinized too close to fake the cause."

"How could you think I could entertain such a notion?" The corners of Scapeli's mouth hinted at upturn. "Besides, we need something more satisfying. The challenge will be planning and carrying out the perfect setup. Whatever that turns out to be, we ... you ... are going to make sure it falls into place like clockwork.

"Mr. Borster's gonna have a vice he's been able to hide till now.   That vice will be bad and it'll become public knowledge right before the Convention.   Once Borster's despicable actions become public, Pritchard will announce his disappointment in his Vice President and his duty to drop Borster from the ticket.   By then, Pritchard'll already have the election sewed up.   Borster'll scream all sorts of charges against Pritchard, and nobody'll believe a word of it.   I'll pick a new running mate who's up to his neck in dirty little secrets, and we'll control his every move.   Life will be bliss."

"I'm gettin' all hot and bothered just thinking about it, Gayle. It's gonna be sweet."

Chapter 9

Friday, September 11, Houston Woods State Park, Ohio, 5:00 p.m.

The Martens and DeCamps had adjacent cabins rented for the weekend. The announcement of Cleve's involvement had lent a more political hue to public perception. Daryl's appearance on The Insomniac Show had ratcheted their notoriety up another notch. Commonguy's hit count was increasing at a staggering rate. Daryl, Cleve, and their wives couldn't begin to absorb all the feedback. Their lives in Carthage were open books. In public, they were bombarded by friends, acquaintances, and well-wishers. Their homes attracted strings of onlookers.

Daryl and Cleve were in the DeCamp cabin to critique this month's proposition and plan an update. As Cleve skimmed through Web postings responding to the last proposition, Daryl's mind drifted back to the night of his appearance on Insomniac, six weeks ago.

*   *   *

Half an hour after Daryl rushed off Kramer's set, he and Racine exited a taxi at their hotel. They ordered room service, but Daryl couldn't eat. He had never considered either the suggestion of running for President or the audience reaction. At midnight, he watched himself on TV, and became even jumpier. They tried to watch movies, but nothing held his attention or made him drowsy. Finally, after 5:00 a.m., he dozed. He awoke at 9:00, grateful to hear Racine had extended their stay another day. He was still stunned, but after sitting at the table in their room for half an hour, staring out the window and absorbing coffee, he became more settled.

Racine grinned at him. "Are your feet back on the ground?"

"I hope so. I felt seasick with them floating all around." He smiled back at her.

She stood behind him and rubbed his shoulders. He relaxed, leaning his head back against her.

"Last night'll trigger another assault on our privacy," he said. "I'm almost scared of what might happen next. Have you talked to Mom and Dad this morning? Is everything all right there? Are the kids okay?"

"Yeah, they're all fine. The kids stayed up and watched, and they're all overboard. And, yeah, everything in Carthage is crazy. I tried to call every five minutes from seven thirty till eight and ended up calling Dad's cell to get an answer. It's the same as it was for us last month. They unplugged their phones at eight."

"Poor Cleve. The Republicans will crucify him."

"I talked to Mel and him this morning, too. He's like a kid in a candy store."

Daryl smiled for the first time since leaving the stage last night. "I think he's looking forward to being lambasted by both parties. He thinks the bigger the fuss they make, the more impact we'll have. Maybe he's right. But I'm not sure I'm up to the publicity."

"You'll be all right, honey. You'll be a celebrity for a while. Heck, you already are. You'll adjust."

"I guess it's what we wanted, but still … I'm worried about you and the kids. You didn't bargain for this. It's gonna be tough on us all, especially the kids. Even Mom and Dad. It's creating a big problem for everybody."

"We're all proud of you and excited about the fame. Yeah, it'll be a pain, but we'll work out some kind of lifestyle we can live with."

"One thing's for sure. I need to be real clear, real fast, about not running for President."

"Talk it over with Cleve, and you two decide how you want to put that to bed. But I agree, you'd better do it soon."

"Good idea. I think I'll call him."

Cleve answered on the first ring. "Hey, buddy, how ya doin'?"

"Hi, Cleve. What's the best way to tell the world there's no possibility of Daryl Marten running for President?"

"I've been thinking about that. If you want to make the most of Commonguy, we shouldn't overstate it. Maybe schedule a short interview with Zach and just say you don't have a plan to run for President, and let it go at that. It'll probably go right up the ladder to national news."

"I should be more emphatic than that. Maybe, 'I know I'm totally unqualified for the presidency and would never consider subjecting the American people to voting for an incompetent person."

"No," Cleve said quietly. "You don't want to go that far. Just a nice little statement of non-intent and let it go. Have you seen any of the morning news shows?"

"No. I'd like to say I hadn't thought about turning on the TV, but it's more like I don't want to see what I hope isn't there."

"Too bad, buddy. It's there. Every network. The clip of Kramer's question, your reaction, the audience reaction. They're replaying your description of how you and Racy met, too. Everybody loves you."

"Crap."

"You're not gonna escape the limelight, buddy. You're a big hit. It'll be great for Commonguy. What we really need to talk about is how to make the most of this to bring about some real change."

"Crap," Daryl repeated. "What'll they do to you in Columbus?"

"If they're smart, they'd better start worrying about what we'll do to them. I'll probably take Commonguy's best proposition, the one that has the most support and would be easiest to implement, and introduce a bill proposing it."

"You're crazy. What would that accomplish? The Republicans and Democrats will join up and rip you to shreds."

"Let 'em try. I don't care. The bill might not stand a chance, but it'll sure get public attention. And that's what we need if we're going to make a difference, more and more noise."

"Which proposition?"

"I don't know. I'm talking while I'm thinking. Maybe I'll introduce a law to make it illegal for lawyers to base fees on percentage of award. That one could be addressed at state level. The public would love it. The politicians would hate it. It could be a real catalyst."

"Now, that's *exactly* what I need right now," Daryl said dejectedly, "a catalyst."

Cleve laughed. "What you need is me right by your side, reminding you how long we've wanted this and how much better it's working than we ever imagined. We're right on the verge. I know you feel overwhelmed, but I also know that, deep down, you want this every bit as much as I do. I really think we might make a difference!"

"Boy, I'm glad I called you," Daryl retorted disdainfully. "I guess I'll see you tomorrow. I'll call Zach to talk about an interview or press release or whatever it'll be."

"Set it up for Monday. We should talk this weekend and be sure what we want to say."

*   *   *

"This is Zachary Forrester, Cincinnati Channel 4 News, with commonguy.com national sensation, Daryl Marten, who appeared on The Insomniac Show last Thursday, and was asked whether he'd consider making a bid for the presidency. Mr. Marten has asked to make a brief statement."

"Thank you, Zach. I want to inform the public that I have no plans to campaign for the presidency. I've received encouragement to do so, but I'm not convinced it would be appropriate. I do want to express my gratitude to all who have supported our propositions and expressed confidence in me."

The brief interview aired nationally that night.

*   *   *

"Hey, Daryl, you here?" Cleve pulled him back to the task at hand in the cabin. Racy, Mel, and the kids had gone to the lodge.

"Yeah, I'm here. My brain was taking advantage of a minute's peace to wander aimlessly."

After working on the proposition for an hour, Daryl asked, "How's your House Bill on lawyers' compensation coming?"

"Like we expected." Cleve had outlined the bill and submitted a request for the official draft to be prepared by the Legislative Service Commission. "LSC's procrastinating, trying to allow time for someone to find a technicality they can use to kick it back, saying they can't draft it. It's time for me to rattle their chains.

"Daryl, how closely have you been watching Web feedback the past couple weeks?"

Daryl knew this conversation was inevitable. "There's no way to read it all. I skim as many blogs as I can."

"What do you think?"

Daryl sighed. "There isn't as much substance addressing the propositions as I'd like. It's mainly comments like, 'I agree one hundred percent,' or, 'You hit the nail on the head.' The adverse postings all pick on lack of detail and impracticality of implementation. We need to address those points."

"What's the most prevalent theme you're seeing?"

"Same as you. Seems like everybody's pushing for us to enter the presidential race. Ludicrous."

Cleve was silent for a minute. "I'm not so sure it's completely off base."

"I know you think it's worth considering, but how could we – how could *I* – ever do that? I don't have an ounce of political experience."

"I have a little. And the one thing I've learned about political experience is it's way overrated. Three things are crucial in a good President. First, integrity. Second, understanding all nuances of each issue and considering them all in making solid, logical decisions. Third, surrounding yourself with experts who conduct themselves the same way, and giving weight to what they say."

"C'mon, Cleve. We couldn't possibly mount a presidential campaign. It'd take millions. We'd have to find financial backers. It'd take a huge staff. We've stood on the principle that we won't seek money. We've stood on morals and ethics, and I've told the public I won't run."

"Actually, you haven't. What you said is, 'I have no plans to campaign for the presidency.' I'm not suggesting campaigning."

"It sure sounds like you are."

"I'm not. I've been rolling this around for a few days. What do you think might happen if you said only that you were willing to offer your services as President if the American public wanted you? That you wouldn't campaign, but that you'd work to get your name on the ballot and publish your platform on the web? No campaign, just an offer to serve if the majority wants. What do you think might happen?"

"I haven't thought about it. What do you think might happen? How would we even go about getting on the ballot?"

"Ballot access is basically just obtaining bona fide signatures. The easy states require one or two thousand signatures, and the hard states take fifty thousand or more. I think it might be possible to get enough signatures with volunteers and a skeleton organization, just you, me, Racy, and Melinda. With the broad support we seem to be getting, it might be possible."

"You're suggesting that we try to get on the presidential ballot in every state, with no staff and no financial investment? Doesn't sound workable to me."

"To me, it sounds exactly like the America we want, that we're working for. It'd be a lot different than traditional politics, but I don't think it's impossible."

"*Surely*, you don't think we could actually win."

"I don't know. It'd make for an historic election, either way. I think the principles and programs we're promoting would win, whether we do or not."

"Cleve, does this conversation make you shake in fear for the safety of your wife and kids?"

"Yes."

"Then why are we having it?"

"I don't know how not to have it. I know you haven't gone as far down this path as me, but it's gnawing at you. I know that sooner or later, if I didn't bring it up, you would. You're reading the same feedback I am, and the question's impossible to avoid."

"Crap," Daryl mumbled. "This update isn't going to be written this weekend. I need time to think. So do you."

"I agree one hundred percent." Cleve grinned. "You hit the nail on the head."

"Jerk."

Saturday morning, Daryl published the September proposition.

Proposition #9: Stop Holding Our Children Back

What is the point of promising a mediocre education to every child in the nation? What is gained by setting the educational standard for every child so low that the least capable and least motivated students can easily meet it? Whereas every child deserves an equal opportunity, the fact that students have differing interests, motivational levels, and abilities cannot be used as an excuse for not offering every child a premium education. Our public system, paced to accommodate the slowest achievers, is a travesty for our best and brightest youth, and ultimately for our nation. Multiple educational paths must be offered.

1. The current level of rigor in our primary and secondary schools should be offered as a choice for students whose interests, desires, and abilities all indicate that the individual isn't likely to choose to attend college.

2. An intermediate level of rigor for grades 4 - 12 should educate students to at least the level of current college sophomores.

3. There must be a highly rigorous path for students whose interests, desires, and abilities cry out for the most challenging education. This path, in grades 4 - 12, should offer the equivalent of a current four-year college education.

4. For the intermediate path, a three-year college program should attain the equivalent of a current master's degree.

5. For the most rigorous path, and at no cost to the student, a four-year college program should be offered that would achieve the equivalent of a current Harvard-quality doctorate.

This proposition is to develop the best educational system in the world by offering every child an opportunity to receive a premium education free of charge and ensuring that no child is automatically pigeonholed into a mediocre educational program. The payoff will be beyond imagination.

*   *   *

Daryl and Cleve met three times the following week. On Saturday, Daryl finally posted the update.

Update, Saturday, September 19

We've observed two repetitive themes in criticism of the propositions we've published. Many question the lack of detail in our propositions. Others question the plausibility of achieving consensus and adoption of laws and programs to implement any of the propositions.

Our propositions lack detail by design. The concepts must be considered before developing details. Does the concept of a proposition hold the promise of sufficient benefit to make it worthwhile? If not, discard it. If it does, then consider various means of adoption and implementation from all angles, evaluating all pros and cons of each possible path. Then create the detail of the proposal, including preparation of adoption and implementation plans.

Our propositions are described in sufficient detail to generate discussion of overall merit. However, the development of the detail required to prepare any of our propositions for practical implementation would require volumes.

Time does not exist for Cleve and me to develop a detailed application, adoption, and implementation plan for any single one of our proposals. In addition, we don't claim to have the expertise to develop the necessary detail. Every one of our propositions would require the involvement of experts in many fields.

Changing governmental policies and programs that have been entrenched for decades would be a grueling process. Pursuit of changes that would redistribute political power or wealth would be excruciating. Initial reactions to such efforts from individuals in positions of power will include ridicule, smoke screening, discounting, and falsification. Any viewpoint that could be manipulated to make the proposed changes seem impossible or preposterous is likely to be shouted incessantly by those who would be negatively impacted.

Launching sweeping changes to programs and policies is only half the battle. Sound transition planning and execution would be crucial to success. The more far-reaching the change, the more time must be allowed for transition. Some of the propositions we suggest would impact national and world economies, international relations, and the fortunes of large conglomerates. Such changes must occur gradually enough to avoid placing impacted entities, large or small, into disastrous circumstances.

In closing, we want to report an action related to one of our propositions. On August 12, Cleve DeCamp submitted a preliminary bill making it illegal for lawyers to be compensated based on percentage of award in Ohio. It appears the Ohio Legislative Service Commission is procrastinating on preparing the official draft. Future updates will report status of this bill.

*   *   *

Sunday afternoon, the DeCamps lunched at the Martens'. After the meal, the eleven family members gathered in the basement on chairs and stools around the ping-pong table for a conference. From down here, they could not see traffic.

Cell phones were turned off. The doorbell would not be answered.

Everyone was seated, Kelsey on Daryl's lap. They all knew the topic. Pressure for a Marten/Decamp independent presidential ticket was everywhere. In addition to the Internet, it was periodically mentioned on television. It was all the talk around Carthage. The stance of the families had been that, so far, there was no such intent. Sitting around the table, no one spoke.

Kyle finally said, "So did we all come down here to play ping-pong, or what?"

"Quit it, Kyle." Rory said.

"All right," Daryl began, "we all know what we're talking about, crazy as it sounds. Cleve and I keep getting more and more people wanting us to put our names on the ballot."

"For freakin' President and Vice President of the country, right?" Kyle interrupted.

"Yeah, for freaking President and Vice President," Daryl answered. "Since the question first came up on Kramer, we've told people we won't campaign for that. But just putting our names on the ballot isn't the same thing as campaigning. Cleve and I are thinking about doing that, just putting our names on the ballot. And then if people want to vote for us they can."

"Do you think there's any way you might win, Dad?" Rory asked.

"It seems like that should be impossible. I mean, there are so many Republicans and Democrats who'll vote for their own people no matter what, it doesn't seem like there'd be enough voters left for us to win. And we wouldn't spend a dime on advertising. The candidates who are really campaigning will spend millions. I don't think we could win."

"Then why do it?" Kyle asked. "If you know you can't win, why bother?"

"We're putting some good ideas out on Commonguy," Cleve said, "and we've got more support than we thought was possible. Putting our names on the ballot will get even more."

"You think we could win, don't you?" Kyle asked Cleve.

"I think anything's possible," Cleve replied.

"We're getting way ahead of ourselves," Daryl said. "What we want to talk about is whether we should put our names on the ballot. What would that mean for all of us? Maybe, sometime down the road, we should talk about what might happen if we won. That's unlikely but, like Cleve said, maybe it could happen."

"How would you get your names on the ballot?" Jeremy asked.

"It's mainly a matter of telling each state we want to be placed on the ballot and then trying to get enough signatures to meet their requirements. Some states only need a few hundred signatures, and some states require over a hundred thousand."

"A hundred thousand?" Rory asked. "How could you get that many signatures? That's more than seven times as many people as live in Carthage. How many states take that many?"

"Only two," Cleve replied. "California and Florida. A bunch require over fifty thousand."

"How in the heck could we get that many people to sign?" Kyle asked. "You think you and Dad are going to make us kids walk around Los Angeles day and night, trying to get people to sign petitions?"

"The way it would work," Daryl said, "is we'd run it from here. Actually, your mothers would do most of the organizing, at least at first, to see if it even gets off the ground. It'd take a lot of volunteers to help out. That's how we find out if we really have any support. If we tell the world we'll put our names on the ballots, but we can only do it if we get lots help, then we'll see what we've got. We'll see if anyone cares enough to volunteer."

Kyle continued to challenge: "So, you're saying Mom and Mel would have to be on the phone all the time to thousands of volunteers, telling them what to do?"

"No. The only way it could work is if we get two main people in each state who have lots of time and will oversee the other volunteers. Your mothers would work with two people in each state."

"So, you'd need a hundred people to work for you for free, and Mom and Mel would just be talking to the hundred then? Right?"

"Right, dufus," Jeremy said as Kyle threw a ping-pong ball at him.

"So when would it all start, Dad?" Jeremy asked. "When do you have to have the signatures?"

"Different states run on different schedules," Cleve responded. "Arkansas is due in mid-November, but we only need a thousand signatures there. Then Nebraska is due in March with three hundred, and then Nevada in April with about six thousand. After that it gets crazy, with about a half-million needed around the country by next September."

Bobby whistled. "A half-million?"

"I know you guys are getting threats," David said. "If you put your names on the ballots will that get worse?"

"Probably," Daryl answered. "That's our biggest concern."

"Nobody's done crap so far," Kyle said. "They're all talk. They never even give their names. There just a bunch of mouthy chickens. Who cares about 'em?"

"Mom, what do you and Mel think?" Rory asked.

"I want to make sure we keep you kids safe," Racine answered. "If we do this, we all have to keep our eyes open and watch what's going on around us. If there's any hint of any danger, we have to find a way and a place to keep safe. But I can't see your Dad quitting on this now. I don't want him to quit."

"I think this whole thing has a real shot at being great for the country," Melinda added. "I'm just like your mom, Rory. I want my kids, and you guys, all of us, to be safe. But I don't want to quit. I *especially* don't want to quit just because some bullies scared us out."

"They're not gonna scare me out," Kyle said.

"I'm not hearing anyone say no," David said. "I know Dad's right about a lot of things and the Party hasn't paid attention to him. I think it's time to show 'em right's right and wrong's wrong. I'm all for it. I wanna help."

"Me, too," Laura said. "I want to help. I could help Mom keep track of her people and the signatures."

"So, if we're all done," Bobby chimed in, "can we play ping-pong now?"

Cleve looked at Daryl. "What do you think, Daryl? Are we done?"

"Looks like it. Let's go up to the study and work on a plan."

Chapter 10

Sunday, October 11, Washington DC, 6:30 a.m.

Gayle Scapeli had developed the habit of looking at updates before reading the new proposition. Public pressure for Marten to enter the race was expanding. If Marten was stupid enough to consider it, he would have to make his move soon. *He just might be far enough off center to go for it.* Scapeli glanced at the update. "Yep, there it is," he said aloud.

Update, Saturday, October 10

The Marten and Decamp families find ourselves at a crossroad. During the past two months we were first stunned, then inspired, by the overwhelming support that materialized, urging us to campaign for the presidency. We have no intention of developing an organization with a paid staff. However, we are willing to offer our personal efforts toward that end. We have decided we will endeavor to place our names on the various state ballots as Independent candidates, myself for President and Cleveland DeCamp for Vice President.

This effort will be a far cry from an active campaign. We stand by our earlier statements that we will neither seek nor accept financial support. Our plan is only to work to get our names on the ballots as we continue to publish propositions on commonguy.com. We will make appearances on televised news or information programs if networks invite us. If it should turn out that a majority of the American people want us to lead the executive branch of the United States, we would humbly, but enthusiastically, provide that service to our country.

Our efforts to gain ballot access will be coordinated by Cleve and me and our wives, Melinda DeCamp and Racine Marten. We will not be able to obtain the half-million signatures required without a great deal of support from persons across the country willing and able to devote their time. To begin with, we will need two full-time, capable volunteers from each state to coordinate the effort in their state.

Persons with experience in obtaining ballot access signatures and who are willing and able to dedicate at least fifty hours per week are invited to email resumes to us. We will reply to the most qualified applicants with additional details and contact information.

Our platform is being revealed month by month on commonguy.com. Thousands upon thousands of people are necessary to operate our government. Should Cleve and I find ourselves at the head of the executive branch, our commitment is to surround ourselves with moral, ethical persons who are proven experts in the fields in which they serve. Every appointee would be required to satisfy us that they meet those criteria. We would place top priority on ensuring that every department and office operating under the auspices of the executive branch conducts its activities morally, ethically, and competently.

We appreciate the encouragement we have received and are excited about moving forward, hand in hand with those of you who believe in the concepts we are promoting.

Scapeli knew Independent bids had never posed a serious threat in presidential elections. This one would be no different. The approach, though unique, made this attempt even more impotent. *No funding, no advertising, no mudslinging. No threat. Keep watching anyway.* He read Proposition #10: Unwinding the Health Care Cost Spiral.

Americans should be satisfied with medical care that places little priority on ordinary, non-life-threatening conditions. Minimize testing, hospitalization, and use of higher cost proprietary drugs. Instead of keeping our Medicare system, expand the Veterans Administration Health Care System to offer free services to all citizens who might seek no cost medical care. Stop trying to prolong life when health conditions are terminal and living situations involve extensive dependence on external care. Instead, accept nature taking its course.

Another unworkable blurb for the impulsive public to laud. Who'd really choose to die instead of getting a free extension, even if bedridden and in pain? Everybody would say, "Forget the pain and taxpayer cost. Give me tomorrow. Give me tomorrow's miracle cure." It'd take an eternity to build confidence in free VA hospitals. End Medicare? C'mon.

Regardless of Marten's unviability, it was time to organize his opposition. Cash by the millions would become available if it started to look like his propositions might receive legitimate consideration. Marten had irritated powerful groups that would be begging to cough up big bucks to squelch him: trial lawyers, the Republican and Democratic Parties, state governments, high-income earners, teachers' unions, and now hospitals and drug companies. Marten's announcement of a presidential bid would incite all of them to hurl money to any opposition. A focal point was needed, and one was ready. Bradley Catcher's campaign was struggling. It had few supporters, no money, and was on the verge of folding. Catcher would eagerly lap up the dollars, regardless of any strings. He wouldn't fully understand where the money came from, but he wouldn't care.

Texas Governor Troy Jorgensen would be the perfect unwitting facilitator. He craved action, and there was precious little of that for him these days. He knew how to wiggle through the maze of regulations to funnel big dollars without disclosing anything. Scapeli had no real influence over Jorgensen, making him an even better vehicle.

Gerald Baron would set up a backdoor contact to Jorgensen, informing him of entities seeking a conduit for distribution of their dollars to fight Marten's absurd ideas. All communications and transactions would be set up by various

Democrats in Scapeli's network, and the funds would find their way to Jorgensen.

Jorgensen would bite hard, seeing not only the opportunity to be a player, but also a spot on the Catcher team in the unlikely event that he might actually win. The attacks on Marten would be designed by the entities with the money, hit from all angles, be relentless, and be paid for, as far as the world would be able to ascertain, by Citizens for Bradley Catcher for President. Marten, with no staff, would unable to rebuff all the attacks with believable, well-constructed responses. His image would tarnish and his popularity nosedive. Anyone clinging to Marten's ideas would hate Catcher, which would also come in handy in November. *Perfect.*

*   *   *

The media was abuzz Monday, anticipating a televised statement of candidacy by Independent phenomenon Daryl Marten. A recorded interview arrived at the network at 4:00 p.m. from Marten's obvious correspondent of choice, young Zachary Forrester. Scapeli never set aside time to watch evening news reports, but he did today.

"This is Zachary Forrester, Cincinnati Channel 4, with Daryl Marten, who has an announcement to release."

Daryl stated his intent to declare candidacy and reiterated his earlier web announcement to the TV viewing public.

Scapeli smirked. *That's the beginning of the end, Marten. You like being on TV? We'll set you up one on one with Regina Wasson and see how you like that.*

*   *   *

The following Wednesday night, Randall Pritchard hosted an informal dinner for a handful of his favorite Republican legislators, a gathering of friends for an evening of enjoyment and relaxation. Politics never came up. Justine was out of town, raising funds for starving African children. Pritchard and Gordon Dresser were the only men not accompanied by their wives. Dresser's companion was Janice Taylor.

Taylor was a knockout. She was twenty-six and held two jobs, secretary for a real estate company by day and exotic dancer at a Washington premier club by night. Janice supplemented her night job, when both the compensation and the companion felt right to her. She was no stranger to climbing the ladder and recognized promising prospects. One night last February, performing her routine at the club, she had caught Senator Dresser's eye. He had bought her a drink after her performance and then taken her out for a midnight dinner. Dresser and Janice had enjoyed lots of time together since that night.

Dresser found Janice not only gorgeous and an ingenious bed partner, but also a smart, confident, witty companion. She was an all-around pleasure. Dresser was showing off by bringing her. He knew better, but had invited her anyway.

Dresser led Janice into the Family Dining Room, the last of the guests to arrive. "Please allow me to introduce Janice Taylor," he addressed the group as they entered. He named each of the ten other guests for her and then, last, President Pritchard.

"Janice, I'm very pleased to meet you," the President said, taking her hand. "Welcome to the White House. I'm happy Gordy brought you. You're a very lovely lady."

She blushed. "Thank you, Mr. President."

"Please. Didn't Gordy tell you this is an informal dinner? My friends call me Rand."

She smiled and repeated, "Thank you."

"Oh, lay off, Rand," Dresser jabbed. "The lovely lady came with me. If we dance later, I'll concede one to you, if you behave yourself ... but only one."

"Never mind him." Pritchard smiled broadly at Janice. "He's always paranoid that somebody's gonna steal his girl."

A large round table had been selected for the occasion. Janice sat beside Dresser, directly across from Pritchard. Pritchard made eye contact with her often and included her in the conversation. After half an hour, she was her normal confident self, enjoying the easy conversation.

"So, Janice, how did you happen to make acquaintance with the distinguished senator?" Pritchard asked.

She smiled, picturing the actual encounter. Dresser spoke up before she could respond. "We met at a night club. I saw Janice and couldn't keep myself from asking her to dinner. Lucky for me, she graciously accepted. I found her irresistible, and since that night, Janice has been kind enough to allow me to continue to see her."

"Gordy," Pritchard replied, "I'm envious. I do believe that before the night is over, there will, indeed, be dancing. And I shall request that one dance, if Janice will permit it."

"I'd be flattered," she replied.

Later, as they danced, Pritchard said to her, "You know, I suspect there's more to the story of you and Gordy meeting than he let on."

She looked up at him, her hand lightly pressed to his lapel, and smiled. "There is."

He waited, then raised his eyebrows and asked, "That's all I get? No more details?"

"Sorry, Rand, I'm Gordy's date tonight. He seemed to want to let the story drop where he left it. If you want to know more, you'll have to ask him."

"I need to persuade you to hold back less from me, Miss Taylor. How would you suggest I go about that?"

"If I were you, Mr. President, I'd make the most of this dance."

He pressed her ever so slightly tighter to him and looked into her eyes. "I will do just that."

She turned her head and lightly rested it against his chest. Without looking up she said, "And why are you not dancing with the First Lady tonight, Rand?"

"She isn't here. She's out of town. Besides, we don't dance."

"Ever?"

"Never. Not for years."

"You dance well. How do you stay in practice?"

"By dancing as often as I can with other ladies. But I can't recall the last time I danced with one so lovely as the one I hold now."

"My intuition tells me this isn't the first time you've made the most of a dance, Rand."

"No, but I've never wanted to more."

"Why? Because I came with your best friend?"
"Because I don't want you to leave with him."
She didn't reply.

Dresser watched from the corner of his eye as he talked with the other guests at the table. He wasn't surprised to see that his long-time cohort had set his sights on Janice. He didn't mind too much. What else could he have expected? *Hell, he'll consider her a present. And presidential favors aren't a bad thing to store up. Anyway, there are more where she came from. Maybe not quite so special, but there are more.* After everyone else had left for the night, including Dresser, Janice remained with the President. It was the first of many nights the two would share.

*   *   *

Thursday night at 11:30, Scapeli walked into Howard's Bar, a noisy all-night dive on the outskirts of Alexandria. He made his way to a dark booth in the back, away from the regulars, sat across the table from Gerald Baron, and ordered coffee.

"Where are you with Wheeler and Herrington?"

"I'm not finished yet, but I can tell you you're gonna love it. If you give 'em the stuff I've got, they'll rape and pillage each other."

"Perfect. Any thoughts on Borster?"

"Probably a sex scandal. I think we could blindside him with a setup and catch him red-handed before he has a clue. Maybe even get him implicated in child pornography. It'd destroy the old boy, but then sometimes life in the big city just sucks. With the right setup, the public would *demand* that Pritchard kick his ass off the ticket."

"I've thought about several scenarios and came to the same conclusion. Come up with a specific plan and let's get back together. What about Marten and DeCamp?"

"They're as squeaky clean as anyone I've ever worked. DeCamp served on his uncle's staff for several years before running for office. Ronnie DeCamp's downfall could be used to incriminate him."

"Was he involved?"

"Nope. But that doesn't mean we can't convince people he was."

"All right. What about Marten?"

"No dirty deeds at all in his past. But he's got an Achilles' heel that'll bring to bring him crashing to his knees."

Chapter 11

Four months later, Saturday, February 6, Carthage, 10:45 a.m.

An early-afternoon, indoor picnic was held at Rob and Donna's house in honor of the Marten/Decamp ticket officially being on the ballot in Nebraska and Nevada, in addition to Arkansas.

After the October 10 announcement, they'd had four weeks to get one thousand signatures in Arkansas. Their first order of business had been to get two volunteer coordinators set up in each of the three states having the earliest deadlines. That had been accomplished in the first week. During the second week, while their supporters were obtaining signatures in Arkansas, coordinators were assigned in all states with deadlines before July.

The week of October 25 found the Marten and DeCamp families in Arkansas. The kids were pulled from school, a first, to experience both the ballot application process and the excitement. On Thursday of that week, Daryl and Cleve presented 3,798 signatures to the election officials in Little Rock, securing the inclusion of their names for President and Vice President on the Arkansas ballot.

By the middle of November, coordinators were in place in every state. Some states had as many as five persons sharing the role. No state had fewer than two. Last Wednesday evening, Daryl and Cleve had flown to Lincoln to meet their Nebraska leaders and receive their petition signatures. They filed them Thursday and flew to Carson City to repeat the process in Nevada. They had obtained over ten thousand signatures in total for the two states and filed weeks ahead of deadlines.

Update, Saturday, February 6

Our volunteers are well-organized and obtaining signatures in every state. In states requiring over 30,000 signatures we still need: California, 146,300; Florida, 92,800; Texas, 66,200; North Carolina, 56,000; Oklahoma, 33,900; Indiana, 24,550; and Michigan, 22,450. The required number has already been surpassed in all other states except Connecticut, Idaho, Illinois, Kentucky, Massachusetts, New Mexico, New York, Oregon, and South Carolina. We are officially on the ballots in Arkansas, Nebraska, and Nevada.

Cleve and I are planning a month-long tour of the continental United States in April. We will make an appearance in each state capital where enough signatures have been obtained and will publicly address our volunteers and supporters immediately after filing the required ballot access documents.

The bill Cleve submitted to the Ohio LSC last August, which would make it illegal for lawyers to base fees on percentage of award, remains stalled. The LSC has not cited any technical issues prohibiting it from proceeding with the legislative draft, but the committee sent Cleve's outline to a House rules committee for further review. This action is a seldom-used tactic to circumvent the mandatory timeliness required of the LSC. The legislature is doing everything possible to stonewall the bill.

After posting the update, Daryl reread the previous three propositions.

Proposition #11: Life Hubs for Permanently and Temporarily Impaired Persons advocated the establishment of life centers for mentally, emotionally, or physically impaired persons. These centers would be accessible to all impaired persons desiring to make use of them. The centers would offer productive work opportunities, socialization, recreation, medical care, psychological services, living quarters, food, and clothing.

Proposition #12 was entitled, "Who pays for Welfare and Unemployment Compensation?" It proposed that all unemployment and welfare administration be by the Federal Government, and that all recipients be required to report for productive work eight hours per day, five days per week. The agency would operate similarly to private employment agencies, and would also utilize available manpower to staff its own positions and other government positions. In addition to providing paychecks to recipient/workers, the agency would provide low cost meals, clothing, child care, and, if necessary sleeping quarters and showers for program participants. No one would get a free ride. Everyone would be required to work, even if the only work available was cleaning parks and roadsides.

*   *   *

While Daryl Marten was reading, 500 miles away in the Queen's Bedroom of the White House, Justine Pritchard placed a call on her cell phone. She waited while the cell phone receiving the call rang four times.

"Justine! I can't believe it's you. Are you all right?"

"I don't know, Clarence. I haven't heard your voice for five years. I needed to hear it again to remind me there's still something soft somewhere inside me."

"What's happened, Justine? You've got what you always wanted. You gave up everything for it."

"Maybe I was always wrong. I have two daughters who act out their own roles when they have to, but, basically, they're estranged. I married a man knowing he'd never be a dedicated husband. I got exactly what I gambled on when I married him: the White House. And I think I was wrong all along."

"What can I do for you?"

"Just talking to you helps. I'd love to be with you again, Clarence. To spend a weekend together, just the two of us, like we used to."

"That sounds like heaven. I'll do whatever you ask, but please, be sure. I know how important the White House is to you. The election's nine months off. I know it looks like it's in the bag, but things can happen. If we got caught, I don't know what that would do. Don't get me wrong, Justine. You say the word, and I'll meet you anytime, anywhere. I'd take you away for good, if that's what you want. Just be sure first. I'd hate myself if I ruined everything you spent your life striving for if the loss of it made you miserable."

"I know. You're right. I need to keep doing what I'm doing. It's harder than I ever imagined. I thought I'd feel good here, but it's all an act, and there's *nothing* I feel good about. Some days I have to steal five minutes just to be alone and relive one of the times you and I spent together. Then I feel a little more human and can go on."

"All you have to do is tell me what you want."

"I'll be all right now. At least for a while. Thanks for being you. I'll always love you," she whispered.

"Anytime you need me, Justine."

"Goodbye, Clarence."

*   *   *

In Carthage, Daryl read the January proposition.

Proposition #13: Is Prejudice and Hate Inborn?

Tolerance is the acceptance, the welcoming, of differences in people. It is genuine respect for others who are, or choose to be, different from us.

1. Tolerance requires acknowledgement that the conviction that defines one's soul has no more intrinsic value than another person's opposite conviction.

    a. One person's ideal that people should reap the rewards of their own efforts is of no greater value than another's belief that those who have wealth should share generously with those who have little.

    b. One individual's commitment to fight to the death for the liberty of oppressed people is of no greater value than another's vow not to take up arms against a militia of conscripted individuals he does not know and has nothing against.

2. Lack of tolerance has resulted in such events as genocide; enslavement; wars; the Crusades; murders of racial minorities, gays, gang rivals, and family members; the Holocaust; on and on.

3. This proposition advocates tolerance toward differences among us, not tolerance for harmful acts.

4. Just as our government can enhance consciousness of racial equality, pride in country, or expectation of a right to privacy, it can elevate awareness of the value of a tolerant mindset.

5. On the national and international level, this proposition is not for lessening our strength but for bolstering our respectfulness. A more tolerant posture by the United States would nudge the world toward increased peace, compassion, and unification.

This proposition is for the United States Government to champion tolerance for differences in people, beliefs, and cultures. Infuse tolerance in every line of every law. Require it in the actions of every department and office. Advocate it to the citizenry and the world. Repeat its merits year after year, decade after decade. Weave the concept into our consciousness so pervasively that tolerance becomes innate in us.

As he finished reading, Racine skirted into his office.

"Have I shown you how happy I am to have you home?" She threw her arms around his neck and kissed him.

"Uh, yeah, you made it really clear last night."

"I did, didn't I?" She beamed.

"I was only gone two days. But I like the welcome home." He pulled her body tight against his and kissed her again.

"I know it was short, but I missed you." She looked up at him. "Everything's so hectic. It's exciting, but crazy busy. Mel does great at staying in touch with all the agencies and organizing all the details. I'm online continuously with our coordinators. They're great, but keeping up with one-hundred-fifty of them is never-ending. Jeremy hardly has time for school, what with keeping the computers and web site running. And you and Cleve are inundated, trying to maintain your careers, keeping Commonguy going, and spending every free second on the phone."

"I know." He continued to hold her tight. "It's hard to believe. Who'd have ever thought it would lead to this?"

"And who knows where it'll go from here?" she replied wistfully. "I try not to think about it. It can be scary."

They kissed again, long and deep, thoughts of the conversation evaporating. "C'mon," she whispered, taking a breath. "Kelsey's napping, and the boys are in the basement. Let's sneak upstairs before we go to Rob and Donna's." Daryl took her hand and followed her quietly out of the office, up the stairs, and into the bedroom, locking the door behind them.

*   *   *

"Hear! Hear!

"Yea!"

"Long live the President!"

The small group erupted into cheers as Daryl carried Kelsey through the Defoe front door, following Racine and the boys. Everyone else was already there, the time spent in the bedroom having resulted in late arrival.

"You all understand it's only three states, and we're only on the ballot, not elected, right?" Daryl grinned at the party.

"Aw, we don't worry about details," Rob said. "Cleve tried to convince us you guys weren't elected yet, but nobody paid any attention. What we all wanna do is look at floor plans of the White House and figure out which rooms'll be ours!"

"Well, you'll probably be living with Randall and Justine Pritchard," Mel said, "and from what I hear, they take two of the bedrooms, so there aren't all that many left. You all might have to double up."

"Pritchard?" Kyle retorted. "Dad's gonna kick his butt. He'd better be asking Dad to design him a new house, 'cause he'll lose the one he's living in now in about a year."

"Enough chitchat," Donna said. "Food's on the table. You guys are late. What were you doing, anyway? Did you miss him that much on his little trip, Racy?"

Racine grinned at her. "Yeah, as a matter of fact, I did."

"Ha! I figured as much." Donna laughed.

"So, how'd they treat you in Lincoln and Carson City?" Drake asked, by now enthusiastic about his son's activities.

"Like royalty. Right, Cleve?" Cleve nodded, mouth full. "I'll bet there were over a thousand, both places. The people working the elections offices were great. They were helpful and seemed excited about us. I mean, there were no state politicians welcoming us, but the people working the offices had to have some kind of Party affiliations, and they still treated us great."

"It was like that in Little Rock, too," Kyle said. "Everybody loved us."

"They loved Dad and Cleve," Jeremy corrected him. "We were just along for the ride."

"I don't know," Rory said. "I watched the faces in the crowd. They were looking at all of us, like they were cheering for each one of us. It felt good."

"I think it was Kelsey," Laura said. "She was really cute up there at the top of the steps, like a natural star."

"Well," Cleve said, "your mother and Racy were looking pretty good, too. Maybe it was all for them."

"Naw," David said. "Everybody knew exactly why we were there. It was all for you and Daryl and what you're doing with Commonguy. The rest of us were just the supporting cast."

"I don't know about that," Daryl said, "but I *do* know there's no other supporting cast I'd rather have."

After lunch, while the kids were watching Ohio State basketball in the living room Danielle's cell phone rang. "Yes, this is Doctor Westmoreland. Can I help you? ... Yes, he's my brother. Why? ... No, I will *not* give him that message! Who is this? ... You'd better never to call this number again." She hung up and glanced at Daryl.

"What'd he say?" Daryl asked quietly as everyone else remained hushed.

"It doesn't matter. It was trash."

"What did he say, Danny?"

She looked at him and breathed out. "He wanted me to tell you it was fortunate you had a doctor in the family, because you were going to need one."

"Have you received calls like that before?" Daryl asked.

"No."

"Are you all right?"

"No! I want to get that jerk!"

"I'm really sorry, Danny. We need to report the call to Sheriff Stone. Okay?"

"All right."

"If any of you ever get calls like that ... and I hope you don't, but if you do ... let me know right away."

"Daryl," Julia said, "this is really a double-edged sword. We're all amazed, and we're proud of you and Cleve, but we keep getting reminded how dangerous it could be for us all. I'm not sure it's worth it."

"We can't stop, Mom. You know that."

"I know, sweetheart. I'm on your side, and I'm trying to be strong for you. The bad stuff makes me backslide."

"Dad! Dad!" Kyle yelled from the living room. "Get in here! You gotta see this!"

"Everybody!" Jeremy added, "Come here. We'll replay it."

The adults rose and crowded into the living room.

"Watch this," Jeremy said and started the replay.

The screen showed a thirty-something man in a wheelchair with a pretty woman and three children at his side. He had no legs. "My name is Harold Ryman. This is my wife, Doris, and my three children, Greg, Janie, and Dillon. I'm a veteran of the Iraq war. I didn't lose my legs in the war. I came home healthy. A few years later I developed pre-diabetic symptoms. Nothing serious, routinely treatable. We weren't rich, so we used the Veterans' Administration medical services and hospitals.

"The doctors either misdiagnosed my problem or didn't care. I don't know which. It doesn't matter. What matters is I didn't get the right treatment or instruction. My condition got worse. My legs became infected. I'm told today by experts that proper treatment would have resulted in complete recovery. The doctors at the VA told me surgery was required to correct circulatory constrictions in my legs. When I awoke from that surgery, and without having ever discussed the possibility, my legs were gone.

"I can't work, and my family is dependent on state support. We've been told by lawyers we have no recourse for recovering our financial losses from the VA. You can imagine what I think of our Veterans' Hospitals."

The screen changed to show an open hospital ward, dozens of beds filled with groaning, uncomfortable patients jammed into one huge room. A voice said, "This is what Daryl Marten wants for all Americans. Why would *anyone* want him? Paid for by Citizens for Bradley Catcher for President."

The jaws of all the adults in the room dropped simultaneously. Drake spoke first. "Looks like somebody's noticed you, son."

Rory said, "Don't worry about it, Dad. Everybody'll know that's a twisted around commercial. They're just starting to get scared because people like your ideas."

Donna replayed the commercial, slowing it down at the end to read the fine print that panned across the screen as the commercial faded out. It read, "The people and situations in this advertisement are fictional and do not depict actual events."

"Bradley Catcher," Kyle said. "I've never even *heard* of him. *Everybody* knows who Daryl Marten is."

"If they didn't before, they will soon," Cleve said.

*   *   *

The following week was doubly difficult. More commercials aired; aimed at making Daryl Marten appear foolish and out of touch with reality. All were paid for by Citizens for Bradley Catcher for President.

Daryl saw two more ads. One ridiculed the consolidation of state functions into national departments, singling out licensing bureaus. It showed Bill Smith from Greenville, Mississippi having his driver's license revoked and being handcuffed and carted off in a police cruiser in front of his school-aged children and their friends for a drunken driving offense that had actually been committed by Bill Smith of Greenville, South Carolina. It then showed intolerably long, slow lines in Chicago, New York, and Los Angeles in driver's license offices, where everyone was being fingerprinted in the process of applying for new federal driver's licenses.

The second ad interviewed a distraught father bemoaning the death of his nine-year-old daughter from food poisoning caused by a large meat packing company owned by a huge, rich conglomerate. The family sued for damages but was unable to recover a cent because the daughter was not a wage earner. The legal fees, based on hourly rates, had been high, forcing the family into bankruptcy. The punitive damage amount assessed the meat-packing company was one hundred million dollars, all deposited directly into a vague government punitive damages set-aside fund.

Both ads ended with the same slogan: "Who would want this to become business as usual in the United States? Only Daryl Marten. This warning against catastrophic policies is brought to you by Citizens for Bradley Catcher for President." The same rapidly panned disclaimer attached to the Veterans Administration ad also followed these two.

Cleve called Daryl after he saw the second ad. "Where do you suppose Bradley Catcher is getting the sudden influx of cash to finance a nationwide TV ad blitz?"

"Who knows? Probably from people who'll lose lots of income if some of our propositions get implemented."

"I'm sure you're right, but why would they choose Catcher for their publicity vehicle? He doesn't seem to have any chance of surviving the primaries."

"I don't know, buddy. Maybe somebody knows things about the Democratic candidates that we don't."

The Martens and DeCamps did their best to ignore the commercials. On Saturday, February 13, Daryl posted the February proposition.

Proposition #14: Survival

Should national governments make decisions based on an overriding goal of preserving human civilization?

1. Governments must understand that, ultimately, what is best for the world population is also best for the people of their nation.

2. Acts of nations and of individual leaders based solely on self-interest work against the overall benefit of mankind.

   a. Rational governments that distribute power (most governments) must restrain dominant individuals from imposing their personal wills.

   b. A handful of rogue governments are controlled by despots or tightly knit radical regimes that resist acting in the interest of mankind. However, responsible governments, acting in unison, can control them without resorting to violence.

3. Clashes between cultures and ideologies are a threat to our future. Various cultures have believed they had a divine right or even a command to overcome others: Christian and Muslim crusaders, Ku Klux Klan over blacks, Arians over Jews, Irish Protestants and Irish Catholics, Sunni and Shiite Muslims; the list is long.

   a. Belief in a right or charge to annihilate another culture or society is arrogant and uneducated. It boils down to this mindset: "I know what is right, and anyone who believes otherwise is wrong."

   b. Considering the number of different customs and beliefs that abound in the world, an opinion that all who disagree with me are wrong belies conceit and thoughtlessness.

   c. Tolerance and acceptance are essential to assure our future. Although each person has a right to beliefs, a

conviction that all others are wrong, or
worse, all others are evil, is dangerous.

d. It is a small step from fervor that others
are wrong, to believing the "others"
have less value or, in the extreme, count
for nothing.   From such passions,
genocide emanates.

4. Cultural   clashes   and   intolerance   can   be
mitigated   through   objective,   broad-based
education.

This proposition is for the United States to
advocate the subjugation of national self-interest to the
preservation of human civilization. We should not be
averse to leading by example, if only in small steps. The
goal is advancement of international cooperation. The
cautious development of more and more multi-national
agencies would lead toward ordered consolidation of
governmental functions around the world.

*   *   *

Sunday afternoon, Daryl's cell phone rang. "Zach! It's
great to hear from you. Have you been seeing the 'blast Marten'
commercials?"

"Yeah, Catcher came out of nowhere with that crap."

"Well, I'm getting someone's attention, anyway. That's
part of the goal."

"You're getting a lot of people's attention, Daryl. That's
what I'm calling about. The network just called me, asking if I
could convince you to do a one-on-one interview with Regina
Wasson. I'm not sure why they didn't call you direct. Maybe
they think I'm you're agent. Ha! But it *is* pretty cool that my
career is tagging along with you. You're pulling me up in the
world, Daryl."

"I don't know about that. After seeing some of these
ads, it's more like dragging you down. Wait! They want me to
do a network interview? To air on one of those current events
programs?"

"Yep."

"Wow! When?"

"I've got a name and number they'd like you to call this afternoon. My guess is they want to do it this month and air it in March. What do you think?"

"With Regina Wasson? That's great!"

Chapter 12

Friday, April 8, Washington DC, 6:00 p.m.

Gayle Scapell was home in front of the TV for the
evening news. Marten and DeCamp were in Montgomery,
Alabama. He'd watched the evening news religiously this
month. Marten was the lead story, a replica of the previous clips
of the week: thousands of cheering supporters on hand to witness
the pair emerge from the state elections office and announce the
successful submission of their ballot request in one more state.

Scapeli had been surprised at how Marten had dealt with
the Regina Wasson interview. It had been a setup. This
interview was designed to be different than any Marten had
participated in previously. Unlike Jeff Kramer, Wasson would
not forewarn Marten of questions or topics. And unlike
Marten's buddy, Zachary Forrester, she would not offer Marten
any opportunity for input in the editing process.

Scapeli's trump card, the Achilles' heal Baron had
found, had been played. So far, Marten had deflected it. *You've
only seen the tip, Marten. I'll explode this on you. You're
finished.* Scapeli replayed the interview. He wanted to
scrutinize it as his first step in blasting the chink in Marten's
armor into a gaping chasm.

He skipped through the first five minutes of the
interview where Wasson had built a rapport with Marten, talking
of his background and family and the development of
commonguy.com. The next five minutes were more interesting,
biting here and there at some of Marten's propositions.

"I'm sure you've seen some of the ads attacking your propositions, Daryl. Do you have a response to, for example, the ad that shows the family of the little girl killed by food poisoning having to file bankruptcy to pay legal fees while a huge payoff was awarded the Government?"

"Yes, I do. The loss of a child to any loving family is devastating, regardless of the cause. Isn't it absurd to claim that a loss like that would be more palatable if only the parents could receive a large amount of money for the loss of the child? To me, that mindset negates the concept of family love and implies that dismemberment of a family is somehow all right if the payoff is big enough. That's just wrong.

"On the other side of the coin," he continued, "any company heedless enough to allow its actions to endanger the lives of the people who use its products must be forced to rectify its practices. This can be accomplished by hitting it so hard financially that it knows it can't survive if it doesn't make changes immediately. In addition, the corporate individuals who made and approved the decisions resulting in the public risk should be punished appropriately for their personal wrongful acts."

"But how would the case ever get prosecuted, Daryl, if the parents know they can't receive any award and would be unable to pay their legal fees? They'd be unable to retain legal services, and there would never be a trial. The company *and* the responsible individuals would get off scott free."

"Every city and county has a prosecuting attorney or similar office, Regina. That office *must* bring to trial any case resulting in death or harm to one of its citizens, even if no plaintiff files suit."

"So you're suggesting the Government force trials wherein the Government would stand to receive huge financial gains?"

"That's a twisted way to interpret our proposition, Regina. The prosecuting attorney's office bringing the suit would not receive any of the money. Large awards would go into the national treasury, earmarked to apply directly and fully to the national debt."

"So, you're saying the winners would be the taxpayers, and the losers would be the trial lawyers, the companies causing the problems, and the families suffering the losses."

"The families suffering the losses are the tragedy. And that tragedy is the loss of the family member. No amount of money can fix that, and throwing money at it is entirely the wrong approach. Making the companies causing the problem pay so much that they know they can't survive if they don't change will prevent other families from suffering similar losses. Yes, the taxpayers gain, which seems fair to me. And yes, some lawyers, ambulance chasers, would lose a potential source of income."

"It sounds like you've had some experiences that have given you an ax to grind against attorneys, Daryl. Let's move on to my next question. Another proposition that's been criticized is your notion of extending VA health services to anyone who's either uninsured or would rather receive free, taxpayer-provided benefits. The ads against this portray the VA system to be, let's say, borderline. Do you really believe the VA hospitals could become a viable option for excellent health care services for virtually everyone?"

"Yes. VA hospitals are not incompetent, as the ad would have viewers believe. Does the system need improvement? Sure. Are the improvements and capacity expansion possible? Yes, but not overnight. It would require a transition period of several years."

"Would it be affordable, Daryl? What would such a far-reaching about-face cost' and who would pay for it?"

"Obviously, it would be paid for with tax dollars. How much would it cost? I can't answer that. Would it cost less than our current methods of handling elderly and uninsured health care? Today's system consists of Medicare and Medicaid and of artificially ballooned billings for health services and insurance to make up for treatments provided to patients who don't pay for them. I believe a nationwide government-operated health care system operating in parallel with private hospitals and insurers would result in quality health care at lower cost than we bear today. An in-depth study would be required to confirm that. What we're proposing is that such a study is worth undertaking.

Then use the results of the study to make decisions that make sense."

"Might such a study be slanted to favor a particular interest group? Insurers or private hospitals, for example?"

"It could be. The department and officials administering the study would have to be responsible and accountable for ensuring the objectivity of the study."

"And, of course," Wasson replied condescendingly, "those officials would have to be above being influenced by billion-dollar drug and insurance industry enticements. All right, let's move to another topic. Your education proposition advocates establishing a three-option path. This will be seen as one path for the smart students, one for average students, and one for those who are, let's say, achievement-challenged. In recent decades the move has been toward inclusion, to make sure *every* student receives a quality education, not just the smart ones. Do you advocate moving away from that approach?"

"What that policy has done, Regina, is downgrade the quality of education our public schools offer to the point that students having either lower abilities or lower interest appear to succeed in gaining the same education as those who could easily do much more. We're not suggesting that any students be automatically sorted into any path. We're suggesting that, in order to keep up with the rest of the world ... even more, in order to allow our best and brightest to give back all they're capable of ... we must offer all our youth educational opportunities that can fully develop their capabilities. Yes, we advocate three levels, none of them lower than our current public school system offers. The decision on which path to pursue would initially be made at the end of the third grade. The decision would be made by the student and parents with input from the educational staff. As students get older, they'd have the opportunity to change paths if the student and parents desired. Obviously, the older a student gets, the more difficult it would be to change to a more challenging path."

"So you don't think this would be looked at as segregating smart kids, average kids, and dumb kids?"

"*I* certainly don't look at it that way. It would create a venue for each student and his or her family to choose a path they feel would result in the most satisfying life for that particular child. Being an auto mechanic, for example, might result in a much happier life for some individuals than being forced into a college prep program, partially completing college, and then never quite fitting into any particular career path."

"I wonder which path you and I would choose for our own children, Daryl. Let's move to another question. Your February proposition is entitled 'Survival.' It begins by saying the United States Government's decisions and actions should not be directed toward the best interests of our own citizens but, instead, toward a concept you call preserving human civilization. You close this proposition by stating, and I believe these words come directly from your text, 'The intent of this effort would be the consolidation of governments around the world.' My read on this proposition is that you're advocating the United States give up our sovereignty to a new world government. I'm having trouble believing that *anyone* in this country would agree with you on this one."

Scapeli couldn't help grinning, watching Wasson angle in on Marten. He was keeping his composure, but you could see him burning inside. With every topic, Regina wormed a little closer to his breaking point. *Setting him up perfectly.* Scapeli watched the remainder of the interview intently.

"Regina," Marten replied, "That isn't the point of the proposition and those are not the closing ...."

"I'm thinking back to nine eleven," she said, cutting him off, "and the number of national governments in existence today that wish anything for the United States other than success and wellbeing. I read your proposition, and it says to me you think if we only educate the people of these countries who wish us harm, if the United States would only step in and educate their people for these governments, and maybe if we would also share our wealth and military secrets with them, then we'll all hold hands and walk off singing together into the future. Maybe it's just me, Daryl, but I don't think *anybody* is going to buy that."

Daryl stared at her in disbelief. He opened his mouth to speak, but she cut him off again.

"We're running short on time, but I do have a couple of questions I need to ask that aren't related to your propositions.

Your longtime friend and running mate, Cleve DeCamp, is the nephew of Ronnie DeCamp, who resigned his congressional seat last year in disgrace. He admitted accepting bribes and other illegal contributions. Cleveland DeCamp worked on Ronnie DeCamp's staff for years while Ronnie was a senator in Ohio, before Cleve himself ran for and was elected to serve as a state representative. There's been talk that Ronnie's illegal activities were going on back when Cleveland was running his staff. Some people are claiming Cleve knew what was going on at the time and might have been instrumental. This runs very counter to your platform of moral and ethical conduct. Do you have any comment on that?"

Now Wasson stopped, looked directly at him, and waited for a response. Daryl was momentarily dumbfounded. "I have no idea where you heard such rumors, Regina. I've heard no such allegations. It's a matter of public record that the offenses committed by Ronnie DeCamp all occurred long after Cleve was no longer on his staff. Anyone can check the record. It's public. You can check the record, Regina. Actually, I'm sure your staff already has, so I don't know how you can make a statement that's so easy to disprove."

"I mean no offense, Daryl. And I'm not making any accusations or charges. I'm only saying there are people who believe Ronnie DeCamp was accepting illegal contributions at that time and that Cleve could have been involved. The inquiry into Ronnie's activities didn't go back that far."

"Yes, Regina, it *did* go back that far, and no illegal activities were found to have occurred."

You're misunderstanding me, Daryl. I'm not saying they did or didn't, only that some people believe the inquiry didn't look closely enough into that period of time and didn't find or report all that happened."

"*Who*, Regina? Who are these people you're speaking of? I've never heard any hint of such charges. I've known Cleve since grade school, and I can tell you with no doubt that Cleve has never taken part in any illegal activities."

"Daryl, you know a reporter can't reveal her sources." She smiled at Daryl and at the camera. "I'm sure your best buddy, Cleve, is a great guy who would never do any wrong.

Let's leave that topic and move on to one last question. Where do you and your family attend church, Daryl?"

Scapeli grinned broadly. You could see it. Marten's jaw dropped. *Blindsided. Blindsided and rattled.*

"What does that have to do with this interview?"

"*Everything*, Daryl. You're a presidential candidate. The citizens of this nation want, and have a *right*, to know everything about their top public servants. With your stance on morals and ethics, I'd think you'd be eager to discuss your Christian heritage. Do you wish to avoid this question?"

"No. I'll answer your question. It's easy for anyone to find that out. My family doesn't attend church. Cleve's family goes to the Methodist Church in Carthage. We don't attend."

"Then how can you expect to be taken seriously as a candidate? This country is overwhelmingly Christian. We've *never* elected a President who wasn't a Christian. I'm sure you know that, which begs the question of why you're even bothering to get your name on the ballot."

Daryl narrowed his focus on her. "I've got a lot to say on this topic."

"I don't doubt that. And I wish we could hear it all, but we only have twenty seconds left. Can you summarize it?"

Scapeli could almost see steam billowing off Marten. He laughed. "What a setup!" he gloated.

"First, Regina, this country was founded on religious freedom, not religious conformity. Second, conclusions about my religious beliefs cannot be drawn simply because I don't attend church. Third, a person's religious beliefs are personal, not public. Actually, they're not even constant but continually developing. The candidacy of Daryl Marten and Cleve DeCamp is based on a platform of moral and ethical conduct and ens...."

"I'm sorry, Daryl, we're out of time. This has been an eye-opening interview. Thank you." The screen cut to commercial.

The interview occurred in late February and aired in early March. It had been perfectly orchestrated, yet here it was, a month later, and Marten was surviving, adding the Marten/DeCamp ticket to an additional state every day.

All right. Raise the stakes. Light a fire under the Southern Baptists and turn 'em loose. Open the attack on another front, too. Catcher would file challenges to Marten's signature lists in all the big states.

*   *   *

Sunday morning, Scapeli sat at his computer, knowing Gerald had already set the wheels in motion for the next thunderbolts to be hurled at Marten. Scapeli's first order of business was to read the new post.

Proposition #16: Terrorize Terrorists, advocated the establishment of a worldwide alliance of nations dedicated to crushing terrorism. Create a superspy intelligence gathering and crack enforcement agency staffed and supported by the alliance. Each nation should prioritize its resource commitment to the cooperative international effort to eradicate terrorism above its own national defense program.

He reread Proposition #15, Prevent Annihilation from Within. Again, international cooperation between all "rational world governments" was expounded as the vehicle for forcing the disabling or neutralization of all existing weapons of mass destruction and for precluding rogue governments and terrorist organizations from gaining access to weapons of mass destruction. This international agency would also be in charge of developing and enforcing safety regulations for the development and use of technologies having catastrophic destructive potential, such as nuclear power.

How could he possibly have gone ahead and issued these propositions after his disastrous interview with Wasson? Both propositions could easily be used to make Marten look even more naïve. It would be easy to convince people that China, Russia, Pakistan, India, Israel, Egypt and a multitude of other nations, would never agree to either elimination of their weaponry or sharing intelligence. *Finishing him off will be a breeze.*

*   *   *

At 9:00 the following Tuesday night, Janice Taylor received a call from President Pritchard, asking her to come to his White House bedroom/office suite. Janice had been hired as a staff typist in the West Wing last November, a month after she'd spent her first night in his suite, the night Dresser had introduced them. Her typing skills were not exceptional, but she had been requested from above; typing skill had not been a consideration in hiring her. Work hours were often irregular in the West Wing. Janice's were more irregular than most. She often left after midnight or worked weekend hours. It was not unusual for her to show up or leave at any time of day or night.

Janice was five-feet-six, one hundred and twenty-five pounds, voluptuous, and beautiful. The attire she wore to work was businesslike: brown, gray, or navy suits, well-trimmed and loose-fitting, purposefully unflattering. She wore her long, wavy, auburn hair pinned up. She wore glasses although she had 20/20 vision. At work, Janice looked as plain as her body and facial features could be made to look.

She carried access credentials, and she often traversed the long corridor between the West Wing and the presidential living quarters. All of her previous visits to his quarters had been prearranged. The call at home and short notice tonight were unusual.

When she arrived, Janice found Gordon Dresser, Senator Goldwyn, and Representative Norton seated around the table with Pritchard, playing poker, smoking cigars, and drinking. They had been at it for a while. Having been traded from Dresser to Pritchard in October, she felt uncomfortable. Her instinct was to turn and leave, but that option wasn't open.

The First Lady was in Tennessee on a benefit trip for the week, not that it made any difference. Janice had never fully recovered from her first and last conversation with Justine Pritchard, here in this room. After that meeting, she knew the trap she was in. She could not speak to anyone of her affair with the President, nor could she put an end to it. She had accepted and was still accepting money from Pritchard, taxpayer money.

She was at his beck and call. Even if he was the President, she didn't like that.

Janice had met Justine Pritchard at midnight on her fourth visit to the President's suite, the week she began working in the typing staff. After spending an arduous hour with Rand in the bedroom, he had asked her to get him a brandy. She had tossed on a sheer robe, leaving it open in front, walked into the study, crossed it, and poured the brandy. When she had turned to carry it back to the bedroom, she was mortified to see the First Lady in the dimly lighted room, elegantly dressed, seated on the sofa beside the bedroom door she had just passed through, staring at her. She had frozen in her tracks.

"Hello, Miss Taylor."

She was unable to reply. Justine Pritchard's voice was neither loud nor soft, holding no trace of emotion. Her eyes locked hard on Janice's. They didn't waver, didn't blink.

"Don't be shocked, Janice. We both know this isn't your first time here. And I couldn't care less what you and Rand do. I'm not displeased he gets his amusement elsewhere. I'm here, now, for one reason. That's to make sure you understand *exactly* what I do care about. And to explain what will happen to you if you disregard that.

"I care about the respectability and propriety that emanates from the White House. Rand's a philanderer. Always has been and always will be. The public doesn't see that. Even if I don't care that Rand spends nights with girls like you, I do care about the level of respect the public has for the White House and its occupants. I won't allow girls like you to tarnish that. What I'm telling you is that you will *not*, under any circumstances, disclose to anyone anything you do here. You won't discuss it with your best friend. You won't discuss it with your next lover, your mother, or your priest. You will never allow anyone even to *suspect* you're well acquainted my husband.

"Here's what will happen to you if you do. As First Lady, I carry some clout, which will remain mine when I become a former First Lady. If I decide that someone – you, for instance – should be unable to secure employment anywhere in the world doing anything whatsoever, you would be unemployable. Your public record would be such that you'd be unable to receive unemployment compensation or any type of government assistance. You'd be reduced to living through illegal means, and even that wouldn't sustain you. After becoming a common street whore, there'd be a tag on you who'd impel every john on to another prospect. Your most challenging tasks would become finding food, shelter, and clothing. Your life would be hell on earth, Janice.

"Now, go ahead and do whatever you please with Rand. But you'd better be deathly discreet. Breathe one word to anyone, and you'll never rid yourself of my resolve to destroy you. Do we have an understanding?"

Janice stood gaping in front of the First Lady, robe hanging open. The bedroom door was not closed. Rand was in there, making no sound. *He hears every word of this! And she knows it!* Janice could not speak, could not move.

"Neither of us is leaving this room till I'm satisfied we have an agreement. Do we understand each other?"

Janice gave one miniscule nod of her head.

The First Lady rose, eyes never leaving Janice's. "Good. You and I will never meet again. But, if you ever break your part of this agreement, you'll fall so far you'll want to take your own life. And you'll know the reason will be that I did *not* break my part. Enjoy the rest of your evening, Janice." Justine Pritchard turned and, like a ghost, flowed out of the room and into the Hall without making a sound, softly closing the door behind her.

*   *   *

Tonight, five months after that appalling confrontation, the option to leave this smoke-filled room didn't exist. This was the White House. This was the President. This was her ticket. She carried a debit card infused with five hundred dollars per day of unreported income, courtesy of the American taxpayer. Pritchard had presented that gift to her at 5:30 in the morning after her third overnight. Janice did have a million-dollar story, but the First Lady had put the fear of God in her. So long as Justine Pritchard lived and breathed, Janice could not cash in on that million. Her ticket was Rand. For the moment, it was here in this room.

"Janice!" Pritchard boomed. "Come in. We're happy you're here! You know Gordy, and this ...." He motioned to his left, "is Senator Goldwyn, Mitch. And this young man is Congressman Rick Norton. He happens to be turning forty today, so we're throwing him a little party."

"Good evening, gentlemen. It's nice to see you." Janice smiled cautiously.

"Janice," Pritchard said, "we invited you up to brighten the atmosphere, enliven the place. We'd like to hire you for the evening to serve us, you know ... drinks and what not. And, what with it being Rick's *birthday* and all, well, you *know* what the perfect outfit would be."

Janice hesitated.

"Don't worry," he said. "These three gentlemen are my most trusted friends. Not one of them will ever breathe a word."

"Rand, can we talk a minute?"

"Sure, Janice, let's step into the bedroom." She followed him through the door, and they stepped behind the wall.

"Rand," she whispered, "I don't do this. I wish we would've talked before you asked me to come up."

"Relax, Janice. These aren't bad guys. They're decent, good ole boys. And it isn't exactly like you don't go along with guys if the guys are okay and the incentive is good. The poker game had a five hundred dollar buy-in. So, there's two grand out there on the table, and it'll be there when the evening's done for you to pick up. Hell, who knows, they might even add to it. Just entertain us while you bring us drinks. I'll go to bed around eleven. Do what you will with the boys after that. Eventually they'll all leave. Then have a nice soak in the Jacuzzi and come curl up beside me and sleep the rest of the night away. Take tomorrow off. It won't be a bad evening. Have fun with it!"

No options. Okay, make it profitable. She would play along. She was pissed off that her freedom of choice had been stolen away, but her best option – her only option – was to push that aside. *Just do it.* She would find a way to deal with her loss of control later.

Chapter 13

Saturday, May 14, Carthage, 5:45 a.m.

Daryl and Racine lay awake in bed, entwined. These moments before rising had become the core that anchored their days. The weeks since the interview with Regina Wasson, had been painful.

Attack ads continued to escalate. In addition to Catcher's relentless pounding, a religious coalition had joined in the castigation. The five-week tour of the nation, one day each in the capitals of twenty-five states, had been grueling. Last Tuesday, Catcher had notified Texas, North Carolina, California, Florida, and Oklahoma he would file challenges to the Marten/DeCamp signature lists. Since then, election offices in those states had become noticeably less friendly.

Cleve had his own problems. Since the tour and filing for ballot access in Ohio, not a single politician in Columbus would acknowledge him. The two friends would have been disheartened, had it not been for the encouragement they continued to receive. The more they were attacked, the more support they received from their families, the Carthage community, and their base of volunteers. Zach had resigned from Channel 4 the day after the Wasson fiasco was broadcast and Cincinnati Channel had 8 hired him the next day. Daryl had posted an update that day.

Update, Thursday, March 9

Last night I watched my edited interview with Regina Wasson. The actual session lasted over three hours, and when it was over, I was displeased with the way portions of it had been conducted. But, I never imagined it could have been twisted so completely out of context as the version broadcast.

After watching, I was unable to sleep. I am still distraught and hesitate to write this in my current frame of mind, but feel an initial response is necessary.

Relative to the attacks Wasson made on our propositions addressing legal services fees, government medical services, world cooperation, and education, the most objective reply I can make is as follows. Scrutinize our propositions, considering each part as well as the overall concepts. Read the updates we have published, and apply the points made in them to the propositions. Then replay the interview. It will be apparent how much the network misrepresented us and misled viewers.

The most inappropriate and deceiving portions of the interview were the personal attacks on Cleve's integrity and on my religious beliefs. The attack on Cleve is easy to respond to. The investigation into his uncle's misconduct was thorough. It is clear from the reports that Cleve could not possibly have been involved. Anyone doubting that is referred to the documentation. It is all public information. All that is required to know the truth is to read the reports.

The religious attack is difficult to address objectively. For now, I will say only that religion is very personal for everyone, and I am no exception. Beyond that, this country was founded on the precept that no one individual or group may impose religious persuasions upon any other.

I have confidence the citizens of this nation can sort fact from media fiction, and for now, my comments on the Wasson interview will end with that.

After the filing tour, Daryl's first order of business had been to further expound on the interview. He met with Zach on Thursday, May 5. That meeting had developed into a recorded session that was aired nationally by Zach's new network on their weekly current events program the following Sunday morning.

The following day, Daryl posted a transcript of that interview as an update. Glancing at it, Daryl relived the session.

"Daryl, Regina Wasson asked several questions relative to the propositions posted on commonguy.com. Would you like to address any of those points further?"

"Yes. Some of her questions were an attempt to ridicule our propositions, along the lines of predictions made in our September 17 update. We anticipated 'smoke and mirrors' attacks and diversion from our actual content.

"For example, Wasson took the proposition to stop lawyers from generating high-payoff trials for their own financial gain, and twisted it to look like a scheme for the government to pursue high-payoff awards to fill *their* coffers. She suggested the reason we published this proposition was that I'd had negative experiences with lawsuits and was trying to get even with all lawyers. Both of these attack fronts were attempts to distract the focus from the actual content of the propositions. And, for the record, I've never been involved in a lawsuit as plaintiff or defendant, either personally or professionally.

"I don't plan to dissect every charge that comes against me or our propositions. We'll respond to comments, pro or con, that warrant further thought and clarification, but our response to baseless attacks will be no response. Although we believe all our propositions merit in-depth analysis, the propositions themselves are not the heart of our candidacy. The core of our platform is conducting governmental affairs morally, ethically, and competently."

"At one point in the interview, it was suggested that your running mate, Cleveland DeCamp, might have been involved in soliciting illegal contributions while working on the staff of his uncle, Ronnie DeCamp. Would you like to address that charge?"

"I want very much to respond to that attempt at character assassination. The financial records of every office ever held by Ronnie DeCamp were thoroughly scrutinized during the investigation of his misconduct. The record is public and shows explicitly that no money was received illegally during any time that Cleve was on Ronnie's staff. Cleve and I invite – more than that, we beg – anyone having any doubt to research the record. Wasson and her network *had* to have been fully aware of the record before they brought the issue up, but they did it anyway. Wasson's statements on national TV are cause for a defamation of character lawsuit. If Cleve believed lawsuit was the American way, he would already have pursued that course. But, he is not of such a mindset."

"Your personal religious beliefs were also criticized. Do you have a reply?"

"I'd like to make several points I wasn't given the opportunity to during that interview. This nation, at its birth, was dedicated to religious freedom. Our constitution and laws have gone to great lengths to ensure separation of religion and state. Our body of citizens has not always been in favor of such separation and, on the surface, might appear to not be in favor of that separation today.

"That deserves a closer look. By most studies, close to fifty percent of Americans profess to be Protestant Christians, twenty-five percent profess to be Roman Catholics, and twenty-five percent do not profess to be either. Consider the makeup of the Protestants. There are millions of Baptists, Pentecostals, Presbyterians, Methodists, Latter Day Saints, and many others. We have significant populations of Jews and Muslims, as well as other non-Christian religions. We also have some professed agnostics and atheists. Considering all the variations in just the Protestants' beliefs on issues such as free will versus determinism, baptism procedures, the significance of faith versus works, the literal versus figurative application of the Bible, and on, it gets mind-boggling to compare all the differences of opinion.

"So, for those who want the United States to retract its fundamental tenet of separation of state and religion, the question becomes: what specific religious practices should be incorporated into our state practices? Should we mandate prayer in our schools and legislative sessions? If so, what wording should be used? Should Christian prayers be forced on Jews and Muslims? Should we require all our public officials to be baptized? If so, what method is acceptable? Must it be immersion? If so, must it be in a natural body of water? My point is this: I believe the separation of church and state has served this nation very well and continues to do so. It protects us from having the religious views of any one group imposed on us all.

"Most people consider their religious beliefs and opinions to be both important and personal. I believe that any one individual's religious beliefs and opinions are of no greater or lesser value than those of any other, whether the individuals are Mormon, Catholic, Jew, atheist, Baptist, or Muslim. Considering the variety of opinions and beliefs, and the fact that some creeds are mutually exclusive of others, they can't all be right. So, who is right?

"I believe the answer to that question, when it comes to governing this nation, is that the question is and must remain irrelevant. All Americans are free to believe what they choose and to live their lives according to their beliefs, so long as they don't harm others in doing so. In running this nation, it doesn't matter whether a Baptist, Pentecostal, Jew, Muslim, Mormon, or Atheist is elected to a particular public office. The day-to-day decisions and actions of government offices should not be based on religious beliefs or customs of the office holder or the religious group he or she belongs to.

"Ethics and morals, on the other hand, constitute a much cleaner set of guidelines. The concepts are clear: treat everyone equally; treat others as you want others to treat you; don't harm others; justice must prevail; don't make decisions you're not qualified to make. These aren't difficult concepts. They're our platform. Religion doesn't play a part in our platform.

"Moral and ethical conduct doesn't conflict with religious conduct, except when one religious group takes action to overcome or influence others. Unfortunately, that happens. It's happened much too often throughout history, and it continues to occur around the world today. Shiite fight Sunni. Protestants fight Catholics. Jews fight Muslims. The list is long. And these fights are not just verbal lashings. They have often been pursued as fights to the death. Moral, ethical conduct does not and cannot condone that course of action. Our platform of ethical, moral, and competent governance requires us to oppose efforts by any religious group to influence or attempt to overcome others.

"To wrap this up, I'll continue to maintain that my personal religious beliefs, as well as Cleve's, are irrelevant to our candidacy. I commit that my decisions would be based on morals and ethics and that I would keep my religious beliefs and opinions to myself. If a voter wants to vote for someone who will uphold religious beliefs identical to his or her own, that voter should not cast a vote for Daryl Marten. Bradley Catcher is a member of the Roman Catholic Church, which represents the greatest plurality of religious affiliation in the United States. If our goal would be to base our elections on religious conformity, then Bradley Catcher should be the next President of the United States."

"That's a lot to chew on, Daryl. Is there anything more you'd like to add?"

"Yes, I'd like to mention some exciting news. As of yesterday, the number of signatures we still need is under sixty-five thousand in California, sixteen thousand in Florida and two thousand in North Carolina. The required number has now been surpassed everywhere else, and our volunteers are knocking themselves out in these three states. We filed in Texas on May second with about two thousand more signatures than required – our biggest test so far. No Independent candidate in recent history has been named on every state ballot. Due to the efforts of our enthusiastic volunteers, we're within striking distance of making history.

"I'd like to close by thanking each of the thousands of volunteers making our candidacy possible. Cleve and I appreciate all your efforts very much."

After the agonizing frustration he'd felt watching the broadcast of the Wasson interview, the segment that had aired that Sunday had been the most satisfying facet of his effort with Commonguy to date.

This morning, Daryl and Racine didn't get out of bed until they heard kids stirring downstairs. Then they rose and enjoyed a leisurely family breakfast before Daryl went to his study to finalize the May proposition.

Proposition #17, Worldwide Economic Growth and Stability, advocated controlling the global economy by cooperative international management. Target the least developed nations and regions for the highest growth rates by

shifting industry to those locations at a reasonable pace.
Eliminate all trade tariffs and duties. Monitor tendencies of
governments, industries, companies, and individuals in positions
to take undue advantage of economic situations, and prevent
such exploitation and profiteering. The United States should
lead this effort by setting our own standards toward this end.

That afternoon Daryl and Cleve held a planning session.
"It looks like the legislature won't adjourn until at least
the middle of July," Cleve said. "I think they'll stretch it to the
end of July if they can, just to make life more difficult for me."
"I can handle filing the last twenty states."
"I know you can, but I don't feel right dumping it all on
you. The April trip was tough enough. The rest will be worse,
more helter-skelter."
"I think I could do it in four stints, a week in late May,
two in June, and one in July. Maybe two road trips and two
flight-hoppers. Racy would have to stay here and work the
volunteers. I'd like to take Jeremy, but he'll need to keep the
computers and web site running. Maybe I'll take Kyle on one of
the road trips and Rory on the other. I'm sure they'll want to go,
and I'd like their company."
"Any idea what all the flights'll cost?"
"What with Alaska and Hawaii thrown in, it'll probably
be at least ten grand."
"I can come up with half. You'll be off work till
August, maybe longer. That's at least four months off. How bad
is this whole thing going to be on your bank account?"
"I don't know. With flights, hotels, time off, and small
stuff, running for President will probably cost around a hundred
thousand. That seems dirt-cheap, considering most candidates
spend millions."
"It doesn't sound dirt-cheap to me," Cleve said. "My
bank account couldn't take a hit like that."
"I'll be all right. The firm did well last year. It'll take
everything I put back last year, and I won't be putting anything
back this year, but we won't have to change our lifestyle. If
running for President only costs me two years of not socking
extra money away, that's not bad."

"What do you think about going back to work in September?"

"If we think we've got a shot, we'll probably need to devote full time till November."

"I agree, and I wouldn't count that out just yet. Wheeler and Herrington are doing their best to destroy each other, and knowing those two, there won't be any reconciliation at the convention. Neither will throw his support to the other, let alone agree to team up on a ticket. Catcher doesn't stand a chance. We'd easily get more votes than him. Everybody thinks Pritchard's a lock, but he's still got five months till the election. He'll probably be fine, but you never know what might happen to blow things apart. Borster's a wild card. And Pritchard's Chief of Staff, Gayle Scapeli, looks shadier and shadier to me every day. I'd love to see him screw up and fall flat on his face."

"Could you have imagined this two years ago?" Daryl shook his head. "Even last May we couldn't have conceived of running for President. You still gettin' threats? Are they getting worse?

"Yes and yes. A week ago, I got a call from a guy who told me what building and what window he was going to shoot me from in Columbus."

"You're kidding. Did you report it? Are the police watching the building?"

"Yeah. And you can bet anytime I'm within sight of it, I'm watching that window."

"Does Mel know?"

"Nope. She knows about the ones she reads on the Internet, or if a call happens to come to her. I don't tell her about any I get, and she doesn't ask. I don't ask her about the ones that come to her."

"Us, too. What a crappy deal to throw at a marriage. It does keep us appreciating each other, though. Not that Racy and I haven't always had a pretty good thing, but we've sure made the most of our time together lately."

Cleve grinned. "Well, we ought to get some kind of windfall from all this craziness. Go for it! You been thinking any about Secret Service protection?"

"Seems to me like we should get it. We'll be on the ballot everywhere and we get enough press to be legitimate candidates. If I understand the process, we'd both get protection around the first of July. I hadn't thought about travel that month, though. I don't know how that'll work. I know I can't pay a Secret Service detail to fly with me."

"I'll look into how it works," Cleve said. "That's the least I can do. I'll get it all figured out by the end of the month."

*   *   *

At 7:00 that same Saturday morning, May 14, before Daryl and Racine were out of bed, President Randall Pritchard, dressed in a black suit, walked into the dining room at Camp David. Justine, dressed suitably for a formal dinner even though nothing of the sort was scheduled, sipped coffee at the table, and gazed out the window.

"Morning, Jussy. Sleep well?"

"Yes, Rand. You?"

"Like a baby." He smiled at her. "You've seemed more relaxed the past couple weeks. Are you finally getting the better of being First Lady?"

"Maybe. It was always such a big deal. I started expecting to be here a long time ago, when you won your first Senate seat. I always knew you had what it took to get here. I wanted to be the picture-perfect First Lady. Always in control. Making the White House social scene the envy of the world. Promoting worthwhile causes. Projecting sophistication worthy of American royalty. I think I tried so hard I made the White House look sterilized. Maybe I *need* to relax more."

"Relaxed becomes you. Reminds me of our younger days."

She sighed. "Thanks, Rand. When's your meeting?"

"Ten minutes. I just stepped in for a starter cup. They'll serve breakfast."

"You're meeting with the Israeli Premier?"

"Yeah, we have to keep them from getting out of hand, at least until November."

"Always politics." She frowned. "Will Gayle be at the meeting?"

"When have I had a meeting in DC without him?"

She shook her head, and the frown deepened. "How did he get so integral to everything? Not just politics. Our lives. Do you do anything he doesn't know about? I have to try hard to keep him from knowing every detail of my life."

"You know I don't consider Gayle a friend. More like a business partner. But we wouldn't be here today without him."

"And he wouldn't be here without you. He worms his way into everything. And does every bit of it under the table. How does one man get so much dirt on everybody? Sometimes I think Gayle Scapeli controls the entire government."

"That makes two of you." Pritchard laughed. "He thinks so, too. I've got to take my coffee and run. You really do seem more like your old self. Softer. More content. I'm glad."

"Thanks, Rand. I hope you have a good day," she said as he walked out.

She *was* softer. Maybe more content. Maybe more melancholy. She knew exactly why. It was the lingering ambiance leftover from her trip to Nashville last month. It was because of Clarence.

She hadn't seen Clarence Clawson since Rand had decided to run for President. Being a proper First Lady, the most perfect and memorable First Lady, had been too important. Planning and making desired impressions had taken over her life. Along the way, she'd become hard and unfeeling, without fully realizing it, sensing there was no other way, no room for mistakes, no room for compassion, no room for relaxation. Eventually, she had succumbed to the unnatural burden, unable to lock up her emotions any longer. She'd been incapable of stopping herself from going back to him.

She had orchestrated the trip. One night in early April, knowing Rand was down the hall in bed with Taylor, she had come apart in her suite and cried like a baby. She didn't know why. She didn't care who Rand slept with. She had no interest in being intimate with him anymore.

She had been lustful with Rand before they were married and for a few years after the wedding. Her desire for him had waned inch by inch with each affair and one-night stand he'd had. He had never tried to hide them; he'd simply expected her to accept that he was not a one-woman man. She had known that when they were dating and had married him anyway. Her own ambition had led her to marry him, and they both knew it. It had been obvious even then that Randall Pritchard was destined for greatness. She had wanted to go along for the ride. For herself.

Whatever interest in intimacy with Rand she'd had left was extinguished when Clarence Clawson entered her life. That had happened twenty-two years ago, not long after the fiasco at the Jansen mansion in Nashville.

It hadn't taken long for Justine to learn Rand had been at the orgy. That was the only time in their married life he had been truly shaken up over the possibility of his career going down the toilet. The day after the fire, she had asked him what was wrong. He'd told her the whole story. That was the weekend Gaylord Scapeli had wormed his way into their lives. Rand thought Scapeli had saved him. For many years she'd believed that, too, but the more she saw Scapeli in action, the more she suspected he had set the whole thing up, fire and all – that he had deliberately chosen Rand as his own vehicle to the White House.

She had met Clarence just over a month after the Jansen fire. She was furious with Rand at the time. The orgy had been the last straw. More precisely, the near miss had been the last straw. His sexual indulgences were threatening the political glory-rise she had anticipated in marrying him. She was disenchanted by his promiscuity, but appalled at the prospect of losing her place in society because of it. Had he been publicly outed, she would've filed for divorce. But he never was.

Not that she was a prude. She enjoyed sex as much as the next girl, maybe more than most. She'd shared a few beds before she met Rand. After they were engaged, though, she had committed to being a one-man woman – until she became so angry about Rand's close call that she wanted to get even, to give him some of his own damned medicine – until Clarence Clawson entered her life.

It had begun by chance near their home in Lexington. She was at the mall by herself at 1:00 on a Saturday afternoon, fuming about Rand and burning away his money, walking briskly, muttering to herself, and not watching what was going on … just being pissed off. Two punks who had heisted a diamond off a jewelry store counter and were beating it for an exit rounded a corner and crashed into her, shoving her to the ground, scattering sacks and packages across the wide mall corridor. She hit the floor hard, severely bruising her hip, gashing the back of her head when it banged on the floor, and spraining both her ankle and wrist.

Clarence had been walking toward her, fifty feet away when it happened. She'd glimpsed him running to help her, but she hadn't noticed him before. He wasn't very noticeable: medium height, medium build, short brown hair, and brown eyes. He had helped her sit and held his handkerchief on her streaming cut until the security staff arrived. The guard escorted her to the medical aid station. Clarence gathered everything she had dropped and brought it to her. The security staff called an ambulance to take her to the hospital. Clarence had followed and stayed with her in the crowded emergency room for three hours. Then he'd driven her home and stayed with her for half an hour, long enough to make sure she'd be all right. He'd promised to stop by the next day to drive her to the mall to get her car.

That evening Clarence had stopped by for a few minutes to check on her and then again Sunday morning. Other than being bruised, stitched, bandaged, and sore, she'd assured him she was all right. Early Sunday afternoon he returned to take her get her car. They had stopped at a coffee shop, where Clarence took her order, picked it up, and brought it back to his pickup truck. It was a pleasant day and they had sat in the pickup and chatted for two hours. She had liked him. He wasn't the type she would have ever been attracted to, but he was nice to her, easy to spend time with. He'd never been married – too shy with girls, he said. He was forty, and she was thirty-seven.

Rand had been in Washington and their girls, ten-year-old Rebecca and seven-year-old Sarah, were spending the week with Justine's parents in Fresno, California, Justine's home town. She'd invited Clarence to dinner Monday evening, in return for his kindness. She didn't cook often, but she knew how, and she had taken pleasure in preparing her chicken marsala specialty for him. They had enjoyed the meal leisurely. They'd talked. They had drunk wine. He'd stayed until midnight, and then offered to check on her again Tuesday night.

"I'm sure I'll be fine, but feel free to stop by. I like your company."

Tuesday he had arrived at 6:00 with Chinese food and a small, wrapped package. She had accepted the package, taken his free hand in hers, and led him to the table.

"Shall I open it?"

"After dinner."

She'd laid the package on the table and surprised herself by stealing glances at it as they dined. When they had finished, each having sipped away two glasses of wine, he'd said, "Come, I'll help with the dishes. Then we'll see what's in that package."

She had smiled and followed him. They'd taken their time with the dishes. When they were done, he'd led her back to the table, seated her, and poured two more glasses of wine. "Don't you want to see what I brought you?"

She'd felt like a kid at Christmas, having to force herself to open it slowly. "It's perfume! It's the same perfume I'm wearing right now."

"I know. I got my first whiff when I helped you at the mall. Then again last night, here at dinner. It was like meandering through a rose garden. I couldn't get it off my mind after I left, and I wanted to let you know how much I liked it."

She couldn't believe she was blushing. "How long did it take you to find this?"

"Not all that long. I found it in the fourth store."

"How long, Clarence?"

"Well, maybe three hours or so. I'm not all that experienced at shopping for perfume."

They had finished their second bottle of wine, and she'd brought another to the table for him to open. They had sat across the corner of the table from each other, close, as they unhurriedly relieved the bottle of its contents. She'd leaned over and kissed him, softly, touching only his lips. He had let the kiss go on for a moment, and then pulled back.

"You're married," he'd whispered.

"Rand wouldn't care," she said quietly, shaking her head. "He'd probably be glad. It might ease his conscience. I couldn't count all the women he's been with since we've been married."

"That's not possible," Clarence said. "No man could do that to anyone as enchanting as you."

"He isn't like you, Clarence. He's nothing like you."

She'd kissed him again. He'd kissed her back. He had stayed the night. He had stayed the next four nights, until Rebecca and Sarah flew back on Sunday.

Clarence lived near Chattanooga, he'd told her. He was a freelance bridge inspector. He inspected small bridges on secondary roads and streets and worked for counties and towns in Tennessee, Kentucky, and Georgia. He spent a lot of time on the road and was inspecting ten bridges that week for Bourbon County. She had ridden with him Thursday morning and watched him inspect and jot down notes. They'd had breakfast first, and then he'd inspected two bridges. They had lunched in the early afternoon. Then he'd taken her home and they'd made love before he went to his motel to write his reports. He had walked back in her front door as the sun set.

She had met him at the door wearing a black, low-cut, flowing evening dress. With no words of greeting, she had wrapped her arms around him and found his lips with a long, passionate kiss, pulling him tight to her. As he had entered, she'd reached over to the wall shelf beside the door and retrieved a package the same size as the one he had given her, wrapped identically. As she had placed it in his hand he asked, "Shall I open it after dinner?"

"Open it now."

They had sat at the table as he unwrapped it. It was a locket, but unlike any in jewelry stores. The locket and neck chain were silver-colored and shiny but not made of silver. The chain was heavy. The locket was half-moon shaped. The hinge and the clasp looked stronger than the locket itself. He examined it, turning it over in his fingers.

"What's this made of, Justine? It isn't silver."

"It's titanium. Made to last."

"I believe that."

"Open it."

The clasp was designed such that even a man had no trouble releasing it. He'd opened the locket. It had a thin rubber seal around its edges and a small red pad inside. "What is it, Justine?"

"Smell it."

"It's you! It's your perfume."

"One drop is supposed to last a lifetime if it's kept closed. They say the fragrance will last a year even if it's open. I don't know how often we'll be able to be together, but I wanted to give you something that would bring me to you anytime you want."

"Where did you find this, Justine? How long did it take?"

"It took a little while." She had beamed at him. "I'm not all that experienced at shopping for perfume lockets."

Their love affair had continued for eighteen years. They'd talked each week by cell phone at prearranged times. They met sporadically, discreetly, when they could work it out. Four times she had been able to spend long weekends with him at his cottage near Chattanooga. The first three years, although their rendezvous were irregular, the affair was torrid. Gradually it had become less intense, more settled. She had never felt guilt over it. She grew to feel more relaxed, more right with the world, when she was with Clarence than when she wasn't.

Then Rand had gotten serious about running for President. It was what she had always wanted. Her ambition had subsided as her relationship with Clarence had deepened. But Rand's talk of the White House brought that ambition back to the forefront. She became more concerned about appearances, about getting caught, public exposure.

Enter Gaylord Scapeli. She had never felt at ease around him, had never trusted his motives. There was little doubt he was behind Rand, pushing him to make the presidential run. That was the only common thread she shared with Scapeli. Then, one Monday afternoon six years ago, when she had arrived home at 2:00 in the afternoon after having spent the morning in Clarence's motel room in Berea, she'd found Gayle Scapeli sitting alone at the dining room table, waiting for her.

"Hello, Justine."

"Gayle, how did you get in? What are you doing here? Is everything all right?"

He held up a key. "Rand gives me keys to everything he has, just in case. Everything's all right, Justine. Do you have a few minutes to talk?"

"I guess so. Is there something we need to talk about?"

"I'm sure Rand's been talking to you about running for President." He looked her squarely in the eyes. "Well, if he's going to do that, he'll have to clean up his act. You and I both know he enjoys women. If he wants to stand any chance, he knows he'll have to give that up. But here's the thing, Justine. And I'm not saying this is fair or how it should be, but, if the voters get a sniff it's the candidate's wife who's sleeping around, reaction will be way worse than if it was the candidate himself."

Justine stared at him. "What are you saying, Gayle?"

"Come on, Justine. I've known about Clawson for years, probably from the beginning. If you care about Rand being president, and I know you do, then today has to be the last time."

"Jesus, Gayle! Where do you come up with this shit?"

"Did I hit a nerve, Justine?" He raised one eyebrow at her.

"Maybe you can tell Rand what to do, but you don't own me."

"No? Let me tell you something, Justine. Rand's chances only get better if he suffers the humility of discovering and having to deal with a lying, cheating wife. You can be cast out, and it won't hurt his bid one bit. I know why you married Rand just as clearly as you do. You saw presidential material in him thirty years ago, and that's what you went for. You knew he'd sleep around with anybody – hell, you knew he was doin' it while you were engaged – and you married him anyway.

"So let's cut to the chase, Jussy. You want the White House as much as he does, probably more. End it with Clawson. Now. Today. You can see that I pretty much know every move you make. If you see him again, you're out, sweetheart. End it today."

"You sonofbitch," she seethed. "You think Rand can't dump your ass in a second?" She knew she couldn't back up her words, but she couldn't hold them in. "I'll talk to Rand, and we'll see who's out. *Sweetheart.*"

"Knock it off, Justine. We both know damned well where we stand. You think I haven't already talked this through with Rand? I know how much you'd like to think you're in control, but you're not, and you *know* your not. If Rand is going to be President, you and I need to get something straight right now. I ruin people. I know more about people who count, power people, than any man alive. I have the dirt that will turn their fortunes. You're just one of many. I don't ruin lives for fun. I do it out of necessity. If you make it necessary to ruin yours, so be it. I don't really give a shit. So, here's the way it's gonna be. If Rand is going to run for President, *you* are gonna to do whatever I tell you. So is he. Now, tell me you're going to break this thing off today."

They glared at each other.

"You sonofabitch!"

"Give me your answer."

"All right," she spat through gritted teeth. "Now, get out of my house and out of my sight."

"I'm leaving, Justine. But don't you forget who's calling the shots. Rand isn't and you know it. And *you* certainly are not."

That was the day she'd begun to harden. She knew she had been a gold digger when she dated and married Rand. She knew her ambition drove her. The fifteen-year affair with Clarence had made her feel more feminine, softer. Her ambition had played less of a role during that time, but it had never left. It flared up when Rand began talking of the presidency, and when it did, the feeling of contentment that came with Clarence began to wane.

She'd continued to call Clarence from time to time after that day, but they never saw each other. As Rand got closer and closer to the presidency, her calls became less frequent. She grew harder. By the time of the election the only thing that mattered to her was becoming the perfect First Lady. She instinctively knew the right social moves and made them all. She understood her tendency to appear stiff and unfeeling, and she worked hard to muffle that. Inside, she had become more callous than the impression she created. She hadn't talked to Clarence since the election ... until the call she'd made in February. And then the second one in April, that night when she'd come apart in her bedroom.

*   *   *

While Daryl and Racine were sitting at the breakfast table with their children and President Pritchard was meeting with the Israeli Prime Minister, Janice Taylor reported to work at the West Wing. At 9:10 she left her workstation and walked to the restroom. From there, she continued down the main corridor to a small meeting room that was usually locked from the main corridor. This morning, it wasn't. She turned the knob and walked into the empty room. The main entrance to this meeting room was at the opposite end, from a secure area of the building. Vice President Borster entered the room from that door at 9:15.

As Janice walked from her work station, she considered the circumstances that had brought her to this meeting. Thursday evening she had received a call at home.

"Miss Taylor?"

"Who's calling?"

"I'm calling for the Vice President, ma'am. He would like to meet with you."

"Why? Who are you?"

"I'm not at liberty to give you my name, Miss Taylor. Vice President Borster would like to meet with you privately Saturday morning in the West Wing. Would you be willing to do that?"

"Maybe. What's he want to talk about?"

"The Vice President is concerned that you might not have been treated decently by President and Mrs. Pritchard and that you might be trapped. He'd like to discuss options that might be open to you."

"He wants to meet with *me* about *that*? Just the Vice President and me? Or would there be others?"

"Just you two, in a private meeting in a secure conference room in the West Wing."

Janice was quiet for a minute. "What time and what room?"

They made the arrangements.

How could Borster know I'm trapped? What's he know about Rand and me? About that bitch and me? Why does he care? Shit.

Borster entered the room alone as Janice sat at the table. He reminded her of the proper, distinguished, gray grandfather she had lost when she was fifteen. He took a seat across the table from her.

"Good morning, Janice."

"Hello, sir," she replied softly.

"I'll not waste time. I'm in a difficult spot, and I believe you are, too. We might be in a position to help each other." He looked her squarely in the eye. She didn't respond. He continued. "I love this country with all my soul. I'm a patriot and want nothing more than to serve America and contribute to her prosperity. Over the past three years, I've grown to know Randall Pritchard, and I'm convinced these are not sentiments that motivate him.

"It's no secret the Administration and the President have ostracized me. I don't want my career end with a whimper. I'm not ready to be put out to pasture. I don't plan to give them the opportunity to remove me from the ticket. I intend to continue to serve as Vice President. And, I expect Randall Pritchard's true colors will soon show. He'll get reelected, but will likely succumb to scrutiny shortly thereafter."

Janice remained silent. He went on. "I'm sure you're wondering what this has to do with you. Unfortunately, in this town, no matter how tightly knit a group of friends might be, one or two talk too freely, and secrets waft out. As it turns out, earlier this week I was told a story of a poker party held in the White House last month – just the President and three of his buddies. And you."

Fear pierced her. *If you ever break your part of this agreement, you'll fall so far you'll want to take your own life. And you'll know the reason will be that I did not break my part.* She shuddered, recalling the words emblazoned in her brain. She forced herself to remain composed. Still, she didn't respond.

"Janice, I know Randall and Justine Pritchard, and I'm sure you must be at least a little frightened. Maybe a lot. I suspect you feel trapped and would welcome a way out. I can offer you that. The process would involve gathering some information on your part. I believe it would be easy for you to do in your unique position. The information would ensure both your escape and my inclusion on the ticket. Do you want to hear more?"

"I'm listening."

Thirty minutes later, as Janice walked back to her workstation, the thought crossed her mind that she could deal with this in more than one way. She didn't care whether Borster was on the ticket or not. *One politician's as bad as the next.* She certainly felt no sympathy for or obligation to either of the Pritchards. *Yes ... it might just be possible. I could come out of this with my freedom and enough money to live luxuriously for the rest of my life.*

Chapter 14

Wednesday, June 15, Rockford, Illinois, 7:00 a.m.

Daryl and Rory had spent the night in Rockford after driving from Springfield, where they had filed for Illinois ballot access and addressed a large crowd of supporters. After finishing an early breakfast, they pulled onto I-39 on their way to repeat the process today in Madison, Wisconsin.

"Dad?"

"Uhuh."

"I know you say the TV ads about you are smoke and mirrors, but do they make you feel bad? I mean, they run those commercials a lot, all over the country, and they all make it sound like you don't know anything. Deep down, does it bother you?"

"Yeah, it's hard sometimes. I try to stay above it, but sometimes when I see one, it makes me want to punch somebody. I know they're just twisting things around, trying to distract people from what I'm really saying. I keep telling myself not to stoop to their level and play their mud slinging game."

Rory grinned at his dad. "I like the one where they say 'Daryl Marten says criminals should earn their keep' and they show this mean dude with a stubby beard and about half his teeth talking to his buddies. He says, 'I earned my keep today, boys. Earned my keep for the whole year, just on my lunch break.' Then he opens his lunchbox and shows them a pile of jewelry. Then you see what he did at lunch. He just walks out the front door of the factory and breaks into a house. He trashes the place and steals the jewels and a bunch of hundred dollar bills and stuffs it all in the lunchbox then strolls back to the factory. Then they say, 'Daryl Marten wants to mainstream our convicted criminals. Do you?' The kids at school like that one, especially the ones who bring lunchboxes."

"Yeah, Rory, that's a good one. I like the one about cooperating with other countries where they have these big Chinese and Russian and Arab guys and a little guy with a red, white, and blue USA jacket. The little guy does all the talking while the big guys just smirk. He squeaks, 'Hey, friends, let's all work together. Let's all share our secrets, get rid of our weapons, and pool our money to protect the environment and help the little countries. Here, I'll go first.' Then it shows him giving all his money, weapons, and secrets to the big guys who just rake it all in. Then the little guy says, 'I wanted to go first just to show you how ethical and moral I am. And tomorrow, I'm going to work on being competent.' Then they say, 'This is how Daryl Marten wants to run America.' I really like that one."

"The nastiest one," Rory said, "is the one about being competent. The guy looks kind of like you, except he has this really stupid expression. He reads parts of your proposition about training and experience. The last thing he reads is, 'This proposition is to declare war on incompetent decision making.' Right after he says that, he stares at the camera, all wide eyed and goofy, and snaps his fingers and says, 'I know what'd be fun! I'll quit bein' a house planner and run for president!' That one's pretty crappy."

"You're right about that. Yeah, sometimes it bothers me when I see those commercials and think about everybody seeing that propaganda. The thing that helps me get past it is confidence in the American people. We're smart enough to sort through the misinformation and figure out the truth. If I'm wrong about that, then everything I'm doing's a waste of time. But I don't think I'm wrong. This country is made up of people who think for themselves."

"I hope you're right. I was still awake last night when the news was on. I heard something about Catcher going after your signatures. Will that be a problem?"

"I don't know. He submitted challenges in Texas, North Carolina, California, Florida, and Oklahoma. We haven't even filed yet in California and Florida. I think he just wants the election offices to know he'll be looking over their shoulders so they'd better not accept any invalid signatures."

"What's an invalid signature?"

"It could be several things. If a person signs more than once, those signatures are crossed off the list. In most states, only registered voters are allowed to sign, so if anybody who wasn't registered in the last election signs, those get thrown out."

"They have to check every signature? Over a hundred thousand? How can they check 'em all?"

"They enter every signature into their computer and cross reference names and addresses. If they make typing mistakes, some names could get dropped even if they're valid. And they investigate practices used in getting signatures. If signatures are bought or coerced, they throw out any they suspect, or they can kick you off the ballot altogether. I'm sure Catcher will push for that."

"Are you sure none of our volunteers did anything wrong like that? You never even met most of 'em."

"Your Mom and Mel were careful about making sure the head people in every state knew the rules and that, if anyone broke the rules, it could cause us to get thrown off the ballot. All we can do is hope everybody did it right."

"If some signatures get tossed out, will we have enough left?"

"We've got more than ten percent extra in every state except the ones Catcher's challenging. Those are the big states, and they carry a lot of votes. Especially California, Florida, and Texas. In Texas we only had about four percent extra. We're still five thousand signatures short in Florida and more than twenty thousand short in California."

"Will we make it?"

"I think so. A lot of volunteers in states where we already filed are helping in Florida and especially in California. I think we'll make it, but Catcher's challenge'll probably create a mess in both states."

"Why's Catcher so all-fired-up? Everybody says he can't win anyway. And none of the other candidates seem like they're paying any attention to you at all. Especially President Pritchard. He's supposed to be ahead. It looks like he'd be the one who'd want you out."

"I think Pritchard wants us to look hopeless. If he notices us, he probably thinks more people will consider us legitimate, and he doesn't want that. I think he's playing it smart. After the conventions, if it looks like we're in the picture, he might start throwing punches. Or he might think we're stealing more votes from the Democrats than from him and just keep ignoring us. Catcher? Maybe he's getting used by groups that feel threatened by us. He probably thinks his only chance is to get his name plastered all over the place. Grab attention. He needs cash and there are probably lots of lawyers, drug companies, insurance companies, and hospitals throwing money at him, but telling him he has to use most of it attacking Commonguy and me."

"Why wouldn't the other two Democrats want the money, Wheeler and Herrington?"

"They don't need it as bad. They have their own supporters and lots of money coming in. They're more worried about each other than anything else. Only one of them will survive their convention. Neither of them thinks Catcher's a threat, even with all his new money. They might think attacking me and our propositions could work against them."

"Catcher seems like an idiot. Why doesn't he just give up if everybody knows he can't win?"

"I know a little about Bradley Catcher. He's young, but he's no idiot. And he's really not a bad guy. It's almost like he knows something nobody else knows. Or like there's somebody behind the scenes driving his campaign, someone powerful. I've thought about it a lot, but haven't figured it out."

They drove in silence for a while. Daryl worried about Racine. This was his third week in a row away. Last week he had gone on the flying trip west to file in Alaska, Oregon, Idaho, Wyoming, and Hawaii. The week before that, he and Kyle had gone to North Carolina and caught up on east coast filing. Monday morning, leaving early for Indianapolis, had not been a happy scene.

That morning, before he and Racy had gone downstairs, Daryl had thought for a moment she was going to pull the plug on Rory going along, no matter how much he wanted to go. In the end, she had delivered a mandate, one of only three or four in their married life. "Don't let anything happen to Rory," she had demanded. "Keep your eye on him every second." Daryl had promised. As he and Rory left, they both hugged her and Daryl kissed her. Racy's perpetual warmth and love had not penetrated the hug and kiss. Daryl couldn't recall a single time he had ever left on a trip with her in such a frame of mind.

He couldn't fault her. Life had become impossibly difficult. He was being targeted by national TV ads making him out to be an ignorant fool. They'd had to disconnect their phones. He had taken an unpaid leave of absence from work. They were living on last year's savings. Racine worked ceaselessly, without pay, coordinating their volunteers. Jeremy invested all his spare time in keeping the website and computers running smoothly. Kelsey wasn't getting the attention she needed. They were continuously bombarded by people they didn't know; driving by, knocking on the door, accosting them in public. Their private lives were not their own anymore. No one complained, but the strain on them all was telling.

Worst of all was the continuous threat of danger. Last week, while Daryl was flying around the west coast, Racy and Kelsey had been the victims of an attempted kidnapping. That Thursday at noon, Racine's guilt had gotten the better of her and she had told the boys they were closing up shop for two hours and going to the park.

While the boys were tossing a football, Racine took Kelsey to see the animals in the petting zoo. It was only a block away and she could see the boys the entire time. Carrying Kelsey, she was halfway back to the boys when a man with a sock hat covering his face leapt out from behind a tree and grabbed her arms.

"Get in the car," he commanded gruffly, nodding toward a sedan parked at the curb with the back door open.

Kelsey screamed. "Jeremy!"

The boys looked up and raced toward them, yelling. As the man glanced at them, Racine wrenched free of his grasp and started running. The man started after her, but tripped on a tree root and thudded to the ground. He cursed, jumped up, ran to the car, slammed the rear door shut, dove in behind the wheel, and peeled away.

By the end of the day, Racine had calmed down. Now, the kids considered the incident great story fodder. However,

Sheriff Stone had posted a round-the-clock watch on the family, to continue until such time as Secret Service protection would be provided. One more snip out of their precious bit of remaining privacy.

The same day, Cleve's family had a similar occurrence. Bobby had been riding his bike when a man tried to abscond with him. Again, a masked man reached out from behind a tree and scooped Bobby off his bike as he rode by. However, kidnapping Bobby was no easy task. Bobby screamed, kicked, and flailed, landing blows on head and ears, and sharp kicks to knee joints. Attempting to silence the wretched warrior by cramming a hand over his mouth, the assailant found his ring finger greeted by an open mouth that clamped and ground hard. Blood spurted as the man yelped and dropped Bobby who landed on his feet, running. Bobby lifted his bike and mounted it in a single motion, and sped off across yards where the man couldn't drive after him. Cleve's home was likewise placed under twenty-four-hour surveillance.

Riding along in silence, Rory seemed to know his Dad's thoughts. "We'll be all right, Dad. When we started Commonguy, we didn't know any of this would happen. Everything'll turn out okay; probably really good."

Daryl smiled at him and ruffled his hair. "You're a good son, Rory. I'm glad you're here with me."

"Mom sure wasn't so glad about that. Man, I thought for a minute she wasn't going to let me come."

"Yeah," Daryl chuckled, "she was pretty riled up, wasn't she." He'd talked to her at least three times every day since they left. The situation was becoming increasingly difficult for her, as it was for them all, but at least her loving warmth was back.

"Dad?"

"Yeah?"

"Do you believe in some kind of God?"

Daryl sighed. "I guess we didn't talk about any of *those* commercials did we?"

"No. They all try so hard to make you seem like such a bad person. But you're a really good person. Everybody who's ever met you knows that."

Ads from a group calling themselves "The Christian Coalition for Americans" had started airing a week ago. They were insufferable. One of them replayed excerpts of him speaking in his televised interview with Zach.

"In running this nation, it doesn't matter whether a Baptist, Pentecostal, Jew, Muslim, Mormon, or Atheist is elected to a particular public office ... The day-to-day decisions and actions of government offices should not be based upon religious belief ... Religion doesn't play a part in our platform ... I'll continue to maintain that my personal religious beliefs, as well as Cleve's, are irrelevant to our candidacy ... Bradley Catcher should be the next President of the United States." The screen caught, or was modified to show – Daryl wasn't sure which – an awkward expression on his face. A deep, slow voice then said, "Is this man an imbecile? America is *not* a godless society. Are these the words of Satan spoken through man? Shun him."

Daryl shuddered, replaying that awful commercial in his mind. It wasn't the only one. *Strength. Stay above it.*

"So, do you?" Rory repeated.

"I'd have to say, I'm not sure, Rory. I'd like to be sure, but I'm not. It seems like there would have to be some sort of being who created all this, the universe, but it's a paradox. Could the creator have just always been there? That's hard to understand too. I hope there's more to life, to our lives, than just chance; that we're here for some reason or purpose and something better is waiting for us when our life here is done. But I just don't know for sure."

"I believe there's a God," Rory said. "I'm just a kid, but I understand your questions. I don't know how to show anybody any answers, but I still believe there's a God. I believe God made everything and has a plan and a better place for us. I'm not sure why I believe that. I just feel it. I always have. I feel it in my bones, like it's part of me."

"I'm glad, Rory. It makes me feel better just to hear you say that."

Rory smiled at his Dad. "I'm really glad Mom didn't go off the deep end and make me stay home. I'm glad I'm here with you."

"I love you, Rory," Daryl said. "I'm glad too."

They were getting close to Madison. Rory was the navigator and he opened the Atlas to the Madison page, preparing to guide his dad to the state offices.

On Thursday Daryl and Rory filed in St. Paul and on Friday in Des Moines. They stayed in Peoria Friday night and arrived home at noon on Saturday. The welcome home hugs and kisses were way more satisfying than those at goodbye last Monday morning. The Martens avoided the TV all day Saturday. They didn't want to see any commercials; they didn't want to see any news. They didn't answer their cell phones. They wanted and desperately needed a day to themselves. The family put all tasks on hold and spent Saturday afternoon in the basement playing games and enjoying being together.

The one thing Daryl had to do was finish and post the June proposition. It was already a week late. He went into his office at 7:30 Saturday night and completed that task. He came out at 9:45 and went to bed with his wife. They were asleep by 10:00.

Proposition #18, Control of Outer Space, promoted the consolidation of all independent national space programs into one international program. Stop the duplication of efforts and all the wasted resources inherent in duplication. At the same time, step up the pace of space exploration. Unimaginable advances have been and will continue to be realized from this effort. Make it a priority, but eliminate the waste.

On Sunday morning, after Daryl got out of bed, he returned one of Cleve's five calls from Saturday. "Sorry I didn't call you back yesterday, buddy. We had our phones off. We really needed the afternoon together. What's up?"

"Have you been watching the news?"

"I haven't had a TV on since Thursday night. I know Wheeler is pounding Herrington and might do him in if the war conduct claims have any truth to them."

"You've been out of circulation too long, Daryl. It's bigger than that now."

"What happened?"

"Herrington hit back. Harder. He says he's got proof Wheeler raked millions from Illinois coffers when he was Governor. If half of what they're saying about each other's true, they're *both* done. It'll be Catcher for the Dems."

"You're kidding. He doesn't stand a chance against Pritchard."

"He couldn't beat *us*, Daryl. The pollsters are starting to talk about us. They're saying all his negative ads are backfiring. They're calling our propositions fresh. Concepts Americans want to hear more about. It's getting more interesting by the day, pal. It's possible November could come down to us against Pritchard."

"That's crazy, Cleve. Even if it did, Pritchard seems invincible. There's never been a more popular incumbent. I'm not sure *anybody* could beat him."

"You're right about him being at the pinnacle. I'll tell you though, Daryl, he's primed for a crash. Anyway, you might want to catch some news today."

"I will. I've also got some big calls to return: Jeff Kramer, Regina Wasson, if you can believe the nerve of that, and Zach. I plan to tackle some of the crap being slung at us next week, and it looks like the perfect venues might be opening up."

"That's great, Daryl! In case you can't tell, I'm excited. Bits and pieces keep falling into place. If it keeps up, this thing could happen."

"We'll keep doing our part and see where it leads. It's been some trip so far."

By the end of the day, Daryl had three televised appearances scheduled. The first was the one he wanted most desperately. It was a follow-on interview with Regina Wasson, on his terms this time. It would be a ten minute, uninterrupted, live telecast interview, and was scheduled for Tuesday night at 6:40. When he had returned the network's call and informed them these were the only terms under which he would appear with Wasson, they had refused. They called back six times before 8:00 Sunday evening. He didn't waver and they finally agreed.

On Thursday he was scheduled for a second appearance on The Insomniac Show. He would be in New York most of the week. It would have to be without Racine this time and he hated that. The following Monday he was set up with Zach.

*   *   *

Regina Wasson looked into the camera. "We have a special treat for you this evening. Daryl Marten is with us. We've dedicated the next ten minutes to a live interview with no commercial interruptions. Welcome back, Mr. Marten."

"Thank you, Regina, and please, call me Daryl."

"All right, Daryl, let's get started. You and Cleveland DeCamp are in the midst of an unconventional run at the presidency. Democratic candidate, Senator Bradley Catcher, has filed charges against your methods of obtaining ballot access in Texas, North Carolina, California, Florida, and Oklahoma. Can you defend yourself against his charges?"

"Let me correct your terminology, Regina. Senator Catcher hasn't filed any charges. He's put election officials in those states on notice that he will challenge the signature lists I submitted. That means the lists will be checked for any duplicate signatures and for signatures from persons who are not registered voters. The election offices will be required to evaluate the practices of the volunteers who obtained the signatures to be sure they obtained the signatures in a legal manner. There are no charges to defend myself against."

"You didn't answer the question, Daryl. I'll repeat it. Can you defend yourself against Senator Catcher's charges of illegal activities?"

"Your question shows that either you don't understand how the process works or you're trying to twist the facts in this interview as you did in our last one, Regina. I answered your question as well as it could be answered. There are no charges to defend against. If you're trying to ask whether we'll have enough valid signatures for our names to appear on the ballots, then my answer is that I hope so, but I can't know for sure. We don't have enough signatures yet to apply for ballot access in California or Florida."

Wasson hesitated, not having anticipated this novice would have the gall to try to turn the tables on her on live, national television. "All right, Daryl. I have a lot of questions and we don't have a lot of time. Since you appear to prefer to skirt the first question, let's try another one. You've been receiving a lot of air time over the past couple of months, courtesy of Senator Catcher, who now appears to be the Democratic front runner. His ads show your ideas to be oversimplified and impractical; impossible to implement. I've read your propositions. All of them. How can you defend the fallacies pointed out in his ads?"

"Let's clear the air, Regina. It should be obvious to anyone watching that you're doing your best to make it appear I'm over-reaching my capabilities. The last time you interviewed me, it was taped. Your network edited that interview to present me in the worst possible light. That's why this interview is live. That's the only way I would agree to appear with you. I will hold my own with you tonight. What the viewers will see this time is me, exactly for what I am. They're free to decide for themselves whether or not they like what they see.

"Now," he went on quickly, giving her no break to intercede, "to respond to your accusation and your question. I did not skirt your first question. You tried to set a trap that didn't work because your trap wasn't logical. Your second question insinuates your personal opinion, and Senator Catcher's, is that the propositions posted on Commonguy are oversimplified, impractical, and impossible to implement. My response is that I believe every one of those propositions has sufficient merit to warrant thorough evaluation.

"If each proposition were to receive detailed scrutiny," he continued, "it might become obvious that some should be discarded. But, I believe many of them would be found worth implementing and certainly possible to implement given an adequate period of time. The bottom line is this. I am offering my opinions to the American public. I believe in the ability of Americans to think for themselves. If a significant majority feel strongly enough that one or more of my propositions deserve further consideration, they'll apply the pressure necessary to make that happen. If they don't, then they don't. I trust the American people and believe in their ability to make reasonable decisions."

"All right, Daryl," her demeanor betrayed her exasperation, "We're running out of time, but I want to ask one last important question. Christians all across the country are aghast at your stance against them. So much so that they've formed "The Christian Coalition for Americans" to prevent you from further degrading faith in the United States. They've gone so far as to claim you speak for Satan. I'm sure you've seen their commercial, Daryl. Do you?"

"Do I what, Regina? Are you sitting here on national TV asking me directly if I speak for Satan? I'd have expected you to use your previous language and ask if I could answer someone else's charge. That's a ridiculous question and I'm tempted to refuse to stoop low enough to even consider responding. But, I've seen how you twist words, so I'll answer you clearly. No, I don't speak for Satan.

"And we aren't out of time yet," he rushed on. "I assume either you're becoming uncomfortable or you want the last minute or two to slant this interview with your own last words. So, if that was your last question, I'll talk for the remainder of our time. If you want to try to twist this interview into some preconceived perception, you'll have to talk over me because I'm not stopping.

"I am not anti-Christian. Nor am I anti-Jew or anti-Muslim. I have nothing but respect for the religious beliefs of all individuals. I have no sentiment that anyone's religious convictions are arrived at in any way other than through arduous introspection, thought, and study. I understand how important religious beliefs are to everyone. My philosophy is that government should not tread on anybody's religious beliefs, no matter what they might be. I believe the only way all persons can be protected in this regard is to ensure that no particular religious concepts are imposed on them by the government or by any individuals participating in government.

"I believe every person has a right to practice whatever religion feels right to them, so long as they do no harm to others. I believe one of the duties of our government is to protect that right. Should the citizens of this country see fit to choose me to head the executive branch, that's the position I'll live by."

As he spoke, Wasson attempted to talk over him, "Mr. Marten, are you an atheist? Answer that question." Louder. "Answer it!"

Daryl's volume rose to avoid being drowned out. "The most critical traits necessary in those governing this nation are high moral and ethical standards and competence in decision-making. Cleve and I don't profess to have all the tools to solve all the issues facing America without a great deal of help, but we do have the ability to recognize those who have the necessary talents and character traits and we'll recruit and utilize them fully."

"Answer the question! You haven't answered one single question! Are you an atheist?" Wasson was shouting.

The network cut to commercial. It was the same commercial that played immediately before the interview; the ad ending with the words, 'Shun him'.

"Marten, you son of a bitch!" Wasson screamed as soon as they were off camera. "Get your damned, sorry ass off my set and don't ever set foot here again."

"Thank you for having me on your program tonight, Regina," Daryl said quietly, looking her in the eye. "It was a pleasure."

"Get out!" she shrieked.

He rose, turned his back to her, and walked out of the studio.

*   *   *

On Thursday night, June 23, at 11:30, Gayle Scapeli was glued to his television set. He watched every second of The Insomniac Show to make sure he wouldn't miss a word whenever Marten appeared. During the monologue, Kramer made several references to the disastrous interview two nights before with Regina Wasson. Scapeli had cautioned against doing the interview live, but had been assured Wasson could handle Daryl Marten. *It could not possibly have gone worse.* It seemed the whole country loved the way Marten had turned the tables on the media. Quick polls indicated even the Christian right was not reacting fervently against Marten.

Unfortunately, Jeff Kramer was not among the circle under Scapeli's influence. Marten's performance on the show tonight would be important.

Fifteen minutes into the show, Kramer said, "Ladies and Gentleman, please welcome back Daryl Marten." Another standing ovation. "Presidential Candidate, Daryl Marten." The audience erupted.

Daryl walked out and the men smiled and shook hands warmly. The audience refused to sit as Daryl smiled and waved at them. "Daryl, you're our most popular guest of the year!" More shouts, cheers and applause.

When the crowd finally calmed, Daryl sat and smiled up at them. "Thank you very much."

"Unfortunately, your beautiful wife, Racine, isn't with us tonight."

"She sends her regards, Jeff. We would've loved for her to be here, but she's very busy coordinating and communicating with our volunteers. It wasn't possible for her to get away for the week."

"That's right. You've been in town all week. I'm wondering," Kramer looked up at the audience, "did any of you happen to see Daryl's interview with Regina Wasson Tuesday night?"

The audience went crazy.

Kramer laughed heartily as he vainly motioned for the audience to pacify. When they finally quieted, Jeff laughed again and said, "Well, that's all the time we have for tonight, folks. Thank you for joining us, Daryl." Laughter.

"Hey, I think they're finally gonna let us talk!" Kramer said. "So, how are you coming along with your ballot access efforts? I understand you still have a few states to go."

"Correct. We haven't filed yet in California, Florida, Michigan, New Hampshire, New York, Vermont, or Maine. Racine told me just before the show that we have enough signatures now in Florida, but we still need around sixteen thousand in California."

"Sixteen thousand? How long do you have left to get them? Will you make it?"

"It's right at ten percent of the total. We need one-hundred-sixty-thousand to file and we have a hundred-forty-four. We want ten percent extra, so our goal is thirty-two-thousand more signatures before August. We want extra signatures to be confident we can survive the challenge Senator Catcher will file." Boos from the audience.

Kramer looked at the audience and gestured as if to say, 'What's that all about.' Then he said, "Yeah, we've all heard about his challenges, which we all now understand, along with

Regina Wasson, are not charges against you." The audience roared.

"Speaking of Senator Catcher, I guess he's somehow now the Democratic front runner. Were you surprised at how Wheeler and Herrington destroyed each other?" Cheers. Kramer grinned at the audience and said, "What, already?!" Then he added, "And the timing, six weeks before the convention, after everyone except Catcher had dropped out."

"Yeah, Jeff. I was surprised at how that all happened. I'm amazed at how detailed and accurate their information on each other appeared to be. I'd have thought information like that would be impossible to get."

"Do you think their mutual annihilation will benefit your efforts to gain the White House?"

"I find myself often reemphasizing our approach, Jeff. It's an unusual angle and the concept seems to roll off people rather than sink in. Your question, 'will it benefit our efforts to gain the White House' carries an assumption that we're *trying* to gain the White House. That isn't what we're about. Cleve and I are working hard to get our names on the ballot to offer our services to the American people in the event they want our services. We've never mounted a campaign. We've not accepted a dime in contributions. We've not placed a single ad, not even in a newspaper. We're really *not* seeking the White House." More applause and cheers.

"I hear you, Daryl, but face it, you're here on national television as you were Tuesday evening with poor Regina," he shook his head, "whom you, the country boy from Ohio, just decimated, by the way." Again the crowd went wild. "Isn't this campaigning?"

"I didn't call you, Jeff. Nor did I call Regina Wasson. You both called me and invited me to interview."

"I guess you're right about that. And then, after she invited you, what you did to her, the professional media icon ... I'm in awe." He bowed to Daryl. More cheers.

"What about Senator Catcher and The Christian Coalition for Americans. They seem to be pulling out all the stops. What do you think about them?"

"I have nothing against Senator Catcher. He's young, but then I'm not old. I believe his record as a legislator is consistent and fairly decent. I've spent a little time reviewing his record, not a lot, just trying to get a feel for what he supports. I've only seen one tendency that strikes me as curious, but it's likely he's simply subverting his own preferences to those of his constituency, which would be admirable."

"And what's that tendency?"

"Senator Catcher belongs to the Roman Catholic Church, but on issues that are priorities with the Church, he's invariably absent for the vote or he abstains."

"Issues like?"

"Abortion for example. When opportunities have arisen to vote against it, he hasn't. He hasn't voted for it either, he's just silent. Also, making birth control available to high school students, back when he was a Vermont senator. He didn't cast a vote. I'm not saying that's good or bad, it just struck me as unusual. Typically, he never misses a vote, but on issues like that, he seems to never cast a vote."

"What about his ads against you? Don't you want to retaliate?"

"I doubt if any of those ads are his ideas. My guess is they appall him almost as much as me. But his campaign desperately needed an infusion of cash and he got it, probably with the caveat that most of the money had to be used to ridicule the concepts Cleve and I are promoting."

"Now that he's the Democratic front runner, do you think the ads will continue or will he turn to Pritchard?"

""He'll have to give attention to President Pritchard. Campaign funding will probably become much more available. But, I'm sure the organizations funneling money through his campaign to attack Cleve and me will continue to do that. My guess is it'll get worse."

"It almost seems to be working against him. I mean, you heard the audience when his name was mentioned." Now a loud and long chorus of boos. Kramer looked at his audience, shook his head, and chuckled. "See there. Is it all going to backfire on him?"

Daryl smiled at the audience and said, "I do really appreciate your support." Cheers and applause. "I don't know whether his negative ads will hurt him or hurt us or help one or the other. For our part, Cleve and I will continue to do our best to ignore the negative ads and keep doing what we're doing; offering our services if the people want us. If they don't, they don't. I'm sure the lives of my family and Cleve's family will be easier if the citizens decide they don't want us. But we're willing to do our utmost for our country if chosen."

"What about The Christian Coalition for Americans? Their ads are barbed with poisonous tips."

"You noticed that, did you? Jeff, I don't really know who they are. I spent an hour or two on the web trying to figure out who's behind the organization and I couldn't trace it. Maybe I could've with more time, but time is a very precious commodity these days. And, in the end, it doesn't matter who's behind it. I'm not going to attack them back or try to expose the individuals driving those ads. As I said, Cleve and I will continue to offer our services. If their ads make people perceive us as the devil incarnate and they don't want to vote for us, that's their prerogative. I believe, and I've said this often, the American people are smart and think for themselves. Our citizens are more than capable of sorting fact from fiction in advertising."

"We really are running out of time, Daryl," Kramer leaned back and held his hands up as if preparing for assault, "and I'm not making that up, honest." Raucous laughter from the audience. "I'm almost afraid to say this after what you did to that poor lady, but I do have one more question I'd like to ask. And this isn't a topic we discussed beforehand. There've been rumors whispered, maybe you've heard them, maybe you haven't, that your family has suffered physical attack recently. Would you like to comment?"

Daryl looked at Kramer without responding for a moment, and then said. "I don't know how hard or how easy the path we've been on for the past year looks from outside. When Cleve and I decided to make public propositions on how we believe our government should function, we could never have guessed we'd be where we are today. We did hope to influence national politics, but thought it was a long shot. We never foresaw becoming *part* of national politics. Had we been able to foresee the results of our efforts in the beginning, we might well have been scared out of ever launching Commonguy.

"I guess what I'm saying, is the past year has been very, very hard. More than once, we considered quitting. Whenever we considered our options, it was never just Cleve and me. Every one of those discussions included not only our wives, but our children, and our joint decision each time was that we would *not* be bullied into quitting." He paused. "Yes, in the past month there were attempted kidnappings of my wife and daughter and of Cleve's seven-year-old son." The audience gasped.

"Fortunately both attempts were unsuccessful and no one was seriously hurt … except for the guy who tried to kidnap Cleve's son. He obviously had no clue what kind of cyclone he was trying to tackle. Anyway, since then our families have been under continuous protection from the local sheriff and we anticipate receiving Secret Service protection beginning in a few days. The question of the safety of our families is a huge concern for us. So is the disappearance of our private lives.

"Regardless, we are not quitters. We'll continue to offer our services to America." A long standing ovation.

"Daryl, I really didn't know those things had happened. I'd truly heard only vague rumors. I'm very happy your families are safe." He glanced at the stage manager gesturing wildly at him. "My stage manager over there has succumbed to heart failure. We're two minutes past time to cut to commercial. Daryl, I can't tell you how impressed I am with you and with what you and Cleve DeCamp are accomplishing. Thank you for joining us tonight and I wish you the very best of luck. Ladies and gentleman, Presidential Candidate, Daryl Marten!" The audience leapt to their feet as the screen cut to commercial.

Scapeli stared in disbelief at the screen. *How can he still be surviving? Building steam? Plan A is dead. Whatever Plan B turns out to be, Marten will have Secret Service protection. With an inside agent or two.* He would see to that tomorrow. He picked up his phone and called Gerald Baron to order the development of Plan B.

Chapter 15

Tuesday, June 28, Washington DC, 6:30

Gayle Scapeli watched the evening news to see the interview taped earlier that day. It was unfortunate that Forrester had jumped networks. He had no control over this one.

"This is Zachary Forrester with Cincinnati Channel Eight News reporting with presidential candidate Daryl Marten. Good afternoon, Mr. Marten, and thank you for joining us. Senator Catcher has challenged your signatures in Texas, North Carolina, and Oklahoma. Have you received any word on the status of those challenges?"

"We did get a report back from Texas just this morning and were pleased to hear their assessment is done and we'll be on the ballot. Their final count showed nine-hundred-thirty-seven more signatures than required. We don't anticipate final word from Oklahoma or North Carolina until early August. We have a generous cushion of extra signatures in both those states, so we're hopeful of positive results."

"After you complete filing, do you intend to conduct a campaign tour?"

"Not in the traditional sense. We've received many requests to appear and speak before various groups. We haven't agreed to any appearances yet, but we anticipate trying to accommodate a half dozen or so in September and October."

"Have you seen recent poll results showing that, if the election were to be held today, the Marten/DeCamp ticket would easily defeat Senator Catcher regardless of who his vice presidential choice might be? The poles also generally agree that if the race were just between you and Randall Pritchard you would present a viable challenge."

"Our concentration right now, Zach, is on gaining ballot access in the remaining states. Cleve and I aren't concerning ourselves with polls. We're committed to doing what's necessary to offer our services to America, if America wants them."

"Assuming the viability of your candidacy continues to grow, would you be willing to debate with the other candidates?"

"Of course, but I'd be surprised if that opportunity presents itself. Regardless of poll results, I doubt either Senator Catcher or President Pritchard will be willing to take any step that would imply they consider me a viable candidate."

"It certainly appears to us you're a viable candidate. Thank you, Mr. Marten, for speaking with us today."

"Shit," Scapeli muttered. The attack ads would be ratcheted up in July and August, but that would probably do nothing more than further alienate Catcher to the populous. If Plan B had to be put into play to deal with Marten, so be it. *I'll decide that in September.*

*   *   *

Jimmy Borster also watched the evening news. Daryl Marten was the least of his worries. Scapeli would undoubtedly destroy Marten's candidacy in one way or another. His immediate crisis was that he was now certain Pritchard and Scapeli were maneuvering to force him off the reelection ticket. Janice Taylor had said she had proof Scapeli had set up the entire Wheeler and Herrington candidacies and had instigated their destruction of each other. She had also told him she had proof they planned to kick him off the ticket. Gayle Scapeli was the most despicable person he had ever known and Borster loathed him

Janice had called Borster on his secure cell phone last Friday and given him this information. Tonight was the first opportunity he had been able arrange to meet with her. At 7:10, he slipped out the back door.

Borster had never liked Secret Service protection and had worked out an arrangement to gain a bit of private time. Periodically he would don a sloppy jacket, dark glasses, and an oversized, wide-brimmed hat that hid his face in a semi-disguise, and sneak out the back door of his residence for an hour or two to walk in freedom. The Secret Service Director had vehemently objected to the unprotected walks, as he had objected to allowing Borster to live in his own hard-to-protect home in Arlington. In both cases, Borster had insisted. The final decisions in favor of Borster's requests had been made by Pritchard.

Few people knew of Borster's unprotected private walks. Gayle Scapeli knew. He had urged Pritchard to approve both of Borster's requests. And Gerald Baron knew.

Curt Willoughby was the senior and most trusted agent of Davidson County Safety Services. From 4:00 until 10:00 every evening for the past week he had been posted in an upper floor room of a distant building with a telescope trained on Borster's back door. Tonight was the second evening Borster had gone out alone since the watch had begun. The first had been nothing more than a one hour stroll. This time, after Borster was out of sight of his security detail, he flagged a taxi.

Willoughby was continuously on the phone, coordinating ground surveillance. Within seconds of Borster entering his cab, a second taxi was hailed. The rider jumped in and said, "Follow that cab up ahead. Stay back, but don't lose him."

After a ten minute ride, the lead taxi stopped at a motel off New York Avenue, one of the low budget ones having doors opening directly outside. Borster exited the cab and looked around nervously. The trailing cab drove a block past the motel, turned the corner where it was blocked from view, and stopped. Its occupant tossed money to the driver, told him to wait, scrambled out, and scurried back to a vantage point where he could see Borster knock on one of the motel room doors. Then he pulled out a digital pocket camera with a high-powered telephoto lens and snapped pictures in rapid succession. A young woman opened the door and Vice President James Borster disappeared behind it.

The photographer found a spot where he was concealed, yet had a clear view of the door to the room. Half an hour later, another taxi pulled up. Borster exited the door abruptly and entered the cab. He was obviously angry. Really angry.

The photographer made a phone call, but remained at his post. Fifteen minutes later, another cab pulled up to the motel room. The woman hurried out and ducked into it. The man shot as many zoomed photographs as he could. The taxi pulled out and the photographer ran to his waiting cab. "Catch up to that cab and follow it."

The destination was a multistory apartment building off Connecticut Avenue. The trailing cab slowed as the woman exited her taxi, and then it drove two more blocks and stopped. The rider got out and ran back toward the building. He noted the address and photographed both the building and the location of the light that came on a minute after the woman entered the front door.

*   *   *

At 9:27, Gayle Scapeli's secure cell phone rang. No caller ID or phone number registered on the display. "Yes?"

At first he heard only a television in the background. Then he made out a whispered conversation. He froze, hearing his own voice, hushed but distinct.

"Calm down, Rand. Marten and DeCamp are not going to threaten your reelection. Herrington and Wheeler destroyed each other, exactly the way it was planned from the beginning. The Democratic ticket is going to be Catcher/Bartolo, like I told you it would be. And that ticket has no chance of posing any threat. What they *will* do is attack Marten and end his bid. Catcher and some special interest groups are going to rip Marten and DeCamp to shreds. Their ads are already making Marten look like a fool."

"We ... *I* ... should take the lead in exposing how disastrous Marten's plans would be."

"No. Officially, this Administration won't acknowledge that a Marten/DeCamp ticket exists. If we notice they're running, we add an ounce of legitimacy to their bid. We won't do that. Catcher will front the attack. If there's backlash, and there will be, he gets it, not us."

"How you gonna control what Catcher does? Which special interest groups? What'll you do if Marten survives it?"

"How many years have I been doing this crap for you? Have I ever failed? Are Herrington and Wheeler out of the picture? You don't need or want to know the details but, believe me, Marten will get annihilated. Catcher will lead the assault and that'll make him even weaker and destroy Marten at the same time. Don't worry about how, Rand."

"All right, Gayle. I'll leave it to you. But I want Marten, and especially DeCamp, gone before the convention."

"You'll like the way it works out. Concentrate on your end. Keep politicking. The economy is going great. International support is strong. You're more popular than any incumbent president. For the next four months, steer this machine where it needs to go. Win it bigger than ever. Start your second term riding the biggest victory margin the United States has ever seen. You go into your second term like that, and you'll be set to establish your legacy as one of the greatest presidents in this country's history. I'll sweep the dirt away. You drive the legacy."

"What about Borster? Have you planned anything for him yet? He pisses me off more every day."

"By the middle of August, the Vice President is going to decimate his own reputation. The Party and the public will demand that you kick him off the ticket."

The phone went dead. "Godammit!" Scapeli seethed. *Janice Taylor! Pritchard and his out of control cock will be the death of us yet.*

Chapter 16

Monday, July 11, Carthage, 7:51 a.m.

The twelve member team of the Marten Secret Service protection detail arrived for introductions and assignment planning. The same process was occurring at the DeCamp household. The Marten detail, ten men and two women, ranged in age from thirty-one to fifty-four. Three persons would be on duty for each family at all times. One agent would always be guarding the residence, leaving two to accompany any family members who left the premises. Daryl would always have two agents with him wherever he went. Anytime four or more might be needed at the same time, team members would work overtime or the two protection teams would borrow agents from one another.

Samuel Eastman, the senior member, was the team leader for both details and he assumed day shift duties at the Marten residence. He was professional, yet considerate and friendly, with a sharp eye that seemed to take in all things at once. He instilled confidence, a sense of trust, and a feeling of safety. He asked to be called Sam, but Kyle insisted on calling him Sammy, which he endured.

Daryl couldn't gain the same feeling of confidence with Brackman Littleton, his day shift guard. He exhibited the same professional manner and, if anything, even more pronounced efficiency at observing surroundings. But there was no friendliness. He was distant. While Sam's eyes seemed to take in everything naturally, Littleton's darted, and Daryl couldn't get comfortable with them. Several times Daryl caught those eyes trained on him, almost as if Littleton was trying to commit his mannerisms to memory. They addressed each other as Mr. Marten and Agent Littleton.

The remainder of the group was generally friendly, especially the day and evening shift agents. They didn't generate an aura of a crack team of sharpshooters always at the ready. They seemed relaxed. They conversed and joked with the family, especially the kids. However, Daryl saw how instantaneously that aura changed anytime a command came to check, or be on the lookout, for something. The night shift agents were more obscure, on duty from 11:00 p.m. to 7:00 a.m. They were efficient enough, but less friendly, less familiar. One of them in particular, Clay Whetstone, the youngest member of the detail, seemed skittish.

That evening, after the family had spent time with all the agents and protection plans had been laid out for the remainder of the month, Daryl posted an update.

Update, Monday, July 11

The ticket of Marten and DeCamp has been determined by the Secretary of the Treasury, in conjunction with the Speaker of the House of Representatives, the Minority Leader of the House, and the majority and minority leaders of the Senate, to be Major Presidential and Vice Presidential candidates. This is the procedure prescribed by law to determine which candidates receive Secret Service protection.

To date, Cleve and I have received no public or private financial contributions and no services from the Federal Government at cost to taxpayers. As much as we would like to continue in that vein, we recognize that it would not be prudent to decline Secret Service protection. We began receiving threats to our lives and our wives' and children's lives six months ago. In the past month, unsuccessful kidnapping attempts have been perpetrated against both our families. In order for us to follow through with our commitment to give the American people an opportunity to vote for us in November, we have no choice, other than to accept the offer of Secret Service protection from the Federal

Government. Otherwise, we cannot be sure we would be alive to receive votes in November.

On Wednesday morning, the Secret Service van departed the Marten residence at 5:30, heading for Lansing. Agent's Littleton and Whetstone were assigned to this trip and conversation wasn't easy.

Daryl sat in front with Littleton, who drove. At first, he tried to make conversation with the agent.

"Sorry I had to get everyone started so early," Daryl said after they pulled out of the driveway.

"We're used to it," Littleton replied.

"Did you guys get some breakfast?"

"Yes."

"Have you been detailed to protect candidates before, Agent Littleton?"

"We aren't permitted to discuss previous assignments."

"Are you married? Do you have kids?"

"No." Littleton watched the road, not making eye contact with Daryl. Whetstone never spoke.

"My middle son, Kyle, can be an ornery rascal sometimes. I hope he hasn't given you any problems."

"No."

"If he gets too cute with you, let me know and I'll tone him down."

"Yes, sir."

"Do you guys have hobbies; do anything for fun and relaxation?"

"When we're on duty we give full concentration to our assignments."

"What about off duty? Surely they let you relax and kick back a little?"

"We're on call twenty-four hours a day, Mr. Marten. We don't kick back."

"Does that kind of life ever get to you? If it were me, I'd have to find some personal time somehow."

"No."

Daryl gave up. For the remainder of the long trip, except for necessary communications like planning a restroom stop, no one spoke. He thought back to his driving trips with Kyle and Rory, and longed for them.

In Lansing, Daryl filed and then spoke to his supporters for fifteen minutes from a yard stage set up for the occasion while the agents surveyed the crowd. Whetstone stood on a front corner of the platform, his presence detracting from the typical jubilation of enthralled supporters. Littleton had selected a third floor window from which to observe the area, keeping Whetstone apprised and directed through an earpiece.

After his speech, Daryl enjoyed lunch with the two lead volunteers from Michigan and a few of their key assistants; the highlight of his day. The agents stood and watched in the background. They ate take-out on the drive home. The party arrived back at the Marten residence late that evening and Racine served Daryl dinner. He'd never been so glad to get home. Unfortunately, tomorrow he would be picked up half an hour earlier than today for the ride to the airport.

The trip to Tallahassee turned out to be less painful. Littleton was present and no different than the day before, but Whetstone had been replaced on this trip by Agent Anita Vandy. Daryl had been surprised when Sam introduced her as the best marksman on the team and one of the best in the Secret Service. She couldn't have been much older than Whetstone and was the best-looking Secret Service agent Daryl had ever seen. Anita was naturally friendly, inhibited only by Littleton's reproachful glances. The bustle of activity at the airports and the fast direct flight combined to make the day more bearable than yesterday had been. Daryl filed with over nine thousand extra signatures. The abundance of supporters, the beautiful weather, and the replacement of Whetstone with Vandy, made the ambiance in Tallahassee much more celebratory than it had been in Lansing. Despite Agent Littleton's presence, it was an enjoyable day.

The Friday evening congregation of the Martens and DeCamps was a comical affair. The DeCamp protection detail escorted them to the Marten residence. Agents were everywhere, practically falling over each other. Anita and Sam were both on overtime duty, in addition to the scheduled agents, concerned that having this entire group together might be especially tempting to anyone considering following through on a threat. Kyle badgered Anita relentlessly.

"Hey, Agent Vandybloomer, is your weapon loaded? Be careful you don't trip over Sammy and shoot yourself in the foot."

"Boy, Anita, this cherry pie is really great! Do you like cherry pie?"

Kyle was scolded for each comment by Racine as well as by Kelsey, who loved to follow Anita around the house. He kept it up anyway.

"Hey, Anita-girl. My buddy, Jack, he's really tall for his age, and really cool, you'd like him. He has this thing for secret agents. He wanted me to ask if you're busy tomorrow night."

She replied good-naturedly, "Tell him my plans for tomorrow night are to arrest Kyle Marten and escort him to the secret agent latrine and give him a swirly!"

"Ha!" Kyle retorted, "I'd like to see you try that one! I've got my own body guard here, Bobby DeCamp. He already beat the crap out of one big jerk who tried to kidnap him. He doesn't carry a gun, but no girl agent is gonna be any match for my guy, Bobby. So you better watch your step, lady."

She just grinned at Bobby and said, "I heard about that. Well, I'm definitely not going to mess with Bobby."

"Anita, don't pay any attention to Kyle," Rory said. "He's only picking on you because he's sweet on you."

"Dang it, Rory!" Kyle retorted. "I'll get you for that."

"Bring it on anytime, bro," Rory chided.

After dinner, Cleve and Daryl went to the Study to review the July proposition. They were excited. This was actually happening! Each day it became more real and yet more unbelievable. They were running for President and Vice President of the United States of America!

Saturday, July 16, one week late, Daryl posted the July proposition, Proposition #19, Sharing Planet Earth with our Grandchildren. All nations should join to drastically reduce pollution and consumption of natural resources. Slow the rapid industrialization of behemoths like China and India. Raise the average quality of life worldwide, in part, by transferring some of the wealth of richer nations' citizens to those of poorer nations. Manage worldwide population growth, not by abortion, which is inhumane, but by conception control. The United States should pursue the organization of an international coalition having authority to set goals, track progress, and enforce adopted mandates.

*   *   *

Scapeli read the proposition Sunday morning. More of the same. Forget about competing with, or defending ourselves against other world powers. Team up with them. *What the hell is wrong with the American public? Can't they read? Don't they understand three-thousand years of history? Can't they think? How the hell can Marten possibly still have a following?*

It didn't matter. Daryl Marten would not be a factor in November. That would be the second topic of discussion with Baron this afternoon. The first would be Janice Taylor and James Borster ... that now being one discussion instead of two.

Scapeli had called Gerald first thing on June 29; the morning after Taylor's recording had been thrust on him.

"Hello, Gayle."

"I've got a top priority assignment."

"What's up?"

"A week ago, I was in the White House, in Pritchard's suite, having a conversation that had to be private. Damn sensitive. Damaging. The idiot, as usual, had a wench in his bed, one wall away from us. I made him talk across the room at the table, whisper, with the TV turned up. But, it turned out his trusted lady had planted a microphone under the table and recorded the whole damn conversation. I found out last night about nine-thirty when my cell rang. I answered it and got a damn recording playing the conversation back to me."

"You want the recording back?"

"And take her out. Same as Girardo last year. She has a brain aneurism. Make sure the same assistant coroner does the autopsy. Get the autopsy done fast, next day, and get her ass underground."

"Who's the bitch?"

Rand thought about the situation, the implications of the recording beginning to sink in. *How could she?* His shoulders sagged. "Can you fix this?"

"I've fixed everything else. I'll do my part. You'd better by God do yours."

"All right." The emotion radiating from Pritchard's gut was one he had forgotten existed. He hadn't felt it since the night of the fire at the Jansen mansion in Nashville; the night that Gaylord Scapeli had entered his world and saved his career. *Panic.*

They left the garden in separate directions.

Scapeli closed out of Marten's ridiculous "share the Earth" proposition and closed his eyes. *Fifteen weeks until the election. Just keep Pritchard from screwing up for fifteen more weeks.*

Gerald Baron had not called him back about the Borster/Taylor conspiracy until three nights ago, July 14. He'd had difficulty unearthing all the pieces of the puzzle without rousing suspicion. Finally, Baron was sure he had it all and had called. Taylor, not qualified to be considered even an amateur, was attempting to run a game. Her marks were the United States President, his Chief of Staff, and the Vice President. *She has no chance.*

During their Thursday night phone conversation, Scapeli and Baron had scheduled a meeting for Sunday afternoon, today, at Patapsco Valley State Park to set the plan. *Janice and Jimmy, your ends begin today.*

"Janice Taylor, late twenties."

Silence. "The Janice Taylor who works in the White House typing staff?"

Now the silence was on Scapeli's end. "How do you know anything about a Janice Taylor in the typing staff?"

"There might be a better way, Gayle. We took her picture last night. Twice. Once at eight when Jimmy Borster went into her motel room and again at eight thirty when he came out."

"What!"

"Yeah. We were tailing Borster on one of his little jaunts. He looked mad as hell coming out of her room. We tailed her home to figure out who she was and spent the wee hours of the morning digging up everything we could find on her."

"Find out what they're up to. Let me know as soon as you've got it all."

During the first week of July, President Pritchard was on a nine nation excursion. It culminated in highly-publicized meetings in Russia and China where he impressed the world with strong arm tactics that, for once, appeared to have an impact on both foreign powers. He'd left Washington the afternoon of June 28, five hours before Scapeli listened to their recorded conversation. Pritchard returned home on Saturday, July 9, busting-proud of building a yet stronger persona, having no clue of the tornado about to strike.

He had several people to contact, but the two most important were Janice Taylor and Gayle Scapeli, in that order.

"Hello, Rand," Janice answered her phone. "I'm glad you're back."

"Can you come over tonight? Nine-thirty?"

"I could tomorrow night, Rand, but I can't tonight. I'm at the airport in a boarding line right now," she lied. "My sister's getting married in Florida tonight, and I have to be at the wedding. I'm flying back in the morning."

"Your sister? You never mentioned any sister."

"There are lots of things about me you don't know. You're always too interested in other activities to ask about my personal life."

"You got that right," he said, chuckling. "Oh, well. I guess I can wait one more night." He was already considering who else he might call for tonight.

"Oh, Rand. I almost forgot. Can you give Gayle Scapeli a message for me this afternoon?"

"Scapeli? What in the world would you and Gayle have to talk about?"

"He left a message for me that he was wondering about this. Just tell him it's for sale."

"What's for sale? What're you talking about, Janice? Gayle won't have a clue what that means."

"Tell him a friend of his wants to buy it. He'll know what it's about. I'm boarding, I have to hang up. Call me tomorrow if you want me tomorrow night." She hung up and turned her phone off, certain that was the last conversation she would ever have with President Randall Pritchard.

"Hello, Rand," Scapeli said into the phone.

"Is the fort still standing?"

"Not exactly. We have to talk."

"What's up? Oh, and I've got a strange message for you from Janice Taylor."

"Let's meet in the garden in back of the White House. This conversation has to be now and it has to be private."

"What the hell?"

"Meet me in the garden in ten minutes."

When they arrived, Scapeli led to a spot where he was positive they couldn't be heard and no one could see their faces or read their lips.

"What the hell?" Pritchard repeated.

"What message did Taylor have for me?" Scapeli demanded.

"That's it? That's the big deal? I could've told you that on the phone."

"Godammit, Rand! What'd she say?"

"She told me to tell you whatever you're wondering about is for sale. And that a friend of yours is interested in buying."

"Shit!"

"Why? What is it?"

"It's a tape, Rand. It's a recording of the conversation you and I had three weeks ago when she was in your bedroom."

"That's crazy, Gayle. We were whispering clear across the living room. The TV was turned up. She couldn't have heard us."

"She planted a microphone under the table."

"No way. Janice couldn't do that. I was with her the whole time. That isn't possible."

"Your powers of observation aren't worth shit. Especially when you've got a hard on, which must be always. She played the damn tape to me. My phone rang the night you took off on your world trek, and what I heard was you and me talking about how we were going to take Wheeler, Herrington, Marten and Borster down."

"That has to be a mistake. Someone's playing some kind of joke. This can't be serious."

"Jesus, Rand. Look at me! Do I look like I'm joking? I'm sure you invited the bitch over tonight. Is she coming? I'm sure she turned you down. That never happened before, right? What the hell do you think her little message was about?"

Pritchard went silent trying to absorb that this could really be happening. Finally, he spoke. "If she wants money, can get it."

"She's gonna sell it to the highest bidder."

"Just get her price and buy it and be done with it. destroy the damn thing."

"She still knows. And it's anybody's guess who already played it for."

"What're you gonna do?" Pritchard was beginning worry.

"I'm going to do my best to fix it, like always. isn't why we had to have this meeting. This meeting what *you're* gonna do."

"What?"

"You're going to keep your dick behind lock and after the election. Nobody, Rand. Nobody! If you think going to die if you don't get it, go visit Justine for You got it?"

Chapter 17

Sunday, July 17, Patapsco Valley State Park, 3:00 p.m.

"Whatcha got?" Scapeli asked.

"Borster planted the idea in Taylor's head to blackmail Pritchard. Talked her into getting something, anything, on Pritchard to give Borster enough clout to force Pritchard to keep him on the ticket. He's scared to death he's gonna get dropped."

"He's right about that."

"They met in May. We come up with May 14. She got you on tape on June twentieth. She spent at least ten nights with Pritchard between those dates, maybe twelve or thirteen. She probably set the mic up every night and got lucky that night."

"God. And Rand never had a clue. Sometimes, I'm amazed I got him elected."

"Nobody ever said you had to be brilliant to be President, just popular," Baron said. "Anyway, she recorded you on the twentieth, but didn't meet with Borster again till the twenty-eighth. It probably took two or three days to set up their rendezvous, but she sat on it for a few days. Probably trying to figure out options. She ended up deciding to take the greedy path."

"So, she's playing my bankroll against Borster's, and she'll retire on the French Riviera?"

"Yep."

"You think she's working anyone else?" Scapeli asked.

"No. She's a novice and she knows it. Hell, she isn't really even a novice. I'm sure she's scared, but thinks she can pull it off."

"So, what do you think?"

"The setup I really like is tricky, but it'd be a thing of beauty."

"Talk to me."

"We want Borster scandalized and Taylor dead. I think we could get both in one hit. We've got pictures of Borster coming and going from his residence alone, half-disguised. On one of those occasions, we have him going into her motel room and leaving half an hour later. I think we can help that happen another time or two before a grand finale."

"You think you can keep him going back?"

Baron grinned. "She's got something he can't resist. It aint sex, but we're the only ones who know that. You could offer her a lot of money, in increments, string her along. Borster can't, but I think we could arrange some back door financing to help him. Some of the cash geyser spewing at Catcher could be diverted to Borster's 'Blackmail Pritchard Fund.' Around the middle of August, just before the conventions, we'd spring the trap."

"Borster'd scream foul at the top of his lungs."

"There'll be enough shit on him by then that even his wife'll be convinced he's lying."

"It hits close to home, Gerald. Pritchard's been bangin' her for months. And we're *not* the only ones who know that. It could come out."

"Yeah, well, sometimes bad things happen when your pecker runs wild. And that's exactly where we are. You want her dead? The opportunist wench who works in the White House typing staff and screws the President's gonna die. I can't guarantee everybody who knows about them will keep quiet. In the end, if that comes out, it's better for Pritchard if she's doin' Borster, too. Makes her look like an evil snake. If people think she was able to seduce even Borster, at the same time she was nailing Pritchard, they'll believe she's a professional blackmailing hooker who deserved what she got. Pritchard'll look sort of like a victim."

Scapeli rolled his eyes at that thought. "All right. Lay out a plan and let's get back together."

"Will do."

"I need to talk to you about Marten, too."

"Yeah, I figured."

"Janice Taylor, late twenties."

Silence. "The Janice Taylor who works in the White House typing staff?"

Now the silence was on Scapeli's end. "How do you know anything about a Janice Taylor in the typing staff?"

"There might be a better way, Gayle. We took her picture last night. Twice. Once at eight when Jimmy Borster went into her motel room and again at eight thirty when he came out."

"What!"

"Yeah. We were tailing Borster on one of his little jaunts. He looked mad as hell coming out of her room. We tailed her home to figure out who she was and spent the wee hours of the morning digging up everything we could find on her."

"Find out what they're up to. Let me know as soon as you've got it all."

During the first week of July, President Pritchard was on a nine nation excursion. It culminated in highly-publicized meetings in Russia and China where he impressed the world with strong arm tactics that, for once, appeared to have an impact on both foreign powers. He'd left Washington the afternoon of June 28, five hours before Scapeli listened to their recorded conversation. Pritchard returned home on Saturday, July 9, busting-proud of building a yet stronger persona, having no clue of the tornado about to strike.

He had several people to contact, but the two most important were Janice Taylor and Gayle Scapeli, in that order.

"Hello, Rand," Janice answered her phone. "I'm glad you're back."

"Can you come over tonight? Nine-thirty?"

"I could tomorrow night, Rand, but I can't tonight. I'm at the airport in a boarding line right now," she lied. "My sister's getting married in Florida tonight, and I have to be at the wedding. I'm flying back in the morning."

"Your sister? You never mentioned any sister."

"There are lots of things about me you don't know. You're always too interested in other activities to ask about my personal life."

"You got that right," he said, chuckling. "Oh, well. I guess I can wait one more night." He was already considering who else he might call for tonight.

"Oh, Rand. I almost forgot. Can you give Gayle Scapeli a message for me this afternoon?"

"Scapeli? What in the world would you and Gayle have to talk about?"

"He left a message for me that he was wondering about this. Just tell him it's for sale."

"What's for sale? What're you talking about, Janice? Gayle won't have a clue what that means."

"Tell him a friend of his wants to buy it. He'll know what it's about. I'm boarding, I have to hang up. Call me tomorrow if you want me tomorrow night." She hung up and turned her phone off, certain that was the last conversation she would ever have with President Randall Pritchard.

"Hello, Rand," Scapeli said into the phone.

"Is the fort still standing?"

"Not exactly. We have to talk."

"What's up? Oh, and I've got a strange message for you from Janice Taylor."

"Let's meet in the garden in back of the White House. This conversation has to be now and it has to be private."

"What the hell?"

"Meet me in the garden in ten minutes."

When they arrived, Scapeli led to a spot where he was positive they couldn't be heard and no one could see their faces or read their lips.

"What the hell?" Pritchard repeated.

"What message did Taylor have for me?" Scapeli demanded.

"That's it? That's the big deal? I could've told you that on the phone."

"Godammit, Rand! What'd she say?"

"She told me to tell you whatever you're wondering about is for sale. And that a friend of yours is interested in buying."

"Shit!"

"Why? What is it?"

"It's a tape, Rand. It's a recording of the conversation you and I had three weeks ago when she was in your bedroom."

"That's crazy, Gayle. We were whispering clear across the living room. The TV was turned up. She couldn't have heard us."

"She planted a microphone under the table."

"No way. Janice couldn't do that. I was with her the whole time. That isn't possible."

"Your powers of observation aren't worth shit. Especially when you've got a hard on, which must be always. She played the damn tape to me. My phone rang the night you took off on your world trek, and what I heard was you and me talking about how we were going to take Wheeler, Herrington, Marten and Borster down."

"That has to be a mistake. Someone's playing some kind of joke. This can't be serious."

"Jesus, Rand. Look at me! Do I look like I'm joking? I'm sure you invited the bitch over tonight. Is she coming? No. I'm sure she turned you down. That never happened before, right? What the hell do you think her little message was all about?"

Pritchard went silent trying to absorb that this could really be happening. Finally, he spoke. "If she wants money, we can get it."

"She's gonna sell it to the highest bidder."

"Just get her price and buy it and be done with it. Then destroy the damn thing."

"She still knows. And it's anybody's guess who she's already played it for."

"What're you gonna do?" Pritchard was beginning to worry.

"I'm going to do my best to fix it, like always. But that isn't why we had to have this meeting. This meeting is about what *you're* gonna do."

"What?"

"You're going to keep your dick behind lock and key till after the election. Nobody, Rand. Nobody! If you think you're going to die if you don't get it, go visit Justine for a change. You got it?"

Rand thought about the situation, the implications of the recording beginning to sink in. *How could she?* His shoulders sagged. "Can you fix this?"

"I've fixed everything else. I'll do my part. You'd better by God do yours."

"All right." The emotion radiating from Pritchard's gut was one he had forgotten existed. He hadn't felt it since the night of the fire at the Jansen mansion in Nashville; the night that Gaylord Scapeli had entered his world and saved his career. *Panic.*

They left the garden in separate directions.

Scapeli closed out of Marten's ridiculous "share the Earth" proposition and closed his eyes. *Fifteen weeks until the election. Just keep Pritchard from screwing up for fifteen more weeks.*

Gerald Baron had not called him back about the Borster/Taylor conspiracy until three nights ago, July 14. He'd had difficulty unearthing all the pieces of the puzzle without rousing suspicion. Finally, Baron was sure he had it all and had called. Taylor, not qualified to be considered even an amateur, was attempting to run a game. Her marks were the United States President, his Chief of Staff, and the Vice President. *She has no chance.*

During their Thursday night phone conversation, Scapeli and Baron had scheduled a meeting for Sunday afternoon, today, at Patapsco Valley State Park to set the plan. *Janice and Jimmy, your ends begin today.*

Chapter 17

Sunday, July 17, Patapsco Valley State Park, 3:00 p.m.

"Whatcha got?" Scapeli asked.

"Borster planted the idea in Taylor's head to blackmail Pritchard. Talked her into getting something, anything, on Pritchard to give Borster enough clout to force Pritchard to keep him on the ticket. He's scared to death he's gonna get dropped."

"He's right about that."

"They met in May. We come up with May 14. She got you on tape on June twentieth. She spent at least ten nights with Pritchard between those dates, maybe twelve or thirteen. She probably set the mic up every night and got lucky that night."

"God. And Rand never had a clue. Sometimes, I'm amazed I got him elected."

"Nobody ever said you had to be brilliant to be President, just popular," Baron said. "Anyway, she recorded you on the twentieth, but didn't meet with Borster again till the twenty-eighth. It probably took two or three days to set up their rendezvous, but she sat on it for a few days. Probably trying to figure out options. She ended up deciding to take the greedy path."

"So, she's playing my bankroll against Borster's, and she'll retire on the French Riviera?"

"Yep."

"You think she's working anyone else?" Scapeli asked.

"No. She's a novice and she knows it. Hell, she isn't really even a novice. I'm sure she's scared, but thinks she can pull it off."

"So, what do you think?"

"The setup I really like is tricky, but it'd be a thing of beauty."

"Talk to me."

"We want Borster scandalized and Taylor dead. I think we could get both in one hit. We've got pictures of Borster coming and going from his residence alone, half-disguised. On one of those occasions, we have him going into her motel room and leaving half an hour later. I think we can help that happen another time or two before a grand finale."

"You think you can keep him going back?"

Baron grinned. "She's got something he can't resist. It aint sex, but we're the only ones who know that. You could offer her a lot of money, in increments, string her along. Borster can't, but I think we could arrange some back door financing to help him. Some of the cash geyser spewing at Catcher could be diverted to Borster's 'Blackmail Pritchard Fund.' Around the middle of August, just before the conventions, we'd spring the trap."

"Borster'd scream foul at the top of his lungs."

"There'll be enough shit on him by then that even his wife'll be convinced he's lying."

"It hits close to home, Gerald. Pritchard's been bangin' her for months. And we're *not* the only ones who know that. It could come out."

"Yeah, well, sometimes bad things happen when your pecker runs wild. And that's exactly where we are. You want her dead? The opportunist wench who works in the White House typing staff and screws the President's gonna die. I can't guarantee everybody who knows about them will keep quiet. In the end, if that comes out, it's better for Pritchard if she's doin' Borster, too. Makes her look like an evil snake. If people think she was able to seduce even Borster, at the same time she was nailing Pritchard, they'll believe she's a professional blackmailing hooker who deserved what she got. Pritchard'll look sort of like a victim."

Scapeli rolled his eyes at that thought. "All right. Lay out a plan and let's get back together."

"Will do."

"I need to talk to you about Marten, too."

"Yeah, I figured."

"The attack ads aren't working.   Catcher's getting weaker, but Marten keeps getting stronger."

"What do you want to do?"

"Hope his popularity nose-dives before Labor Day. If it doesn't, go to Plan B."

"Take him out?" That was Scapeli's standard Plan B.

"Yeah."

"Professional assassin on this one?"

"Probably."

"I'll put some options together. You got help on the inside?"

"Yeah."

"I'll need details."

"I'll get you a contact, Gerald."

"All right, I'll get to work on my end."

*   *   *

The Marten and DeCamp families spent the last two weeks of July preparing for California. Both families would fly to Sacramento on Tuesday morning, August 2nd and fly home the evening of August 4th. The volunteers were setting up a rally to begin Tuesday evening and culminate Wednesday evening after the filing. On Wednesday morning, there would be a breakfast for the candidates' families and a thousand of the volunteers.

Sam had convinced Daryl and Cleve that the most cost-effective, safe way to get the eleven family members and eighteen agents to California was to travel aboard a Secret Service jet. The kids were ecstatic. The only damper would be the presence of Agents Littleton and Whetstone.

The entourage arrived at the Cincinnati airport at 7:30 in the morning and landed in Sacramento at 9:30. The party occupied an entire floor of a wing of the Sacramento Sheraton Grand near the State Division of Elections offices. The State hadn't approved the requested gathering of supporters on State grounds, so it was held in Capital Park.

The trip was a magnificent success; a fitting crown to all the effort put into obtaining nationwide ballot access. The volunteers were ecstatic. The committee had arranged for television coverage, which captured the elation of the affair's participants. More than twelve-thousand extra signatures had been obtained. Daryl received confirmation from North Carolina and Oklahoma in time to announce they had survived Catcher's challenges in both states. Everyone had a grand time; the volunteers, Daryl and Cleve, their wives, and the kids. Even the agents, except for Littleton and Whetstone, seemed imbued with a festival air.

The two weeks following the California trip were blissful compared to the preceding eight months. All the work had come to fulfillment. Little had to be done during the middle of August. Lost family time was made up. Concerns for family safety were alleviated by the presence of the Secret Service. For the first time in a long time, facing the day was not an insurmountable task.

Daryl posted the August proposition a week earlier than usual, on Saturday, August 6, instead of a week late, as the last two had been.

Proposition #20: Removing Our President's Handcuffs

Concern over getting reelected distracts from an officeholder's attentiveness to performing the duties of their elected office. The orderly introduction and full implementation of comprehensive programs by the President of the United States requires more than four years. These facts combine to favor longer, single-term limit, presidencies.

1. Setting up an administration is a tremendous and costly effort.
   a. Half of a four year term can be consumed before a complete administrative staff is in place and operating smoothly.
   b. Two years into a first term, focus of an administration tends to shift toward reelection.
   c. An efficient, smooth-running organization, concentrating on performing its function, is hardly attainable.

2. Limiting presidents to a single term would free them from the influence of reelection considerations.
3. Combining single term limits with longer terms would allow a president to systematically implement his campaign commitments.
4. Relationships with world leaders would become more consequential if the officeholder was certain to be less transient. International program development would become more productive.

This proposition is to enable our presidents to contribute more to the betterment of the nation and the world by changing our constitution to set the term of President to eight years with a limit of one term.

*   *   *

Like many others, Jimmy Borster read Daryl Marten's propositions on Sunday mornings. He couldn't help but admire Marten. Some of his ideas were far-fetched, but some might work well. Marten had become a viable candidate with no paid staff, no financial contributions, no advertising, and no political experience. He would be no match for Pritchard, but would do better than Catcher. It was almost inconceivable, yet there he was.

If Pritchard actually replaced him on the ticket, he would consider offering assistance to Marten. But that was *not* going to happen. He had a third meeting scheduled with Janice Taylor tonight. The first two meetings had been infuriating. This one promised to be much more satisfying.

She had blindsided him at the first meeting. When she had called him and told him she had Pritchard and Scapeli recorded; speaking of the catastrophe they had orchestrated for Wheeler and Herrington, and of the one they were planning for him, he'd been sure he had exactly what he needed.

However, when he went to her motel room, she spent the first ten minutes stammering about how she wanted to get out of the country and needed a lot of money to do it. It took another five minutes to get a clear picture of what she intended to do: pit him against Scapeli in a bidding war for the recording. He couldn't believe it. The whole thing had been *his* idea. It had not been about money. It was to have been her way out of the trap she was in and his way of ensuring his place on the Republican ticket. That night, though, the scheme became entirely about money.

He had tried to explain there was no way he could compete in a bidding war with Scapeli and Pritchard and their bottomless slush fund. At first, she stayed calm, telling him he would be able to find a way, instructing him to find a way, to get the money. That went on for ten minutes, before the meeting turned into a shouting match. She refused to play the recording for him, saying she would play it as soon as he agreed to try to get the money. He'd wanted to physically beat her. In the end, he left, taking her ultimatum with him. She gave him a month to come up with a minimum bid of five million dollars. He had stomped out, livid.

He spent the next two weeks plotting ways to get the cash. He could come up with one million of his own, but that would be a last resort. It wasn't close to meeting her demand anyway. He had backers who disliked Pritchard enough that they would help keep him on the ticket. He was sure they would contribute another million and a half, but that still wasn't enough. Besides, the only way to get them to contribute would be to let them know about the recording. Then it would get used, which, if Janice's claims were true, would jeopardize Pritchard's reelection and defeat the purpose of the whole charade.

Then, on July 21st, the answer had come to him in the unexpected form of Democratic Texas Governor Troy Jorgensen. The Governor called that afternoon, saying he was in town for the night and had heard some talk that Gayle Scapeli was trying to convince Pritchard to drop Jimmy from the ticket. Jorgensen said most of the major Democratic supporters had already conceded the November election and were worried about what Scapeli might be able to get away with if Pritchard didn't have the moderating voice of Borster at least trying to keep the audacious Chief of Staff in check. Jorgensen asked Borster to meet for a private dinner that evening in his hotel room to discuss how an unofficial consortium of Democrats might be able to help.

He had accepted Jorgensen's offer to meet feeling more excited than he'd let on. It had turned out that what the Democrats had to offer was money. Lots of it, to be used in any way Borster felt necessary to ensure his spot on the ticket. Jorgensen declined to identify the sources of the cash. Borster got the impression he didn't know. Regardless, the funds could be used entirely at Borster's discretion, without going through any account having Borster's name on it. It wasn't Jorgensen's money and he was not being paid by, nor was he a member of, the organization providing the money. He was an intermediary, technically invisible, but able to commit to immediate transfers of up to three million dollars into a special account.

"Troy, this could be a fortuitous meeting. I'm not at liberty to give the details, but we have a situation where a substantial sum of money would guarantee my place on the ticket and without the money, I am almost sure to be dropped."

"How much do you need?"

"Five million is being asked, but I might be able to make it happen for less."

"How soon would you need it?"

"As soon as possible. Definitely before the convention."

"What form? Would a check made out to the right entity work?"

"I doubt it." Borster looked concerned. "It'd probably have to be cash. But, I'll try to make three million work."

"Three million in cash? I think I could get that done, but I'd sure hate to be the delivery boy."

Borster had called Janice that night. "I'll try to get the money. I have a source. But, I have to hear the recording first." Janice had set a 9:00 meeting time for the following night, Friday, at another budget motel; this one way out on Allentown, near Andrews Air Force Base. She had called him back five minutes later with a room number.

He knocked on the outside door to the motel room at 8:54. She let him in.

Gerald Baron took the pictures himself this time, hiding in the trees across the road, and listened to their conversation on his receiver.

"How much can you pay?"

"Two and a half."

"I said five."

"You said you'd play the recording if I agreed to try to get the money."

"Are you trying to get five?"

"I'm doing the best I can."

"Can you get five?"

"I think I can get three."

"Not enough. Are you trying to get five?"

He seethed. He wanted to rip her hair out. "I'll try. If the recording's worth it."

"Okay." She walked into the bathroom and came back with a pocket-sized player. She pushed a button and played the recording.

Borster was astounded. The voices were soft, but the recording was clear. Scapeli's and Pritchard's voices were easily distinguishable. Scapeli claiming to have set up the entire fiasco with Wheeler and Herrington. Promising to eliminate Marten from the race. Claiming to have a plan to get him off the ticket with some sort of set up. It was unbelievable. If he could gain possession of that recording, and get it released by a third party after the election, Pritchard would quickly become history, possibly go to prison, and James Borster would become President.

He attempted to conceal his elation. "All right, I'll work on the money."

"What's your offer now, tonight?"

"I can't get you the money tonight."

"How soon can you get it to me?"

"How do you want it?"

"Fifty thousand in one hundred dollar bills and the rest deposited in a Swiss bank account. I'll give you the account number and I'll hand you the recording when the deposit is confirmed. How soon can you get it?"

"Give me two days."

"How much?"

He waited a moment. "Three million, maybe a little more."

"Not enough," she retorted immediately.

"I can get four. That's it," he shot back.

"Not enough."

"What the hell do you want?"

"Five million's the opening bid."

"Janice, you're crazy."

"I told you I'd give you a month to come up with five million. You've got a week left."

"You've got no idea what you're playing with."

"One week."

Borster left almost as angry as when he had left the first meeting, but this time there was excitement mixed with the anger.

Baron called in a report.

*   *   *

Ten minutes after Borster left the room, Taylor telephoned Gayle Scapeli.

"Yeah."

"It's Janice Taylor. What do you have for me?"

"You don't know what you're doing, Janice. Bring me the recording."

"I have a buyer."

"Who."

"Funny. It'll cost you five million."

"Bullshit."

"I've got a buyer and I'll tell you this, you won't like who it is."

"When's your buyer giving you the money?"

"As soon as you don't bid."

"What the hell do you want, Janice?"

"Five million. You've heard the tape."

"I'll give you one."

"I'm calling my buyer."

"What's their offer?"

"Five million."

"Bullshit, Janice! What's their offer?"

"Four right now, but they're gonna get five."

"Maybe four and maybe in a few days," he surmised. "I'll give you two and a half. Tonight. And you give me the recording tonight. And if I ever see you or hear your voice again, you're dead."

Silence. "I gave him one week to get to five. I'll get back to you after I get his answer."

"Fuck you." Both phones clicked off.

She sat on the bed in the motel room for an hour, shaking. *I can't do this for another week. Borster's right, I'm crazy.*

*   *   *

Borster called her at 7:00 Friday evening, July 29. He had worked hard on Troy Jorgensen all week and got a commitment for up to six million.

"This is Janice."

"It's Borster. I've got it."

"Five million?"

"Yes."

"When?"

"I can have it to you by the end of next week. Sunday, the seventh."

Janice sucked in a breath. "I have to call my other buyer. I'll call you back."

She clicked her phone off, took two deep breaths, and dialed Scapeli.

"What?"

"It's Janice."

"So?"

"I've got the five million."

"And?"

"Do you want the recording?"

"Five and a half. Same deal. Tonight and I get the recording tonight. And you're dead if I ever hear from you again."

"I'll call you right back." She clicked her phone off and redialed Borster.

"Janice?"

"I've been offered five and a half."

"*Goddammit*, Janice! You're gonna get yourself killed. Stop with the greed!"

"How much?"

"Six. And that's all I can get."

"I'll call you back."

She hung up and called Scapeli.

"What?"

"I've got six."

"Go to hell." He clicked off.

She called Borster.

"I can't go any higher, Janice. Six is all I've got."

"It's yours."

He closed his eyes. This was it. *Just follow through. In six months I'll be President. Pritchard will be impeached. Scapeli will be in prison. Behind bars! How sweet that day will be.* "I need until next Sunday. Can we make the exchange then?"

"Let's do it Sunday night. At one of the airport hotels. I'll let you know the details."

*   *   *

At 7:30 Sunday evening, August 7, James Borster walked briskly out the back door of his residence, disguised more heavily than usual and carrying a briefcase. Four blocks away he hailed a taxi and headed for the designated hotel near Ronald Reagan Washington International Airport. He hurried through the lobby, took the elevator to the second floor, and knocked on the door of Room 238 at 7:58. The deadbolt clicked and the door opened.

Borster hurried in and surveyed the room. All the lights were on. A laptop rested on the small business desk, awaiting input. Janice, apparently in honor of the occasion, wore a sleek black dress with a shear shoulder scarf.

"How do you want to do this, Janice?"

"You brought the source bank and account information with you?

"Yes."

"The cash is in the briefcase?"

"Yes."

"Give me the briefcase and sit at the computer." He sat. "The screen's up. Type in the information it requests."

He did. She stood behind him, shifting her weight from one foot to the other and tapping her fingers together nervously, almost twitching. The receiving account information had not been displayed on any screen Borster had seen. When Borster finished typing the required information, she leaned over him and, hand trembling, pressed the enter key.

She had been assured the transaction and the account identity would be known only to her and anyone she gave the information to, but novice blackmailer, Janice Taylor, had not been careful enough. Her first step had been to research Swiss banks on the Internet. Her second step had been to call the bank she had selected. She had followed their instructions scrupulously to maintain secrecy of the account information. She had never suspected her phone had been bugged and all conversations had been monitored.

"It'll take a few minutes for the confirmation to come back." She motioned to the reading chair in the room. "Make yourself comfortable while I check the cash." She sat on the bed and opened the briefcase. It was 8:05.

At 8:02 the room air conditioning fan had kicked on and the solenoid valve of a small, concealed, high pressure carbon monoxide canister had opened, releasing its contents into the intake of the fan. Taylor and Borster, intent on their business, didn't notice or care about the functioning of the room air conditioning equipment. Temporary seals on the door and the back side of the bathroom exhaust grille kept the carbon monoxide concentration in the room from diluting. Within one minute the compressed gas canister was empty and fifty cubic feet of the odorless, toxic gas had mixed with the room air. The carbon monoxide concentration in the room reached one percent and the fan turned off.

At 8:06, sitting in the chair, watching Janice sift through bundles of one hundred dollar bills, the Vice President felt light-headed and nauseated. He saw Taylor blink her eyes slowly and shake her head, as if trying to stay awake. She seemed to be having trouble concentrating.

His head was thumping. For a moment, he suspected his emotions were triggering a physical reaction; too much adrenaline. *No, something's wrong*, Borster thought sluggishly. He watched in a stupor as Janice slumped over onto the briefcase, not fully comprehending the motion and unable to do anything about it. His chin nodded down onto his chest.

At 8:10 Gerald Baron and Curt Willoughby, gloved, dressed in maintenance uniforms, and carrying large tool boxes, unlocked the door to Janice Taylor's room. As soon as they were inside they pulled oxygen masks out of their toolboxes and donned them.

They had made sure Janice's room would have no other guests nearby by accessing and manipulating the hotel's computer system. Taylor was booked into an end room with the door not visible from the main corridor. The three rooms nearest hers were reserved by occupants who never arrived. The two rooms adjacent to those had non-working components, one the air conditioning, the other a toilet, and they would not be occupied for the night. Baron had made sure the hotel's closed circuit security surveillance camera system was not working.

"Let's get their clothes off and shoot 'em up," Baron said. "We've got ten minutes."

Baron and Willoughby stripped the limp victims, throwing their clothes on the floor. Curt injected speedball, a mixture of heroin and cocaine, directly into each of their veins, just as Borster and Taylor would have done if administering it to themselves. The overly potent dose of the injected drug would keep Borster unconscious for at least two hours. Taylor's triple dose would kill her in less than one. Gerald laid the injection paraphernalia case on the table. It still contained two hits of the drug, another hit for each of the victims to make it appear the party was to last a while. The cause of death in the Coroner's report on Taylor was already determined; cardiac arrest induced by drug overdose.

Willoughby tied Borster to the bed, lying on his back with arms and legs outstretched, to the four bed posts. He tied Borster's wrists using his necktie and her scarf, then one ankle with his pants and the other with her pantyhose. Then he fashioned a makeshift blindfold by intertwining her black underpants and bra and secured it tightly around Borster's head, making the scene look as kinky as possible. Baron and Willoughby pulled the limp body of Janice Taylor face down on top of Borster and spread her legs over his.

Baron retrieved the recording and player from Taylor's purse and placed it in his tool kit. Then he set the cash laden, briefcase on the floor and the arm strap and hypodermic needles on the table. Willoughby pulled the seals off the bathroom exhaust grille, turned on the exhaust fan, and retrieved the carbon monoxide cylinder and its outlet tubing from behind a plumbing access panel in the wall.

The laptop beeped. Janice Taylor would never see the confirmation. The money from Bradley Catcher's campaign contributors would be split and deposited within the hour, half in one of Gaylord Scapeli's personal accounts and the other half in a Davidson County Safety Services account.

Baron and Willoughby performed a final room arrangement, an obvious drug intensified sex rendezvous. They placed their masks in their toolboxes and put the laptop in its case. Carrying the case and toolboxes, the hit men exited the room, deftly pulling off the door seals, rolling them up, and slipping them into their maintenance uniform pockets on the way out. They quickly descended the adjacent stairs and left the building, certain no human eyes or cameras had detected their presence.

At 9:48, the Secret Service received an anonymous tip from a woman on an untraced phone line claiming a sighting of the Vice President entering room 238 of the hotel with a young woman. The security entourage arrived at 10:01.

Pounding. Pounding. Pounding. Pounding. *Head's splitting.* Pain. *Can't move. Splitting in two! Can't see. Throat so dry. Water. Water! Freezing. What's on me? Crushing me! Can't talk.* Pounding. Pounding. Jumbled sounds. *Where am I? Who am I? Can't breathe. Suffocating! Get off me!* Pounding. Aching. Pounding. Muffled voices. Shivering. *Freezing!* Pounding. Pounding on a door.

"Mr. Vice President! Are you in their?"

Pounding. *Why can't I see? Can't move! Get off!*

A door opening. Gasping. Voices … louder … clearer.

"Holy Mother of God!"

Chapter 18

Saturday, August 13, Washington DC, 6:30 p.m.

Gayle Scapeli watched the news clip from his office.
"This is Zachary Forrester with Presidential and Vice
Presidential Candidates Daryl Marten and Cleveland DeCamp.
Thank you for joining us this evening, gentlemen. Many folks
are anxious to know whether you'll be making public
appearances over the next two and a half months."

"Thank you for inviting us to speak," Daryl replied.
"Yes, we've scheduled one appearance per weekend during
September and October. We'll speak on Labor Day here in
Cincinnati; then Detroit, Pittsburgh, Chicago, Stanford
University, New York City, Dallas, Denver, Jacksonville, and
lastly in our home town, Carthage, Ohio."

"Do you have an agenda for the appearances?"

"First, we want our supporters to see firsthand who we
are. We'd like them to meet our families. We'll talk about each
of our propositions, two or three at each outing, then open up for
questions, and then allow a couple of hours to mingle and meet
folks one-on-one. We're excited about the gatherings."

"As am I," Zach said. "I received word last night I'll be
assigned to cover each of your trips."

"That's great, Zachary. We like having you with us."

"Are you now officially on the ballot in every state?"

"All except California. We received word from Florida
late last week that our volunteers had obtained more than enough
valid signatures to overcome Senator Catcher's challenge. We
won't know for sure about California until around Labor Day,
but we believe we'll overcome that challenge, also."

"Representative DeCamp," Zach turned to Cleve, "do you think the events of the past two months involving the front running Democratic and Republican tickets will have an impact on your independent bid?"

"I'd prefer our destiny be determined on our own merits rather than the fortunes or misfortunes of others, Zach. But, yes, it's possible the withdrawal of both Democratic front runners might result in some voters who would've voted for the Democratic candidate to do otherwise."

"Do you think the Marten/DeCamp ticket is likely to pick up those votes?"

"We'll probably get some and the Republicans will get some."

"Then you don't think the events of last Sunday will be disastrous for President Pritchard?"

"President Pritchard and the Republican Party have a strong head of steam built up," Cleve sidestepped the reference to Borster. "My guess is they don't consider either the Democrats or us a significant threat."

"Were you surprised to see the mutual destruction of Senators Wheeler and Herrington?"

"Politics can be very nasty. It isn't uncommon to witness one candidate undercut another, but I don't recall ever seeing two candidates so thoroughly and simultaneously destroy each other. I didn't anticipate that."

"What about the events regarding Vice President Borster last Sunday? Were you shocked?"

"At first I was, Zach. But the more I've thought about it, the more I'm convinced things might not be what they appear. I know the Vice President. I can't say we're close, but I've been acquainted with him for several years, and he's maintained an impeccable reputation for a lifetime. I have no way of knowing what really happened that night, but I'm not sure the Vice President actually committed any scandalous acts."

"You're saying you think he was framed? You think the whole thing could have been a set up?"

"I'm really not saying anything other than I'm not yet convinced James Borster is guilty of the accusations being leveled against him. Isn't that supposed to be the American way? Every person is presumed innocent until found guilty under due process of law?"

"If he were to eventually be found innocent, do you think his political career could survive?"

"I doubt it."

"Do you have any comments on that, Mr. Marten?"

"I don't know the Vice President, but I've learned over the years that Cleve DeCamp is the best judge of a man's character I've ever met. When it comes to knowing who to trust and who not to trust, I don't doubt Cleve's opinion."

"I have one last question. What do you think of your chances in November?"

Daryl and Cleve both smiled, and Daryl said, "The whole basis of Commonguy is optimistic idealism. We're optimistic, Zach!"

Unfortunate, Scapeli thought. They seemed like decent guys, not really stupid, just misguided. And way too naïve. One would think, especially after the political events of the past two months, that they would either be smart enough or wary enough to stand down.

DeCamp was right about Borster on both counts. He was innocent and his political career was over. The Night Sky tabloid that had hit newsstands across the country last Sunday night had been published the Friday before, with a final copy cut off time of midnight Thursday. It had blared clear front page pictures of a disguised, but recognizable Vice President James Borster being let into two separate motel rooms by Janice Taylor; the paparazzi at work. The world had proof that last Sunday night had not been their first rendezvous.

Taylor's autopsy report had been released Tuesday afternoon; dead at twenty-seven of a drug overdose. She had been buried Thursday, following a hushed funeral attended by immediate family only.

*   *   *

Borster had been taken directly from the hotel to Walter Reed National Military Medical Center. He was so distraught, he'd been kept sedated for two days. By Wednesday he had calmed down enough to be debriefed. He denied taking drugs or having sex with Taylor despite the position she died in and despite the tabloid publications and their damning photographs. He had no idea how the drugs had entered his system. He admitted going to two motel rooms previously to meet her, but, in both cases, only to attempt to retrieve a recording.

He had claimed to be delivering the fifty thousand dollar package to purchase a recording she possessed that could have been damaging to President Pritchard's reputation. Yes, he had heard the recording. No, he was not in possession of it. No, he was not at liberty to divulge the content of the recording. No, the President had never been aware of the recording. Yes, he was aware that no recording had been found in the hotel room where Taylor had died sprawled on top of him.

He recalled entering her room, handing her the briefcase, watching her look through it, and waiting for her to give him the recording. He remembered nothing more until his horrendous wakening. Yes, the money was his personal money. What bank had issued the bills? On this question he stumbled, obviously lying. He simply couldn't tell it all; couldn't implicate Jorgensen and the financial backers, whoever they were. Jorgensen had not stepped forward so far, which meant he would probably deny any involvement. It would be pointless to relay the conversation between Scapeli and Pritchard that was on the recording. No one would believe a word of it. He was trapped, humiliated, and hopelessly broken, all at the hand, he was positive, of Gaylord Scapeli. In his entire life, he had never hated so vehemently as he now hated that bloodsucker.

On Tuesday, the Democrats demanded his resignation. The Republican Party followed suit on Wednesday. He was discharged from the hospital Thursday morning while Janice Taylor was being buried. With charges pending, Borster returned to his residence under his own recognizance. Pritchard never talked to him, but sent a messenger Thursday afternoon requesting his resignation. On Friday morning, August 14, Vice President James Borster tendered it, effective immediately.

*   *   *

At the Democratic National Convention, Senator Bradley Catcher had no opposition. He was chosen unanimously to be the Democratic Presidential Candidate. He named forty-five-year-old Arizona Senator Gil Bartolo as his running mate. He and Bartolo had become allies in the Senate over the past five years. They were nearly the same age, both Catholic, and agreed on almost all issues. Bartolo complimented the ticket, being from the opposite side of the country and Hispanic.

The Democrats struggled to package a meaningful platform. They decided against calling further attention to Marten and avoided dealing with the independent candidate's propositions. Confoundingly, it was also problematic to attack the Republican Administration's strategies when all was going so well for the nation.

In the end, they settled on emphasizing traditional Party lines; better medical care for the poor and uninsured, protecting jobs from exportation, making Social Security and Medicare well, raising the quality of the educational system, better detection of terrorist activities, and reduction of the deficit through eliminating waste. They also included a couple of hooks suspiciously similar to some of the Commonguy propositions; vaguely defined tax reform, preserving the environment, and the one they hit hardest, improving the level of integrity in government.

In addressing integrity, the convention speeches were generic except for a few vague references to problems the Democratic Party had corrected; obvious references to Herrington and Wheeler. However, everyone in the country knew they were calling attention to the Republican Administration's recent, highly-publicized scandalous acts.

The Republican Convention opened in a subdued tone, not mentioning James Borster, but giving due solemnity to the disgrace ... on the first day. Enthusiasm was gradually incited and, by the next to last day, unbridled boasting over the current exceptional state of domestic and foreign affairs, and over the outstanding accomplishments of President Randall Pritchard, had flipped the atmosphere to one of zeal. Their platform was vigorously touted and amounted essentially to one short, but emphatic, line: "Give us more of the same!" On the last day, when Pritchard named his new running mate, charismatic California Governor John Lawrence, the zeal became frenzy.

*   *   *

The Marten/Decamp Labor Day rally at Riverbend Music Center in Cincinnati was inspiring. The afternoon was sunny, 76 degrees, with a light breeze. Twenty-thousand wildly enthusiastic supporters filled the pavilion to capacity. The Secret Service protection detail kept itself inconspicuous. Beginning at 1:30, Daryl spent five minutes presenting his family, relating an anecdote with the introduction of each member. Cleve then did the same. Racine explained how Commonguy came into being and what the first few months had been like, when support began to appear. She finished by announcing that Friday they had received word they had overcome the Democrats' challenge to ballot access in California, completing their effort to be placed on the ballot in every state. The crowd roared.

Daryl discussed their first proposition, the concept from which all the other's ultimately derived: why it was important to approach everything giving primary consideration to impact on the long-term thriving of mankind. Cleve talked of their tax reform proposition. Melinda, having taught third grade for twelve years, addressed the education proposition. Daryl closed the presentation with a recap of what the past few months had been like for their families.

The volunteers had set a ticket price of two dollars per person to cover the cost of renting the facility. From 2:30 until 4:00, two of the volunteers drew ticket stubs on stage, inviting the holders of the tickets drawn to come to the stage, introduce themselves, and ask any of the family members any question they wished. The families then descended to the area in front of the stage and visited with their supporters, discussing whatever topics were raised. Zach and Channel 8 were present all afternoon. At 6:30 he interviewed the families. Afterward, the families went with a group of volunteers to a reserved viewing area to enjoy a late picnic and watch the Labor Day fireworks over the Ohio River. It was an extraordinary day.

The event in Detroit the following Saturday was even bigger. The day was overcast, but the crowd was 5,000 stronger and even more enthusiastic than Cincinnati's. Both families reveled in the September activities. They traveled together on a charter bus. They spent time together preparing for the rallies.

The children spent weekdays together, being tutored, since attending public school before the election had been vetoed by Sam. The two families were congealing into a single unit. Even the Secret Service staff was becoming part of an extended family circle, except for Littleton and Whetstone, who remained and distant.

On September 11, after the Detroit rally, Daryl posted their next proposition.

Proposition #21: Political Parties, the Embodiment of Antagonism

Political parties usually come into existence to support or oppose a central issue. The first two parties, the Federalists and the Anti-Federalists, were opposed on the issue of centralization of power. The original focus of the Republican Party was opposition to the expansion of slavery. Once in existence, parties expand their platforms, often with little more rationale than to oppose whatever the other party advocates.

1. The longer a party exists, the more it becomes a power machine for getting people elected who commit to further solidifying party power. Constituents' concerns become secondary to expanding party clout.

2. Public officials would more faithfully represent their constituents if the power of political parties was held in check. That could be accomplished though election reform.

   a. Eliminate all paid political advertising.

   b. Establish a transparent election administration, a monitored organization whose sole purpose would be to ensure the dissemination of complete and unbiased information on all candidates and issues to all voters.

   c. Negate the impact of wealth and financial contributions on elections by setting low limits on campaign spending and making that amount available to all viable candidates from public election funds.

   d. Terminate the Electoral College system for presidential elections in favor of election by popular vote.

3. There would be tremendous resistance to these changes, but this is America. Ultimate power does still rest with the citizenry. The people need only be sufficiently unified and insistent to exercise that power; that is, the people must be deafeningly demanding.

This proposition is to shift from government driven by politics toward truer representative government serving a well-informed citizenry by implementing comprehensive campaign reform.

*   *   *

Scapeli read the proposition and shook his head. He had watched the news clips from Cincinnati and Detroit. He had listened to and read articles by prominent political analysts, who should have known better, as they gave credence to the viability of the Marten/DeCamp ticket and their propositions. Disdainfully, he looked at the poll results he held in his hands.

Catcher was essentially out of the race, predicted to land less than 15 percent of the vote. Pritchard was currently predicted to carry a slim majority of the vote, just over 50 percent. Marten was projected to carry almost 30 percent, robbing about equally from Catcher and Pritchard. Little more than 5 percent were reported as undecided; unheard of this far in advance of an election. Pritchard had not suffered a significant setback during his entire first term. There was no reason to expect one now, so long as the aftermath of the Borster scandal remained in check. Scapeli was nervous.

The Borster situation bothered him. It wasn't the former Vice President himself. The old man understood he would only make his own life worse by trying to convince people of a set up. The police kept poking around, refusing to put the case to bed. They did not have a scrap, but they seemed unable to accept as happenstance, that the hotel security camera control panel had been fried by a lighting storm two days before the incident.

The storm had been real enough. When the cops began to dwell on the coincidence, Scapeli had lit into Baron for how he had dealt with the security system. But the fact was Gerald had done it right. When Baron had fried the control panel, he had been on the premises on a legitimate heating unit repair call. No one had seen him during the sixty seconds it had taken to access and disable the camera system. He had shorted out the surge protector, making it appear defective, and then, during the height of the storm, hit the panel with a power spike that simulated a lighting surge.

No suspicious persons or activities had been reported by anyone the night Borster went down or the week before, while preparations had been made. No one could have figured out the control panel repair parts delivery delay had been sabotage. The police had no evidence that hinted at any outside foul play.

Scapeli knew Baron had made no misstep, but had chastised him anyway. That was the only occasion over the entire span of their association he had ever spoken harshly to Gerald. The harsh words had not become a problem. Baron had let it roll off and the rebuke was history.

The other hitch that nagged at Scapeli was the inexplicable persistence of individuals who were publicly standing by Borster in the face of all the irrefutable evidence. His wife appeared convinced beyond any doubt he was completely innocent. Democrat, Troy Jorgensen, of all people, Pritchard's old friend and the unwitting pawn used in the setup, had stated he would never believe Borster guilty of either drug use or infidelity. And DeCamp had said on national TV *he* wasn't convinced Borster was guilty.

One blunder in the next six weeks could easily cost Pritchard ten points. Marten could easily pick them up. And the persistence of doubts about Borster's culpability, their refusal to die, could become a catalyst for an unraveling. *Unbelievable. It could happen.* He reached for his cell phone.

"Hello, Gayle," Baron answered.

"Eliminate him."

"Done."

Scapeli hung up.

Chapter 19

Wednesday, September 28, Tijuana, Mexico, 3:30 a.m.

A small Cessna aircraft landed by moonlight at a little-used grass airstrip 6 miles southeast of Tijuana. It lifted off five minutes later, less its passenger. Basilio walked into the City before dawn, nothing in his pockets except twenty-five, twenty dollar bills, a pen light, and a key. Not a soul in Tijuana knew Basilio. He carried no credentials, so no one could ever identify him.

He spent the morning inconspicuously taking in his surroundings. At noon he walked into the appointed dive for lunch. He sat at a small table under a grimy window and spotted the man at the bar matching the photograph he had committed to memory. Basilio ordered and ate. At 12:30 he stood up, looked squarely into the eyes of his contact, walked out, crossed the street, and leaned against the wall of a ramshackle grocery. Five minutes later, the contact walked out of the greasy tavern and sauntered two blocks south, where he rounded a corner and climbed into the driver's seat of a dust-covered panel truck.

Basilio stayed put for ten minutes, hat pulled low over his face. Then he moseyed down the street, climbed up into the open back of the truck, and pounded his fist on the front wall of the cargo bed. The driver started the truck and rumbled onto the street. Basilio left the rear overhead door up, exposing the emptiness of the bed to the outside world. As the truck left town, bouncing along the rough road, Basilio opened the trap door in the floor, scrunched flat on his back in the coffin-like compartment, pulled the door closed six inches above him, and slid the underside latch-bolt into place.

The steel floor of his casket was overlaid with a folded, worn, stinking blanket that absorbed little of the shock as the truck pounded along. Basilio did not care. After an hour, the truck slowed and stopped. He heard the muffled sounds of border officials half-heartedly going about their jobs. They did not climb up into the open empty bed.

The truck traveled the smoother highways of the United States for forty five minutes and stopped. The driver got out and slammed the door. Ten minutes later, Basilio slid the latch-bolt over, shoved the door open, and wormed his way up into the world. After stretching to loosen his limbs, he jumped down out of the bed, feet landing on the earth of Escondido, California. He surveyed his surroundings, determined he was where he was supposed to be, and walked ten blocks to a parked, brown Chevy pickup truck. He pulled the key out of his pocket, unlocked the door, started the engine, and drove off, heading for Interstate 15 and north.

Basilio was Venezuelan, but lived in Columbia in his brother, Videl's, compound. Videl's business was reaping money. For the most part, cash influx was generated in the drug trade, but Videl didn't limit his services. He would take any job if it carried a high enough payoff. His operation was small time compared to Columbia's kingpins, but, still, he counted money in millions of U.S. dollars. Basilio, at twenty eight, was the most formidable combatant, the most audacious commando, in Videl's band of thirty desperados. He was fearless, icy in the midst of mêlée, and the deadliest shot Videl had ever seen.

Basilio had killed many men and a few women and children. He'd kept track until he had notched up sixteen. Then, on his twenty-second birthday, Videl's gang engaged in a turf shootout in a slum section of Neiva, Colombia. Basilio gave up counting that day, unable to decide how to count victims pumped full of holes by multiple rounds from different directions. He had received his most prized birthday gift during that shootout. A bullet grazed his left cheek and clipped off his ear lobe. He esteemed the scar the bullet had left and the unbalanced appearance the missing earlobe created. The battle scars intensified the level of respect deferred him.

Basilio had been in the United States four times before. Each time, when he left, the U.S. population had been reduced by one. This trip eclipsed the others. Never had Videl been offered so much money for a single operation. Videl's renegade outfit had been selected for its success rate. It had never failed to deliver, so far as anyone on the outside could ever find out. Videl had selected Basilio for this particular task for an even better reason. He had never failed to deliver, period.

Basilio drove the rusted out, but well-tuned, pickup north until 6:00 Wednesday night; when he arrived at a truck stop north of Los Angeles. He paid for a sparse meal, a shower, and a change of clothes, and spent the night there in a rented bunk. For the remainder of this sojourn in America, his uniform would be blue jeans, a black tee-shirt, and sneakers.

On Thursday morning, Basilio drove to Bakersfield and parked the rust bucket in a mall parking lot. He opened the glove box, pulled out the only loose item in the cab, another key, got out of the truck, and locked it. He walked through the mall, out the other side, and into one of the chain restaurants lined up along the highway. After a late morning breakfast, he walked out, crossed the highway into a strip mall lot, and found the green Ford Taurus where it was supposed to be, in an area full of parked cars. He unlocked it with his new key and headed north toward San Francisco.

Two hours later he stopped at a rest area and sauntered around, stretching his legs and inconspicuously dropped the key to the pickup truck in the tall grass along the fence at the back of the property. Basilio slept nine hours Thursday night at a rent-by-the-hour, no-questions- asked, dump of a motel room in San Jose. On Friday morning, he drove ten blocks from the hotel and parked the car on a run down, dead-end street. He retrieved a third key from the glove box, locked the car, and walked twelve blocks to the bus stop. He boarded the bus and rode to the station where he dropped the key to the Taurus in a restroom trash container. Then Basilio boarded another bus. Its destination sign read *Stanford University*.

Walking the campus, Basilio looked much like any Hispanic student, just more scarred than most. He ate lunch at a deli and ambled past the Frost Amphitheater, abuzz in preparation for tomorrow's speakers, then past the Stanford

Memorial Auditorium, where he would spend the night. He committed everything to memory. At 1:30 he entered the Green Library where he spent the afternoon at an isolated study carrel, appearing intent on a stack of books. At 7:00, he walked to a student dining area and lingered over dinner. An hour later, he went to the Jackson Library where he spent the next four hours. Then he left for the Auditorium.

The Auditorium was one of the older buildings on campus, built in 1937. It was empty this late at night. Basilio glanced around, ducked into the tree shadows, and sneaked to the service entrance in the rear. His key worked and the code he had memorized disarmed the alarm. So far, everything that was to have been set up had been. Not a single glitch. The dim security lights in the corridor were perfect, creating enough light to see, yet not betray his presence through any windows. The door to the attic stair was unlocked. He entered and used his pen light to see the rest of the way.

When he reached the top of the stair, Basilio could see the window at the opposite end of the attic, a double hung wood window, already open with the bottom sash solidly braced up. He walked gingerly to it, testing each floor board, noting those that creaked. Ten feet to the right of the window, he saw a wooden box four feet long and ten inches square, lying on the floor against the wall. He opened it and extracted the components of the CheyTac Intervention M200 sniper rifle. Basilio assembled the precision weapon by the light of the moon shining through the window, assisted by his pen light.

Basilio examined the rifle and worked with it for fifteen minutes, memorizing its feel. A more accurate long range rifle didn't exist. His target would be less than one thousand yards from him. This precision instrument was deadly accurate at twice that range. He made sure it was loaded with five rounds … he would need only one … and placed it on the floor away from the window. Then he sat in a corner, leaned against the walls, rested his head on arms folded over his knees, and went to sleep.

He woke at dawn. He found a five gallon bucket and positioned it four feet back from the window where he could sit without being seen, yet have a clear view of the stage in the distance. He had a direct line of site to about a quarter of the stage at the end nearest him. The few tree limbs that might have obstructed the path of either his vision or a hurtling projectile had been cleared. The target would be standing on that part of the stage, beckoning the M200.

Basilio waited silently and watched. The event was to begin at noon. By 10:00, he had spotted his signal man. Right on cue, the man looked directly at the window for ten seconds. The man couldn't see Basilio, but had confirmed the security system at the Auditorium had been disabled at the appointed time last night. He knew Basilio was there, waiting for his signal. At 11:56, the two families walked onto the stage. Basilio cradled the M200, staying back from the window.

Three minutes later Basilio lay dead on the attic floor, his face unrecognizable, and Rory Marten was convulsing and bleeding out on the stage, as his mother screamed for a doctor

An ambulance was standing by, a standard Secret Service Precaution. The medics were already on the move. Within ten minutes of the bullet ripping Rory's leg apart, he was gurneyed into the Stanford Hospital emergency room. Daryl, carrying Kelsey, and Racine rushed in behind the medics. Five minutes later, Jeremy, Kyle, and the DeCamps, arrived along with six of the Secret Service detail under Anita's direction. Sam stayed on the scene to direct the remainder of the protection staff and police in securing the area.

Daryl spotted the boys with Anita and the DeCamps and left Rory, Racine, and the doctors momentarily, taking Kelsey to Melinda. He pulled Jeremy and Kyle tight to him and said, "The doctors have the bleeding under control." His eyes bored into Anita's. "Where are Littleton and Whetstone?"

"Not with me. Probably with Sam."

"Keep them away from us."

She looked at him questioningly, "Do the doctors know anything yet?"

"They've stemmed the blood flow and given him a transfusion. He's unconscious and they've got the convulsions stopped. They're taking him to surgery now to find out how bad it is and fix what they can."

"What happened, Dad?" Jeremy asked, trying to talk over the lump in his throat as Kyle stood by, wide-eyed.

"I don't know. Sam will figure it out. I've gotta get back to Rory and your mom." He ordered Anita, "Keep them safe."

"I will. Go to Rory."

By 6:00, Rory was out of surgery and recovery and was situated in intensive care. He had lost a lot of blood. The bullet had shattered bone and done extensive muscle damage. In time, after more surgeries and a lot of therapy, it would heal. He would remain in intensive care overnight and might be ready to move to the floor tomorrow. The hospital would provide a secure area for Rory and the families, a space that could be safeguarded by the Secret Service.

While Rory was in surgery, the Hospital Administrator, Benjamin D'Angelo, along with the Chief of Staff, Dr. Timothy Quast, entered the surgery waiting room. They introduced themselves and promised to provide any service the group might need. They gave Daryl twenty-four-hour contact information and asked for a meeting that evening after Rory was out of recovery.

When Rory was out of surgery, after friends and relatives had been called and updated, Sam asked for a conference with the four adults. He'd already briefed the protection detail. The kids wanted to hear the discussion. Daryl asked Sam if he objected. He didn't.

Sam briefed the group in a conference room offered by Administrator D'Angelo. "The assassin shot from an attic window of the Memorial Auditorium."

Daryl interrupted abruptly, "The building behind us, across the street?"

"Yes," Sam gave Daryl a questioning glance and continued. "It appears he shot just when you saw Rory's seizure and bent down to catch him. Rory's seizure and that motion saved your life and cost Rory a bullet to the leg. Anita spied him right before he shot, but by the time she could aim and fire, he got a shot off. I'm sure he'd have finished the job with a second shot if she hadn't taken him out. We don't know who he was. He was Hispanic, possibly from Latin or South America. He had no identification on him. The only things in his pockets were three-hundred-seventy-six dollars, a key to the service entrance of the Auditorium, and a pen light.

"We think he entered the building overnight and the weapon he used was planted in the attic beforehand. This hit was planned in advance ... well planned. We don't know how he intended to get away. The man was bold and cool. It's possible he was going to walk out of the building and board a bus. He was an ice cold professional.

"What concerns us most right now is this guy didn't do this on his own. Whoever hired him is still out there and still has the same motive, probably intensified. And, the dead man isn't a lone wolf; possibly a member of an organized band of assassins. He should *never* have been able to pull this off. But he did. Daryl, our advice is to cancel the remainder of your public appearances."

"Done," Racine pronounced, almost before the words left his lips.

"I agree," Daryl said.

"So do we," Cleve added.

The children did not miss or utter a word.

"That doesn't mean our candidacy is over," Daryl said, "but we won't put our families in any more danger."

"Good," Sam said. "I'll meet with the team overnight and we'll develop a plan by morning. In the meantime, the hospital is clearing out an area for you all for living quarters for at least the next couple of days. Anita will pick up your things from your hotel rooms and bring them this evening."

They filed out of the conference room somberly, Sam bringing up the rear, Daryl in front of him. As Daryl reached the door, he stopped and turned to face Sam. He spoke softly so none of the others would hear. "Sam, did you hand-pick every member of this protection team?"

"I had input on each member. Why?"

"What about Littleton and Whetstone? Did you pick them? How well do you know them?"

"I didn't know them before this assignment. I knew everyone else on the detail, except Anita. Those three were assigned from the Director's office. They were available and highly recommended. I checked their records, and there was no reason to hesitate. Why?"

"Anita's a godsend. I owe her my life. But, I'm not comfortable with Littleton and Whetstone. They don't fit. The other agents are almost family friends, but not them. They don't have much of a rapport with the rest of the detail either."

"The others all knew each other before this assignment. They probably feel like outsiders. I'm sure they're not as comfortable as everyone else. What are you suggesting, exactly?"

"I've spent more time with Littleton than any of the others. And I've been around Whetstone a lot. They're not friendly. Hardly even cordial."

"They're not supposed to be. They're supposed to be professional and, from my perspective, they have been. Truthfully, the rest of us have come closer to crossing the line than they have. Your family and the DeCamps are likeable people. We're supposed to be your protection, not your friends. We've been more like friends than we should've. It's possible that hampered our judgment. Maybe we missed things we shouldn't have by being too relaxed, not concentrating intensely enough on our job."

"Sam, just before the gunshot, I saw Littleton. I think his demeanor caught my attention. He did something, looked up. Up and back to his left, toward that Auditorium window. He looked at it and held his look for a second, then turned away. I followed his look to that window and thought I saw something right before Rory's seizure. Sam, I'm not sure Littleton didn't signal the guy."

Sam looked hard at Daryl for a minute. "Daryl, that's not possible. I understand you don't feel as comfortable around Littleton and Whetstone as the rest of us. I told you I saw Littleton's record and found no reason to object. That was an understatement. I scrutinized his record with a fine-toothed-comb. Whetstone's and Anita's, too. Specifically *because* I had no personal experience with them. And because of the importance of this assignment. It's not possible anyone could've served in the Secret Service as many years as Littleton, established a record as untarnished as his, and then committed what you're suggesting. Whetstone wasn't quite as impressive, but only because he hasn't been around as long. It isn't possible, Daryl. Wipe the notion out of your head."

The rest of the group had walked on before realizing Daryl and Sam had stopped at the door. They were now all looking back at the two of them. Daryl stood firm at the door, looking Sam squarely in the eye. "I don't trust them, Sam."

"You're going to have to rely on my judgment, Daryl. I'm responsible for the protection of you and your family and I *will* ensure your safety. Danger will *not* come from within."

"You didn't keep us safe today." Daryl turned to rejoin the group.

*   *   *

Gayle Scapeli had to create the appearance that this day was like any other. He was in his West Wing office, resisting the urge to turn on his television. The news would come to him. *Patience.*

An urgent rap on the door.

"Yeah."

The door burst open and Greg Jolsen entered breathlessly. "Flip on your TV! There's just been an attempt on Marten's life! One of his kids got shot."

The shock on Scapeli's face was genuine. Not the anticipated … the required … report. He grabbed his remote and turned on the television, already set to CNN, which was in the midst of the breaking news story.

"As Presidential Candidate Daryl Marten was about to speak at a rally at Stanford University, an assassin shot at him. At the same time, his youngest son, Rory, standing at his side, was struck by a seizure. As Marten reacted to help his son, the bullet pierced his son's leg. The Secret Service killed the assassin before he could get off a second shot. The eleven-year-old boy has been rushed to Stanford University Hospital. We have no reports yet on his condition. No one else in the Marten or DeCamp families has been reported to be injured, but the scene remains chaotic. We'll take you to the scene when we return."

"This could give Marten the boost he needs to become a factor in November," Jolsen voiced the political reality of the situation. There were no sentimentalists on the staff of the Pritchard Administration. "I've got to go. We'll have to come up with some kind of statement. Do you want to see it before we go public?"

"Yes."

Gerald Baron was watching the news, waiting for the story. When it broke, he couldn't believe his eyes. *Failure! There'll be hell to pay for this!* When the deal had been made, it had seemed ironic; five million for the assassination, the same amount requested by Taylor on her trek to her grave. Two million had been paid in advance with three to follow this afternoon, after confirmation of the assassination. Baron had no clue what organization or person was performing the service. He knew only his intermediary, and he knew him only by a variety of aliases. Though he didn't know the man's true identity, he had worked through him on previous occasions; all extremely sensitive and nearly impossible ... and all executed to perfection.

He knew Scapeli would be calling soon; knew what was coming, and began to evaluate options. He braced himself.

The call came at 3:57. "You failed."

There was nothing to be gained by pointing out that no one could have predicted the seizure or the instantaneousness of the return fire from the Secret Service.

"Yes."

"*You shot the kid!* Now it's *way* worse than before. And you cost me two million doin' it."

"What do you want me to do?" As if he didn't already know.

"Finish the job."

"Yes."

"You've got two weeks."

"Yes."

Scapeli hung up on him. *Shit. On my own.* Scapeli would have nothing to do with further planning. There was three million left to complete the job. He would get that, when the job was done, but could not ask for more. His intermediary would not be heard from again. Baron sent a message through the standard path, beginning with a cell phone call, but knew there would be no reply. The two million was gone, as was his most reliable means of carrying out impossible missions. *On my fucking own.*

* * *

By 8:00 the Marten/DeCamp entourage had settled into its quarters and Ben D'Angelo and Dr. Quast stopped by. The Administrator asked what they would all like to eat and telephoned the order to his staff. D'Angelo and Quast sat and talked with the temporary tenants until the food arrived. They briefed the group on what to expect of Rory's recovery process. He would need to remain hospitalized for at least a week before he would be ready to begin a series of reconstructive surgeries. They explained the services the hospital could offer the group during their stay. They asked Daryl and Cleve to keep the staff posted on the times various members of the group might depart and on the times friends and family might arrive.

Daryl liked both men. They felt genuine. Both offered telephone access around-the-clock and made sure everyone knew how to find their offices. Daryl took them up on their offers. He had several private conversations with D'Angelo on Sunday afternoon and Monday.

Daryl asked Zach to come to the hospital for a brief press release Sunday afternoon. The interview was broadcast live from the hospital conference room, interrupting regularly scheduled programming.

"This is Zachary Forrester, Cincinnati Channel Eight News, reporting from Stanford University Hospital in California, with Presidential and Vice Presidential candidates Daryl Marten and Cleveland DeCamp. As the world is aware, an attempt was made on Candidate Marten's life yesterday. The attempt failed, but eleven-year-old Rory Marten, standing at his father's side, was shot in his left thigh. Yesterday afternoon, Rory underwent surgery here and is recovering."

"Mr. Marten has asked to address the American people in the aftermath of these events. Mr. Marten."

"Thank you, Zachary. As I'm sure everyone can imagine the past thirty hours have been traumatic for us. We're encouraged and relieved by doctors' reports that Rory will heal. Over the past year, Cleve and I have received many threats. This incident confirms the danger is real. At the urging of the Secret Service, we've decided the risk associated with further public appearances prior to the election is too high. While our candidacy will remain alive, we regret that we must cancel our remaining scheduled public appearances before Election Day.

"Although we won't be visible, we'll issue two more propositions on Commonguy before the election and we'll continue to post updates. Cleve and I remain at the service of the people of this nation and again wish to express our appreciation to all who've given us such extraordinary support."

"Thank you, Mr. Marten," Zach took over. "We continue to wish you and your families the very best and we intend to remain available to you as Election Day draws nearer. I'm personally overjoyed to hear Rory will recover. I know firsthand what a treasure that young man is."

Daryl, Cleve, and Zach talked in private after the interview. "We haven't decided for sure what we'll do or where we're going from here," Daryl told them. "We might not go home. We'll decide tomorrow. I need you both to know I have some concerns about our security detail. I might be paranoid, but I'm not convinced there wasn't inside knowledge of the assassination attempt. Maybe even inside help. I need to tell you both it's possible the Marten half of this team might decline further Secret Service protection."

They both looked disbelievingly at Daryl. "After what happened, you'd go without protection?" Zach asked.

"At the very least, they didn't protect us," Daryl replied. "I haven't mentioned this to anyone except the two of you, and I won't force a move like that on Racine. We'll decide on a plan tomorrow and I'll let you both know what we're doing no later than Tuesday. Cleve, you and Mel should decide between the two of you what's best for your family. We're a solid team, but until the election, we should probably avoid being in the same place at the same time. And Zach, I'm asking you and Channel Eight to hang with us through the next five weeks. I consider you a close personal friend and, if you're willing, you'll play a part in whatever we do."

"I'll stick with you all the way," Zach said. "I'll do anything I can to help. I can't speak for the station, but my guess is they'll jump to be at your service."

"I agree we should split up," Cleve said. "We'll try to arrange for separate accommodations tonight, and probably leave town for somewhere Tuesday."

"Don't worry if you don't hear from me Monday, guys. I'll be in touch with both of you before nine Tuesday morning."

On Sunday evening the DeCamp family left the hospital for a suite at a hotel near the airport, taking their portion of the security detail with them. Sam, Anita, Littleton, and Whetstone were among the group remaining with the Marten's. Littleton was even more focused on Daryl. Whetstone was even jumpier than before. Sam and Anita watched them all incessantly.

By noon Monday, the Marten plan had been set and was known by all family members, except Rory. Daryl asked Sam for a private meeting at 12:30 in the conference room.

"What's on your mind, Daryl?"

"Sam, my family has decided to decline further Secret Service protection."

"What! You can't be serious. Not after what's happened."

"I can't convince myself somebody on the detail wasn't involved in setting it up."

"If you're that concerned over Littleton and Whetstone, I'll relieve them of duty."

"I appreciate that, Sam, but if I'm right, if one or both of them were involved, then it goes higher than them. One of your superiors made sure they were placed on this detail. If that's the case, my family's safer carrying out our own plan, severing all ties with the Secret Service."

"You can't really believe the government itself is attempting to assassinate you."

"I'm not saying it is. I'm not even saying I believe anyone associated with the government was involved. All I'm saying is I think it's possible. I can't rule it out."

"Daryl, you wouldn't last a week!"

"I'm not convinced I'll last any longer with Secret Service protection than without it."

"You can't."

"The Government is required to *offer* me Secret Service protection. I don't have to *accept* the offer."

"That's right, you don't. But Daryl ...."

"Our decision's made. Actually, and don't take this personally, I need to ask you and your detail to clear out of here by three o'clock this afternoon. We need you to be far away from the hospital, not watching us. I need your people out of Stanford."

"No, you don't want that."

"Sam, I know you have our best interest at heart, but I demand it. Leave us."

"You're giving me no choice? What about Cleve's family, their protection?"

"I don't know. They're making their own decision. You'll have to ask Cleve and Mel what they want. Will you be gone by 3:00?"

"I *have* to talk you out of this, Daryl."

"Don't waste your breath. It's done, Sam. Leave us. Don't make me deal with it publicly."

"All right," Sam replied, shaking his head. "We'll go."

Chapter 20

Tuesday, October 4, Stanford University Hospital, 3:43 a.m.

Hidden in an inky, shadowed patch of darkness, Racine wrapped her arms around Daryl, clung to him, her cheek against his chest. His left arm was draped over her petite frame, his hand on the small of her back, pressing her against him. He held Kelsey in his right arm as she tilted her head to touch his forehead, one of her arms around his neck and the other her mother's. He felt his wife's soft cheek moistening his shirt, and he ached.

He couldn't see the taxi three blocks away, but knew it was there, lying in wait to abscond with the two roses of his life. Kelsey, never at a loss for words, didn't utter a sound. Daryl knew exactly what Racine was thinking, feeling. She hadn't asked for any of this, had only gone along with it for him, and she was scared. He also knew her trepidation would find no voice. He almost wished she would try to talk him out of continuing this madness. Maybe she could convince him to quit. She would not try.

"You have to go, sweetheart," he whispered in her ear. She nodded her head against his chest, released the embrace, and wiped her tears.

Racine held her arms out to Kelsey and spoke hoarsely. "Come on, baby." Kelsey lifted her arm from her father's neck and reached out to her mother for the transfer. "You find a way to let me know you're okay," Racine said quietly, voice stronger, eyes demanding.

"I'll keep in touch," Daryl replied, his speech becoming more difficult. "I'll be all right. Everything will work out." He hoped he sounded surer than he felt.

For one last moment, he held her gaze. He inhaled her sweet scent and fixed his eyes on her tense, Hispanic face, storing her in the recesses of his mind. The wide dark brown eyes and thin tawny face were Racine's. The long, stringy blonde hair and the worn, oversized, gray hooded sweatshirt engulfing her were not. She wrapped a dull burgundy scarf over Kelsey's head and face, turned, and hurried away, out of the blackness and into the dimly lit drive monitored by hospital security cameras. They didn't look like his wife and daughter. *Good.*

They would get away. The unseen taxi would take them to the train station. They would walk in the main entrance, exit a side door, and hurry two blocks to another waiting taxi. This one would take them to a rundown strip mall in a seedier part of town, to a lot that Zach had cased and made sure had no working cameras.

Zach would be watching from the shadows to protect them, to make sure they drove off in the rental car. After they were safely away, he would take their taxi to the bus terminal and catch a bus back to his hotel. The rental car wasn't in his name. Daryl didn't know whose name it was in, only that Zach was confident it couldn't be traced to him. That was good enough for Daryl.

He watched Racine carry Kelsey away, round the street corner, and disappear from sight. His chest was caving. Step two of the escape was in motion. Step one had begun last night and was not one bit easier than this. Step three was in process inside the hospital right now, with neither he nor Racy present. It was the hardest of all.

Last night Jeremy and Kyle had made their break with the help of their grandparents.

Daryl's parents and Danielle had flown from Cincinnati to San Francisco on Sunday morning. Rory had been in the intensive care unit of the hospital when they had arrived. Monday morning, Rory's condition had been upgraded to fair, easing tensions.

By noon on Monday, Daryl and Racine had devised the plan for their family's disappearance. Four tickets were purchased for flights back to Ohio with a transfer in Denver. In Denver, Jeremy and Kyle would not make the transfer flight after the short layover. Instead, they would disguise themselves and catch a taxi to the bus terminal. They would eventually wind up at the bus station in Butte, Montana.

The plan had been communicated in a hurry, outdoors in the park across the street from the hospital, where the family could talk without fear of eavesdropping. Daryl's parents had grimly agreed to perform their roles: to obtain and pack the boys' disguises, get the plane tickets, oversee the first portion of the journey, and then, the hardest part, to continue to Ohio, leaving their grandsons to fend for themselves in Denver.

Jeremy could be counted on. Monday afternoon he had wrenched details of the Denver airport, the bus terminal, and the bus trip from the Internet and committed them to memory. Kyle had shown surprising support for his older brother. Listening to the plan, Kyle had been attentive and supportive, drawn to the adventure. He was impressed by the confidence placed in Jeremy, and in Jeremy's unhesitating commitment.

The foursome had left for the airport at 5:00 Monday afternoon amid a quandary of emotions. The grandparents were angst-ridden. Everyone they loved was involved in this mess, and the outcome was far from certain – especially for their eleven year old grandson, Rory, lying in a hospital bed – even more so for their only son, Daryl.

Once the plan had been set, Jeremy and Kyle had shown only dogged determination to perform their part. Daryl had no doubt that fear was there, not far from the surface, but neither boy had displayed any sign of it.

Daryl knew his wife, knew her insides were twisting apart. The son she always worried most about was lying in a hospital bed, sedated, unaware that his entire family was leaving him. Her other two sons were setting out on their own, feeling their way through a twelve hundred mile maze with no experience to draw upon to navigate whatever perils might lie ahead. She would have to flee with Kelsey and protect her, without her soul mate and source of strength by her side. On the outside, she was composed and unwavering.

On Wednesday the family would be reunited, except for Daryl. Racine and Kelsey, disguised, would be waiting at the Butte bus station for Jeremy and Kyle to arrive. The four would drive eighty miles to a ranch owned by a friend of Danielle's. Danielle was critical to the plan and would already be there with Rory.

One of Danielle's friends was a doctor from Chicago. They had met at a conference eight years ago and had since attended several coinciding events, sharing accommodations. Neither made any pretense of being monogamous. They liked and understood each other and had grown to depend on one another for support and getaway companionship. He owned a remote ranch an hour and a half from Butte that had an airstrip. Few people knew of their relationship, but Danielle habitually confided in Daryl. He knew of her companion and the ranch, although he didn't know the man's name. Daryl had thought that the ranch would be the perfect place, if Danielle and her friend would be willing to help. They were.

*   *   *

Rory lay sedated in his hospital bed. He half-woke after Daryl, Racine, and Kelsey left his room.

"Hey, Aunt Danny," Rory mumbled. "What're you doin' here?" Then, disheartened, "Did I have … a seizure?"

"You fell and were hurt." Danielle smiled at her nephew.

Rory touched the cast on his leg, and asked, as he had the previous times he'd awakened, "I hurt my leg?"

"Yes, but it'll heal and you'll be fine." That was all he needed to know for now. "You're in Stanford University Hospital. We're going to move you to a place where I can look after you myself for a few days."

"Cool." He looked around. "Is anybody else here? Where's Mom and Dad?"

"They already left and are going to meet up with us." It was only a partial lie. *At least your mother will be meeting us. If all goes according to plan.* "We're going to fly on Uncle Rob's plane. The nurse will give you some medicine. You won't remember much."

"Okay, Aunt Danny."

The nurse injected something into Rory's IV. He drifted away. Two orderlies entered the room, and the group rushed the bed to the elevator and down to the emergency entrance where Rory was loaded into a waiting ambulance. Danielle hopped into the rear compartment beside him.

"I don't know where I'm supposed to take you," the lone driver said. "They told me a doctor would be riding with a kid and would tell me where to go. Are you a doctor?"

"Yes. Turn left on the street, and I'll tell you where to go from there. Turn off your radio. There's no need for speed, and leave the lights and whistles off."

This patient is nowhere near ready to leave the hospital. None of Rory's doctors had been willing to authorize his release. She'd had to sign him out, as his pediatrician. The action she was taking violated all her training and instincts.

Danielle had called her brother-in-law, Rob Defoe, early Monday afternoon to ask him to fly to California with a stash of medical supplies. Defoe waited in the one-room shack that served as a flight house at the private grass air strip near Sonoma, forty-five miles northeast of San Francisco. He watched the ambulance pull into the gravel drive. In the brightly lighted interior of the ambulance, Rob could see the surprise on the driver's face when Danielle unfastened Rory from the gurney and the medical support equipment, tilted and lifted him out of the ambulance, and landed him in the wheel chair they'd brought with the special leg support. As the driver got out to help, Danielle turned and said something to him. The man shrugged his shoulders, got back into the ambulance, and drove off. As soon as the ambulance turned out of the drive, Rob ran out to help.

Rob and Danielle whisked Rory to the six-seat dual engine aircraft, hefted him into it, and collapsed and loaded the wheelchair. Rob scrunched into the pilot's seat while Danielle secured Rory into one of the rear seats, with his injured leg propped as comfortably as she could make it across the adjacent seat. She hoped the heavy dose of Demerol she'd injected through the IV during the drive would last for the flight. If her nephew woke before they got him out and situated in a bed, this would be a painful experience for all. Danielle fastened herself in one of the middle seats, facing back toward Rory. The low eastern horizon was a pale mixture of pink, orange, and sky blue, lit by a sun that hadn't yet shown itself.

Rob started the engines and turned to Danielle. "Okay, Danny, you're going to have to give me some idea where I'm going so I can point this thing in the right direction."

*   *   *

At 4:20 Daryl stood in the doorway of Rory's empty hospital room. His family was gone. Kyle and Jeremy were somewhere on a bus headed for Montana. Racine and Kelsey were in a taxi, driving away from him. Rory, injured and not nearly ready to be discharged from the hospital, was with Danny, heading toward an airplane that would fly them away.

He'd had to make that decision on his own. The Hospital and Rory's doctors had refused to sign his release. His parent's had initially argued vehemently against taking Rory out. Racine was incapacitated by the decision and couldn't make herself support either option: keeping him in the hospital or checking him out. Danielle had told Daryl she had the authority, as Rory's pediatrician, to sign over responsibility for the child to herself, but from a medical perspective it was clearly the wrong move and the action would be judged as medically incompetent if she was ever called to task for it.

The point he'd argued with them all was not a medical one. If the family stayed at any known location, even at this hospital, and if the Secret Service had insiders taking action to kill him, no one in the family was safe. If he went into hiding and the rest of the family didn't, the family was in even greater danger of being used as pawns to flush him out. If only one family member was left at a known location – Rory in a hospital – then *he'd* be the one who'd become the pawn.

In the end, although none of them had held fast to a stand against him, not a single one had supported turning Rory over to Danielle's care away from a hospital. The decision had been his alone, just like the decision to discharge the Secret Service detail. Daryl hated everything about this plan. *No options.* He had to fight to suppress fear. And guilt. *Keep going.* It was time for step four. *I have to talk to Cleve.*

Chapter 21

Tuesday, October 4, San Francisco, 4:55 a.m.

Daryl exited the taxi at a small, all-night diner a half mile from San Francisco International Airport. Cleve had ordered Sam to let him leave the hotel unaccompanied and was waiting in a dark, rear corner booth. Daryl skirted past the three people at the bar, sat across from Cleve, and whispered the Marten plan to him.

"Do you and Mel have a plan?"

"Yeah. You know there's a branch of DeCamps in Ottawa, right? My Grandpa's brother's clan."

"Yeah, you have a second or third cousin in Parliament, I think."

"Right. The family there's politically active in Ontario about like we are in Ohio. We keep in touch and compare notes occasionally, especially my cousin George. He's a Member of Provincial Parliament in the Legislative Assembly in Toronto. We had several conversations yesterday. I told him what's going on here. He arranged protection for us from the Royal Canadian Mounted Police. They have a Protective Policing group that safeguards politicians and dignitaries."

"How will you get to them?"

"They're coming for us. Today at one-thirty. As soon as I get back to the hotel, I'm doing the same thing you did. I'm declining Secret Service Protection. I'm gonna tell Sam to keep his entire group sequestered at the hotel under his eye till six tonight. By then we'll be on the ground in Ontario."

"Where in Ontario?"

"We don't know. I asked George to let Protective Policing pick our location, wherever they can protect us best till after the election. Here," Cleve slipped Daryl a scrap of paper. "If you call this number or email this address, you'll reach Protective Policing. Use this password and they'll put you in touch with me."

"All right. Sounds like you're covered. I called Sheriff Stone yesterday and he's calling in whatever help he needs to protect our relatives in Carthage. Jeremy will keep Commonguy up and running from his location and I'll post on it when I can. I've got a half dozen cell phones with two hours prepaid time. Nobody can call me, but I can call out. I'll be stingy with calls, but I'll let Racine and you and Zach know I'm alive."

*   *   *

Gerald Baron had not slept Saturday night. He spent the night considering options, and plotting. None of Davidson County Safety Services' nine agents knew anything about his part in the attempt on Marten. The seven men and two women had been involved in clandestine operations of all sorts. They'd each been players at one time or another in snuffing out a life that had become a problem to someone with money and power, usually to Gayle Scapeli. However, assassinating a Presidential Candidate was huge. This one had been all Gerald Baron. It needed to stay that way. He'd do this himself.

Sunday he had researched. He'd discovered everything he could about the events surrounding the shooting. He'd studied the facility layout and the current operations of the Stanford University Hospital. He'd found out what he could about the make up of the Secret Service detail. He knew there were two agents on the inside and that he might have one opportunity to get information from them. He only had contact information for one of them and he would conserve that call until the optimal time.

Everyone, both families and the Secret Service detail, was holed up at the Hospital. The boy was still in intensive care. It appeared certain he would be in the hospital for at least a week, maybe for months. The hospital had set aside a secured suite for the entourage. Baron was sure the Secret Service would keep it that way, everyone together in one easily monitored and controlled location, at least for the next several days.

It was anybody's guess where they might go from the hospital. Baron surmised, and Marten had confirmed via news conference, there would be no more public appearances. The best opportunity to take him out would be upon either departure for, or arrival at their October living quarters destination, wherever that might be.

After the day of research and the previous sleepless night, he had been exhausted. He knew he'd have to be well-rested and sharp to carry out whatever action would become necessary. On Monday he would book a flight for Tuesday to San Francisco and spend most of the day developing options. Upon arrival Tuesday, he would call Littleton to find out when the group planned to leave, how they would split up, and where they would go. He went to bed at 9:30 and slept fitfully, finally giving up and rising at 5:30 Monday morning, feeling as if he hadn't slept at all.

*   *   *

Tuesday afternoon at 5:00, Brackman Littleton's cell phone vibrated. He stepped behind Whetstone as inconspicuously as he could, unclipped the phone, glanced at the number and clicked it off. *Worst damn timing in the world.* The situation was unfathomable. Sam Eastman had the entire security detail penned in a hotel conference room. They'd been there since 9:00 this morning. Lunch had been brought in. Restroom breaks were granted only in pairs and his assigned escort had never been anyone he needed it to be.

Marten had declined protective services Monday. Now it appeared DeCamp had done the same thing and wanted to make sure no one knew where they were going. And Eastman, the idiot, was actually forcing that to happen. Littleton had been expecting a call from someone, he didn't know who, ever since the bungled shooting. He had no clue why the call had taken so long to come, but there wasn't a damn thing he could do about it now. He knew Eastman was watching him and was sure Marten had fingered him as the reason for declining protection. *This whole operation couldn't possibly be any more of a disaster.*

Sam Eastman had not discounted Daryl's concerns. Even before Marten had brought it up, he'd had an eye on Littleton and Whetstone. Although he hadn't wanted Daryl to know, he, too, had thought their attitudes had seemed off kilter. Since the conversation with Marten, he had watched them even more closely, out of the corner of one eye. He saw Littleton's attempt to conceal the phone call. *Inconceivable! Marten was right!*

The biggest problem Eastman had to deal with was that this had come from above. He didn't know who to report to; who could be trusted and who could not. He hoped the Martens and Decamps had good plans. They would need them. Sam bleakly conceded that Marten had also been right in deciding they'd be safer without Secret Service protection than with it. He would at least help them get a decent head start. He'd keep this group sequestered in this room until 9:00 tonight, three hours longer than Cleve had requested, regardless of any orders he might receive to the contrary.

Baron cursed Littleton. And Scapeli for not giving him the second contact. *No help.* He took a cab to the hospital. From a distance, he watched the windows of the block of rooms set aside for the candidates and the Secret Service staff. He watched from 6:00 until 7:00 and saw no signs of any activity in those rooms. He saw no signs of any security activity beyond normal anywhere, and began to feel uneasy.

A scruffy-looking, late teen boy walked toward the entrance and Gerald approached him. "Hey, kid, want to make fifty bucks?"

Baron walked into the hospital, sat in a chair facing the reception desk and looked at his watch as if waiting to meet someone. He picked up a paper and appeared to read, but held it low enough to peer over. The scruffy kid walked in and asked the receptionist, "Is Rory Marten still here?"

The receptionist eyed him, glanced at her coworker, then back at the kid. "Yes, he's still here, but no one is allowed to see him."

"I was just wondering," he said. "it doesn't seem like much security around here for that bunch to still be here. That sure was something, wasn't it?"

"They're all still here," the receptionist repeated fidgeting with her ear.

The kid turned and walked on to see whoever he had come to see. As soon as he turned the corner the receptionist picked up the phone and whispered urgently into it.

Son of a bitch. They're gone! Baron sat for another two minutes and then slowly rose and sauntered out of the main entrance, looking around for the benefit of the receptionist, looking for whoever had stood him up. He walked five blocks and called Littleton again and again, was sent immediately to voicemail. *Shit.* He hailed a taxi, went to his hotel room, and opened his laptop. One could find out a lot on the web. There had to be clues to their whereabouts.

Finally, at 9:12, Littleton answered Baron's umpteenth call.

"I've been try to reach you since 5:00. What the hell's goin' on?"

"I've never seen anything like it. Marten declined Secret Service protection yesterday and DeCamp did the same thing this morning. Then the damned head of this assignment, Sam Eastman, locked up the whole detail in a conference room from nine this morning till ten minutes ago. He intentionally kept us all from knowing where they're goin' or how they're traveling. I don't think *he* even knows."

"Shit, did they all leave together?"

"I'm telling you, I don't know *anything*. The DeCamps left the Hospital Sunday night and we all checked into this hotel at the airport. The last I saw of anyone was before nine this morning when we all got locked up."

"What's your detail gonna do now?"

"Hell if I know. I guess we're stayin' here in the hotel tonight. We'll probably all fly back to Washington tomorrow. Who knows?"

"Who else is on the inside? I need to talk to him."

Silence.

"Give me a name!"

"Can't."

"You guys are completely useless." Baron clicked his phone off and turned his attention back to his computer.

After another sleepless night of checking airline, train, and bus ticketing information, and browsing chat rooms of potential interest, Baron determined they had all disappeared into thin air except for the two boys, Jeremy and Kyle, who had been ticketed to fly back to Ohio yesterday. And except for Marten.

By 6:00 Wednesday morning, Baron had determined Marten was on the run. Yesterday morning, he had been driven out of San Francisco by one of his supporters, headed for Nevada to spend the night at another's home. This morning he would be transferring to yet another. The trick was going to be to get a step ahead of him ... before October 15. *Ten days.*

Marten was traveling without his family. It was impossible to tell where the wife and daughter went. Or the kid who got shot. They might all still be in San Francisco, maybe even still at the hospital. More likely closer to home, nearer the older boys. As a last resort, he would draw Marten out by threatening to do in his family. It would have to be a threat he could back up. Like it or not, he was going to have to involve Curt Willoughby in this fiasco; at least have him confirm the boys were back in Carthage. In the meantime, he had to find Marten.

In visiting thirteen chat rooms spawned by Marten supporters, he had discerned Marten had spent Tuesday night somewhere around Spring Creek, Nevada. The destination for tonight was Mount Pleasant, Utah. On Wednesday at noon, Baron boarded a flight for Salt Lake City. He rented a car and drove seventy five miles south to Nephi, where he checked into a motel. He showered, walked to a restaurant for dinner, returned to his room, researched the web for two hours, and went to bed, unable to keep his eyes open any longer.

Baron was awake and dressed by 5:00 on Thursday morning, searching the chat rooms. Finally, after 7:00, he found something.

Daryl Marten spent last night with us. He's an impressive person with great ideas. He misses his family terribly and is worried about them. He wouldn't say anything about where they are. Rita Mullins picked him up after breakfast. She's driving him to Colorado today. To Cortez, I think. He's going to stay with one of the volunteers down there tonight, Sue Twittleby, or something like that.

So satisfying. As soon as Baron was on the road, he called Willoughby.

"Hello, Gerald."

"Hi, Curt. Did you find the Marten boys?"

"No. They got on the flight in San Francisco with their grandparents, but they didn't get off in Cincinnati. Looks like they ditched the last leg and got off in Denver."

"The grandparents got off in Cincinnati without them?"

"Yep. And I'll tell you, the grandparents are being guarded by an army. So is his sister's family, the DeFoes. They seem worried about somebody getting to the relatives."

Shit. Can't use the family. Find the bastard. "All right, Curt. I need you to do something else for me."

"What's up?"

"I need you to find me a Sue Twittleby, or a name that sounds something like that, in or close to Cortez, Colorado."

"Okay. I'll check it out and get back to you by noon."

At 11:20, Willoughby called him back. "There are seven Twitterly's listed around Cortez. No Twittleby's. Looks like two of them have women at the house named Sue."

"Great." He got the addresses. *This might not be so tough after all.*

Baron drove fast and checked into a motel in Cortez at 4:00, with luck an hour or more ahead of Marten. He spent half an hour on the web digesting the city map and the areas around both residences that were homes to a Sue Twitterly. The two houses were twenty minutes apart. The first one he cased had two boys, ten or twelve years old, playing ball in the front yard. He drove by it three times memorizing the layout of the lot and surrounding area and imagining the interior of the house. No sign of Marten or any other adults. Then he headed across town to check out the other place.

Ten minutes later, the boys' mother pulled in the drive with a passenger. "Hi, Mom!" the boys ran to greet them. "Hi, Mr. Marten! Is Rory doing okay?"

"Hello, boys." Daryl smiled at them. "Rory's okay. It'll take some time, but he'll be okay."

"Do you think there'll be any shooting around here?" the smaller boy asked, wide-eyed. "We saw this guy driving past, looking at the house."

"Past here? Our house?" Sue asked uneasily.

"Yeah," the older boy replied. "He drove past three times. Slow. Looking at the house and all around, but mostly at the house."

"How long ago?" Daryl asked.

"'Bout fifteen minutes."

Daryl looked at Sue. "I'd better move on. I'm not sure it'll be safe for your family if I stay. Is there a bus station in town?"

"There's a bus that goes to the main station in Durango. I think it leaves in about ten minutes, though."

"Can we get there before it leaves?"

"Maybe, if we hurry."

"Let's go. The boys should come with us."

They all piled in the car. On the way, Daryl said, "After you drop me off, call the police and tell them about the suspicious car. Ask them to watch your house tonight."

There was no sign of anyone home at the second residence. When Barron returned to the first, as he approached, he saw a car pull in the drive. The two boys he'd seen playing before got out behind the woman who had been driving. He saw one of them tug on her arm and point at him. *Just kids. Nothing to worry about.* He drove past, looking out the corners of his eyes. To his dismay, he saw no sign of Marten. He traveled back and forth between the two residences until it was dark, trying to vary his route. En route back to the first house, he noticed headlights in his rear view mirror that seemed to be tailing him from a distance. He made a few turns and watched the car get closer.

Shit! He gunned it hard zigzagging around a half dozen blocks. When he was sure he was two turns ahead, he made a quick U-turn, parked along the curb behind a line of cars, and cut the engine and lights before the follower turned onto the street. He slid down in the seat, keeping his eyes just high enough to see out the window. *A cop. Reported! Probably those damn kids.* Marten was obviously not at either house. *I've got to get my stuff from the motel and get out of town.*

In Durango, Darryl boarded a bus for Grand Junction. He didn't like taking public transportation. He purchased sunglasses and a hat in Durango and wore the hat pulled down low. He didn't speak to anyone. Was he being followed? Was he endangering his supporters by allowing them to help him? How could he *possibly* have been found so quickly? He arrived in Grand Junction at 11:00 on Thursday night and decided to take a chance on one more bus to Denver. He purchased a ticket with cash and slept sitting on a bench in the terminal with one eye half open, waiting for the 7:00 Friday morning departure.

At 6:00, he walked outside, away from anyone within earshot. He pulled one of the cell phones out of his bag and punched in a number.

"Zach?"

"Daryl! I was getting worried. Are you all right?"

"Yeah, but I need your help."

"Anything."

"Can you meet me at the bus station in Denver today? Can you get there without anyone knowing?"

"Sure. What do I do when I get there?"

"Just check us into a room for a couple of days. Somewhere off the map. Get us in without using your name if you can."

"I've got a couple friends in Denver. I'll get one of them to get a room for us."

"Perfect. Don't tell them any more than you have to."

"I'll tell 'em I'm meeting a girl."

Baron left Cortez at 11:30 on Thursday night, headed for Durango. An hour and a half later, he was asleep in another motel room. He was up at 6:00 on Friday morning, looking for clues on the Internet. Nothing. Everyone had disappeared. What other leads could he pursue? Maybe that Channel Eight news kid would give him a clue. He used a fake name and called the station. No, he wasn't in. No, they didn't know when to expect him back. No, they were not at liberty to give out his location. So, the kid was involved. He called Willoughby.

"Yeah, Gerald?"

"Curt, I need you to locate a news reporter for a Cincinnati TV station, channel eight, Zachary Forrester."

"The eager beaver who does all the Marten interviews?"

"Yeah. Don't bother calling the station. They're tight-lipped. I need to know where he is. Find him and let me know by noon."

"Will do."

Willoughby called back two hours later. "Forrester checked out of a hotel in San Francisco this morning and booked a flight to Denver. He should be arriving there in ten minutes."

"Great. Find out where he's staying."

Baron checked out and headed for Denver. He would be there by midnight.

He had several conversations with Willoughby on the trip. Forrester had disappeared. He had not turned up anywhere in Denver. Baron checked into a motel near the airport and called Curt one last time. Still nothing. "Find out who this kid knows in Denver. Put the whole staff on it. All night if you have to, whatever it takes. Make a list of everybody he knows. Get me the addresses of any who live around Denver. And find out if any of them booked a motel room anywhere around Denver for tonight."

By 10:00 on Saturday morning, they had identified five of Forrester's acquaintances living in the Denver area. One of them had booked a room Friday.

Daryl and Zach's room was on the second floor on the front side of the motel. At noon, Zach left the room to get sandwiches. He walked to the elevator, punched the down button and glanced out the window. Something caught his eye. He looked closer. There was a man in a car parked straight out from their room, staring at their window. He turned and ran back to the room.

"Don't open the curtain. There's a guy parked in front of our room. Call me paranoid, but he looks like he's staking out the place."

"Let's get out of here," Daryl said. "They packed in two minutes, descended the back stairs, exited the back of the building, and ran across neighboring lawns to a back street. After scurrying five blocks, they hailed a taxi and headed for the Denver bus terminal.

At 1:00, the curtains to the motel room were still closed. No one had peered out. Baron walked nonchalantly into the motel and took the elevator to the second floor. He walked to Room 227 and listened at the door for five minutes. No sound from inside. He banged on the door. "Hey Zach, you in there?" Nothing. He tried again. Finally, he gave up and went to the front desk.

"Hi," he said casually to the desk clerk. "I'm Jerry Sherburn. My buddy Lloyd Rustin is supposed to be in 227, but I couldn't get an answer. Has he checked out?"

The clerk checked his computer. "No, he hasn't checked out. Do you want me to dial him up?"

"Please, if you don't mind."

"No answer, sir. Maybe he stepped out to lunch."

"All right. Thanks. I'll stop back later."

Baron walked back to his car. *Shit! Got away again.* He drove around the area for half an hour, looking for them. Nothing. *Try the bus terminal.*

Baron arrived there at 2:12, nine minutes after the bus carrying Zach and Daryl had left the station. They had rushed into the terminal and glanced at the schedule board for the next departing bus. It was headed for Fort Collins. They paid cash for two tickets, purchased a hat and a pair of sunglasses, for Zach, and boarded the bus.

They formulated a plan as they rode. In Fort Collins they took a taxi to a sporting goods store in a shopping mall where they bought a small tent, two light sleeping bags, two backpacks, and more gear and supplies than they could carry. Then they hired a taxi to take them to State Forest State Park.

Arriving at 7:45 on Saturday evening, they registered under false names, convincing the park attendant they had no identification to show. Armed with their camping permit and four days rations, they had their taxi driver deliver them to the North Michigan Reservoir south side campground. In the twilight, they hiked a half mile trail to the most remote campsite on their map. Then they trekked back to where the taxi had dropped them off, reloaded their backpacks, and lugged their

remaining supplies to the campsite. Except for them, the entire
south side camping area was vacant. They set up camp by
moonlight and flashlight. By 10:00 they had a decent campfire
going and the tired, hungry pair roasted hot dogs and drank
water. By 11:00 they were both asleep.

On Sunday morning, Daryl pulled out one of his cell
phones and made several calls. For the first time in over a week,
he could honestly tell people he felt safe. He made calls to
Racine, Cleve, and his parents, talking for two to three minutes
to each. He didn't tell any of them where he was or that Zach
was with him, only that he was safe. Neither Cleve nor Racy
spoke of their locations. Both told him they were all fine and the
escape plans had worked well. Zach and Daryl enjoyed the
warm, calm day, the protected seclusion, and each other's
company. They told each other their life stories. They relaxed.

*   *   *

On Saturday night, Gerald Baron felt the first twinges of
panic. It was a new feeling for him. He'd lost his quarry. *Not a
trace.* He called Curt Willoughby.

"Hello Gerald. Did you find Forrester?"

"I never saw him. I'm sure he was there, but he's on the
run and got spooked. My mission's getting intense. I didn't
want to involve the staff, but I've got no choice. I'm going to
need you to bring everybody in on this. For the next week we've
gotta drop everything and do whatever it takes to get Forrester.
Leave three people at the office and tell 'em to man it round the
clock. You and everybody else get to Denver, pronto. Catch the
next flight. When you get here, split up and visit every one of
Forrester's friends here. Get everything they know out of 'em. I
don't care what you have to do to get it. Put the three at the
office on the task of finding him, nothing else. Check
everything. Get into the bus terminal and train station camera
systems and scrutinize every camera tape, starting from eight this
morning."

*   *   *

On Monday morning Zach's boss at Channel Eight called him.

"This better be important," was Zach's greeting. "I've gotta keep it short."

"You might be in danger, Zach. We received calls from two people in Denver saying they know you and they've been accosted by people looking for you. One of them was beaten in the process."

"All right," Zach said. "Thanks." He clicked his phone off and relayed the message to Daryl.

*   *   *

By late Monday afternoon, Willoughby reported to Baron that the office had found a person they thought was Forrester on video at the bus terminal. He was purchasing tickets at 1:27 on Saturday with a guy wearing a big hat and sunglasses. Forrester picked up his own disguise and they got on a bus to Fort Collins. And they found them on the Fort Collins bus station video getting a taxi. They never found anything showing them come back to the station.

The staff of Davidson County Safety Services spent Monday night in Fort Collins. On Tuesday they spent the day riding taxis and interrogating taxi drivers. Shortly after 2:00, Willoughby reported to Baron, "We found a driver who took two men in hats and sunglasses to a mall and dropped 'em off at a sporting goods store. He gave us the name of a driver who picked up two campers at the same store Saturday afternoon and took them to a campground in State Forest State Park. It's a huge park with campgrounds scattered all over the place. The driver who took 'em is off today, but we're locating him now."

The driver was in Denver for the day. Davidson County Safety Services waited impatiently in front of his home. Baron called the camper registration office claiming to be a relative of a Zachary Forrester relaying an emergency message, but was told there was no record of anyone by that name registered in the park. The campground office told Baron they always checked identification of campers checking in.

The taxi driver finally arrived home Tuesday night at 10:30. He told the two agents he had delivered the campers to the North Michigan Reservoir area campground. Baron called the campground office again. The night guard answered. He confirmed that two campers had registered Saturday night at 7:45 and headed for the Reservoir; Ron and David Christianson. Baron decided to remain in Fort Collins overnight. He and Curt would leave at 5:00 on Wednesday morning for the state park while the remainder of the team awaited further instruction. Overnight, two members of the team would create map and satellite image binders of the North Michigan Reservoir area.

*   *   *

On Monday, while Davidson County Safety Services was searching out taxi drivers, Daryl and Zach spent the day planning for escape, just in case. They scouted the surroundings. Around mid-afternoon, they topped a hill a mile and a half southwest of their campsite, near the southwest border of the park. They saw, another mile away, a small, unkempt grass runway. As they walked to it, Daryl made a phone call.

*   *   *

On Wednesday morning at daybreak, Gerald Baron and Curt Willoughby walked into the State Forest State Park registration office and told the attendant they had emergency information they had to get to Ron and David Christianson. Their mother had been in a life-threatening accident.

"Yep, your cousins are registered here," the attendant told them. "It's possible they could have left. Campers are supposed to sign out when the leave, but some don't."

"Do you know where they camped?"

"Campers are free to choose any open site they like. Hey, Willie," she asked a disheveled man walking in the door, "Do you know where those two guys who checked in Saturday night for North Michigan set up?"

"They pitched tent up on the point, as far away from people as they could get."

The attendant pulled out a park map. "You can drive to the campground, but you have to hike the last half mile to get up to the point." She showed them the point and the path on the map.

"Thanks, we'll find them," Baron said.

Wednesday morning was crisp, clear, and still. The campers sat silently on logs around the fading campfire, enjoying the peaceful morning, heating water for coffee. The quiet was interrupted by the faint sound of a car coming up the road. Zach had a pair of binoculars around his neck, courtesy of their visitor who'd arrived late yesterday afternoon. He focused them on a spot in the road that wound toward the parking area. It was the one spot along the route that could be seen clearly from the campsite. The car passed through the opening. "It's the same car that was parked at the Hotel Saturday. Same guy driving."

"Let's go," Daryl said. Within three minutes, the trio gathered the gear they considered critical, and abandoned their tent, remaining paraphernalia, and campfire. They rushed stealthily off to the southwest.

The two men from the car hurried just as urgently, and just as quietly, up the trail toward the campsite, each carrying a rifle and a binder. As the pair neared the campsite, they stopped. They smelled the campfire as they silently studied the maps and images in the binder. After a few minutes of pointing and nodding, they readied their weapons and checked the silencers.

They crept toward the campsite. One-hundred-fifty yards from the site the path forked. Baron took the path leading directly to the camp and Willoughby took the one that circled up around it and came in from the back. They inched closer. Five minutes later they could see each other on either side of the camp. Nothing moved at the camp except the flickering flames boiling water. They waited another three minutes. Nothing. Just as Baron was about to call out to the campers, he caught a glimpse of far off color in motion.

He turned his head to toward it. "God damn it!" He bellowed. He pointed at the distant figures, three of them, running clumsily, crossing a grassy spot at the top of a hill carrying, awkward backpacks. "There they go!" he shouted. "C'mon!"

Willoughby yanked his rifle up to his shoulder as the trio began to disappear over the crest of the hill and fired a futile, long distance shot. Then Baron and Willoughby took off after them. After running along a path for a quarter of a mile, they came into a clearing where they again glimpsed their quarry running and stumbling in their attempt to escape. "Hang on a minute Curt," Baron said, breathing hard. "Let's be smart about this. They can't get far on foot and we're probably not gonna catch 'em on foot. They can't know anything about the area and we have everything right here with us. We'll be able to see them for a while yet. Let's figure out where they'll wind up. We'll outfox the bastards."

They leafed quickly through the maps. There was nothing close ahead of the three. The small town of Gould was over two miles beyond them. They probably heard the car coming, got spooked, and were running blind. That would work against them. "Let's look at the satellite images and find the best way to head 'em off," Baron said. Then he saw it. *"Son of a bitch!"* He screamed.

Willoughby had never seen Baron lose it in all the years they had worked together. He scanned the image Baron was staring at. He saw what appeared to be a grass airstrip. The escaping trio was headed straight for it. They stood silently and watched as their quarry crested another far off, low ridge and disappeared over it. Five minutes later, they heard a motor start. Three minutes after that, they saw a twin engine plane rise above the ridge as it traveled away from them.

Curt jerked his binoculars up. "I can't see the letters,"

"Forget it. It's Robert Defoe." *How in the hell am I going to get him by Saturday now?*

Chapter 22

Wednesday, October 12, Gould, Colorado, 8:38 a.m.

"Where to, boys?" Rob asked, still breathing hard as he
retracted the landing gear.

"To my family," Daryl huffed.

Two and a half hours later the Piper Seneca V made its
second landing in just over a week at the Montana ranch. When
they saw Rob's plane unexpectedly descending to the strip
everyone ran out of the house, all except Rory, who wheeled
himself gingerly onto the front porch. When they saw Daryl hop
out of the craft, the runners redoubled their speed. Rory, elation
overwhelming pain, grinned from ear-to-ear.

Daryl group-hugged his wife, carrying Kelsey, and his
older sons for a brief minute, spied Rory beaming on the porch,
and sprinted to him. They clutched each other, tears streaming
down their cheeks.

*   *   *

That night, in the White House, Justine Pritchard was
furious. When Rand's last whore had met her doom, Justine
knew he'd been shaken. From what she could tell, Rand had
been chaste since July … until last Friday night. He'd actually
gotten desperate enough two weeks ago to visit her room, trying
to find a way to suggest sharing a bed for the night. She'd given
him no in.

Her hard-heartedness had increased by the day, since she
had last seen Clarence in May. She needed him desperately.
Her personal torment was assuaged a bit by watching Rand

suffer his own. Then, last Friday night, he'd brought another young tramp to the White House for the night. The little Aphrodite had returned every night since, vaporizing Rand's pain, which intensified Justine's. Tonight, after thirty-four years of placing social status above everything, of sacrificing all to reach this pinnacle, she was losing it. Becoming engulfed, now, way too late, by an overwhelming certainty that this was not the life she needed or even wanted, Justine felt her strings snapping, one by one, and zinging wildly about.

At 11:00, elegantly dressed as always, she angrily left her quarters and stormed into Rand's suite. She knew no doors would be locked, which enraged her even more. She banged open the door to Rand's bedroom and turned on the light. Her eyes shot fire at the young woman who wrenched her head up from Rand's chest when the light blazed on. "Wait in the other room," Justine spat.

The horrified woman's mouth opened, trying, but unable to speak, as she pulled the covers up to her neck.

"For God's sake, you don't think I've seen this before? Get out and wait in the study. I have to talk to the President." Disgust for both cavorters poured from the words as they left her lips.

The young woman shot out of bed and wrapped herself in a shear robe in one lightning motion as she darted for the door.

As she whisked past, Justine said disdainfully, without turning to look at her, "You know the last whore who slept in this bed is dead, don't you?"

"*Justine!*" Pritchard roared, "What the hell are you doing?"

"You're absolutely determined to destroy it all, aren't you? Even the great Gayle Scapeli can't make you stop. God knows, he controls every other move you make, but even *he* can't keep you from bedding anything in a skirt!"

"*What do you want, Justine?*"

"I want you to be a man instead of Gayle Scapeli's puppet. Make your own damned decisions! Maybe even try to think with your brain instead of your penis."

"What are you talking about? You barge in here out of nowhere, at midnight, to scream about Gayle Scapeli?"

"Didn't he *order* you to quit with the whoring? Didn't he tell you you're blowing everything? *Stop it!*" She was livid.

"You're not making sense, Justine! What're you so upset about? You afraid we're gonna lose?"

She was pushing buttons, punching his sensitive places. "You're so weak. You do everything he says, except you're not strong enough to even do that without your brandy and your sluts!"

"*Shut up, Justine!* You couldn't care less who I sleep with and you know it. You haven't given a damn since your first fling with Clawson."

That froze her for a second. He had never uttered that name before. She'd often wondered if he knew. Then she became fiercer than ever. "You know nothing about Clarence Clawson." Venom dripped from her lips. "He's more of a man than you could be in five lifetimes."

"That's *bullshit*, Justine!" He paused, regaining an ounce of control. "You don't want this conversation. Drop it. Go to bed."

Infuriating! He was trying to be superior. She'd never been so out of control in her life. Her face was beet red, hate streaking from her dark eyes, fingernails at the ready, as she stood before her husband in her black evening gown. Justine renewed her attack, thrusting daggers at what she could only guess to be true. "You think I don't know what Scapeli's done? What you've done with him? You're blackmailers and murderers! Scapeli didn't have enough dirt on Borster and look what happened to him and your *last* wench. You're President because Scapeli made you and that's it. He set the whole goddamn thing up twenty-three years ago. Your sugar daddy planted that orgy in Nashville and he set the fire and he got you out. Not cause he wanted you to be President. Cause he wanted a president who'd be his puppet!" She was screaming. "*And that's exactly what you are!*

"*Shut the fuck up, Justine!*" he shouted back. "You're the damned *queen* of closet skeletons! You think I don't know how he kept *you* under control? He used your own damn dirt on you! You're not a bit different than me or anyone else."

"At least my dirt was my own and not something he created and threw on me! At least I wasn't so stupid and sex blind to just fall in that asshole's trap!"

"How can you *possibly* still believe that, after seeing him in action all these years?"

"What are you talking about? That bastard's never been able to set me up."

"You're a fool. Where do you think Clarence Clawson came from?"

That took her aback. After a moment she said, more controlled now, "You're crazy. You're so eaten up by his control, you can't stand to think I might not be in the same hole as you."

"I'm telling you, Justine, he set you up just like everybody else. His name's not even Clarence Clawson."

"You crazy bastard," she said, seething.

He looked her squarely in the eye and she saw a flicker of intense gratification in his expression. "His name is Gerald Baron. He's Scapeli's right hand man in that security company back in Nashville."

"That isn't even possible," she retorted disgustingly. "You'd *know* that if you knew how we met."

"I know *exactly* how you met. You thought he saved your ass at the mall when those thugs staged the robbery and knocked you down. That pair of thugs was paid by Gayle Scapeli. They were all trailing you around the mall, waiting for just the right time. *I* knew they were gonna do it before it ever happened."

"You want to hurt me so bad you're making shit up, you lyin' bastard. Clarence took me to work with him. He's a bridge inspector. I spent weekends at his cottage in Chattanooga. We've lasted for years, decades. It wasn't just a week or a month or a year. He's the most precious thing in my life. And me for him. It's not just me. I see it and feel it in him every time we're together, every time I hear his voice. We're the only real things in each other's lives."

There was a moment of silence. Justine watched her husband's anger melt away. His expression turned into one of pity. As she stood over him, full of hate, anticipating his next spiteful outburst, he said quietly, miserably, "I'm sorry, Justine. His name is Gerald Baron."

Justine spoke just as quietly, but with disdain, "No. You're wrong. You hate being Scapeli's puppet so much you want it to be. But you're dead wrong." She turned and walked out of the bedroom and through the study, past the girl of the week, whoever she was, without glancing at her.

After several minutes the young woman crept back through the bedroom door.   Pritchard looked at her despondently. "Do yourself a favor. Go home and don't ever come back. Get dressed. I'll get you a ride. But remember this. What Justine said about the last woman who shared this bed? That's true. If you ever think about talking to anyone about what happened here tonight, before you open your mouth, remember the last person who did that is dead. It wasn't my doing, but she's dead just the same. If you say anything to anybody about tonight or any of the other nights, you risk the same fate."

The First Lady did not sleep that night. She did not go downstairs to breakfast Thursday morning. Instead, she stayed in her bedroom, trying to work up nerve.

*   *   *

Neither did Gerald Baron sleep that night in his motel room in Fort Collins. He gave up trying at 4:00 Thursday morning and got up, showered, and dressed. He turned on his laptop and tried to find something – anything – that might give him a clue to Daryl Marten's whereabouts. He picked at the web, with no result. His cell phone rang at 8:00. He glanced at the number and tried very hard to reorient his mind-set. It took five rings for him to feel he stood any chance of pulling it off.

"Justine! You can't believe how good it feels to hear from you."

Silence.

"Justine?"

"Gerald Baron?"

Now it was he who was silent.

"Is this Gerald Baron?" she insisted.

More silence. She had her answer. She clicked her phone off, sat on her bed, and stared at nothing the rest of the day.

Baron couldn't absorb it. He had always feared that call would come. It was crushing. His affair with Justine Pritchard had been pure deceit from the beginning. He'd been paid handsomely to seduce her, and had pulled it off perfectly. However, over the course of time, she'd done something to him, brought out something he had not suspected existed. It had become as if he had two lives. One was the life he lived. The other was a dream. He could shut the dream out for weeks, months, or years at a time. But whenever she reopened it, color came into his black and white world. Now, with one phone call, in one instant, the dream evaporated in a puff of smoke.

He tried to force himself to concentrate on finding Marten, but found the effort impossible. At 10:00, he called Curt Willoughby.

"Yeah, Gerald?"

"Take everybody back to Nashville on the next flight. Then have everyone work round the clock today and tomorrow. Find any scrap of a clue to the whereabouts of Forrester, Daryl Marten, Cleve DeCamp, or Robert Defoe. I'm staying here. Call me with whatever you find.

On Friday morning, Baron's phone rang at precisely 8:00. Justine. He knew he shouldn't answer, but couldn't stop himself.

"Yes."

"You owe me."

"Yes."

"I want him gone."

"Yes."

"You've got three days."

He didn't respond.

She hung up.

*   *   *

On Saturday, October 15, Daryl posted Proposition #22: Lobbyists: Who is for Sale and What is Your Price?

Persons or groups who attempt to influence executive, legislative, or judicial decision-making are a threat to representative government.

1. Public servants are charged to uphold the Constitution and act in accordance with the best interests of the citizenry, not to make decisions to benefit a particular person or group in return for a reward.

2. Auditing of contributions and gifts received by candidates and officeholders would reduce the likelihood of public officials being beholden to contributors.

   a. All candidates and officeholders should be audited annually for receipt of gifts and donations.

   b. The full value of all gifts and gratuities received by public officeholders belongs to the taxpayers, not to the receiving individuals. Accepted gifts must either become the property of the government or may be kept by the officeholder in exchange for fair value paid to the government.

3. When applying to be placed on any ballot and again upon being elected, all candidates and officials should be required to submit to auditing of all contributions and gifts accepted.

   a. Annual audits should continue for the term of office and five years thereafter to guard against bias in return for promise of future reward.

   b. The requirement for audited disclosure should extend to gifts and gratuities received by the office holder's family members.

4. Any finding of receiving undisclosed favors or rewards from any entity that benefited from action taken while in office, would constitute a

criminal offense and subject both the office
holder and the donor to incarceration.

Decision-making by public officials under the
influence of special interest entities is a corruption of
representative government.   This proposition is to
eliminate that corruption.

*   *   *

On Sunday morning at 6:00, Gayle Scapeli read the
proposition. Then he called Baron.
"Yeah?"
"You missed your deadline."
"I have him in my sights."
"When?"
"I'll bring you proof of his death tomorrow. His head if
you want it."
"I want the proof to be public; a news report."
"It won't start that way, but I'll bring you proof."
"It had better be solid."
"I'll call you back later today with details, after the
mission's accomplished."

*   *   *

At 9:12 on Sunday night Gayle Scapeli's cell phone
rang.
"Yes."
"It's done. I did it myself. I blew his brains out two
hours ago in Mexico, near Villa Ahumada. He won't be found
for a while, but I've got photographs and positive identification.
I'll bring them to you tomorrow. Can we meet at Patapsco
Valley?"
"Where are you now?"
"El Paso, getting ready to board a flight to DC.
"Meet me at ten in the morning. Have the spot cleared
out before nine. Should I have Wasson report his death by
assassination at Villa Ahumada?"
"You can if you want. It's done."

This conversation held no hint of the familiar aura of camaraderie between the two men.

*   *   *

At 9:45 Eastern Standard time, Sunday, October 16, Regina Wasson's solemn face interrupted regularly schedule television programming.

"We have very distressing breaking news. We've just learned from reliable sources within the Mexican Government that they've recovered and positively identified the body of Presidential Candidate Daryl Marten. He was shot to death less than three hours ago near Villa Ahumada, Mexico, one-hundred miles south of El Paso. We have correspondents en route to the scene, and will report additional details as they become available. Again, very sad news. Presidential Candidate Daryl Marten has been assassinated, dead at the age of forty-four. Our heartfelt sympathy is extended to the Marten family and their friends."

*   *   *

Gaylord Scapeli arrived at the Monday morning rendezvous ten minutes early. He hurried toward the picnic table, eyeing the manila envelope lying on it, beckoning him. Gerald Baron sat across the table, anticipating Scapeli's early arrival.

"This had better be real, Gerald," Scapeli warned curtly as he approached the table. Somebody claiming to be Marten posted an update on his web site right after Wasson announced he was dead. Probably DeCamp, but the network president is giving me a ton of grief about not being able to confirm the assassination."

Scapeli was worked up. It had been a long time since his youth in Cabrini Green where he had learned to unemotionally and instantly recognize situations for what they were. This morning, that defining character trait was one step below being foremost in his psyche. It should not have been.

As Scapeli reached for the envelope, Gerald Baron, in one smooth, fast motion, lifted his handgun off his lap, pointed it at Scapeli, and shot him between the eyes. Scapeli collapsed, three days to the hour after Justine had delivered her ultimatum. Baron rose, retrieved the envelope, walked to his car, and drove away, leaving the dead body of Gaylord Scapeli to whoever might find it.

Chapter 23

Sunday, October 16, a remote ranch in Montana, 7:48 p.m.

Within a thirty second period, four cell phones rang: Racine's, Danielle's, Rob's, and Zach's. Cleve, Drake, Donna, and Zach's boss were each calling in a frenzy after hearing Regina Wasson report that Daryl had been assassinated. The conversations were all frantic.

"That's not true. He's standing right here in front of me. We're nowhere near Mexico. It's a lie."

After making assurances, everyone tried to keep the conversations short. Racine ran to Daryl and clutched him. "Do you have any idea what those calls would've done to me if you hadn't been right here? Don't leave me. If anything happens, it happens to us all."

At 8:15, Daryl posted an update.

Update, Sunday, October 16

This is Daryl Marten, in person, issuing this message to the world at 10:15 p.m. Eastern Standard Time. Thirty minutes ago, Regina Wasson reported on national news that I had been assassinated. That is not true. I am alive and well and believe I am currently safe. Attempts have been made on my life and I have been pursued, but the attempts have not been successful. On Monday, I'll issue a video for press release.

The household did not settle down until after midnight. It began to stir Monday morning before 6:00 and was bustling by

7:00. At 8:00, Zach and Daryl were ready to shoot the video session.

"This is Zachary Forrester, reporting from an undisclosed location with Presidential Candidate Daryl Marten. It's currently 10:30 a.m. Eastern Standard Time on Monday, October seventeenth. Here is Daryl Marten."

"Thank you, Zach. For reasons unknown to me, it was reported on national news shortly before ten o'clock last night that I had been assassinated. Obviously that report was false.

"I don't know who wants me out of the way or who wants the people of this nation to believe I'm dead. There are some seemingly obvious possibilities, but I have no information that points to any particular responsible party. Hopefully, we'll all know who's behind this madness soon. In the meantime, I ask everyone to not jump to conclusions.

"As the election nears, I urge all Americans to cast your votes based on the qualifications of the candidates and on your confidence in each candidate's likelihood of acting in your best interests. If you're considering voting for the Marten/DeCamp ticket, please do *not* cast your vote out of feelings of sympathy or suspicion or anger. Stay above the mêlée and cast your votes, dispassionately, for the candidate you believe will best serve you and this nation.

"I'm sure everybody wants to know who's behind the terror aimed at my family. Believe me, *no one* wants to know more than we do. But we won't form opinions or suspicions from inconclusive evidence. We thank everyone for your concern. We also thank Zach Forrester and Channel Eight for allowing us to provide facts to you."

The interview was received by the station at 11:17. By 12:05, it had been sent to the network in New York and was aired as breaking news. Five minutes later, on another network, a trembling Regina Wasson reported another breaking story.

"At 11:15 this morning, the body of Gaylord Scapeli, Chief of Staff of the Pritchard Administration, was discovered in Maryland's Patapsco Valley State Park, fatally shot in the forehead. A passerby discovered the body near a picnic table and notified the police. Homicide detectives arrived at approximately 11:30 and pronounced Chief of Staff Scapeli dead at the scene. She wiped her cheek with a shaky hand. "This is Regina Wasson reporting live, breaking news."

As word of Scapeli's death exploded through the mesh of Washington, an exhaling breath of relief was palpable beneath the surface postures of shock and grief. The lone exception was Randall Pritchard. Gayle Scapeli had been the motivating force behind him for more than twenty years. Pritchard, now on his own, felt more lost than free.

That night, at 8:00, President Pritchard delivered an address.

"Good evening. I come before you tonight grieving the loss of a brilliant statesman and a close personal friend, my Chief of Staff, Gaylord Scapeli. He was fatally shot this morning by an unidentified gunman who remains at large. Gayle will be sorely missed by all he came in contact with while running the day-to-day activities of the White House. In my estimation, Gaylord Scapeli was the most influential Chief of Staff ever to hold that position. Without his support and boundless determination, I might never have occupied the Oval Office.

"I vow that this heinous act will not go unpunished. We *will* find the assassin and any and all persons accessory to Gayle's murder, and they *will* be brought to justice.

"It will be difficult to move forward in the coming days, but move on we must. If this crime was committed in an attempt to weaken this presidency or the Republican Party in advance of the coming election, the perpetrators will find that we are stalwart and will become even stronger. But, for tonight, I join with all of America in mourning the loss of one who served this country so faithfully. I ask all of you to remember Gaylord Scapeli in your prayers.

"Thank you and good night."

At the conclusion of the address, Pritchard immediately left the Oval Office and walked to his living quarters. Justine, having watched the address, was waiting for him.

"You'd think Scapeli was a saint after watching that."

"He did a lot for us, Justine."

"He destroyed us."

"We wouldn't be here if it hadn't been for Gayle. I know it and you know it. Everybody knows he was the prime mover in this Administration."

"Where are *you* in that formula, Rand? *You're* the President. Don't you think *you* should've been the prime mover? It looks like you'll *have* to be now."

"*Come on*, Justine. I know you're upset that he handled you, but the man was *murdered* today. Can't you leave it alone for one day?"

Fire spat from her eyes. "*Upset?* That bastard has made what's left of my life hell! I wanted him dead so bad I could taste it! Just like half the politicians in Washington. You think Jimmy Borster isn't feeling the sweetness right now? You asked people to pray. I can see Jimmy on his knees right now, giving thanks to God for answering his prayers. That's what I'm doing."

"*Stop it!*"

"How do you think you'll *ever* find out who was behind it, Rand? Everybody he ever came in contact with had motive to kill that son of a bitch!"

"*Enough!*"

"How you gonna find the killer, Rand?"

He took a step toward her, fist balled.

"Do it," she said quietly. "Hit me. Beat me. Beat me till I tell you who killed him."

His face was fire red. She could see how much effort it took for him not to strike her. "You're mad," he growled through gritted teeth.

"Maybe I am," she whispered. "Maybe the two of you drove me mad." She paused. "I know who killed him. Do you want me to tell you?"

"You're mad," he repeated.

"No. It'd be easier if I was. Do you want to know who killed him?"

"You couldn't possibly know."

"I know."

"All right, Justine." He snarled at her. "You tell me who killed him."

"It was Gerald Baron. Clarence Clawson."

"You'd love that to be true, wouldn't you? You're dreaming. You aren't worth that. Not even close."

She hated her husband at that moment almost as much as she hated Scapeli. "He did it, Rand. He did it for me. I called him Friday and told him to. I gave him three days to get rid of that fiend. He did it. And today Gayle Scapeli's in Hell."

"No."

"Yes. Go after him. Tell the FBI to find Gerald Baron and ask him if he killed Scapeli. He'll admit it. He'll tell them how he did it."

"And that's what you want? You want Clarence Clawson sentenced to death?"

"Yes. He deserves it. And he knows it."

"Get out of my sight."

"Just a few nights ago you wanted to share my bed, Rand. Tonight's the night. I'll sleep in your bed tonight."

"*Leave me alone!*" he shrieked.

She smiled wickedly at him, turned, and walked away.

By Thursday, political allies who Scapeli had browbeaten were scattering from Randall Pritchard like passengers jumping from a sinking ship. At first, Pritchard struggled to function. The double punch of losing Scapeli's motivating direction and suffering Justine's venom put him in a tailspin. He named Elaine Kosovich acting Chief of Staff. He gave little guidance to her or to Greg Jolsen, but did his utmost to make a show of all being under control.

Pritchard had not mentioned Gerald Baron to the FBI, but someone else, an anonymous female caller, had tipped them off, fingering Baron. Justine had turned out to be right. Baron had been easy to find, readily admitted to the murder, and told the FBI exactly how he did it. He even turned over the murder weapon. However, he'd been tight-lipped on anything more than that. Not a syllable about why.

Pritchard was almost incapacitated by anxiety over what Baron might reveal. Baron surely knew the worst, Wheeler and Herrington, the Catcher set up, Borster, Janice Taylor, in addition to the attempt on Marten's life. Worse, Justine seemed to have some kind of spell over him. Was Baron, or Justine, simply biding their time? *He can connect Scapeli to everything.*

Can he tie me to any of it? What if he tries? How much crazier will Justine get? How far will he go in carrying out her scheming? It was paralyzing.

Throughout the week of Scapeli's death, the only Presidential Candidate actively campaigning was Bradley Catcher. Pritchard did not make a single public appearance after his address on October 17, eulogizing Scapeli. Catcher was making the most of it, chucking ad money as if it were being sucked into his war chest by a black hole. It took the entire week for his staff to realize that, since Scapeli's death, cash had stopped flowing in.

On Wednesday, October 19, one day before taking an extended leave of absence, Regina Wasson retracted the network story of the previous Sunday night, claiming Daryl Marten was dead. She didn't reveal her source, but said network investigators had searched Villa Ahumada, Mexico, and found no evidence that Marten had ever been there. She also stated the source for the Marten story had recanted.

On Saturday, Daryl Marten posted an update.

Update, Saturday, October 22

We all have experienced a volatile political campaign process this summer and fall. There is no solace to be gained by anyone from the circumstances that befell Senator Wheeler, Senator Herrington, Vice President Borster, or Gayle Scapeli.

Cleve DeCamp and I have advocated change. If this advocacy has contributed to the strife, we truly regret that. However, all the turmoil and scandal reinforce our conviction that the United States Government and its leaders desperately need an infusion of ethics and morals. We retain our belief that the ideals espoused by our founding fathers and embedded in our constitution can help this nation soar if ardently pursued and carefully applied.

We feel compassion for those who have suffered from these ill-fated events. We sincerely hope the nation and its leaders are rounding the corner to a more prudent approach to governing. We wish well being to President

Pritchard and to Senator Catcher, as well as their families and staffs, as we approach Election Day.

On Tuesday, October 25, with the election just two weeks away, several poll results were released. The consensus was that Pritchard and Marten were in a dead heat and Catcher continued to lose ground. The poles put the popular vote at approximately 40 percent each for Pritchard and Marten, 10 percent for Catcher and 10 percent now undecided. Pritchard's decline was attributed to his loss of Washington insider support since Scapeli's death. Marten's rise was attributed to the attempt on his life and his son being wounded. Catcher's continuing decline was attributed to his negative advertising.

While poll results were being issued and debated, Gerald Baron was being interrogated by FBI psychological guru, Thomas Marker. Marker was convinced there was much more to learn from Gerald Baron than just his reason for killing Gayle Scapeli. However, that question was the starting point. If he could get Baron to open up on that question, then a geyser of information would follow.

Chapter 24

Wednesday, October 26, the Oval Office, 7:24 a.m.

"We have to go on the offensive now, today, Sir, or we're going to lose," Greg Jolsen beseeched the President. "We're in a dead-heat with Marten and his numbers are rising while ours fall. We have to turn it around now or we'll be the first incumbent administration ever to lose to an independent."

The President was recovering his resolve by the day, getting stronger, digging out the old Randall Pritchard, the savvy politician of 25 years ago, before being taken over by Scapeli. He would overcome the onslaught. *Throw at me what you will. Gayle Scapeli, Justine Pritchard, whatever.*

"So, what do you want to do?"

"Get you in front of the public. We need you to make some enthusiastic, live appearances. We need to get tons more ads on the air lauding the economy and our healthy international respect."

"All right, let's do it. We've got plenty of money. Step up the ads. I can make appearances Friday, Saturday, and Sunday if you can schedule them."

"I'll get on it right away," Jolsen committed.

Beginning Thursday, Pritchard's television ad time quadrupled. On Friday, several new spots were released. One showed a robust, friendly President Randall Pritchard being cheered by a jubilant throng. The voice-over compared before Pritchard to after Pritchard jobless rates, household incomes, housing sales, and gross national product statistics, all of which had improved dramatically. Another showed the democratic candidates blasting away at each other, displaying them all in the same disastrous light. First Wheeler and Herrington delivering mutual death blows, then the Democratic National Chairman in a scene taped before the Wheeler-Herrington debacle, imploring Catcher to step aside, citing his youth, inexperience, lack of support, and lack of funding. Another was a barb on deceitful advertising, showing two of the more blatant attacks on Marten, first, Catcher's ad ridiculing him on the veteran's hospitals, and then one comparing him to Satan, not a Catcher ad, but lots of people would mistake it for one.

On Friday night, Pritchard made a live appearance in Washington, Saturday night in New York City, and Sunday afternoon in Miami. All had huge crowds in attendance and an abundance of television cameras. The speeches were nearly identical. They all started and ended with emphatic recountings of accomplishments attained during his term of office. In between, he addressed two topics. First, without mentioning names, he talked around shortcomings of the Democratic Party and its untrustworthy leaders. A small part of this theme was devoted to policy and platform, while most of it was devoted to integrity, primarily the Democratic lack thereof. The second topic, again without mentioning names, addressed the essential ingredient of experience in presidential leadership.

Pritchard put on a show of exuberance. The crowds were lively, sparked by lots of planted enthusiasts. He did everything right. The old Randall Pritchard, the embodiment of American leadership and statesmanship, was back! With or without Scapeli and Justine, he was still, and always would be, *the* American politician.

While Pritchard rebounded, Bradley Catcher nose-dived. Catcher's campaign management was accustomed to cash raining on them from the sky; they had gotten careless in spending and tracking. After grasping the depth of their poor status in the polls, they conferred on Wednesday, October 26, to consider expanding and redirecting their ad campaign. The Catcher campaign's financial brain trust spent eight hours ferreting out their spending limits. Finally, in disbelieving panic, they concluded that, at current rates of receipts and expenditures, their coffers would go negative in three days, plunging at a rate that would bankrupt a millionaire every day. As it turned out, their conclusions were too optimistic.

On Thursday morning, the Bradley Catcher for President organization put all efforts toward pulling ads across the country. However, even applying the brakes as aggressively as they could, their well was dry on Monday morning, October 31. No money was left for payroll or all the bills pouring in for services already rendered. Many staffers, already disgruntled, walked out the door. Advertising ground to a halt.

On Friday, October 28, a five minute spot from the Marten family was aired during a special program highlighting the unique events of this presidential election campaign. Zach had shot and sent the Martin segment. It opened with Daryl speaking.

"I think most of the nation is aware of our propositions and philosophies for governing this country. However, I don't believe many of you are as familiar with my most prized treasures, my wife and children. I'm proud to present them to you." He glanced toward Racine as the camera panned to her.

"Hello. I'm Racine. I'm first and foremost a wife and mother. That role is and will forever remain my passion. The past year has been a roller coaster ride that's now engraved on my soul. My children and I journeyed with Daryl from the beginning, starting with posting their philosophies of good government on Commonguy, through appearing on the Insomniac Show, through the decision to offer to serve the nation, through being threatened, through gaining ballot access, through attempted assassination, through physical separation, and ultimately to finding our way back together. I can't say I would've been in favor of launching Commonguy, had I known all that would happen as a result. My family has been in grave danger, and I would never have chosen that.

"Regardless, today we're all in one piece, we're together, and Daryl is a viable candidate for President of the United States. I stand emphatically at my husband's side and will give him every ounce of my love and support, whatever the outcome on Election Day. This wonderful brood of children might not offer exactly these same words, but each one of them is filled with the same sentiments. Now, because Jeremy won't tell you this, I will. Computers and websites require technological whizzes to keep them operating. Our miniscule campaign staff had one techy, who kept it all operating all the time. Here he is."

"Hello, I'm Jeremy and I'm seventeen. We kids have been on the adventure of a lifetime. We've visited many states and been on stage at rallies. We've been in the heart of this crusade and learned firsthand how the system works. It works, at least it works for us, because there've been so many people eager to believe in and work hard for a good cause. When Dad first told us some states require over a hundred thousand signatures, just to get on the ballot, we were sure it'd be impossible. What we didn't know was there'd be so many people helping.

We've flown on a Secret Service jet. Kyle and I traveled over 500 miles, by ourselves, disguised as punks. Well, I guess that isn't all that much of a disguise for Kyle," Jeremy said, grinning. "We were there on the stage when Rory got shot and we were there in the hospital when he was in surgery.

"Dad let us help ... no, he made us help ... decide what the family would do at critical times. We did sort of make fun of Dad at first for just throwing his opinions out on the web. But, it turned out maybe he was right. Maybe what this country needs *is* some fresh ideas, sort of a rebirth. Anyway, we're just as proud of Dad as he is of us. Now, and I apologize for doing this to you, here is my brother, Kyle."

"Don't let Jeremy con you," Kyle said. "He would never have gotten through that five hundred mile trip if I hadn't been there to show him the way. Anyway, I'm Kyle. I'm fourteen and available for all you girls," he flashed a broad smile. "I'm no good at that techy stuff, like Jeremy is. My bag is football, basketball, and baseball. I want to say a big hello to all my friends back in Carthage. Look! I'm on TV.

"But, I agree with Jeremy on a couple things. I don't like to do that, but once in a while he has a point. It's been a heck of an adventure. We've been really scared and we've been really happy and we've been everything in between. We helped Mom keep her mind occupied before Dad got here. Sometimes, we had to think really hard to come up with things to drive her nuts, but we were always up to the task. Okay, I'll turn it over to my little brother, Rory, now. He's the famous one."

Rory sat in a recliner, a light blanket covering his legs and his third generation cast that had been fashioned from whatever materials Danielle could lay hands on. Danielle had been dumping all the antibiotics she could into Rory, along with more pain killers than she liked to prescribe. By the end of the first week at the ranch, Rory's leg had shown signs of infection. The reason the replacement casts had been necessary had been to allow room for increasing swelling. Rory needed more intense medical treatment than she could give him here, and they all knew it. He needed to be in a hospital, and the sooner the better. The plan was to leave the ranch via Care Flight on Election Day morning, headed for University Hospital in Salt Lake City. Tonight, his leg was throbbing, but Rory handled it well.

"Hi. I'm Rory and I'm eleven. Like Jeremy said, sorry about Kyle. He gets carried away sometimes." He grinned. "Yep, I got shot in the leg. That was four weeks ago and it's getting a little better. I'm actually glad everything turned out the way it did. I got shot, which is a bad thing, but I still have my dad. I'll take that bullet any day.

"So the candidate's kid experience has been different for me. It's been something to watch everybody and all the problems that come up and see how they get handled. I watched Dad and Cleve act like school kids when they started Commonguy and then started getting feedback. I watched Mom and Dad go all crazy about being on Jeff Kramer and watched Mom turn red when they put the camera on her. Everybody should've seen how hard Mom and Mel DeCamp worked, keeping up with all of the volunteers, and how dedicated Jeremy was at keeping Commonguy going all the time. Kyle and Kelsey helped keep everybody laughing just by being their normal selves. Whenever Mom or Dad got stressed out, one of them would always come up with something to make it better.

"Anyway, now I'm watching everyone talk to a TV camera and pretty soon I'm going to watch us all on TV. It's been cool! Now, here's my little sister, Kelsey."

"I'm Kelsey and I'm five. I've never talked on TV before. My Daddy is running for President. If I was you, I'd vote for him. He's a very nice man."

The camera went back to Daryl. "I know I've promised I wouldn't campaign, but I won't turn down that pitch from Kelsey. Now you all know what really makes my world tick. If Cleve and I should happen to be elected, we'll work diligently to serve all of you. However, the most important thing in my life will always be this group who you've just met. I wanted you to meet them because we come as a package deal.

"There's another person here who deserves mention. When Cleve and I launched Commonguy, we'd not yet met a young man named Zachary Forrester. Then, when things began to pick up steam, the first media person to contact me was Zach. He asked for an interview. We did the interview and, thanks to his efforts, it was aired nationally. That was the initial boost that kick-started the trek that resulted in us being where we are today."

"Zach has supported us and covered our story from the beginning. When he saw his first network treat us poorly, he resigned and was immediately picked up by this network. Zachary quickly became our friend, and I've grown to trust him as much as anyone I know. He's as close to being a member of our family as one could be without being born in. Zach played a part in our escape after the shooting. When I felt unable to stay ahead of my pursuers, Zach jumped into the foray. I don't believe I'd be alive today if he hadn't. Zach, I know you're supposed to be the professional reporter, but do me a favor and make a few personal remarks."

"All right, Daryl. The station might allow me one minor discretion. It's obvious that covering your candidacy has been, and will be, a boon to my career. That's a good thing, but it's not what's important here. You and Cleve have attained a phenomenal achievement, regardless of the outcome of the election. I'm honored, proud, and humbled to have played a small role in it. Above all, I treasure the friendship you and Cleve and your families have extended me. You're all extraordinary people and I'll be forever at your service.

"I'd like to add one more thing. I don't want to close this out harshly, but I've got to say this. This is to the man who was after you in Denver and in State Forest State Park." Zack looked fiercely into the camera. "I saw your face. Clearly. Twice. You were after my friend. I'll be keeping my eyes open for you. *Nothing* would be more satisfying than identifying you to the authorities."

"I'm sorry folks. I couldn't keep that in. This family would bring out the protective instincts in anyone."

*   *   *

Sam Eastman watched the news clip and smiled. He liked them, too. He admired Daryl and Cleve for having the fortitude to decline protection and then the wherewithal to stay ahead of a professional assassin. Even though he was a member of the media, Zach was a good, young man. In spite of his longtime Washington ties, Sam hoped Daryl and Cleve would win.

Something nagged around the edges of his mind after watching the segment. What were Zach's words? "This is to the man who was after you in Denver and in State Forest State Park. I saw your face." That would have been between October 4, when they split up, and Daryl's October 15 update. Right after that, in rapid succession, came the false assassination report on October 16, Scapeli's murder on October 17, and the arrest, out of the blue, of Gerald Baron on October 21. *Could there be a connection? "I saw your face. Clearly. Twice."*

Sam had heard that Thomas Marker was attempting, unsuccessfully, to extract information from Gerald Baron. Sam had met Marker a year and a half ago at a seminar. They were barely acquaintances, but Marker knew who he was. On Saturday afternoon, Sam found Marker's home phone number and called him.

"Hello?"

"Hello. This is Secret Service Agent Sam Eastman. Is this Thomas?"

"Yes. Hello, Sam! It's been a while. What can I do for you?"

"Did you happen to see the clip of Daryl Marten's family last night?"

"Sure did. This is an election for the record books, isn't it? I think I heard you were on Marten's protection detail."

"I was. They're even more impressive and likable in person than on TV. Did you catch the end – the part where Forrester said he saw the pursuer?"

"Yeah. I'm not sure I'd have proclaimed that to the world if I were him."

"Zach's as remarkable as the Martens in his own way."

"So, what does this have to do with your calling me, Sam?"

"Well, I'll tell you. After I heard Zach say he could identify the guy, I got to thinking about the sequence of events over the past two weeks. I guess, I'm wondering if Scapeli's murder and the attempt on Marten might be related."

"Are you suggesting Gerald Baron was the man Forrester saw?"

"I don't have a lick of evidence to support that, but I was wondering, if I could get Zach to come to Washington, what would you think about asking him that question?"

"I wouldn't be opposed. So far, Baron's been a hard nut to crack. He gave himself up with no fuss at all, willingly gave us the details, but won't even *hint* at why."

"What led you to him, Thomas?"

"An anonymous tip. A woman called one of our receptionists and asked her to give the Director the message that Gerald Baron, owner of Davidson County Safety Services in Nashville, Tennessee, committed the murder."

"That company sounds familiar," Eastman said. "Wait, wasn't that Scapeli's old company?"

"Yep."

"Interesting. Any idea who the caller was?"

A brief hesitation, then, "Nope."

"Thomas, the longer we talk, the more I want to get Zach here."

"You get Forrester here and we'll put Gerald Baron in an old-fashion line up and see what happens."

"I'll do my best."

Half an hour later, after struggling through four obstinately resistive people at Cincinnati Channel Eight, he finally coerced the station manager into calling Zach and telling him Sam Eastman wanted to talk to him about identifying Marten's pursuer. Ten minutes later, Sam's phone rang.

"Sam Eastman."

"Hi, Sam. It's Zach. You wanted to talk to me?"

"I sure do. I watched you on TV last night and heard you say you got a good look at the guy chasing Daryl. Well, we've got a man in custody we'd like you to take a look at. See if it's him. Would you be willing to come to DC to do that?"

"I'd love to if I could be sure I wouldn't be seen in public. I won't take any chances on leading anyone to Daryl."

"We could have a Secret Service jet bring you here and take you back. On the ground, you'll ride in a limo with tinted glass. We'll load and unload you inside government hangers and enclosed carports. Sun rays won't find you."

"All right," Zach committed. "I'll find a way to fly to an airport away from here where you can pick me up. If I fly in privately, can I avoid going into a public terminal?"

"How about an Air Force Base?"

"That could work. What about Schriever, in Fort Collins? When would you want to do it?"

"Monday?" Sam asked.

"I'll see what I can set up and call you back."

On Monday afternoon, October 31st, at 4:00, Zach was in a Secret Service facility in Washington with Sam and a profile artist, working up a sketch on the man he saw. When it was finished, it looked a lot like Gerald Barron. He'd already filled Sam in on how his sightings of the man had occurred. The line up was scheduled for 10:00 a.m. on Tuesday.

There were ten men in the line up, a varied group. Two had some features similar to Baron's. Zach took one look through the one way glass and said, "That's him. Number seven. Who is he? Did you arrest him for attempting to assassinate Daryl?"

"No, it's an unrelated case," Sam said. "After I saw you Friday night, I just had a hunch about a connection between the two crimes. I wanted to play it out. Looks like the hunch was right on."

"You talked me into coming all the way out here and you're not gonna tell me why you arrested him?"

"We can't yet, Zach. I can tell you this, though. We *will* charge him with complicity in the attempted murder of Daryl. You can take heart knowing you made that happen. I'll clue you in on everything as soon as release of information is cleared."

Ten hours later, Zach was back at the ranch in Montana.

*   *   *

Tuesday afternoon was grueling for Gerald Baron. Now, there were two interrogators. Thomas Marker, the mind extractor, and Secret Service Agent Sam Eastman. Marker noticed Baron's eye twitch when Sam walked in the room. Baron knew who Eastman was.

"Gerald," Marker began, "we know more now than we did when you and I talked yesterday. In case you're wondering about that line-up this morning, you were positively identified in a stake out of Presidential Candidate Daryl Marten at a motel room in Denver. Then you were identified again in pursuit of Marten in State Forest State Park in Colorado. Those facts, along with our investigation of Secret Service Agent Brackman Littleton, are going to piece this puzzle together, with or without your cooperation."

Baron remained composed. "Go ahead and work on your puzzle. I couldn't care less what you do or don't figure out."

"That can't be true, Gerald. You had a productive, rewarding relationship with Gaylord Scapeli for over thirty years. He was your source of livelihood. You provided him with the information and control he needed to maintain his power base. You were obviously going after Marten, and you were failing. It's possible this failure was all it took to topple your lifelong relationship with Scapeli, but I'm finding that hard to believe.

"Now, there's another angle we've been looking into," Marker continued. "And this is the one we're really interested in. There's a woman in this picture. Over the years, you kept control over all the vices that can get a man in trouble, bring him down. And that includes women. Oh, you bedded a skirt now and then, maybe on a short vacation, or maybe in the line of duty. But you never let a woman get to you; get in the way of your work, your career. Except, we're thinking, maybe for one.

"We haven't identified her yet, but we know she's there. She's been there for a long, long time. Probably never for any uninterrupted stretches. But intermittently. Maybe for twenty years or more. We don't think different women. Just this one."

Baron was being interrogated without being physically secured. He wore no chains. Marker, though no longer young, was fit and not worried about holding his own with any man one on one, at least for the two seconds it would take reinforcements to burst into the room. He wanted his subjects free to allow their body language to speak. Baron's gave away a hint of increased difficulty in remaining nonchalant.

"What can you tell us about her, Gerald?"

"You're dreaming up a ghost, Marker. There ain't no girl. Never has been. But, you guys go ahead and spin your wheels. I hope you put in ten thousand hours and spend a million bucks trying to find a ghost. How stupid do you think I am?"

"Well, at least that's a response. That's progress. But she's no ghost. She's real. She's out there. And we're gonna find her. She's probably not involved in all this mess you created. Hell, you've probably got her completely fooled about your line of work. But, in the end, maybe she's more important to you than Scapeli was. And he might just have died because of that."

"God, do you ever get tired of listening to yourself, Marker? I sure as hell do."

"I'd rather listen to you, Gerald, but since you won't talk," he shrugged his shoulders, "somebody has to."

"What about Sam over here? Can't he talk for a while?"

"You don't want me to talk, asshole. I'm not as politically correct as my friend Thomas. I spent enough time with the Martens to develop a healthy respect and fondness for them. You went after them. All I want to do is nail your ass."

"Yeah, I heard the kid got shot on your watch," Baron goaded him. "Tough break, Agent."

"You're goin' down, Baron."

"Me and Mr. Marker here've been all through that. I don't give a shit. And I couldn't care less how many different things I go down for. Pile up a hundred charges … a thousand. It don't matter. I'm only gonna die once."

"Okay, Baron. I see where you want this to go. Well, I'll tell you where I want it to go. I want you to suffer. And from what I've seen this morning, there's one thing you seem to care a lot about. You don't want us to get to your woman. You lie and say there is no woman. Did you forget about the locket you wore in here? That's one expensive sealed titanium locket. On the outside, it only smells like you. It smells a lot like you; like you've worn it constantly for 20 years. But inside … it smells just like her, inside. She's no ghost, Baron. I'm going after her. And when I find her, I'll figure out *exactly* how to use her to make you suffer most, and that's what I'll spend every second doing."

"Go to hell, Eastman."

Baron was near perfect at keeping his cool, but both interrogators saw it was no longer effortless. They'd found a nerve. "See there, Gerald," Sam said, "it's not so bad talking to Thomas after all." He turned to Marker. "I'm gonna leave you two alone and put a team on getting his girlfriend. Then, I'm going to pay visits to Littleton and Whetstone. Have a good day, gentlemen."

Sam had met with the Director Saturday morning before calling Thomas Marker. If there was infiltration into the Secret Service, and if it went as high as Director Clyde Leonard, he no longer wanted this career anyway. Sam had explained the facts he knew to Leonard, the additional circumstances he suspected, and the investigative actions he wanted to pursue.

The Director had listened stoically and, after hearing it all, expressed confidence in Sam's deductions. Leonard committed to debriefing Agents Littleton and Whetstone personally on Sunday. Then, he would question Deputy Director Franklin Morganstern, who had insisted Littleton and Whetstone be assigned to Marten's protection detail.

Littleton had caved under pressure and admitted he had planted the gun at Stanford Memorial Auditorium, seen to tree-trimming for a clear shot, provided the key and security code for the Auditorium, and signaled the shooter. However, he had not implicated Whetstone, or anyone else on the detail. Whetstone was even more skittish during his grilling than he had been when sequestered in the hotel conference room. Surprisingly, the twitchy twerp never cracked, never admitted to knowing anything, and refused to implicate Littleton.

On Wednesday, Sam began an independent Secret Service investigation of Gerald Baron, his business, his personal life, his past and recent activities. Information was difficult to find. Between the time of Scapeli's murder and Baron's arrest, Davidson County Safety Services had evaporated. Every employee had disappeared without a trace, probably all out of the country, each likely with a share of the defunct company's bankroll. The building the company had occupied for more than 25 years was vacant, stripped clean. Not even a waste can remained.

The company had no landline phones. Communications had been conducted on secure cell phones. All financial transactions had been electronic. The firm kept a checking account at a local bank. Bank records showed the account never held more than several thousand dollars, enough for a few days operation. Deposits came not from identifiable clients, but from Swiss banks. Except for those veiled deposits into the checking account, there was no record of company receipts. Tax records of the business and all its employees showed the company broke even, more or less, every year. Each of the employees, including Gerald Baron, reported incomes of 75,000 dollars per year, give or take 25,000. There was no record anywhere of any clients.

What Sam wanted most was Baron's cell phone records. Sam assigned four people to researching cell phone accounts in the Nashville area that had ceased activity on, or shortly after, October 17. On Thursday, they discovered several. Five of them listed calls on October 10th, 11th, and 12th made from the Fort Collins, Colorado area. One of them logged calls beginning on October 4th from San Francisco and then, throughout the next few days, from Nevada, Utah, and Colorado. The calls to and from that cell phone followed the path Zach had described; Denver, Fort Collins, State Forest State Park. That was the one. Sam wanted all the records for that phone account.

On Friday afternoon, November 4th, at 1:30, after overcoming legal resistance, Sam presented a subpoena to the cell phone service provider for the records of the desired account. By 2:30, he had a complete printout. The name of the account holder was Clarence Clawson, a person who appeared, upon detailed investigation, to be a phantom.

The phone record went back more than fifteen years. Most of the calls were secure cell to secure cell. The times of the calls and locations of the sending and receiving towers were on the printout, but most of the numbers of the phones on the other end were not listed, not permitted to be identified even to the cell phone provider. One of the numbers listed as being called on October 5, matched one Sam had brought with him; Littleton's. He called Leonard and told him what he had. Leonard agreed to send an electronic communications guru, Jason Smith, to Nashville that evening and to issue a Secret Service directive, requiring the service provider to assign staff to fully cooperate with Smith on Saturday.

Sam was at Smith's side beginning at 7:00 on Saturday morning, November 5. They started with the more recent calls and worked back, extracting identities of the account holders of the cell phones on the other end. By 9:30, they had identified the most often called phone number in Washington DC, averaging over one call per week. That number first appeared about the time Pritchard had been elected. Another frequently called number, predating the first one, also was logged at about one per week. That phone was sometimes, but not always, in Washington, and had its last call listed at about the time the first number initially appeared. By 10:00, they had the holder of those two phones identified. No surprise. Both had belonged to Gaylord Scapeli.

By 1:30, they had identified two more phones of interest. The calls to these two were sporadic, sometimes going well over a year between calls and sometimes having several calls within a given week. The peculiarity that drew their attention to these two numbers was the pattern; the same as they'd found with Scapeli's two phones. There was a cutoff date between the appearances of the two numbers. One had not been used before Pritchard's election and the other had been used only after that, just a few times. They spent an hour trying to extract the identity of the holder of the more recently used phone with no success.

They finally gave up and tried the earlier phone. That one was easy. By 2:45 Sam had the identity of that account holder.   He couldn't believe it.   Justine Pritchard!   *The girlfriend!*

Chapter 25

Sunday, November 6, a ranch in Montana, 10:00 a.m.

Daryl posted his last update before the election. Within two hours, it was reported word-for-word by every network.

Update, Sunday, November 6

I want to take one final opportunity before the election to express our appreciation to all who have supported us and our propositions.

The past year has been extraordinary. We could never have imagined what it would bring. Although it has been grueling, it has also been rewarding. We have met many people whom we now cherish as friends. We have learned much about this country and have grown stronger and more committed than ever to the betterment of the nation and the service of her people.

The past five months have been politically turbulent. At such times, it is crucial for the citizens to be heard. Tuesday will present your opportunity. Take advantage of it. For each office to be filled, vote for the person you believe will serve you best. Vote on the issues placed before you. Hundreds of thousands of men and women have fought and died to give us this opportunity to jointly determine how we shall be governed. Don't take their sacrifice for granted. Honor them by making the most of that privilege and duty they preserved for you. Vote.

*   *   *

As Daryl posted his update, Thomas Marker and Sam Eastman were, again, interrogating Gerald Baron. "Good morning, Gerald," Marker said. Baron didn't reply. He looked uneasy.

"Have you ever heard of Clarence Clawson?" A quick dart of the eyes. Marker and Eastman saw it and interpreted: Yes.

"Since our last meeting," Marker continued, "Agent Eastman has been researching cell phone records. He found none registered to any Gerald Barron from the Nashville area, but he did find one registered to a Clarence Clawson. That one followed the locations where you were seen during the second week of October."

"I've never heard of Clarence Clawson."

"We also have the phone records of four employees of Davidson County Safety Services and they all knew him well. Lots of calls."

"You don't have shit."

"We have calls from Clawson's phone dating back more than fifteen years to Gayle Scapeli."

Baron's body language and voice were calm and controlled, but his eyes betrayed nervousness. "So?"

"Have you carried a cell phone for the past year, Gerald?"

"If you haven't figured that out, then you're damn poor investigators."

"And where is that cell phone?"

"As I said ...."

"All right, Baron," Marker said, "we'll stop playing games. We know your cell phone account was in the name of Clarence Clawson. We found records of a few calls over the past four years between your phone and one cell phone we couldn't identify. That's the one we want to talk about." Baron's eyes showed a glint of hope. The corners of his mouth, almost imperceptibly, turned up.

"We have all the other names we want. We even have calls between you and Secret Service Agent Brackman Littleton." Another nerve pricked. "That's right, Gerald. We have plenty of evidence to charge you with conspiracy to assassinate Presidential Candidate Daryl Marten. We also know you were in Washington at the time of Janice Taylor's death and we're investigating that. But let's talk about this unidentified phone number."

"Good luck, assholes." he looked directly at Sam.

"Oh," Sam chimed in, "we *know* who was on the other end of the conversations; we just want to talk to you about the phones.

The eyes flickered hatred. "Bullshit."

"Have you ever met," Sam leaned in, almost whispering, "First Lady, Just ..."

As soon as the word, "Lady", left Eastman's lips, Baron lunged for him, up and over the table.

That was the reaction they wanted. Certain confirmation. Sam dodged to his right while Marker shoved Baron's head down hard as he dived over the table. Baron's face cracked down onto the floor, nose broken, blood gushing from it. The door to the room crashed open as three armed guards rushed in, pinning and cuffing Baron before he could regain his senses.

Eastman placed two calls. The first was to Director Leonard to schedule a 9:00 meeting.

*   *   *

On Sunday afternoon at 1:25, Clyde Leonard and FBI Director Wells Carter were seated in the President's residence office in the White House. Their unusual appointment with the President and First Lady was scheduled for 1:30. Together, on a conference call with the President at 10:30 that morning, they had requested the meeting, indicating urgent national importance involving both he and the First Lady and relating to the assassination of Gaylord Scapeli and the attempted assassination of Daryl Marten. At 1:35, President Pritchard, followed by his wife, entered the room.

Impersonal greetings were exchanged. Secret Service Director Leonard spoke. "We requested this meeting because it's important that both of you know where the investigation of Gaylord Scapeli's murder has taken us and where it's likely to lead. Eventually, both your names will appear in a report, which will likely become public. We felt you'd need to know what we know as far in advance of the election as possible. The facts and probable future developments are problematic. You shouldn't offer us any comments this afternoon. We're not here to ask questions or confirm information. If you have questions for us, we'll be straightforward with you.

"I'll start by saying we've long been aware of Mr. Scapeli's methods. Frankly, he was a blackmailer. Worse, he often orchestrated circumstances that, once played out, gave him leverage to compel persons and officials at all levels to do his bidding. His network of influence was phenomenal.

"Here are the facts we know," Leonard continued. "Gerald Baron killed his long time associate and mentor Gaylord Scapeli. Scapeli and Baron maintained their alliance until the day of the murder. Baron's company was financed by Scapeli, probably from a secret Government slush fund, in return for Baron's execution of delicate and risky political sabotage missions.

"Baron arranged the assassination of Daryl Marten and pursued him for a week after the unsuccessful attempt. The Secret Service is implicated in the plot. Our Agent Brackman Littleton planted the weapon and signaled the shooter. Deputy Director Franklin Morganstern, under direction from Scapeli's network, made sure Littleton was placed on Marten's security detail. So, the United States Secret Service, under my directorship, is implicated in an assassination attempt on a presidential candidate. Regardless of the outcome of this election, I'll tender my resignation on November ninth and will cooperate fully with the investigation.

"Also, Baron was in Washington at the time of Janice Taylor's death. We suspect the entire circumstance, including Vice President Borster's presence, was a set up, conceived and executed by Scapeli and Baron.

"We're aware, Mrs. Pritchard," Leonard went on, "you've been a long time acquaintance of Baron's. We have no reason to believe you were involved in his activities or had any knowledge of them. It's probable you were deceived for many years, another of Scapeli's unwitting victims. Whatever the case, your name will appear in an official report that will likely become public.

"Mr. President, your situation is the most difficult. Your name will be mentioned early and often. I'm asking you nothing this afternoon, but many questions will be asked as this case unravels. Your relationship with Scapeli dates back to the time your political career took off on the track that eventually brought you to the White House. It's no secret Scapeli was pivotal to your advancement. You'll be asked how much you knew about his illicit activities and whether or not you approved any of them.

"Sir," Leonard continued, "I wouldn't presume to advise you on any actions to take, either now or after the election. We felt it important that you know, today, where this investigation stands and where it's likely to lead. Do either of you have any questions for us?"

The President stared at them, seeing through and beyond them, his mind projecting where the next year would take him, what his options might be. Both he and Justine had listened to Leonard in stone cold silence, not flinching, not moving.

Justine spoke first. "Baron told you about me?"

"No," Leonard replied. "We found you as a contact, researching phone records. We couldn't identify your number on calls from the last four years; your phone's security protection is too high. We identified your old phone number, before you were First Lady. Those calls went back many years on his phone records, in an account registered to Clarence Clawson."

"Does he know you found that? That you've identified me?"

"Ma'am," Leonard replied, "that was the one and only bit of information he's reacted to since we arrested him. At the mention of your name, he attacked our interrogator. Baron had to be forcibly subdued, suffering a broken nose in the process."

"Good," she replied icily. "How, exactly, did you come by his name as a suspect in Scapeli's murder?"

"One of our receptionists received an anonymous tip and the caller asked her to give his name to me."

She looked Leonard directly in the eye and said firmly, "You're welcome. Now that he knows you have my name, does that torment him?"

"It appears so. We put him on suicide watch."

"Would you deliver a message to him?"

"If you wish."

"Justine, stop it," Pritchard said quietly, returning to the conversation.

"Tell him we are *not* even," she directed, ignoring her husband.

"Yes, ma'am."

"Tell him to stay alive and suffer through his trial; hear the judge and the American people tell him how loathsome he is. Tell him to live to hear the people pronounce his death sentence, to die at their hand, not his own. Tell him I despise him from the pit of my soul." She looked Leonard in the eye. "Tell me you'll tell him in person. Today. Tell him those were my *exact* words. Then you can stop the suicide watch. He won't take his life."

"Shut up, Justine!" Pritchard demanded.

"You tell him that, Clyde."

"I'll tell him, Mrs. Pritchard," Leonard said quietly. "As soon as we leave. Do either of you have any other questions?"

Neither responded.

"All right, then. Please," Leonard glanced at each of them, "contact either Wells or me anytime if you wish to talk." The two men stood. Neither the President nor First Lady did. Leonard and Carter turned and walked out of the room.

As soon as they were gone, Justine rose without a word and left the President alone. She walked to her bedroom, where she remained until Monday morning.

Pritchard began mulling over options. *What would Scapeli do? With him gone, who do I trust most?* After an hour, he placed a call.

"Rand?" the self-assured female voice answered.

"I'm going to need your help. Can you be at the Oval Office tomorrow morning at seven-thirty?"

"I'll be there. I've been wondering if you'd call."

"It's been too long, Lynn. It'll be good to see you."

Pritchard called another number. "Yes, Mr. President."

"Clyde, I've been thinking over your accusations against Gayle Scapeli. I'm not saying you convinced me, but everybody knows he was shrewd and could be ruthless. Sometimes he *did* take actions without my knowledge. I can't believe he would've gone so far as to authorize an assassination attempt or a setup of Borster, but I'm willing to allow an investigation and offer my full cooperation. However, I can't allow you, or Wells Carter, or anyone from either of your agencies, to jeopardize national political stability the day before a presidential election. You are to ensure that any charges against Gayle remain under wraps until after the election. Do you understand?"

"Sir, I'm not sure I can..."

Pritchard cut him off. "I'm ordering you, Director. I'm declaring the containment of any and all information insinuating that Gayle Scapeli might have been involved in any illegal activities to be a National Security issue until Wednesday. Chaos will ensue if your charges are made public before that. The stability of the nation would be at risk if you allow any of this to leak out. If that happens, if you violate this order, you'll be charged with treason."

"Mr. President, I'm not sure it can be contained. It may be too late."

"Director, I'm not asking you to do your best. I'm ordering you. *Contain it!* Whatever it takes. Do it."

*   *   *

Sam Eastman's second call that morning had been to Cincinnati Channel Eight. Five minutes later, his cell phone signaled a return call.

"Zach, I need you back in Washington right away. This thing could break today or tomorrow. Your immediate availability for testimony could be critical."

"Okay. Same set up? Schriever Air Force Base?"

"That'll work. Can you be there by one?"

"Yeah, one your time."

*   *   *

At 5:00, inside a closed hanger at Andrews Air Force Base, two passengers transferred from a Secret Service jet to a bullet proof limousine. As they pulled out of the hangar, Sam leaned close to the two travelers. "The situation has become treacherous since we talked this morning. The President has classified all information relative to Scapeli and his killer, Gerald Baron. He's claiming it to be a matter of national security. He's ordered Director Leonard to make sure no part of it becomes public before Wednesday."

"He still thinks he's got the election sewed up as long as he keeps Scapeli's crimes secret," Zach surmised. "He intends to deceive America into reelecting him."

"I have a plan," Sam said. "Officially, I'm on my own, but I have to do what I can or I'll never be able to live with myself. I've scheduled a meeting tonight at seven with two high-ranking politicians. I'm glad you're both here. It'll be a precarious encounter and I'll need you both to stand your ground."

That turned out to be an understatement. The meeting lasted until after 11:00. It was harrowing, beset with numerous agitated sidebar debates, and punctuated with sporadic shouting and threats. After the guests of honor left, Sam could only hope a few hours contemplation would buoy whatever patriotic spirit the two politicians had left in them to overcome their cronyism.

* * *

Secret Service agent Anita Lynn Vandy, Lynn to her closest friends, entered the Oval Office on Monday morning at precisely 7:30.

"Good morning, Sir," she said professionally.

Pritchard stood to greet her. "Lynn! It's great to see you. When was the last time, four months ago? That fund raiser in New York?"

She relaxed and smiled. "It was memorable a night."

"Quite. But, as much as I'd like to relive old times, I've got some serious business to discuss. You can imagine how big of a blow it's been to lose Gayle Scapeli. We trusted each other with everything. The man was a magician. He could make anything happen."

"I've been worried about you, Rand. I know you lost your right hand. And I know how damaging it could be if some of Gayle's activities became known. If there's a way I can help, I want to."

"That's why I called you. I need an invincible force on my side today and tomorrow. And, after the election, I'll need a new Chief of Staff. Someone who could pick up where Gayle left off. I believe you're that person, Lynn. What would you think?"

"I'd be honored, Rand. I'm not saying I could fill his shoes, but I'd work hard to accomplish whatever you need. I'd be committed."

"I have no doubt about that. That's why you're my first choice. There are some immediate issues to deal with. Let's sit at the table."

The intercom interrupted them, which was highly unusual. "I'm sorry, Mr. President," came his executive secretary's voice, "but Senator Dresser and Governor Jorgensen are at my desk and insist they have urgent business that can't wait."

Gordon Dresser's voice interrupted over the intercom. "Rand, this is critical. The election could be at stake. We *must* talk to you."

Silence. Then, "I'm meeting with the Secret Service right now, Gordy. Will five minutes be enough? That's all I can spare."

"Yes," Dresser lied. "How soon will you be ready for us?"

"You can come in. Agent Vandy can hear anything I hear."

Dresser hesitated at that response. "Thank you, Sir. We'll be right in. We have a couple of associates with us."

Leaving no time for a reply, Dresser and Jorgensen headed for the Oval Office door as Secret Service agent Sam Eastman escorted Zachary Forrester and Daryl Marten behind them.

As the group entered, five jaws dropped: Daryl's, Zach's, and Sam's upon seeing Anita Vandy and Anita's and the President's upon seeing them. For a moment no one spoke.

Sam broke the silence, looking squarely at Anita. Daryl could see Sam's mind clicking the pieces into place as he spoke. "You were in on it."

Daryl's adrenalin was pumping, but his lack of sleep made his mind stutter. He saw Zach going through the same painful process of fitting the pegs into the holes, and saw Zach catch up to Sam the same time that he did. They both turned toward Anita, stunned.

Pritchard glared at Dresser. "What the hell are you doing?"

Gordon looked confused briefly by Sam's comment. He quickly came back to the moment. "We need to talk to you, Rand."

"You already said that," Pritchard snapped at his old friend. "What do you want? Make it quick."

"There's a serious problem, Rand."

"Dammit, Gordon, if you've got something to say, say it!"

"Please, Rand. Troy and I are trying to avert disaster."

"Looks more like you're creating one. Get on with it."

"How could you possibly..." Daryl cut into the conversation, staring at Anita.

All heads turned to him, surprised anyone would interrupt the President.

Anita returned the stare, expressionless. "You're way too naïve," she said coolly. "You could never handle this job."

"I welcomed you in my home. You were our friend. You played with my kids. Rory..." he choked. "This can't be true."

"You've gotta back out of this, Daryl."

Now it was Dresser and Jorgensen dropping their jaws. Everyone else in the room understood the exchange.

Sam shot daggers at her. "How could I have missed it?"

"You put too much faith in your people, Sam. You were easy."

Pritchard cut in. "You've got ten seconds, Gordon."

Dresser gave his pal a compassionate look and said quietly, "It's all going public, Rand."

"What are you talking about?"

"Everything. The assassination attempt. The setup of Borster. The manipulation of the democratic candidates. Scapeli's control of all of it. Your complicity."

That rendered Pritchard speechless. Vandy immediately assumed her new role. "You've been misinformed, Senator. You don't have a clue what Gayle Scapeli might or might not have directed. Even if he was involved in any of those actions, President Pritchard would've had no knowledge. He would *never* have permitted anything of the kind. And you, of all people, know that."

Jorgensen took over. "That's very good, Agent Vandy. What do you think we'd guess you two were discussing when we walked in? Tell me, why, exactly, are you here this morning?"

Pritchard looked at Dresser and Jorgensen. "What the hell are you trying to do? You brought Marten," his tone was one of disgust, "the news media, and the Secret Service in here? Into the Oval Office? Under the pretext that you, my most trusted friends, are offering me a *lifeline*? Get 'em out of here! *Now!*"

"Rand," Jorgensen replied, "you've got to step back and listen for a second." We *are* trying to save you. At least as much as that can still be done. Mostly, we're to save you from yourself. You can't do what you're setting out to do to this country. If you don't stop, you'll do damage that can't be fixed. You've gotta stop!"

"Troy, you don't have a goddamned clue what you're talking about. I don't know what you guys think you know, but you don't know *shit*! Are you telling me you believe *this* idiot," he nodded in Marten's direction, "and his teenage reporter? And *Eastman*, the guy responsible for not preventing the shooting? He's obviously trying to make up for his own negligence. I can tell you for *sure* he's committing treason. I'm getting Leonard on the phone right now. Eastman you'll be behind bars in ten minutes."

"*Rand!*" Dresser shouted at him. "*Stop this!*"

"You're *all* committing treason!" Pritchard fired back. "Leonard knows it. He knows everything and he knows the security of this nation is at stake if the unfounded charges you're talking about become public accusations one day before a presidential election. He knows it's treason for anyone to attempt to wreck our democratic process by playing on hearsay like that. Now, I'm telling you to get out of my office! *Right now!* All of you!"

"How can you possibly consider yourself a patriot?" Daryl said contemptuously. "Who do you think you're fooling? Everyone in this room knows exactly what you've done. Lie about it all you want. We *know!* You might be able to hide it from the people for the next few days, maybe even for another month. But you can't bury it forever. What do you think will happen when it does become public? You'll be ripped to shreds."

"You *idiot*! You don't think information can be contained. John Kennedy was shot over half a century ago and the public *still* doesn't know what happened. And believe me, what happened *is* known. It was known and documented within a month. Did the public ever find out? *Hell no!* Now *get out*!"

Zach looked loathingly at the President. "It won't be like that this time. The public already knows. It's being broadcast right now, as we speak. We were up half the night last night taping. It's airing right now," Zach lied.

Daryl knew what Zach was doing. They hadn't discussed the possibility of bluffing. It was true, they had been up half the night and taped it all, with the weight of Secret Service Agent Samuel Eastman adding credence to the testimony. They had sent it to Channel Eight. Channel Eight had forwarded the piece on to the network. However, it wasn't being aired, at least not yet. He wasn't sure it would ever be aired. For the moment, that didn't matter. The ruse worked.

"*God Dammit!*" Pritchard roared. "*I'll have Leonard's head!*"

"*Rand!*" Dresser shouted back at him. "This is over! Marten's right. This isn't JFK. It can't be squashed."

"He isn't right about *anything*," Pritchard snarled. "The only way to save this country is to keep it out of *his* hands."

"And do what?" Daryl stepped toward the President. "Every decision you made as President had only one goal: to advance Randall Pritchard. You don't care squat about the citizens of the United States. You care about yourself and that's all."

Pritchard now stepped toward Marten, face reddening. Vandy took a step and so did Eastman and Zach. It looked like a brawl was brewing in the Oval Office.

"*Hey!*" Dresser and Jorgensen shouted in unison, bringing a moment of pause to the group. Jorgensen quickly added, "Let's all sit down at the table and talk this through, like we're almost civilized."

"It's being broadcast now?" Pritchard croaked.

"Troy's right," Dresser said. "Let's talk it out in some kind of order.

Pritchard's shoulders drooped a notch. His eyes spewed hatred at Daryl. Then he turned, walked to the conference table, and sat at the head. Agent Vandy sat beside him. Daryl sat at the opposite end, Zach taking a seat to his right and Eastman to his left. Dresser and Jorgensen sat on one side, a chair between them.

Gordon spoke quietly. "Rand, there appears to be proof that Scapeli order Marten's assassination, culminating in the shooting of his eleven-year-old son. The same for Borster. It appears provable it was a set up. And it might not be provable yet, but it looks like Scapeli managed to manipulate the rise and fall of the democratic candidates. No one is going to believe you didn't know what was going on. They're going to come after you, Rand, whether you win or lose this election."

"What he said about it being on TV right now," Pritchard said nodding toward Zach, "Is that true?"

"I don't know," Gordon said. "Eastman made a strong enough case to Troy and me on the phone yesterday that we felt compelled to meet with them last night. For your sake. For the country's sake. We spent four hours with them in a shouting match. When we left, they said they were going to tape a piece overnight and send it to the networks before seven this morning. I assume they did. I don't know whether it's being run right now or not."

"It doesn't matter," Jorgensen added, looking intently and empathetically at his old friend. "Look at it from outside, Rand. Hell, look at it from Gordy's and my seats. And we're your oldest friends. Untold damage has already been heaped on the country. An assassination attempt on a presidential candidate sanctioned by a sitting President? A setup of the Vice President to destroy his career? A setup that involved the premeditated murder of an innocent citizen? Sanctioned by a sitting President? The systematic manipulation of the opposing party candidates to ensure a one-sided election? Sanctioned by a sitting President? Rand, look at it! In the United States of America, for Christ sake! The world's bastion of freedom and democracy! How much harm has already been done?"

"Mr. Pritchard," Daryl could not bring himself to address this man as Mr. President, President Pritchard, or even, Sir, "I *am* a patriot. Even if I had no stake in this, there's *no way* I could sit by, knowing what I know, without screaming the truth to everyone. Even under the threat of a false charge of treason, under a silence order directly from the President to me, I'll scream it to the world. *Because* I'm a patriot! I can't and won't allow you to do this to the citizens of my country. You'll have to kill me to stop me." As he made that last statement, his laser eyes flicked away from Pritchard's and directly to Anita Vandy's.

Daryl saw the armor begin to crack. He saw Pritchard fighting it with all the will he could muster, but shame was beginning to creep in. He thought he even detected an ounce of respect showing through the façade. "And I'll tell you another thing," Daryl spoke quietly now. "No, our interview isn't being aired. Yet. It's been sent to the network. It was sent with my order not to be made public until I authorize it. That was a concession I made to your friends, Senator Dresser and Governor Jorgensen. They stood by you last night and they're standing by you now. They know this will go badly for you. They're doing what they can to help you keep an ounce of self respect. And they're doing everything in their power to minimize the damage to this country, which they still love. Follow their advice."

Pritchard looked at Vandy. She looked down. He said, "Give me a few minutes with Gordon and Troy."

"I'll wait until noon," Daryl replied. He stood up. Zach and Sam followed Marten out of the Oval Office. Anita Vandy exited through the President's private door.

*   *   *

At 11:45 Monday morning, eighteen hours before polls would open, all news networks released a breaking story.

"According to White House sources, the late Chief of Staff, Gaylord Scapeli, and his long time associate and confessed killer, Gerald Baron, have both been implicated in the attempted assassination of independent Presidential Candidate Daryl Marten. They are also suspected in the murder of White House staff typist Janice Taylor. Miss Taylor was found dead on July

31 in a motel room with former Vice President James Borster. Our sources indicate the Borster/Taylor episode may have been a setup orchestrated by Scapeli and Baron and that the former Vice President might be guilty of no wrongdoing.

"Baron reportedly killed Scapeli as a result of a breach between the two life-long collaborators brought about by the failure of the attempt on Marten's life. Both the FBI and the Secret Service are investigating the affairs of Gaylord Scapeli and Gerald Baron. It is expected that complete reports of the investigations will be released to the public after due process of law. Baron is currently incarcerated in a maximum security facility.

"It's also reported that an investigation is being opened into whether Scapeli masterminded both the rise and the demise of Democratic presidential hopefuls Garner Wheeler and Richard Herrington.

"Gaylord Scapeli has been an associate of President Randall Pritchard from the early days of his political ascent and was vital to his attainment of the Oval Office. Although all of this information was released by the White House staff, President Pritchard has not personally commented on any of the accusations against his Administration nor has he admitted to prior knowledge of any of the alleged conspiracies of his former Chief of Staff."

By noon, Justine had seen the news. She'd already determined her next step, but the dire announcement only reinforced it. By 2:00, without so much as leaving a note for her husband, she was on a government jet en route to Fresno, California. Home. Her parents were gone, but Sarah, their youngest, lived in the old house where Justine had grown up. Justine no longer felt anything inside. No vengefulness, no compassion, no pride, no shame, no ambition. Nothing. She was an empty shell. She'd called Sarah and told her that she was coming home and that she hoped they could revive some kind of relationship. Sarah had told her the doors would be locked. She was not welcome. She left for Fresno anyway.

By 3:00, the Democratic Party had settled on the appropriate response to the public announcement of Scapeli's corruptness. Allowing Catcher to hold a press conference was not an option. There would be no sidestepping the ensnaring questions. "Did the Republican Administration actually dupe the Democratic Party by choosing their candidates? "By handpicking candidates they knew were fatally flawed? "And then handing over the secret details by which they would destroy each other? "Did the President's Chief of Staff pick you, Senator Catcher, out of all the Democrats in the land, because his opinion was that, out of them all, you would be the weakest possible opponent? "Was your Democratic campaign, Senator Catcher, funded through Republican maneuvering with the caveat that a significant portion of the funds be directed toward vilifying independent candidate Daryl Marten, whom Scapeli considered the most significant threat to the reelection of President Pritchard? "Why do you believe, Senator Catcher, that your money tree suddenly lost all its leaves upon the death of Gayle Scapeli? "Where exactly, Senator Catcher, did your funding come from? "Do you even know?"

Within a few days of Scapeli's murder, the Democratic Party had figured all this out. However, having to respond to those questions today, one day before the election, on the day the President was self-destructing, would do more damage than had the actual occurrences. After all the inconceivable disasters of the past three months, the Democratic Party was poised to take over the White House via election eve default. No, the only option was the release of a public statement, delivered presidentially by Bradley Catcher, worded as carefully as possible in the miniscule amount of time available to prepare it.

Their taped press release aired at 3:15. On the fifth take, Catcher had performed it well enough to broadcast.

"My fellow Americans. I stand before you resolutely. There is no denying the presidential campaigns of this election have been plagued by catastrophe. Every single campaign. I take heart in the fact that the difficulties suffered by my organization over the past few weeks were not due to dishonesty or lack of ethics on the part of anyone on my staff. Considering that we became an unexpected frontrunner very late in the game, I am *extremely* proud of my staff and the presence they were able to establish and sustain for many, many weeks. I sincerely thank and congratulate each and every person who has faithfully served on my staff. I stand here today, still a frontrunner, because of their unwillingness to give up, because of their profound belief that, in spite of all the adversity, we can … that we *will* … prevail in this election.

"I am, by nature, a compassionate person. I am not unsympathetic, even toward those who ensnare themselves in their own webs. However, sympathetic or not, some actions simply are not acceptable, especially from our highest public figures.

"Three hours ago, I heard, along with the rest of you, charges that the current administration is responsible for the premeditated murder of a United States citizen, for the deceitful, libelous ruination of the career of one the greatest living statesmen of their own Party, the sitting Vice President, and for the attempted assassination of a political opponent. These are *incredible* accusations, made on the eve of Randall Pritchard's bid for reelection to the presidency. We've waited over three hours to hear his personal response, his rebuttal, his *disavowal*. But nothing. *Not one word.* Not even an acknowledgement that these accusations have been made.

"Considering these fantastic charges came to the forefront on the most critical day of his political career, and absent his *immediate* response, I see only one logical conclusion. I will not claim that which I don't know. I will not say I believe the President was complicit in any decision-making that led to these unthinkable actions. I *will* say his lack of response lends credence to a conclusion that these actions did happen and that he may have been aware that they were in progress as they occurred. At the very least, a sitting president *must* accept responsibility for the actions of his staff, whether he was aware beforehand or not. And I'll stop at that.

"Tomorrow, all of us, we citizens of the United States of America, will elect our next President. Today, our election process, potentially our very political stability, is in disarray because of the charges leveled against the current Administration. Where do we look now, amidst all the chaos, for leadership we can depend upon? We *must* look to that which we know.

"Say what you will about our great Party machines. They've been with us for centuries. Major political parties have been at the forefront of this country for more than two hundred years. Are they perfect? No. Can we count on them to guide us through unforeseeable future circumstances? Look back at what they've taken us through in the past and the answer is obvious. Yes, we can count on our political parties and the system they work within. It works, America. It's proven itself in the past and it can be counted on in the future.

"We *cannot* allow heat of the moment reactions to cause us to put the political future of this nation at risk. And that's exactly what would happen if we let the acts of one administration, however appalling, lead us away from our tried and proven institutions and into a future that would turn on nothing more than chance. Let us not turn our backs, *especially* in tumultuous times, on that which we know works. We *must* keep our heads about us. Thank you."

Daryl, Zach, and Sam watched Catcher's press release on a television in their suite, deep within the Secret Service building. Zach looked at the other two, "He thinks he's just been gifted the presidency."

"I've got news for him," Daryl retorted. "I've had all I'm going to take from our great political party machines. Let's shoot a five minute introduction to the tape we made last night and send it out for airing. I'm exhausted and I'm sure I look it, but let's shoot it anyway."

The cameraman and equipment the trio had used to record the exposé last night had been on standby all afternoon, just in case. Daryl had wanted to wait to see if Pritchard would step to the plate and take responsibility. He hadn't. Now Catcher and the Democrats were attempting to twist the Pritchard Administration's criminal deeds into votes for them, in spite of their own failings. Daryl made his decision. Daryl Marten's last pre-election message to the voters hit the air waves as breaking news at 5:40.

"Good evening. I'm Daryl Marten, independent candidate for President of the United States. Yesterday morning, I left a ranch in the Northwest on a flight to Washington. When I arrived, I met with Secret Service Agent Samuel Eastman and news reporter Zachary Forrester. Last evening, the three of us had a grueling four hour meeting with Tennessee Senator Gordon Dresser and Texas Governor Troy Jorgensen that lasted until midnight. After that, Sam, Zach, and I spent four hours taping and editing a video report that will follow this introduction. Then, early this morning, the same five of us who grappled last night, met in the Oval Office with Randall Pritchard and Secret Service agent Anita Vandy, who was an accomplice in the assassination attempt on my life and the shooting of my son. At that meeting the President of the United States threatened to charge me with treason if I released the report you are about to see. After the meeting, my two associates and I proceeded to a location we believe is safe for the time being.

"The tape you're about to see explains everything Agent Eastman, Zachary, and I know to be fact, relative to the charges against the Administration made public earlier today by the White House. I'm authorizing its airing at the risk of being prosecuted for treason. I authorized it because I am *done* making allowances for the unethical and immoral conduct of the leaders of this nation. I do not accept that this must be the way our government conducts business. If I'm in the minority in this opinion, so be it. Regardless, I've had all I can take. Deceitful … criminal … leadership of this nation is not acceptable. Period.

"The act that pushed me beyond my limit and resulted in my decision to release this tape was Senator Catcher's press release this afternoon. Zach said it best. 'He thinks he's just been gifted the presidency.' I hope everyone has his press release recorded. Play it again. Listen to the rhetoric. Then ask yourself why Senator Catcher, why the Democratic Party, chose a taped press release instead of a live press conference. If you had the opportunity to ask Senator Catcher a question or two, what would you ask him? 'Senator, were the Democratic presidential candidates actually selected and then destroyed by the Republican Chief of Staff? 'Are you the Democratic candidate today only because the Republicans chose you, knowing you would be easier to beat than any other Democrat? 'Where did your campaign money magically appear from, Senator? 'And why, exactly, did it dry up as soon as Gaylord

Scapeli was assassinated?' I don't know about the rest of America, but United States citizen Daryl Marten has had enough.

"I *refuse* to concede that this nation must be run by behemoth political parties. I refuse to concede that the top public servants in this country cannot be honest, ethical, and moral. I refuse to be attacked and lied about endlessly, without speaking the truth. And I refuse to stand by and watch this great country, the United States of America, my home, get less than the best from its leaders. I *will* do everything I can, as one mere man, to help fix the problem.

"In closing this introduction, I admit that I, too, am issuing a taped press release instead of holding a live press conference. And, lest Senator Catcher accuse me of doing the same thing I denounced him and his party for, I'll lay my reasons on the table. They are entirely selfish reasons. First, I wish to live. I have no protection and the Administration of the President of the United States has attempted to assassinate me once already. Second, the President has told me in person that if I release this tape, I will be charged with treason, and I prefer to keep my freedom for as long as possible.

"Please watch the following segment. Everything Sam, Zach, and I state in it is true. Think clearly about the state of this nation tonight. Then, tomorrow, do your duty. Vote your conscience."

The taped segment detailed dates, locations, names of involved persons, and actions. The whole story was told, everything that was known to be true. It took into account everything seen, by Zach, Sam, and Daryl and everything confirmed by the testimony of others, including Gerald Barron, Clyde Leonard, Gordon Dresser, and Troy Jorgensen.

The remainder of the television night was consumed by political experts attempting to unravel the impact the days events would have on tomorrow's election. Virtually every expert landed on the same final theme: Bradley Catcher had hit on the pulse that would carry the day. The political climate was calamitous. People would stick to what they knew, to what they had become comfortable with and dependent upon. There would be no mass migration away from political parties tomorrow.

There was no consensus on whether the winner would be Pritchard or Catcher. If only Pritchard would make a statement early in the day denying any knowledge of any illegal acts ordered by Scapeli, he could salvage the Presidency. If he didn't, then welcome, President Catcher. Registered Republicans unable to bring themselves to vote for Pritchard would not vote. Registered Democrats would vote for Catcher. Daryl Marten had made himself the greatest wild card in the history of United States Presidential elections. But fear not, come Wednesday morning, America would not wake to find that her president-elect had no Party affiliation.

Daryl watched the evening news from the suite in the Secret Service building, resting on a couch. At 7:30 he lay down on it. The next thing he was aware of was that it was 7:45 Tuesday morning, Election Day. A thought flitted through his mind as he woke. *I am still alive.*

Epilogue

Inauguration Day, January 20

The day was cold, but sunny and calm. President Elect Daryl Marten stood in front of the cheering throng with his wife and children to his right and the DeCamp family to his left.

When he had sluggishly wakened back on November 8, after twelve hours of exhausted sleep, it had all felt like a dream … a dream that had begun when the Marten and DeCamp families had decided to seek ballot access. It had taken an hour to shake the surreal feel of that morning. To believe voters were considering him on that day as they marked their ballots. To realize the effort and strain of getting to that day was over. To release the pent up pain inflicted by his decision to keep his son away from the medical attention he needed so desperately. Now, that day, election day, seemed like another dream unto itself.

By 2:00 that Tuesday afternoon in November, all voices of the media, citing exit polls, were steadfastly sticking to their prediction that Party politics would prevail. The prognosticators split half-and-half between Pritchard and Catcher, or, more precisely, between the Republican Party and the Democratic Party. Early television network declarations began to spew shortly before 5:00. The picture portrayed was that the big party machines were invincible, regardless of the lack of viability of any particular candidate.

Vermont, Massachusetts, Connecticut, and Rhode Island were declared for Catcher, giving him the first 26 electoral votes. The fact that Marten was a close second in each state was downplayed. Within ten minutes, West Virginia, Florida, and South Carolina were declared Pritchard states, putting him in the lead by 40 electoral votes. Marten was again second, close, and downplayed. No networks declared any states for Marten before 7:30. The networks were eager to declare any state for a major party candidate early, but unwilling to declare one for the independent until it was impossible for him to lose.

Then, when it was mathematically impossible for him to lose, Delaware was begrudged to be a Marten state, followed in rapid succession by Maryland, New Jersey, Maine, Virginia, and New Hampshire. By 8:15, Marten had a narrow lead with 49 electoral votes. Shortly before 8:30, with 43 percent of the New York vote reported and Catcher leading Marten by 4 percent, Catcher was declared the winner, putting him back in the lead with 57 electoral votes. By 9:00, Texas was declared for Pritchard by similarly early indications. A few minutes later, Kentucky and Tennessee were declared for Pritchard placing him in the lead with 93 electoral votes.

No candidate made a single public appearance all day. Pritchard had been veiled from the public and the media since his Sunday morning meeting with the FBI and Secret Service directors. Catcher didn't dare risk being bombarded with public questions. Marten was satisfied he had already done everything in his power to fulfill his promise that his supporters would have the opportunity to vote for him if they desired.

Shortly after 9:30 Georgia, North Carolina, Alabama, and Wisconsin were declared for Marten, putting him ahead of Pritchard by 5 electoral votes. Within five minutes Pennsylvania, Ohio, and Illinois were declared for Catcher, with none of those states yet reporting 40 percent of the vote and Catcher leading by less than 3 percent in all of them. At 10:15 California was also declared for Catcher. That brought his total to 210 electoral votes.

As soon as California was declared for Catcher, network anchor Dennis Helms, substituting for Regina Wasson, began explaining the process of electing a president when no candidate receives the required 270 electoral votes necessary to win.

"The only candidate who could still mathematically win this election outright is Senator Bradley Catcher. However, it appears likely that, although he will have a majority of the electoral votes, his count will not reach the required two-hundred-seventy. In that case, the election will be determined by the House of Representatives. They are not bound to consider either popular or electoral votes cast. They can elect whichever candidate they desire. Considering the House is heavily Republican, it's possible they would choose President Pritchard, regardless of yesterday's allegations. With California going for Catcher, the independent, Daryl Marten, no longer has any chance of being elected."

While Helms educated the nation on the anticipated process, Missouri, Indiana, Iowa, Michigan, Louisiana, Minnesota, Arkansas, Nebraska, Oklahoma, New Mexico, and Nevada were all added to Marten's tally. The precinct reports from Pennsylvania, Ohio, and Illinois came in faster, their rural areas catching up with the early returns reported from the cities. By 10:45, Marten had wrested the lead from Catcher in all three of those states, a potential swing of 62 electoral votes. By 11:30 it was obvious all three would go to Marten, rather than Catcher. Between 11:45 and 11:50, Marten became mathematically unbeatable in both Colorado and Arizona, pushing him over the magic number of 270 to 272. Marten's final tally turned out to be 297 electoral votes.

Neither Pritchard nor Catcher called Marten to either concede or congratulate him. Nor did either make any public appearance after the outcome was determined. It was as if the Party machines had closed their doors, the world having come to an end. The media was glum. How were they to deal with a clean slate President?

At midnight, a live feed was transmitted to Cincinnati Channel Eight and immediately rebroadcast on all major networks.

"Good evening. I'm Daryl Marten. Like most of you, I've observed today's election proceedings on a television screen, filtered by the media. I've received no communication from either Randall Pritchard or Bradley Catcher. I speak to you under the assumption the media reports we've been watching are accurate enough to conclude that I will be your next President. Until it's evident that the current Administration is transitioning smoothly to the next, I'll make daily televised progress reports.

"Prior to tonight, I've experienced five earth-shattering moments in my life. Each required a life-commitment of me. Those were the moments I spoke my marriage vows and the moments of the births of each of my children. Tonight I add a sixth. And based upon my thirty-five-year association with Cleve DeCamp, I assure you he makes the same commitment alongside me.

"Here are my vows to the American people. I will continuously act in your best interests and those of your children and grandchildren. I will act morally and ethically, with transparency, honesty, and integrity. I will not accept incompetence in my Administration or in the divisions, departments, offices, and individuals who comprise it. I will assemble an Administration that's non-partisan and will strive ceaselessly to enjoin both major parties to progress toward goals that will benefit us all.

"I am honored and humbled that you have elected me to lead the Executive Branch of the United States of America for the next four years. Cleve and I will conduct the affairs of the Executive branch such that four years from now you'll have no doubt your placement of trust in us was well-founded. Our families are no different than your families. Acts that will benefit you will benefit us and acts that will harm you will harm us. We don't stand over you. We stand with you, on the same playing field. We dedicate the next four years of our lives to service to the people of the United States of America. Thank you and goodnight."

While waiting to take the oath of office, thoughts of the past weeks continued to whisk through Daryl's mind. Many key positions in his Administration remained open, but most had been filled with good, qualified individuals: Republicans, Democrats, and independents. Since the election, James Borster had been cleared of any wrong-doing and had accepted the office of Secretary of State. Greg Jolsen had accepted the position of Chief of Staff of the Marten Administration and Elaine Kosovich had agreed to remain in her assistant position. Samuel Eastman had replaced Franklin Morganstern as Deputy Director of the Secret Service. Zachary Forrester was about to become the youngest, most enthusiastic, most dedicated Assistant to the President for Communications in the history of the United States.

Troy Jorgensen, after several heart-to-heart discussions with Daryl, had renounced all party affiliation and accepted a new staff position, on par with and independent of the Chief of Staff. He would be responsible for enhancing cooperation between political parties. For every partisan issue or bill, his charge would be to work with Congress to ensure the interests of the American people were at the forefront, ahead of partisanship, local interests, or special interest groups. He was to make extensive use of the media to keep the American people acutely aware of the details of proponents and antagonists positions on all issues that hinted at partisanship or special favor.

Much had come to light between Election Day and Inauguration Day. Clyde Leonard and Wells Carter had visited Gerald Baron immediately after their meeting with the Pritchards' on November 6 to relay Justine's message to him. Baron had displayed no reaction whatsoever. However, the next morning, he had requested a pen and a journal. He spent the next week detailing his entire association with Gaylord Scapeli, describing every plan and every action they had participated in together. He named every accomplice. After handing the journal to Sam Eastman, he stoically awaited his trial, not speaking to anyone.

After the election, carrying out the duties of the Office of the President became tortuous for Pritchard. He didn't have Scapeli. He didn't have a First Lady, a wife. His Vice President was useless. He had been served legal notice he would be indicted for a long list of criminal acts as soon as his term of office ended. He had then delegated all activities he could to Greg Jolsen and Elaine Kosovich. The two of them had provided Daryl invaluable assistance with the transition.

The most difficult ordeal of the past ten weeks tugging at Daryl's mind was personal. Today, five members of his immediate family were at his side. His wife and three of his children were standing. His youngest son was seated, missing his left leg. The father's decisions to tout his philosophies of government to the world, place his name on the ballot for President, and extract his son from ready access to vital medical resources, had ultimately cost his son his leg. Even though thoughts of blame or need for forgiveness were foreign to Rory's mind, those matters would haunt his father for years to come.

It was time. Daryl focused his mind on the present, on the oath of office he was about to take. He absorbed the magnitude of the moment. Stepping forward to speak his oath, Daryl Marten recommitted himself to endeavor to realistically and relentlessly mold a more ethical, responsible government. A government that would pave the way to a better day for the United States of America. For the people. For his children and future grandchildren. For everyone's.